MOUNT HAVEN

Also by Melanie P. Smith

<u>Warrior Series</u>

Dusk

After Dark

Serendipity (Anthology)

Dawn

Shadows

Intrepid (Anthology)

Chaos

Exposed

Progeny

<u>Novels</u>

Hidden Lakes

MOUNT HAVEN

by:
Melanie P. Smith

MPSmith Publishing

Dedication:

This book is dedicated to former

Salt Lake County Sheriff's Office K9, Knight

And his handler, R. Lee Smith

Retired Captain Lloyd Prescott

I met my friend Lee Smith back in 1972. He was a tall, good looking deputy with blond hair and a ready smile. But Lee was much more than that. Lee was a 'go to' guy in any kind of potentially deadly situation. His calm demeanor was converse to his ready smile, laugh and a somewhat distorted sense of humor. Later in his career, Lee served in the Salt Lake County Sheriff's K-9 Unit. His dog, Knight shined as one of the best German Shepherds in the Unit. Back in the early days, we trained our own dogs, unlike today when police dogs are trained by professional trainers, then purchased by law enforcement agencies. Lee put his heart and a tremendous effort into training Knight and the dog was one of the best, both in the day-to-day work, and also in K-9 competition. Lee was also on the Sheriff's Pistol Team and set records that held for over twenty years. Later, Lee climbed the professional ladder and eventually retired as a Captain. His leadership was exemplary because of his 'lead by example' attitude. I could go on for a long time about my friend Lee, but it would suffice to say that if my life was on the line, I could breathe a lot easier if Lee had my back.

Captain Kris Ownby

Lee Smith was much more to me than my Sergeant, Lieutenant, and Commander. He was my mentor and good friend whose leadership and courage fostered my character and competence into a successful law enforcement career. I will be forever grateful for his inspiration to stand tall for what is right and not what is popular. I'll never forget Lee saying, "I don't require Deputy Sheriffs to be nice, I require them to be civil." Thanks, LeeRoy... On You!

Retired Lieutenant Scott Bannon

I met LeeRoy prior to my law enforcement career with Salt Lake County Sheriff's Office and was greatly influenced from day one. His guidance and knowledge led me along a career path that I will be forever grateful. As a leader, he took the time to identify my greatest values, and was always willing to support me with guidance throughout my career. In my eyes, LeeRoy was the ideal leader which was to lead from the rear forward, rather than to drag others along from the front. My judgement of other leaders throughout my law enforcement career was always based on LeeRoy's admirable leadership skills. Your friend always, Scott.

Sergeant Matthew Visher

Lee Smith taught me and countless others what a true police officer is. For me, Lee is one of the greatest police officers of our time. Lee always treated me like a son and taught me to always speak my mind. Lee is a person that people are drawn to and want to be around. If I were to describe Lee Smith, three words that come to my mind are: pride, honor and integrity, but I'm just honored to call him a friend.

Detective Ben Pender

Captain LeeRoy Smith was my Division Commander in West Patrol. I consider myself very fortunate to have worked for him. "He was really one of the good guys". Captain Smith was more than a great Division Commander, he is truly a great friend and someone I have admired throughout my career.

Chapter One

Officer Rowdy Cooper took a sip of coffee as he slowly maneuvered his truck through the industrial park. They'd had a rash of burglaries in the area and Admin was putting pressure on the graveyard guys to catch the perps. Burbank, the hotshot captain over the Investigations Bureau, insisted it was one guy acting alone but Rowdy wasn't buying it. He just didn't see how one guy could steal that much merchandise in such a short amount of time. He was certain there were at least two, maybe three guys acting together. The latest numbers circulating the precinct were upwards of sixty thousand in cash and merchandise missing, and the number was growing weekly. Chief Steven Griggs was furious. He wanted the burglars caught, yesterday! The Mayor had been pushing for a resolution before, but after last night he was on the warpath. Mayor Gregory Adams was all about politics. When one of his largest contributors got victimized, heads rolled. Currently, Chief Griggs' head was the Mayor's primary target. Rowdy hated politics and he hated threats even worse. So far, Griggs was handling the pressure.

Mount Haven

Rowdy didn't envy the man. He liked Chief Griggs, far more than he had ever liked his predecessor. Griggs was a street cop at heart. He looked out for his men, but demanded hard work and dedication in return.

Rowdy aimed to please. He was an officer of the law and believed in equal justice for all. Which is why his entire squad had made catching the burglar a priority weeks ago… without pressure from the mayor. They'd spent every free moment they had patrolling the commercial areas of the city, trying to catch the burglars in action. Unfortunately, Sweeney Industries was hit last night. Tens of thousands of dollars' worth of equipment was stolen and Theodore Sweeney was beyond livid. To make matters worse, Sweeney was not only a campaign contributor, but a close friend to Mayor Adams. Adams of course blew a gasket when he heard his financial backer was the victim of a crime. Catching the burglar had become a priority, not only for the police department, but for the Mayor's office as well. Rowdy loved being a cop. He loved catching bad guys, which is why he loved working the graveyard shift. He was a hunter of men. His current prey was nothing more than an interesting challenge. The burglars may be clever but as with all criminals, they were getting cocky. Sooner or later they'd get caught - they all did. This time, Rowdy was determined to be the one doing the catching.

He shot a glance to the back of the truck then slowed even more to survey the area. Knight was getting antsy. That was all Rowdy needed to know. Something wasn't quite right and the trouble was close by. Knight, an eight-year-old German Shepherd and Rowdy's K9 partner, was never wrong. Rowdy's life had been saved more than once because Knight sensed something Rowdy had missed. As he made a right turn onto Amelia Avenue, Knight went nuts. He was pacing back and forth with so much force the truck began to rock. Rowdy spotted a beat up old pickup parked on the side of the road and immediately grabbed his mic. He could see from here that the bed was full of expensive equipment. He was going to need backup and fast. He glanced around, but couldn't see his suspect; or suspects. The truck cab was obviously empty. Maybe the perps were still inside the building.

"Kilo 3," he spoke into the handset as he pulled his truck to a stop blocking in the suspect vehicle. He usually preferred the element of surprise, but he'd already lost that with Knight in the back making so much noise.

"Go ahead, Kilo 3," the dispatcher replied.

"I'm in Chesterfield, Amelia Avenue on a burglary in progress and I need a back." Rowdy rattled off the address, the plate number and a brief description of the truck. Dispatch asked for an available unit, but received no response. The fine hair on the back of Rowdy's neck stood up and an uncomfortable tingle ran down his spine. He needed to free Knight; they were going to have to handle this on their own. The bad guys weren't going to wait for help to arrive.

"Charlie 1, I'm clearing the shopping center but I'm a ways out," Sergeant Stratton replied, tension evident in his voice. "Leave this call assigned to Charlie 52, he'll clear when he's finished." Sirens could be heard in the background. "Who do we have closer?" he demanded as he accelerated onto the roadway, tires squealing in protest. "I want a back for Kilo 3 and I want it now."

"Charlie 63 is on a parking problem a few blocks away, but I haven't been able to raise him," the dispatcher advised.

"Charlie 63," Sergeant Stratton bellowed across the airwaves. His tone conveyed his impatience. No one in their right mind would ignore Stratton at a time like this.

"Charlie 63," came the reply.

"Clear your detail and respond to Amelia Avenue immediately," Stratton took a deep breath in a futile attempt to rein in his fury. "I'm on my way. Do not leave the scene until I approve it, personally." The radio went silent for several seconds. Everyone listening knew what that meant. Officer Davis had some explaining to do. Rowdy never asked for a back unless there was trouble. There was no excuse Davis could give that would save him from the Sarge's wrath. Ignoring a fellow officer's call for assistance was taboo. Ignoring it to remain on a parking problem was unforgivable, but not unexpected from Gary Davis. The man was a dinosaur. He should have retired years ago. Even in his prime, he'd been lackluster at best. Now he was useless, occupying an allocation that could go to someone who actually wanted to work. Rather than force the issue, Admin transferred him back on the street six months ago, hoping it would force him out. No such luck. The man was out of shape, lazy and stubborn. He put the men he worked with at risk, but was too arrogant and bullheaded to retire.

"10-4," Officer Davis reluctantly agreed. He knew he was in trouble. He knew he should have responded to assist Officer Cooper, but he hadn't wanted to get involved. This call was bound to be a cluster and Davis wanted no part of it. He had heard the call for help the instant it came across but he'd silently waited, hoping someone else would step up and respond so he wouldn't have to. He was too old for this shit. Nobody knew it yet, but he'd finally decided to pull the plug. He was just waiting for the retirement board to send him the final paperwork. Just a few more days and he'd be moving to sunny Florida to live a long, happy and relaxing life. He certainly wasn't going to put himself in harm's way over a stupid burglar. Dynamo Officer Rowdy Cooper would just have to fend for himself. He had to obey his sergeant's order to respond to the call, but

Stratton couldn't control how quickly he got there or what he did when he finally arrived.

* * * *

Rowdy slid from the truck mentally cursing recent budget cuts. How many times had his sergeant put in a request for remotes to operate the back gate on all their K9 trucks? But no, the department couldn't afford it. So here he was, putting his very life in danger to get to the back cage and release his dog… manually. Rowdy paused when he heard a noise to the right. Knight began to bark and growl, circling the truck even faster now. Rowdy pulled his weapon and surveyed the area. Danger was lurking in the shadows; he could feel it all the way down to his bones. Knight was only confirming what Rowdy already knew: they were sitting ducks and on their own. Man he wished his dog was outside that truck right now.

Rowdy took another step forward then hesitated. Every instinct he had told him to stay close to his vehicle. He glanced to the right again, then made a decision. He needed his dog. Before he could second guess himself, Rowdy pushed his back against the cold metal siding of the truck and silently took another step. Once he reached the back panel, he slowly reached his arm around and fumbled for the release. Within seconds, Rowdy's fingers slid over the spring loaded lever and the gate swung open. Two things happened at once: Knight sprang from the truck, and a shot rang out. Rowdy's leg exploded in pain, he'd been shot in the thigh. Knight didn't hesitate for a second. The well trained dog disappeared, engulfed in darkness as he sprinted toward the shooter. Rowdy was torn. Should he follow Knight, or stay and deal with the second suspect? He focused on the sounds around him and made his decision. He was on his own until he neutralized the threat to his right. Rowdy reached into the truck and grabbed a spare leash, wrapping it tightly around his leg. If he was lucky that would slow the flow of blood oozing from his wound.

Rowdy forced himself to ignore the pain and focus on the sounds around him. Gravel occasionally crunched underfoot as the suspect drew closer. The guy was approaching from the rear and slightly right of his K9 truck. Rowdy smiled and started to relax. He could handle this, just a regular day at the office. He instantly changed his mind when he heard the unmistakable sound of a hammer being cocked. Rowdy froze in place and silently waited for just the right moment to act. Another shot rang out, but he was prepared for it. He fired back, positive he'd hit his mark. The man lunged from the shadows and fired again. A second bullet struck Rowdy in the chest. He always wore a vest so he was protected, but the force of the impact knocked him to his knees. He raised his gun and fired again. This time he knew he'd hit his mark, but the man still kept coming. Rowdy fired again, aiming for the man's head. Maybe the suspect was wearing a vest, too. Without street lights, it was too dark to tell if the guy was bleeding. Rowdy's final shot hit its mark a second too late. As the suspect went down he pulled the trigger. One last round echoed into the night as pain exploded through Rowdy's head, then his world went black.

* * * *

Officer Davis heard what sounded like gunfire. He was torn… rush in to help, or claim he'd gotten lost? He was already in trouble, but could he live with himself if Rowdy Cooper died because he wasn't there? On the other hand, he never had been that good at shooting. He barely qualified when they were forced to go to the range. Who was to say he could even save his fellow officer anyway. It was more likely he'd just die too, a second casualty in this senseless war on crime. And for what? Property the owners would just turn into their insurance company anyway. But he was too close to risk a detour now. Someone might see him and then he would be in trouble. He took another turn, slowly inching his way onto Amelia Avenue, and immediately slammed on his brakes.

The scene before him made him physically ill. Cooper was lying on the ground, bleeding profusely. Another man was spread out a few yards away from the K9 truck. Well, Davis assumed it was a man. The body was face down in the gravel. Blood was seeping from somewhere beneath it, creating a tiny blood river that slowly cascaded over dirt and small rocks before it finally settled in a pool next to the sidewalk. Davis sat, mesmerized for a full minute before he pulled his attention from the growing puddle and glanced around. Rowdy's K9 partner was on alert, guarding another man who was huddled in a fetal position on the ground. The dog was growling, hair standing up, clearly in attack mode. There was no way Davis would be getting out of his car. He was terrified of dogs as it was, police dogs took that fear to a whole new level. He cringed when he heard a car door slam and swung around to see his sergeant running to Rowdy's aid.

"Officer down," Sergeant Stratton barked over the radio. "I need additional backup and a medical chopper, now!" The radio went silent for a moment as he studied the dog. "I also need someone familiar with Cooper's dog to respond. We have a slight situation here." The man being guarded by the dog was on the ground screaming like a girl. There was a black handgun lying just out of reach. Stratton could see what looked like blood splattered around the area near the gun. He glanced back at Rowdy's K9 partner. The dog was standing perfectly still, but leaning slightly forward, clearly waiting for a reason to attack again. His ears were pulled back and his hair was standing straight up as he focused intently on the suspect. The guy slid no more than an inch backwards. Knight growled, a low vicious sound that grew in volume and intensity with each passing second. The suspect froze in place and started to cry. Stratton knew he needed help. He looked at Davis in disgust. The wuss was still cowering inside his cruiser. No help there. He'd deal with Davis later. For now, he needed to do what he could for Rowdy and hope the dog didn't kill the other suspect before help arrived.

* * * *

Sergeant Andy Cooper's car fishtailed as he took a corner too fast. Rowdy was in trouble. And when he got his hands on that no good Davis... Coop didn't finish the thought, he was too busy trying to get his car back under control. Okay, he had to slow down. He'd caught air going over that railroad crossing. But his kid brother was in trouble. The instant Rowdy asked for a back, Coop knew it was serious. Rowdy had Knight and that was usually enough. Coop could count on one hand the number of times Rowdy had asked for backup and every one of them had been ugly. His brother had good instincts. They both did. They'd gotten them from their father, the best cop Coop had ever known. "Come on Rowdy, get on the air and tell us everything is under control."

He slowed to take another corner then accelerated. He was entering the commercial side of the city now. There would be very little traffic out here at this time of night. His heart dropped to his stomach when he heard Stratton's traffic. "Officer down," could only mean Rowdy, especially with the follow-up. Knight was on the loose. Coop barely slowed as he took the turn onto Amelia Avenue. The instant he saw the scene, his breathing became labored. If he didn't get a grip, he'd go into a full panic from the shock. After shoving his car into park, he threw open his door and ran. Rowdy was lying on the ground, not moving. There was so much blood. Could his brother even live after losing that much blood? He slid to a stop then dropped to his knees as he tried to blink back the moisture gathering in his eyes. "Rowdy," he choked out as he slowly reached down and pressed his finger against his brother's neck. There was a pulse, but it was so weak.

Coop stood and ran his hand through his hair. Stratton was better with medical emergencies than he was. It was best to stay out of his friend's way. His brother was in good hands and right now Coop couldn't think. He had to turn away from his brother's helpless body if he was ever going to calm down. It was the hardest thing he'd ever done, but he turned his back to his brother and glanced around the darkened area. He immediately spotted the other man. He was a few yards away and had been shot in the head. At least Rowdy had time to fire back. Was there only one suspect or had Rowdy been ambushed by multiple threats? That's when Coop snapped back into cop mode. Stratton was taking care of Rowdy, but he needed to make sure they were safe. They were sitting ducks out here in the open. He slowly surveyed the area until his focus landed on Knight; who was still guarding the other suspect. Coop forced himself to move forward, hoping he could control Rowdy's dog. "Good boy," he said softly as he approached. "Very good boy, Knight," he said, pausing to wait for the dog to react. He felt vulnerable and too exposed but he also knew Knight would warn him if there was another threat.

Coop let out the breath he hadn't realized he was holding when Knight's ears perked up and he stopped growling. The man on the ground misread the situation and began to crab walk backwards. Coop spotted the gun just a few feet away. The situation was getting worse by the second. He unsnapped his own gun and pulled it from the holster, not knowing if the man was going to lunge for the gun or simply back away from the dog.

Knight refocused on the man and started to growl again as he inched forward ready to attack.

The guy yelled at Coop, "Get that thing away from me." He pivoted and pushed onto his hands and knees then lunged forward in an attempt to flee. That was all Knight needed. He sprang through the air, sinking his teeth into the back of the guy's thigh. Coop was surprised at the grace and precision of the dog's attack. He'd never actually seen Knight in action before.

"Not the brightest thing you've ever done," Coop said, amazed at the man's stupidity. He shook his head as he slid his weapon back into his holster. "Stop fighting or you'll make it worse," Coop ordered as he moved forward to kick the gun further out of reach.

"Get him off," the man screamed. "Get him off!" Then he began to sob.

Knight disengaged from his target, circled once then crouched, hair standing on end as he resumed an aggressive posture; waiting for his prey to make his next move. "How many of you were there?" The suspect didn't respond. He was frozen in place, staring intently, as Knight released a low guttural growl. "Answer me," Coop demanded. "Was it just the two of you? Or were there more? I'm not calling off the dog until I get an answer. And don't lie to me. Knight here can smell a lie a mile away. You don't even want to know what he does to liars."

"No," the man said, then screamed again. "Just us two."

"Knight," Coop said, trying to sooth the dog as he approached. "Good boy," he coaxed taking another step forward. He glanced over his shoulder when he heard the helicopter approach. He didn't have time for this. He needed to be with Rowdy. He needed to know if his brother was still alive. Coop was so focused on the problem at hand that he didn't even hear the other cars arrive. So he was taken by surprise when Officer Johnson, another K9 Officer, stepped up beside him.

"I've got this, Coop," Johnson said softly. "Knight knows me and we've trained for this." He held up a leash. "Go on, you need to head to the hospital. Rowdy's in bad shape. Chacon can help me with the suspect." The cop cocked his head to the side, signaling a second officer that was standing beside him.

"Thanks." Sergeant Andy Cooper nodded and turned back toward the helicopter. He reached it just as they were about to load Rowdy inside. He took a step forward, but was stopped by Sergeant Stratton.

"No, Coop," his friend said soberly. "Let them do their job." He pulled on Coop's arm, guiding him back towards Rowdy's truck.

Coop looked around and for the first time realized just how many cops had arrived. Where were these guys when Rowdy had needed them? He pulled away from Stratton and marched to Gary Davis' vehicle. The coward was still inside. "Get out," he demanded. "Before I help you out."

"Coop," Stratton warned. "I'll handle it. He's my guy. I'll take care of it."

Coop didn't budge. "He's a disgrace to the badge," Coop spit out. "The man has no business being a cop."

"I know," Stratton agreed, taking Coop's arm and pulling him in the opposite direction. He scanned the area and called out to one of his men, "Hey, Lockman."

A uniformed officer turned and immediately jogged over to his sergeant. He paused when he saw Coop, not sure what to say. Before he could think of something that didn't sound lame, Stratton addressed him.

"You got the new guy with you again tonight?" Stratton asked.

"Uh… yeah," he said turning back to his sergeant. "Why?"

"I need you to transport Sergeant Cooper's car to the office. I'm taking him to the hospital as soon as I deal with Davis. I also need to arrange for someone to secure Rowdy's stuff."

"I'll take care of it," Lockman said. "Sergeant Morris just arrived," he pointed to another K9 truck. "It sounded like his Unit would be taking care of Rowdy's truck and his dog. I'll just go find him and make sure," then he turned back to Coop. "We're all sick over what happened here tonight. Give our best to Rowdy when you see him and tell him we're all here for him. Anything he needs, all he has to do is ask."

"Thanks," Coop said softly. He was grateful for the support and Lockman's optimism. Rowdy wasn't gone, yet. Coop knew his brother's chance of survival wasn't good, but he wouldn't give up hope. He couldn't. He wasn't sure he could take another loss. Rowdy had to pull through this. Coop needed him. Both sergeants looked up when Chief Griggs approached.

"Andy," he said as he placed his large hand on Coop's shoulder in support. "We need to get you to the hospital. Let me find you a ride."

"I'll take him sir," Stratton said, glancing around. "But I need to deal with Davis first."

Chief Griggs' face hardened. "I'll deal with Davis." He inhaled a long, deep breath. "I realize I'm stepping on toes here and I'm sorry, but as Chief I'm pulling rank. I want to handle this one personally."

"No offense taken," Stratton said, relieved. He wanted to handle Davis himself but he was also afraid he'd do physical damage to the man; which would definitely get him fired. This way, he could get his friend to the hospital and still know Davis would pay for being inept. Chief Griggs wasn't known for his patience with incompetence.

"Go on," Griggs told Stratton. "Get Cooper to the hospital. We'll handle things here."

"Thank you, sir," Coop said as he turned and headed to Stratton's car.

* * * *

Rowdy slid his eyes open then groaned. His head was killing him and the light coming through the window wasn't helping. He tried to cover his eyes with his arm, but realized he was attached to all kinds of wires.

"Rowdy," Maggie said, rushing to the side of the bed. "Finally," she choked out.

Coop stood and closed the blinds, realizing the light was bothering his brother. Once the blinds were closed, he moved to the wall and flipped the switch. "See if that's better," he said moving in behind his wife. The only light in the room was a soft glow seeping in through the open door.

Rowdy cautiously opened one eye, then the other. "You look as bad as I feel, Coop." He tried to push himself up, but stopped when his head began to throb even more. He glanced at Maggie. She looked exhausted. "What happened?" he asked, trying to remember how he'd gotten here.

"You don't remember?" Coop asked, worried.

"The burglars," he finally said. "Is Knight okay?" He was concerned for the mutt he loved like family. He'd completely lost track of his dog once Knight took off after the first shooter. Rowdy had been too busy dodging bullets. He forced his mind to concentrate. Had Knight been shot, too?

"Knight is fine. Johnson's keeping him at his place until you get out," Coop said, moving closer to the bed. "What do you remember?"

Rowdy thought for a moment. "I remember patrolling the industrial park. We'd been working it for weeks. But with the Mayor breathing down Griggs' back, we all split up. Morris had the whole Unit working that night but individually, you know? We all had the dogs to back us and we had strict orders to call it in immediately if we spotted anything suspicious."

"That answers why you called for backup so quickly," Coop told him.

"I'm going to go get a nurse," Maggie said, tension in her voice.

Once the door closed, Rowdy turned to his brother. "Is she okay?"

"No," Coop sighed. "This has been rough on her. She's not sleeping or eating for that matter. She refuses to leave your side. I thought I was bad but with every passing day, Maggie has gotten worse."

"Every passing day?" Rowdy asked, furrowing his brow. "How long have I been here?"

"Two and a half weeks," Coop said, pulling a chair closer to the bed then sinking into it. He scrubbed his hands across his face, then moved one hand back to rub his neck, letting the other one drop to the arm rest.

"Seriously?" Rowdy asked worried about the toll this ordeal was taking on his brother. "And the two of you have been here the whole time? Who's watching Bryan?"

"He's staying with Maggie's mother," Coop admitted. "This has been hard on him, too. Marsha said he's not sleeping. I've stopped by every day but he's withdrawn and won't talk to me. He's only eight, he doesn't know how to deal with something like this. Hell, I'm thirty-four and I don't know how to deal with it. What kind of example is that for my son?"

Mount Haven

"I'm sorry, man," Rowdy said, horrified at what he'd put his entire family through. "Why don't you grab Maggie and head home for a while? I mean, I'm okay now so go take care of your family."

"You're my family," Coop said, shaking his head. "We'll take off in a while. But first tell me what you can remember. Then I'll update you before the doctor arrives."

"There's not much to tell," Rowdy said, thinking. His head was killing him, but he could remember everything. "I pulled up and spotted the truck. It had some equipment in the back and I knew it had to be our burglars. I called for a back but nobody was available, so I figured it was up to me and Knight. He was going nuts in the back of the truck. I got that feeling, you know the one, I was sure danger was lurking."

"Yeah," Coop agreed. It was like an extra sense. A lot of cops had it, and the good ones always listened. It's what kept them alive.

"Anyway, I felt like a sitting duck. I knew I had to get Knight out of the truck and instinct told me not to go out in the open and drop the cage. So, I stuck close to the vehicle hoping it would hide me enough to hit the release. Knight flew out the back and took off. That's when I knew there were at least two of them. At about that same moment, the guy shot me. My leg was on fire but I couldn't go after him and Knight - there was a second threat and he was headed my way. The second suspect fired and missed. I shot back. I was so sure I'd hit him but he just kept coming… firing at me the entire time. He struck me in the chest, but the vest took that one. It did knock me to the ground, hurt like a bugger. I fired off another shot and I know that one hit him, but it still didn't faze him. The guy must have been wearing a vest or something. That's when I knew my only option was a head shot. I aimed and fired off one more round, then my head exploded and I think I must have blacked out."

"He wasn't wearing a vest," Coop told him. "I might be in trouble for telling you this before you talk to the DA and Internal Affairs, but you hit him every time. He was hyped up on meth. Your first round wasn't fatal. It caught him in the shoulder. The second one was a little off, barely missed the heart, but it would have been fatal and should have stopped him. Obviously the head shot did the trick. The investigators figure he went down instantly. Just dumb luck he got off a round before he went down."

"I take it the last shot got my head?" Rowdy said soberly. He was lucky to be alive.

"Yeah," Coop said, forcing a smile. "Lucky for you there's nothing vital in there."

"Funny," Rowdy said, grinning. Before he could come up with a smart reply the door opened and Maggie returned with a man who Rowdy figured must be the doctor.

"So, my patient has finally decided to wake up," the doctor said cheerfully. "How do you feel?"

"Like I got shot in the head," Rowdy grumbled. "Killer headache and I can't move with all these wires."

The doctor smiled. "Yes," was all he said as he studied Rowdy intently. "I see the lights are off, was that your doing?"

"It was mine," Coop told him. "When Rowdy woke up, the light was too painful."

"Well then, I guess you're not going to be too happy about my light test. Can't be helped. Are you hungry?" The doctor asked as he flicked on a pen light and forced open each eye. Once he finished, he began pushing and prodding, making Rowdy uncomfortable.

"No," Rowdy said. "Not really." He closed his eyes and waited for the pain to subside.

"That's to be expected," the doctor said taking a step back. "Everything looks good. I'll have the nurse bring something in for the headache. Just press the button and let the staff know when you get hungry. For now I want to keep you on broth or Jell-O. I'll give you a pass tonight if you don't think you can stomach anything but I expect you to eat in the morning." Then he turned, nodded to Maggie, and left.

Rowdy gave Coop a questioning look. "That was odd."

"Actually, it was pretty normal for him," Maggie said, lowering herself into the chair Coop had vacated. "The other doctor is more personable. I mean that one's okay, but he doesn't really tell you anything earth shattering or helpful."

A uniformed officer stuck his head into the room. "Hey Rowdy," he said grinning, "Glad you're back among the living." He turned to Coop. "The Chief's been informed of the patient's condition. I also called Troy. He's on his way."

"Thanks, Martin," Coop said, turning to stare out the window.

"Coop, do they have to do this now?" Maggie asked, clearly distraught. "I mean, Rowdy just woke up. Do you really think he's up for a long interrogation?"

"No," Coop said soberly. "But it's not up to me. And it's not up to Rowdy, either."

Rowdy took Maggie's hand. "Hey, Magpie. I'm good. Stop worrying about me. This is procedure. I signed up for it when I took the job."

Maggie nodded and brushed away a tear.

Coop straightened. "I'm going to go downstairs and wait for Troy," then he turned to Maggie. "He's the union rep. I can't be in there with Rowdy, but Troy can. I want to talk to him before they get started."

Rowdy smiled. "You want to give him orders and tell him what will happen if he doesn't obey."

Coop smiled. "That too," then he disappeared out the door.

"Hey, Maggie," Rowdy said once he was sure Coop was gone. "Talk to me, those dark circles under your eyes aren't only for me."

"I don't have dark circles," she protested, but knew she probably did.

"Seriously? They're as black as Toby's butt." He grinned, satisfied that had gotten a rise out of her.

"Rowdy Cooper! You are awful," she scolded. "I'm amazed the ACLU hasn't broken down your door yet."

"What?" Rowdy asked innocently. "That rangy mutt of yours has the blackest butt I've ever seen." He was referring to their son's black lab, Toby, but he knew she would still take offense. "Anyway, I may be politically incorrect, but I've never violated anyone's civil liberties. I'm irreverent about everyone equally," he shrugged. "It's just part of my charm," then he sobered. "Don't try to change the subject, Mags. What's wrong?"

Mount Haven

Maggie stood and walked to the window. She wanted to look out, but knew the sun's glare would hurt Rowdy's eyes so she turned back to face him. "I'm a mess and I hate it. I hate what I've become. I can't sleep, if I do I have nightmares. I practically have a panic attack every time Coop heads off to work. I'm a cop's wife. I'm supposed to be strong. I knew his job was dangerous when I married him. I signed on for this. Coop loves being a cop, it's in his blood. It's all he's ever wanted to be and I'm putting him in danger. I try to be strong, but he can see right through me. I know I'm a distraction. I'm a weak, sappy wife. Everything I've always hated, I've become." She was crying now. "But I don't know how to stop it."

"Mags," Rowdy said softly. "Come here," he held out a hand. Maggie hesitated then moved forward, dropping back into the chair and taking Rowdy's hand. "You're being too hard on yourself. You're human and you had a scare," he smiled. "So, ten percent is about me, ninety percent about Coop? That makes me feel better already."

Maggie narrowed her eyes at Rowdy. "More like forty/sixty," she inhaled. "You scared us, Rowdy. We were both sure we were going to lose you, but we pretended otherwise. Coop's been so worried. You're the only family he's got left. And then his blubbering, weak wife goes off the deep end and he doesn't even have me for support. I'm such a failure. I keep telling myself to pull it together. I know it's not helping. I know the odds are in his favor. It's far more likely that Coop will work for thirty years and never get injured than it is that he will get killed in the line. But no matter how logical I try to be about this, I still can't sleep. I can't eat and when I do sleep the nightmares are awful."

"Tell me about them," Rowdy urged, worried. He'd never seen Maggie like this and it surprised him. She was always so spunky and confident. She was the perfect cop's wife, even when his brother joined SWAT. She knew the risks and still supported his decisions. No wonder Coop was so out of sorts.

"Sometimes they're about you. Sometimes they're about Coop. Mostly they start with you and then turn into Coop," she started to elaborate.

"What do you mean?" Rowdy asked.

"They are always about one of you getting shot. The worst ones are when I'm there. Either you or Coop get shot, and I rush to you to try and stop the bleeding. Whether it starts out as you or Coop doesn't matter. It always ends up being Andy. The ending, before I wake up, is always one of two endings. It's either me and Bryan dressed in black standing over Coop's casket, or I'm sitting on the floor next to him trying to stop the bleeding when he dies. I'm covered in blood and I start screaming. I can't hide them from Andy because if it's the last ending I actually wake up screaming. If it's the first ending, I wake up sobbing uncontrollably."

"Well," Rowdy said slowly. "I don't think it takes a professional to analyze this for you. My encounter has you worried you're going to lose my brother. I'm not surprised by your reaction, why are you?"

"You always knew I was weak?" Maggie asked, horrified.

"You're not weak, Magpie." He pulled her hand to his mouth and kissed it in comfort. "Coop is your life, just like you are Coop's life. I envy the connection you two have. It's that rare, forever kind of love just like my parents had. Giving birth to Bryan only made that connection stronger. Sure, you've always known Coop had a dangerous job but watching me go through this has brought it closer to home. We both know how devastated you would be if anything ever happened to my brother. I think those fears have always been there, in the back of your mind. This has just brought them to the forefront. It's natural to worry about the man you love. Especially when he's a cop. But Mags, Coop is a sergeant now. He's not out in the thick of things. Sure, he runs into danger occasionally but it's not the same as it was before. When you start to panic, just remember that. Most of the time Sergeant Andy Cooper is off having coffee and harassing his men. Your husband used to be on SWAT. He's well trained, very tactically savvy and he's not out responding to the dangerous calls anymore. This will pass, I promise. You're always going to worry and you should. But don't let it control your life. Give it time."

Maggie wiped her face and stood. "I need your bathroom before the world arrives to harass you. I really wish I could stay and protect you, or that Andy could be there. I don't like this," she scowled. "I really don't like this at all."

Rowdy smiled. "Take a breath, momma bear. I'm okay with it. Troy will be there. If it's too hard on me, he'll insist we take a break. If I know my brother, he's threatening the man's life as we speak. If Troy lets the interview go too long, he'll answer to Andy Cooper."

Maggie did smile at that. "I agree, your brother is one of a kind."

Coop stepped back into the room, relieved to see his wife smiling. Not the fake, forced smile she'd been giving him for weeks, but a genuine smile. "That I am," he said, moving to Maggie and enfolding her in his arms.

Maggie wrapped herself around Coop and held on. "And I'm the luckiest woman in the world." She went up on tiptoes and kissed him lightly on the lips.

Coop wiped the moisture from Maggie's face. "You've been crying," he frowned. He hadn't been gone that long. What had he missed?

"Only a little," she said, stepping away and moving into the bathroom.

Coop turned to Rowdy but before he could say a word Chief Griggs entered the room.

"I'm glad to see you're awake Cooper," Griggs said as he scrutinized Rowdy.

"Thank you, sir," Rowdy said, but he didn't move. "Unfortunately, I can't move yet so the interview will have to take place like this."

"That's not a problem," Griggs said, glancing around for a chair. "Michelle Tingey from the District Attorney's office will be conducting the interview today. She has assured me she will not take too much of your time."

Both Coop and Rowdy relaxed. Michelle Tingey was good at her job. She was also very pro law enforcement. If she was doing the interview it would be quick and to the point. Rowdy should be cleared in matter of days.

"I've approved Lieutenant Christensen from IA to sit in," Griggs continued. "However, I am not allowing him to ask any questions at this time. He can take as many notes as he likes, and he's been told he can ask for clarification if necessary, but he will not be conducting an interrogation today. I don't see a need for it and I won't allow my people to hamper your recovery."

"Thanks," Rowdy said, unsure how to respond. They all watched as Maggie slipped from the bathroom and left the room, closing the door softly behind her.

"Do you have any questions before we start?" Griggs asked.

"I do have one question," Rowdy said, glancing from the Chief to his brother. "I don't know if you can answer it though."

"What's that?" Coop asked.

"Coop, you said I've been out for over two weeks. Why is that? I mean the doctor came in for about two minutes, but he didn't say if I have brain damage or why I've been out cold for so long."

"I can answer that while you get Michelle and Troy Nelson. He's going to sit in as Rowdy's rep," Coop told the Chief.

"Okay," Chief Griggs said with a nod. "I'll be right back."

"The bullet hit you in the side of the head," Coop began. "You had lost a lot of blood already because of the leg wound. But then you had internal bleeding in your brain. After a couple MRIs they decided to operate. Once they removed the bullet, the doctors had you in a medically induced coma for the first ten days. They said it was necessary for your recovery because of the bleeding and the drainage tube," Coop grinned. "They assured me they would pull the tube before all your brains leaked out, but we'll have to wait and see if that's really true."

Rowdy smiled. His brother was finally starting to get back to normal. "The rest was up to you. We've been worried because the doctors had no idea how long it would take you to come out of the coma. The longer it took, the lower the odds that you would ever wake up."

"No wonder Maggie's so upset," Rowdy realized. "She's worried about you."

"I know," Coop admitted. "But I don't know how to help her. I keep wondering if I should just find another profession."

Rowdy was floored by that. Coop could never be anything but a cop. "I think maybe you are just as messed up by this incident as she is. Don't do anything stupid. She'll come around. And if she doesn't, then you can think about a different career. I'd hate to see you make a rash decision and regret it the rest of your life."

Coop didn't make any promises. He didn't have time to say anything. Chief Griggs and the small group entered the room and Coop excused himself. He had a lot to think about. But he was certain of one thing, Maggie wouldn't simply get over this. He was starting to believe some kind of change was the only thing that would help. He was also worried about Rowdy. They didn't know the extent of his damage yet, but the doctors had pretty much guaranteed Rowdy would not recover completely. If he did, it certainly would not be in time to return to work. The department's policy was extremely restrictive. They only had three months from the time of the incident to apply for a medical retirement. If Rowdy didn't act within that time frame, he was screwed. That wasn't nearly enough time for his brother to recover. Coop figured there was about a ninety nine percent chance Rowdy would have to take a medical retirement from the department. He worried the blow was going to be more than Rowdy could take. Coop wasn't the only one with cop in his blood.

Chapter Two

Six months later...

Rowdy shifted, trying to find a comfortable position for his leg. It was killing him, but he didn't want to force Coop to stop again. He reached into his pocket and slipped out two Tylenol, wondering for about the hundredth time that day if this was such a good idea. The ranch had to be a rundown disaster by now. Their grandfather on their mother's side had left it to them almost a decade ago. Rowdy studied the two pills, debating.

"Just take the damn pills already," Coop said, handing Rowdy a fresh bottle of water.

"What?" Rowdy asked, jerking around to face his brother. "Oh yeah, thanks," he answered absently as he twisted the lid and gulped down the pills. "Do you even know where you're going?"

Coop refused to justify that question with an answer. He glanced at Rowdy then back to the road as he rolled his eyes in exasperation.

"Okay. Fine," Rowdy said, shifting again. On top of the leg pain, he was starting to get a headache. He just hoped it didn't turn into another migraine.

Coop studied his younger brother for several minutes then pulled into a small diner.

"What are you doing?" Rowdy demanded.

"I want coffee," Coop said with a shrug. He climbed from the car and raised his arms in a long body stretch. "It's kind of cool, you want a jacket?" Coop opened the back door and pulled a large sweatshirt over his head.

Rowdy climbed from the car holding onto the open door for support. His leg was slowly getting better, but after the long ride it was stiff. He needed to get his bearings before he tried to walk or he'd fall on his face.

"You know," Coop said as he grabbed Rowdy's jacket and cane then casually pushed the door closed. "I never realized just how stubborn and pigheaded you really were until now." He reached the passenger side of the car and held the cane out for Rowdy to take.

"Confident and determined," Rowdy corrected, taking the cane in disgust. He hated the thing and was doing everything in his power to ditch it for good. He had no doubt that he would... someday. At first the doctors were afraid it would never heal completely. They couldn't determine if he was having trouble walking because of brain damage or the bullet that had lodged in his thigh. Rowdy was sure it was the bullet and he was right. The

Mount Haven

surgery to remove the fragments had been extensive and caused some nerve and muscle damage. In addition to that, he had suffered minor brain damage. Nothing too severe, but he still had excruciating headaches and sometimes he had trouble concentrating. The damage was bad enough to force him into a medical retirement. Chief Griggs promised he could have his job back once he recovered fully. Initially, that gave Rowdy something to work towards. He loved being a cop and couldn't see himself as anything else. Yet six months later, he still walked with a cane. Reality began to set in. His career was over and it was time to decide what he wanted to do with the rest of his life. He was just grateful that Knight was old enough to retire with him. Otherwise he would have had to turn his best friend over to a new handler.

Rowdy pulled on his jacket and turned to face his brother. "Are you sure this was a good idea?"

"Positive," Coop said cheerfully. "And anyway, if it turns out to be a disaster I can always blame you. It was your idea in the first place."

"I can see how that would be important," Rowdy grumbled, "having a scapegoat to blame for your whims. When I suggested it, Maggie was still having nightmares. I thought it might do her good to get out of the city."

Coop scowled. "Maggie still has nightmares. She just thinks she hides them from me and they no longer haunt her every night."

Rowdy came to an abrupt stop. "She said she was better."

"She is better," Coop told him, pressing his hand to Rowdy's back to give him a gentle nudge. "That term is relative. She's started to do that more often… tell partial truths. She doesn't want me to worry and she thinks her reaction to all this makes her weak."

"And Bryan?" Rowdy asked. "How was he this morning before you left?"

"The same," Coop said with a sigh, even more worried about his son than he was his wife. "So for my family's sake, I hope the house is at least livable and the place is salvageable. I know Mom always talked about it like it was paradise, but there had to be a reason she left."

"There was," Rowdy grinned. "His name was Pappy Cooper."

Coop smiled too. "Yeah, they were something weren't they?" He held the door for Rowdy. "I don't think it'll matter how old I get, I'm going to miss them forever."

"Me too," Rowdy said, pausing to walk down memory lane. He had needed his mother these past few months more than any other time in his adult life. And he knew if his dad were here, the transition from cop to nobody would have been easier on him somehow. Thinking about his father was always a jumbled mix of pride and sadness. Maybe it was better Pappy wasn't here to see this. It would have killed his father to see Rowdy wounded to the extent that he couldn't return to active duty. Pappy Cooper was the proudest father ever when his boys decided they were going to follow in his footsteps and join the force. Rowdy could still remember his first day on the job. His father couldn't stop smiling. Rowdy tried to shake off the sadness and frustration as he glanced at his brother. "When I'm ninety, sitting on the front porch of that big ranch house, surrounded by grandkids, I'll still be thinking of Mom and Dad."

"You do realize you have to have a wife before you can have grandkids, don't you?" Coop smirked. "Is the terminal bachelor thinking about settling down? And anyway, I'm the oldest, I get the ranch house. You get the cottage."

"Yeah whatever," Rowdy said. "I'm the invalid, you'll cave."

"Don't count on it," Coop said, knowing he would but not wanting to admit it to Rowdy. He'd give anything to make his brother happy again. The last six months had been the hardest six months of his life. Maggie still wasn't herself, Bryan was not only struggling with his homework, but he was getting into fights at school. And Rowdy? He couldn't remember the last time his brother laughed. Not just a smile or a chuckle to humor him, but truly laughed. His brother used to be so full of life before he got shot. Rowdy was always the most relaxed, fun-loving guy Coop knew. That was probably why they got along so well. Now, he was all about determination and hard work. At first Rowdy was determined to make a full recovery and get back to work. Once he was forced to retire, his brother had gone into a deep depression. Then one day, he started with the determination again. He worked his leg too hard. Two months ago he had caused so much muscle damage, the doctor had ordered him to stop completely for three full weeks. Now, Rowdy was back to pushing himself. And it was rare for him to even take an aspirin. That was how Coop knew it was time for another break. Rowdy downing a couple Tylenol meant he was suffering. And as usual, he suffered in silence.

"What's with the frown?" Rowdy asked. "If it means that much to you, I'll let you have the ranch house. I'll build a new mansion on the lake instead. The chicks will dig it."

"Funny," Coop said grabbing a menu.

"I thought you said we were stopping for coffee." Rowdy scowled as he picked up his own menu. "You seriously cannot be hungry again." He knew this stop was for him because of the Tylenol. But if Coop thought they were going to take another long break just so he could rest, his brother was sadly mistaken.

"If you didn't notice, that last place was a dive," Coop said studying the menu. "I barely gagged down half my sandwich before I gave up."

Rowdy grinned. "I noticed."

The waitress stopped at their table then glanced around. "I couldn't help but overhear you two." She glanced back again, then leaned forward. "Don't order anything hot. The cook's a nephew of the owner. He thinks he's a master chef, but he's really a dud."

"Good to know," Coop said, grinning at Rowdy.

"The only exception is the pie," she continued. "Mrs. Clayton makes the pies fresh daily and they are to die for."

"I'm sold," Rowdy said, handing the menu back to his brother. "I'll have a slice of cherry pie with a large scoop of vanilla ice cream and a glass of milk."

"Make that two," Coop said, adding his menu to Rowdy's then passing them to the waitress.

"Good choice," the friendly woman said with a wink. "You boys just passing through?"

Coop shrugged and leaned back against the bench. "Not sure yet. Our family's from here, on our mother's side. We inherited some property a while back but up until now haven't had a chance to see it. We're here to check the place out."

Mount Haven

"Brothers?" The waitress asked, studying the two men more closely.

"Yeah," Rowdy said grinning. "We both got looks, but unfortunately for him I got all the brains."

"You wish," Coop said, enjoying Rowdy's playful demeanor. "I got the looks and the brains. You, little bro lucked out, you inherited mom's sweet spirit." Coop laughed out loud when Rowdy rolled his eyes in disgust.

"I'd say neither one of you missed out on the ego gene," she laughed. "I'm Gina and I've been here all my life. How long since your kin lived around here? I might've known them."

Coop hesitated. The woman had to be in her sixties. Maybe she had known his grandfather, or maybe his mom? "My mother moved a long time ago. Followed her one true love to the big city. Grandpa stayed until the day he died. We were lucky though, he visited often. He died nine years ago."

"Then I should know him. What's his name?" Gina asked.

"Donald Walker," Rowdy said softly, watching for a reaction.

"No kidding!" Gina said, excited. "That would make you two Charlie Walker's boys. Well, I'll be," she said with a smile. "I should have guessed. You look just like your daddy. How are those two anyway? Since Donald passed we haven't heard a word about them."

"Mom passed away seven years ago; cancer," Coop told her. "Dad went two years later; heart attack. Although Rowdy and I believe it was really a broken heart. He wasn't the same without Mom."

"I'm so sorry," Gina said, astonished that both of their parents had died so young. "Skip, go get Joe."

"Gina," Skip whined. "I'm working. How many times have I told you, I can't be interrupted while I'm working? This is art, it is culture, it's..."

"It's crap," Gina said impatiently. "Go fetch Joe, now."

Skip let out a huff, then slipped outside letting the door slam in his wake.

"Sorry about that," Gina said, still intrigued. "His daddy spoils that kid rotten. Mark had aspirations and dreams. He took off the day after his eighteenth birthday, headed for the big city, off to college to make it big. He succeeded, too. Mark works for Microsoft, which means Skip will probably never work a day in his life. He's what they call a trust fund baby. Anyway, Joe is going to be so happy to see you."

Just then an ancient man walked through the back door. "Gina, what'd you do to get Skip all fired up again?"

"Joe," Gina said, moving to wrap an arm around the old man's waist. "Guess who these boys belong to?"

Joe straightened, then squinted, took a step forward, then squinted again. "No idea," he finally admitted as he lowered himself slowly into a chair and waited.

"Charlie Walker's boys," Gina practically squealed. "They're here to check out Donald's old place."

"You don't say," Joe said, leaning forward to get a better look. "Which one of you's Coop and which one is Rowdy?"

That took both of them by surprise. "I'm Rowdy, the ugly one over there is Coop."

Joe laughed. "Cocky as always I can see."

"I take it you knew my grandfather well," Coop said, a little uncomfortable that an old man he had never met seemed to know so much about him.

"Don and I were best friends, practically since birth," Joe said, lost in memories. "He sure loved that girl of his and when she had you two, his life was complete. He'd be so thrilled to know his boys finally came out to see the place. It was his pride and joy, you know?"

"Mom called it a little slice of paradise. Which is why we never understood why grandpa always came to us. If it was so great, you'd think Mom would have wanted us to see it. That she would have wanted to spend time out here," Rowdy said still confused about that.

"Charlie did love that old place, but it brought back too many memories. Oh, there were plenty of good ones, but visiting the ranch always reminded that girl of her mother. When Lydia took off with that rich womanizer, it broke Donald's heart. Which in turn broke Charlie's heart. She adored her papa and never did forgive her mother for abandoning him like that. Lydia didn't much care for small town life, but Donald adored her and thought the feeling was mutual. Having her take off with another man crushed him. Charlie was already married to that handsome cop of hers. That there was a whirlwind romance if there ever was one. Anyway, the ranch reminded your mother of Lydia. She couldn't stand to be there and didn't want you boys to get caught up in all the drama of the past.

So, Donald went to see you every chance he got." He snapped his fingers. "Problem solved."

Both Coop and Rowdy grinned. The man was a character. Coop could just imagine this old coot and his grandfather sitting around town gossiping about their families. "Gina says your son has done well for himself. You must be proud of all his accomplishments."

Joe huffed. "Mark, I'm proud of. That one in there, waste of good air," he contemplated. "I always thought Gracie and I would leave the place to Mark and see the world. But Mark didn't want anything to do with the food industry. I get that, he had his own dreams to chase. But now what am I supposed to do with this place. The town needs somewhere to eat. Not that Skip hasn't run most of them off. The boy couldn't cook a cheese sandwich if his life depended on it. Gracie's pies keep the place going, but the arthritis got her hands. Some days she can barely move." Joe seemed to realize he was airing his family business. He shook his head then turned back to Coop. "You know how to get out to Don's old place?"

Coop rattled off the directions.

"Then you're all set," Joe turned and called to Gina. "Help me to the house. I need to check on Gracie and my back's had enough for one day."

"My pleasure," Gina said, wrapping an arm around Joe's waist to guide him toward the door. "You two don't worry about the bill. It's on the house today. Just be sure to stop by before you rush out of town and let me know what you think of the place. I'm as bad as the old cat, but curiosity's always been my worst vice. I have to know if we'll be seeing you two around on a more regular basis."

Mount Haven

"We'll do our best," Rowdy said, not wanting to commit to anything. "Do you need any help with the old man?"

"Nope," Gina said. "I got it. He's a lightweight. Don't you worry and drive careful, that upper road gets washed out after a storm. It should be fine, but it rained a few days back."

"Thanks for the warning," Coop said as he pulled out his wallet. He might not be charged for the meal, but he'd be leaving a generous tip.

* * * *

Coop spotted the large red barn just in time to catch the turn off. Directions around here were something out of an old western novel. No addresses, just things like 'take a left at the Benson's old barn' and 'turn right when you reach the three willow trees'. He was amazed he'd found the place so quickly. He slowed the car to a crawl as he maneuvered around the large holes in the old dirt driveway. He could already see the place was going to need some work, and about a ton of gravel to make the roadway usable. He glanced at Rowdy; his brother was unusually quiet. "Not too bad, all things considered," he finally said, hoping for a sign from his brother one way or the other.

"The ranch is like a paradise," Rowdy finally whispered. He turned to Coop and smiled. "Mom was right. Look at this place. Sure the road needs work and I have no doubt the house is going to be worse, but look at that view."

Coop smiled. Rowdy was right, the view was magnificent. "I wonder how much is ours," he said absently, trying to take in the majestic land and miss pot holes at the same time.

Rowdy shrugged. "No idea. I'm sure there's a way to find out though. If the place doesn't have fences, the surveyor's office should be able to come out and mark the boundaries for us."

"Does that mean you want to stay?" Coop asked hesitantly. This move was perfect for Coop and his family, he just wasn't sure that Rowdy was going to adjust to small town life as easily. Coop on the other hand was set if they decided to make the move. He'd already talked to the Mayor of Mount Haven, Jon Herlin. The man was a friendly sort and was pushing Coop to accept his offer and take over as Chief of Police. Mayor Herlin had flown out to Chicago three times and upped the salary twice in an effort to close the deal. But, Coop wouldn't commit until they saw the ranch and Rowdy agreed to join him. He held his breath, waiting for his brother to respond. He was desperate to hear what Rowdy thought of the place.

"Maybe," Rowdy finally answered softly. "Let's not get ahead of ourselves. We still need to see what condition the house is in and I need to check out the cottage Mom talked about. No offense, but I'm not living with my brother."

"Fair enough," Coop agreed. He too wanted to see how much work they had ahead of them. They rounded a small bend in the driveway and the house finally came into view. Coop's breath caught in his throat. The thing was massive. Surely too large for a family of three. "Uh, I'm pretty sure there's room for you in the main house, bro."

Rowdy laughed. He too was awestruck and a little intimidated by the sight. "How did we not know about this?" he finally asked.

Mount Haven

"I mean, when Mom told us she inherited the ranch, she acted like it was no big deal. I feel like the Kennedys or something."

Coop laughed. He could relate. "I have no idea. I guess because gramps never let on he was loaded. I mean, he had to be in order to afford all this." Coop was surveying the property. In addition to the house, there was a large barn to the left and an even larger stable area. Their grandfather must have been very successful at whatever he did. "Let's see what the place looks like inside. But from here, I don't think we have as much work ahead of us as we originally believed."

"I don't see the cottage. Where did Mom say it was located?" Rowdy asked as he unfastened his seatbelt and opened the door to stand. Coop had brought the car to a stop directly in front of the main house.

"Over there I think," Coop said, pointing to what looked like an overgrown pathway. "She said it had a wonderful view of the lake, so it has to be over there somewhere. I think the trees are just obstructing our view."

"I think that's a good thing," Rowdy said, straining to find some indication the cottage was in that direction. "I mean, if we are both going to live here, we're going to want our privacy. I wouldn't want the place to be right in your backyard."

Coop laughed as he handed Rowdy his cane. "If I didn't know better, I'd take offense to your attitude. You're acting like you don't like me or my amazing family."

"I prefer to love you from a distance," Rowdy said. He flashed his brother a teasing grin as he turned toward the mansion's front door. "Okay, let's see what we've got here."

Coop slid in the key and relaxed when the lock smoothly released. He swung the massive door open and reached for a flashlight. Hopefully once they opened some windows there would be enough light inside to see their way around.

The home was still furnished but there was dust everywhere. It was obvious the place had been deserted for a number of years. As the two brothers made their way through the large foyer, to the study and eventually to the kitchen and dining area they were thinking the same thing… the place was perfect.

"Mags is going to love it here," Rowdy finally told his brother when he reached the top of the large flight of stairs. His leg was hanging in there so far, but the test would be going back down. The two of them moved silently to the first door and Rowdy swung it open. The bedroom was large, but obviously not the master. They continued down the hallway, opening door after door. There were four bedrooms, two baths and a large area that would be perfect as a game room for Bryan. The last door they came to was the master suite. Rowdy let out a soft whistle. "Yeah, like I said, Mags is going to love it."

"It's going to be a lot of work to clean up the house, but I'm not complaining." Coop let out a deep sigh. "I was afraid the roof would be falling in and I'd have to replace all the windows. Maybe chase a few raccoons out of the living room. We got lucky, brother. I think someone came in and winterized the property. I bet gramps knew it would be years before Mom did anything with the place and prepared for the worst."

"Grand dad always did plan ahead," Rowdy agreed.

Mount Haven

"Now let's go find that cottage and see if it's going to work for your needs as well," Coop said, turning to head down the large staircase.

"You don't have to ask me twice," Rowdy said, unable to hold in his excitement. He'd been more than a little skeptical of Coop's plan at first. Sure, he was the one that initially suggested it, but that was back when Maggie wouldn't even leave the house. Bryan wasn't much better. Since then Coop's family had seemed to be healing, whereas Rowdy was getting worse. Not being able to work out for three full weeks had almost killed him. When Coop approached him with this idea, Rowdy thought his brother had lost his mind. Now, if he was honest, he couldn't wait to move in. Hopefully the cottage was livable. He knew if the place wasn't up to Coop's standards, he'd be fighting a losing battle. Coop would never live in the big house and allow his brother to rough it in a small dilapidated cottage.

The two men slowly made their way along the overgrown path. Rowdy was about to give in to the pain and find a rock or something to rest on when the trees opened up to a large, albeit overgrown, garden area. There was a substantial grass yard to the side. It was sprinkled with dandelions and wildflowers but salvageable. The overgrown path flowed into a flat concrete walkway that led to a brick and stone structure. When his mother talked about a cottage, Rowdy envisioned a small one room shack. This was no shack. It was a house. A western style rambler that sat high on a hilltop that overlooked the lake. "It's perfect," Rowdy said, grinning from ear to ear. "Let's go check out the inside."

Coop was smiling, too. The pathway would need work but the cottage didn't look any worse than the main house. Sure, it was dirty and would need weeks of cleaning before it was livable, but nothing was broken. No windows or walls needed to be replaced. "The patio is going to be great in the evenings," Coop grinned. "The picture of romance. Should come in handy while you seek out that wife, the one that's going to make all those grandkids possible." Coop laughed at Rowdy's scowl then slid in the key. The lock opened with ease. As the two of them stepped inside, Rowdy began moving curtains. Dust quickly filled the room and Rowdy coughed but continued to move from window to window letting in light as he went.

"Slow down, man," Coop said, moving in front of Rowdy and continuing down the hallway. In addition to the large family room, the kitchen and a spacious dining room, the cottage had three bedrooms, one and a half baths and the master, which also had an adjoining bath. Coop spotted another door at the end of the hallway. "I wonder where this goes," he said as he pushed open the door. The instant he stepped inside he grinned. "Man, this would be perfect for a weight room. We can move all that gym equipment in here so you can work out any time you want."

Rowdy took a cautious step forward then he too was smiling. This place was perfect. The room was spacious enough that all his expensive equipment would fit with room to spare. "Yeah," Rowdy finally said. "I do want to move to Mount Haven."

Coop spun around to face his brother. "Are you sure?" He swallowed and started again. "I mean, really? You want to move here, for you I mean? Not just because you can see it's what I want, but you want to move halfway across the country because it's what you want?"

Rowdy smiled and nodded. "Take a look around you. How could I not want this? It's amazing. I wish we'd known it was here before." A shadow crossed Rowdy's face and Coop instantly understood.

Mount Haven

"Don't go there, man," Coop said, refusing to think about how things might have been different if they had moved here years ago, or even last year for that matter. But they both knew that never would have happened. Neither man would have willingly left the department they loved. The department where their father had worked most of his life. A department where their family was loved and respected.

"I know," Rowdy said, shaking off the cloud that threatened to swamp him. "We both know that even if we'd seen the place years ago, neither one of us would have made the move. We're only doing it now because I messed up and ruined all our lives."

Coop moved to stand beside Rowdy. "No," he said, choosing his words carefully. "We both know that's not true. Everyone knows that's not true. A couple thugs got high and brought weapons to the party. Then they decided to go on a crime spree. What happened to you, could have happened to any of us. The only reason you lived through it is because you are a better cop, a better shot, than most."

"Lucky me," Rowdy said, turning to head back outside. He needed fresh air. This conversation had taken a turn he wasn't willing to travel. And for about the thousandth time he wondered if they all would have been better off if he hadn't survived that night. Once they were standing in the spacious front yard, Rowdy turned to Coop, determined to shake off the gloom. "Now what?" He found a large rock and leaned against it, taking the pressure off his bum leg. "I mean, do we go back to town and call Maggie? Do you need to head over to City Hall and accept the job? What?"

"If you don't mind, I think we should spend the night here in town," Coop said, leaning against a large tree. "I can stop in and finalize things with Mayor Herlin tonight. In the morning we can make arrangements for the utilities to be turned back on. I was worried we would have to deal with well water, but I don't think that's the case. We'll need to arrange for power, water and gas for sure. After that, I guess we head back to Chicago and start packing and selling."

"Sounds like a plan," Rowdy agreed. "I think Maggie is going to be relieved. Bryan? He might be another story. Moving from the big city to a small town might be a little hard on the tyke."

"You don't think we're doing the right thing for my son?" Coop asked, worried again.

"I didn't say that," Rowdy disagreed. "I think it is the right thing for Bryan. I'm just saying he might not agree at first. It was more of a warning than anything. Don't expect Bryan to jump for joy when you call home tonight. He's going to lose all his friends and the only home he has ever known. Sure, he needs the change and he'll make new friends out here but that doesn't mean he's going to make this easy on you. After all, you're not changing careers, just locations. He's still worried about you being a cop."

"I know," Coop agreed. "But that's all I know. If I could move out here and be a plumber, don't you think I'd do that? For my family, I would do anything."

Rowdy decided to go for broke. "I know you would," he began. "I also know you'd be miserable. You are a cop, Coop, whether that means being the chief in a small town or a SWAT cop in the big city, your blood is blue and always will be. I really wish you would stop feeling guilty because you're still on the job and I'm not. I'm never going to have that again. Just because my career is over, doesn't mean yours has to be. I'm okay with that. I've accepted things, this is what I have. I'll figure my life out. I'll learn to do something else, something that makes me happy," Rowdy smiled and shrugged. "Anyway, if I'm moving to Podunk I at least want to know they have a good Chief of Police. Us invalids need to feel safe," Rowdy smiled, but there was no light behind it. He did feel like an invalid and he hated it.

Coop felt the change and didn't know how to respond. He knew his brother felt vulnerable and helpless but Coop knew he wasn't. And with time, Rowdy was going to find his place again. Life wouldn't keep his brother down forever. "Let's head back. I can't wait to call Maggie." The brothers started down the overgrown path. "You do know if you insist on living in that cottage alone, Maggie is going to make me repair this pathway. Probably before she lets me do anything else."

Rowdy laughed, Coop was right. "It shouldn't take much to fix that up, and we can hire out the driveway. I'm thinking if we just spread out some gravel to fill in the holes, that will do for now. In fact, the noise will alert us to visitors. Maybe we can find someone while we're here in town and get on their schedule right away. That way it should be finished by the time we get back."

"Agreed," Coop said as he kept pace with his brother all the way to the car. He wanted to be close just in case Rowdy stumbled. One day Rowdy wouldn't need his attention, but for now he was going to be there whether his brother wanted him to or not. Which is why Coop never could have made this move without Rowdy. The two men talked about plans all the way back to the car then continued to discuss improvements and repairs as they made their way to town. Once they arrived, they found a small hotel and checked in for the night.

* * * *

Reese took another sip of vodka and studied his friend. Cole was engaged in another tantrum. For the millionth time since childhood, Reese wondered what it would be like. How would it feel to lose control the way Cole frequently did? Would experiencing that kind of uninhibited emotion feel exhilarating and powerful, or weak? He just didn't know. He'd never been allowed to show emotion, ever. Reese scowled as that old unsettling question returned, pounding through his head like a freight train. Did he maintain such unwavering control as an adult because he wanted it that way, or was his father still influencing his decisions and his actions? He liked to tell himself it was his own choice, but in times like this he wasn't so sure. He would never admit it to anyone, but sometimes he envied his longtime pal. Envied his freedom, envied his family and envied how secure Cole was in everything he did.

Reese threw back his head and downed the last of his scotch. Then, he stood and moved to the French doors gazing into the darkness. Thinking about his father always did this to him; the instant anger mixed with a feeling of inadequacy. He hated the man with every fiber of his being but he would never be rid of him. The old man made sure of that. There were plenty of company spies still on the inside, watching his every move. Which made tracking down Victoria an even bigger priority. He needed her money to cover the bad business risks he took three years ago before the wrong person caught on. The debts were also coming due and the company just didn't have that kind of expendable cash. The mighty Carlton Weathersby was going to discover Reese's mistakes any day now. And when he did, there would be hell to pay.

Reese turned just as Cole slammed down the receiver and then picked up the phone and violently tossed it to the ground. "I gather your investigator's lead didn't pan out," he said coolly returning to the couch. If there was one thing he knew, it was how to handle Cole Hughes. Paramount was remaining calm and collected.

"The incompetent fool," Cole growled. "I've paid that man over fifty thousand to find the spoiled brat and he hasn't found shit." Cole stood and practically stomped to the recliner positioned across from Reese. "Seriously, truck stop waitress?"

Reese frowned. What was Cole talking about? "I thought the last lead was some floosy sniffing around Devlin Parker." Parker was one of the richest men in the country. His family's development firm was said to net over a hundred million annually. It was exactly the type of man Victoria would seek for refuge. Cole's sibling would never sacrifice comfort, not even on the run.

Cole tossed a folder on the table in front of Reese. "That woman cannot be my sister." Technically Cole and Victoria were step-siblings but the family had dropped the step titles years ago. Piper, his father's current wife, believed it made them a closer family unit without them.

Reese slowly moved forward and retrieved the file. The instant he opened it, he knew Cole was right. Victoria, or Tory as Reese liked to call her, might be able to color her hair and add a few pounds, but she couldn't have aged fifteen years that quickly. Sure, she'd been in hiding for just over three years now but still. He tossed the file on the table and waited. Cole was the most impatient man he knew. He wouldn't have to wait long for an explanation.

"Now the moron wants to check out some waitress that worked at a truck stop in hicktown Nebraska for six months before dumping the joint and moving on. I mean really. Can you imagine my sister waiting tables? The idea is ludicrous."

Reese agreed. He couldn't picture Victoria Alexander lowering herself to wait tables, especially not for dirty, low class truckers. The idea made Reese shudder with revulsion. He could only image Tory's reaction if anyone even suggested the idea. "So the trail's gone completely cold?"

"He had one other lead, but the guy dismissed it. I told him to get on it right away. It seems some dark haired damsel in distress showed up in Texas a few months back and charmed her way into the life of the local oil tycoon. Sounds like something Victoria would do. Rumor has it, the family adores her and the locals are thrilled to have such a sweet, vivacious thing living in their community." Cole hesitated; Reese was not going to like the rest of the story.

"Go on," Reese said, knowing his friend was hiding something. "Tell me the rest."

"Well, you're not going to like it Reese," Cole said with a sigh. "It seems this woman, who called herself Alexia Torrin, got married last week."

"To the oil tycoon?" Reese said, seething. If this was the lead they'd been waiting for, if his Tory had up and married some Texas oil man, heads were going to roll.

"To the oil tycoon," Cole confirmed. "Apparently they live in a fortress that's nearly impossible to access. My guy has his people scouring the area for anything on the woman, but so far they've come up empty. What if it's her?" Cole hated to ask, but had to. It wouldn't stop his plans, not in the least, but it would be an obstacle for Reese.

Reese shrugged. "Then we've finally found her," he said, trying to maintain his calm façade. Right now, he was anything but calm. His stomach felt like a typhoon was raging inside and it took all the willpower Reese possessed not to throw one of Cole's tantrums.

"But if she's married…" Cole let the sentence hang in the air, not sure how to finish that thought.

"People have accidents every day," Reese said calmly. "If this man married my woman, it's unfortunate but easily rectified."

Cole smiled; he hadn't considered that. Getting to a man who lived in a fortress would be difficult, but not impossible and more challenging than the bimbos they'd been playing with lately. Taking the life of a rich oil tycoon, now that was going to be fun. "I'm in," Cole said, significantly more cheerful than he had been just moments earlier. "Just remember our deal," he added, watching his friend closely. "I get her first. One night alone with the conniving princess then she's all yours."

Reese cringed inwardly. He was still trying to find a way out of the bargain they'd struck but so far, nothing was coming to him. "I'm well aware of our agreement Cole," he smiled. "It seems you're the one forgetting the terms."

Cole squirmed. He knew the terms, but he'd struck the deal before he'd met Sissy. His future wife was delicate and innocent, exactly what Cole wanted in a lifelong mate. Allowing Reese Weathersby anywhere near her, even for one night, was out of the question. And if he was honest with himself, the idea terrified Cole. He'd seen firsthand the kind of sex Reese enjoyed. The trauma would kill his precious Sissy for sure. Okay so Cole enjoyed rough sex as much as the next guy, which is why he had no intention of curbing his extracurricular activities after the wedding. But he could never allow Reese the privilege of performing those heinous acts on his woman. "About that," Cole began slowly. "I'd like to renegotiate the terms."

"Fine with me," Reese said with a cocky grin. "You don't want to share, I'm not sharing." Which was fine with Reese. It resolved his problem completely. He had never wanted Cole to touch Tory in any way. He had only made the bargain to protect what was his in the first place. The only thing Cole had ever been denied in his life was Victoria. His father clearly did not understand his son. The restriction had made the prize even more enticing for Cole. He had craved the girl since the moment he'd met her. Reese had been a little put off by that. At the time Victoria had been a fourteen-year-old child, entirely inappropriate for a twenty-six-year old man. But as she matured, Reese wanted her with the same desperation Cole did. Reese knew the only way to keep his friend away from his wife was to strike a deal. Cole could have one night with his step-sister, then it ended. Once Reese married her, Cole would never so much as look at the woman again. In return, Cole had to agree to give Reese the same amount of time with his future wife. After the wedding, their spouses were off limits forever. Now that Reese had met the woman Cole planned to marry, the bargain didn't seem fair. He had absolutely no desire to touch pretty little Sissy Carter. The girl was weak. Doing her was going to be a chore, not a pleasure.

"Now wait just a damn minute!" Cole said, angry now. Reese was not going to deprive him of one night with Victoria. He'd wanted it for too long. He needed the release. He needed to conquer the cocky princess and put her in her place once and for all. Being deprived of the opportunity for so many years had made it the single most important thing in his life. He would not give it up.

Reese shrugged, hoping Cole couldn't see just how important this was to him. "It's your call," he added as he reached out and poured himself another scotch. "You want to renegotiate the terms, we'll renegotiate. Just remember, I get what you get. You want even five minutes with Victoria, I get five with Sissy." Reese appeared calm and nonchalant on the outside, but inside he was annoyed. His next words were condescending and meant as a subtle reminder that the two of them didn't keep secrets. "I guess you two haven't set a date yet. I mean, I'm sure as your best friend you would have told me if time was running out." Reese knew he had Cole now. Cole's father, Peter, had let it slip that the wedding was in six months. And forcing Cole to agree to time with Sissy was the one and only bargaining chip Reese had with his friend. He wasn't willing to compromise on this one. And with any luck, Cole's need to protect his future wife would outweigh his need for a night with Victoria.

"Who told you?" Cole finally asked, never taking his eyes off Reese. He knew his friend well. The guy already knew Sissy had set the date for next spring, which gave him just over six months to find a solution to this untenable problem.

"Does that matter?" Reese asked, careful not to show Cole how much he was enjoying this. He'd won the battle and they both knew it. But gloating over his victory would only make the situation worse. Cole was his equal when it came to competition. And in this instance, caution was his only defense.

"I guess it doesn't," Cole admitted. "You know I would have told you, sooner rather than later." He'd lost this one, but he didn't have to give in easily. "You still planning to be my best man? That was another deal we made, brother. No going back on your word. Sissy is counting on it."

"You sure she'll still feel the same once we've settled on new terms?" Reese asked, unable to resist rubbing Cole's nose in the problem.

Cole wasn't sure, which was why he had to convince Reese anonymity was the only possibility. "I was thinking she wouldn't have to know it was you." He was holding his breath, not willing to let Reese know just how important that clause of the deal was to him. If Reese knew, he'd capitalize on it for sure.

"Interesting idea," Reese said, considering. That actually would make the whole ordeal more enjoyable. "But does it go both ways? Neither woman knows who her attacker is?" He knew that would be a deal breaker for Cole. But he couldn't agree too readily or Cole would get suspicious.

"No," Cole said immediately. "And you know why. Part of the deal was that Victoria has to know she's being punished for denying me what was rightfully mine to take. That is the whole point. That's not necessary with you and Sissy. And doing it this way only makes more sense. I'm confident Sissy will report the attack, her parents will insist. We can prevent Victoria from doing that, not you and me but my father and Piper will. Dad would never believe that I would harm his princess in any way. And Victoria's mother, please. Piper's so caught up in letting my dad handle everything unpleasant that she'll run from the possibility. Her only goal in life is to find a suitable mate for her precious little girl, and you my friend are suitable. Piper will worry a scandal will change things."

Reese smiled outwardly now. Cole was right about his family and the situation. "I'm more than suitable, my friend. And I'll think about it."

Cole knew that was all he would get for now. It would just have to be enough. "So, I'll let you know when the incompetent PI sends word." His spirits lifted. They were close, he felt it deep in his bones. They were closing in on his nuisance sister. In no time at all their plans would become a reality. "We still on for Friday?" Cole asked casually as he poured himself a shot of vodka.

Reese stood. "It's all arranged. I have a meeting that afternoon but it shouldn't take long. Do not start without me," he warned, narrowing his eyes at his oldest and dearest friend. The two of them had a lot in common, which is why they had stuck together for so long.

"I already gave you my word, Reese," Cole reminded him, annoyed now. "One time, just that one time years ago, and I have to hear about it for the rest of my life. Give it a rest already. You're starting to sound like your old man."

And... bull's-eye. Reese decided to let that one go. Cole was only trying to even the score and Reese wasn't going to take the bait. Not today, he had too much to think about without dwelling on his father or himself. And there were still preparations to make for their upcoming event. Friday was going to be memorable. And with any luck, this new lead would pan out and he would have his woman back before the desperate need to strike again hit either of them. He stood. "I'm heading out, that Inception stock I gambled on seems to be panning out. I need to meet with Todd before he heads home. If we're lucky, it will give us just enough cash to keep dear old Dad in the dark a little while longer."

"Hope it all works out for you, man," Cole said seriously. He knew what a tyrant Carlton Weathersby was. Cole had considered taking the man out more than once, he'd only held back because he knew one day Reese was going to take that step himself. And Cole knew his friend needed that release as much as he needed his time with Victoria. He would never deprive Reese of something so important. Just like he knew Reese would never deprive him of time with his sister. Which brought him back to his dilemma. What to do about Sissy and Reese. There had to be a solution, Cole just hadn't thought of it yet.

* * * *

Maggie glanced in the back seat and frowned. Bryan was still scowling, arms folded angrily over his little chest as he watched the world go by. Toby was patiently lying across the seat with his head resting against the door. He'd finally realized that no matter how hard he tried, his best friend was not going to pay him any attention. Bryan loved that dog. Watching her son shut him out broke Maggie's heart and made her doubt their decision even more. She hoped they were doing the right thing. She knew it was right for her and Coop. It was even right for Rowdy, but was it right for an eight year old boy who was already struggling? At least back in Chicago he had his friends, or did he? Maggie shifted back around, pulled her knees to her chest and pondered. Bryan and Troy had been so close all their lives. Lately, Bryan barely talked to their neighbor. Instead, he was hanging out with the school bully and picking on smaller kids for kicks and giggles. Never in a million years would she have guessed Bryan would act that way. He'd always been such a kind, happy kid. Not anymore. She had to believe getting him out of Chicago was the best thing for him, even if he didn't like it. If he was constantly in trouble at eight, would he be out of control at twelve or thirteen? No, they couldn't risk it. Moving away was the only option.

Coop knew Maggie was worried. He was too, but they had to do something, and this seemed like the right course. Bryan would adjust and maybe in a few months, once they were settled, Troy could come out for a visit. Coop knew Bryan was avoiding his friend out of spite. Maybe with a little distance and a calmer environment they could conquer whatever demons had latched onto his happy, fun-loving boy. He reached across the front seat and linked hands with his wife. The contact settled his nerves, the way it always did. Maggie looked up and smiled but continued gnawing at her bottom lip as she concentrated on the scenery flying by. Coop frowned as he questioned this decision for the millionth time. The small family continued on in silence, each deep in thought, as they made their way from Chicago to Montana to start a new life.

* * * *

The instant Coop pulled onto the long drive, Maggie's spirits lifted. "It's amazing," she said softly, turning to look at her husband. "Coop, it's so beautiful."

Coop smiled. He loved Maggie like this. She was like a kid at Christmas time. Her smile was so big, it was a wonder she could speak. "I knew you'd like it," he said as he gave her delicate hand a squeeze.

"I love it," she said turning back to lower her window. "I had no idea. I mean you guys took a few pictures, but they did not do this place justice." Maggie undid her seatbelt, climbed onto her knees then leaned out the window. She raised her arms high in the air and yelled, "whew-hoo."

Coop laughed, then glanced in the mirror to see his son's reaction. If he hadn't looked at just that moment, he would have missed it. Bryan was smiling and he had a glint in his eyes that Coop hadn't seen in nearly a year. The instant Bryan realized Coop was watching he sobered and rolled his eyes at his mother's antics. Coop relaxed. Bryan was going to love it here, just like he, Maggie and

Rowdy would. They had made the right decision. He was sure breaking through his son's defenses was going to take time and a lot of hard work, but at least now he knew the old Bryan was still in there somewhere.

Coop pulled the car up to the house and frowned. Where was Rowdy? He'd left at least an hour before Coop had. He should be here by now. Coop stepped from the car and walked around to get Maggie's door. The moment she looked at him, she knew something was wrong.

"What?" she asked, worried now. The mood change had put a damper on her enthusiasm.

"Rowdy should be here by now. He left long before we did. Even with constant breaks for Knight he should have arrived already."

"I saw a turn off about two hundred yards back. Does that lead to the cottage? Do you think he went straight there instead of stopping at the main house?" Maggie asked, clearly hopeful.

"I'll check it out but I doubt it," Coop said, turning to open the door for Bryan. "Come on son, I have to go find your uncle. Grab a few necessities and help your mother. While I'm gone the two of you can negotiate for space," he winked at Maggie. They had already decided to give Bryan the spacious bedroom upstairs and the adjourning room as a game room. He was old enough that once he made some new friends they would need a place to hang out.

Bryan gave his father a dirty look, reluctantly grabbed two bags and stomped to the front door. His heart was racing and his stomach hurt. Had something happened to Uncle Rowdy? He hated feeling so panicked but he loved Rowdy. What if something bad had happened to him again? What if he was dead?

Mount Haven

"Oh, this should be fun," Maggie said sarcastically. She gave Coop a quick kiss, grabbed a box and followed her son to the front door.

Coop waited for Maggie to unlock the door and enter the house before he pulled away. Where in the world could Rowdy be? He reached for his phone and dialed his brother. No answer, the thing went directly to voicemail. His body tensed and he put a little more pressure on the gas pedal. He would not panic. Rowdy was fine. He had to be.

* * * *

Rowdy let out a string of cuss words that was sure to shock the devil himself. He knew he should have traded in this POS for a truck before leaving Chicago. *Too late now*, he berated himself and wondered how in the world he was going to get out of this one. His phone was dead and the charger was packed away somewhere out of sight. Knight was antsy and needed a break and Rowdy's leg was killing him. Not to mention the massive migraine that had been gradually worsening with each passing second. He figured he had about five more minutes before he was down for the count. Just enough time to let Knight pee on a few trees. He wouldn't be stranded forever, but his dog might be stuck in the backseat for a while before help arrived. With any luck, the two pills he'd just forced down would start working soon. He knew eventually Coop would get worried and track him down, which didn't do a thing for his aggravation. He hated being a burden to his family. He hated the fact that Coop had to worry about him all the damn time.

Rowdy slowly climbed from the car, latching Knight's collar to his leash. Once he was sure there was nobody around, he'd let

Knight run and explore. His dog could be aggressive if startled but mostly he was protective of Rowdy. That had gotten worse since the shooting; even his dog thought he was weak. But Knight was smart and never disobeyed a command. If someone showed up and surprised them, Rowdy simply had to call Knight's name and he'd come, no questions asked. Too bad he couldn't find a woman with that same trait. Rowdy laughed out loud. Maggie would slug him if she ever heard him voice that particular desire. He glanced around one more time then unlatched the leash and let Knight run. The path was becoming uneven and he'd left his cane in the backseat of his car. He wasn't comfortable pushing it any further. Just another thing he hated about his pathetic life. Nine months after his injury and he still needed the stupid cane on uneven terrain. Sure, his leg was getting stronger but at this rate he'd never lose the thing. He'd just transition from an invalid to an old man.

Rowdy leaned against a large tree then used his forefingers to massage his temples, wishing the migraine would subside just a little. In his condition, even if his car miraculously started he was in no shape to drive. He was going to have to rely on his brother. He wondered how long before Coop got tired of babysitting a grown man. Coop had a family of his own to worry about, he shouldn't be burdened with Rowdy's problems too.

Rowdy waited as long as he dared, then whistled loudly. Knight immediately came running. The moment they reached the car, Knight leapt into the back seat, circled twice then plopped down and waited. "Sorry boy, nothing I can do. Car won't start. You'll just have to be in charge until Coop finds us. Once we get to the ranch I promise I'll feed you." Rowdy slid into the passenger's seat, reclined the seat as far as it would go and closed his eyes. He didn't know if it was wishful thinking or if the medication was finally beginning to work, but the pressure behind his eyes felt like it was subsiding. Unfortunately, the nausea had set in.

Mount Haven

* * * *

Coop pulled the car in behind Rowdy's vehicle and frowned. He'd expected his brother to jump out cussing for taking so long. He pulled his keys from the ignition and approached the driver's side. Knight stood, instantly on alert. Coop glanced at the dog then immediately moved to the passenger's side of the car. He pulled open the door and crouched. "How bad?" He asked, glad Rowdy had pulled to the side of the road before landing in a ditch.

Rowdy slowly opened one eye then immediately shut it again. "The car or the head?" he finally asked.

"What's wrong with the car?" Coop asked, frowning.

"No idea," Rowdy said, pushing himself up and snapping the seat back in place.

Coop ran his hands through his hair and considered. He could get Rowdy and Knight to the ranch no problem, but what about all Rowdy's stuff? Coop knew the trunk was packed full. "Give me a minute," he said turning and moving away. "Hey babe," he said when Maggie finally answered. "Has World War Three been settled or is Bryan still acting up?"

"Bryan is up in his room complaining about the bed, the dust, the curtains, the carpet… oh, and don't forget the color of the game room. Apparently, only a sissy would spend more than five seconds in that room and only if forced to do so by their evil mother," Maggie said with a sigh.

"Did he help at all?" Coop asked. He thought bringing Bryan out to help transfer Rowdy's things might make him feel gown up but if he was still giving Mag a bad time, Coop was not going to reward him.

"Actually he did," Maggie said, sounding more like herself. "He took care of everything before his alter ego surfaced. Did you find Rowdy?"

"I did," Coop assured her. "But we have a problem. Rowdy's got one of his migraines. From the look of him it's pretty severe, but I have a bigger problem. His car broke down. I'm going to need to get Rowdy home then come back out and unload his trunk. I'm not comfortable leaving the car full of his personal belongings out here on the side of the road all night. In the morning I'll ask the Mayor who to call to get the thing towed. A town this small may not even have roadside service."

"And you wanted Bryan to help?" Maggie asked, knowing what Coop was doing. She hoped it worked; Coop was going to be disappointed if Bryan gave him attitude instead of respect.

"I do," Coop admitted. "But not if he's going to bring his attitude with him. That's the last thing I need to deal with right now."

"I'll talk to him before you get here," Maggie promised. "Then we can decide."

"It's going to take me a few minutes to get Rowdy into the car. I haven't seen him this bad for months," Coop admitted.

"I knew he shouldn't have driven out alone," Maggie said, worried. "But he's so stubborn -he wouldn't hear of it when I offered to join him. The long trip had to be hard on him."

Mount Haven

"I know," Coop said, equally frustrated with his little brother. "But he's a grown man and we can't control his decisions," Coop laughed. "We're having a hard enough time controlling our eight year old."

"Yeah, well sometimes I think Bryan's an angel compared to that stubborn oaf of a brother you have," Maggie vented. "Just get him home and bring him up to the big house. He's staying in the guest room whether he likes it or not. And that is not negotiable. I'll have it ready when you get here." With that, she hung up.

Coop was laughing as he approached Rowdy. Man he loved that woman. His brother tried to stand, but nearly fell over. Coop barely had time to grab him before he stumbled to the ground. He silently wrapped an arm around Rowdy's waist and led him to his car. Once Rowdy was securely in place, Coop returned to retrieve Knight's leash, water dish and chew toy. "Come on boy, let's get the old man home. And if you're good, I might have a juicy package of hot dogs waiting for you. Dad will never know, he's incapacitated."

"You get to clean up after him if you feed him that crap," Rowdy mumbled. "There's dog food in the trunk."

Coop slid behind the wheel and pulled onto the road. "I know," he finally answered. "But this way, I'm his hero and you're the strict disciplinarian that makes him eat dry dog food for dinner. I like my place in the pack."

"We both know I'm in no shape to stop you tonight but you will not ruin Knight's diet just because we are neighbors. I mean it Coop," Rowdy scowled. "I spoil that dog enough. No donuts, no ice cream. I will not let you feed that crap to my dog. We don't need two lazy, overweight mutts on the farm. You and Maggie have already ruined Toby. That's not what I want for Knight. Just because he's retired, doesn't mean he needs to be a heart attack waiting to happen."

Coop was about to object but changed his mind, Rowdy was in no shape to have this conversation. "Do dogs even have heart attacks?" Coop asked with a grin.

"Did you grab my gun?" Rowdy changed the subject. He didn't want to leave the weapon vulnerable.

"I did," Coop said, glancing at Rowdy. He was worried about his brother. They all thought the headaches were getting better. Now he wondered if Rowdy had just been hiding them from him and Maggie so they wouldn't worry. "Did you take something for it?"

"About an hour ago I think," Rowdy said, cracking one eye to look at the clock. He tried to do the math, but gave up. "I took two pills at eight fifteen. Then I puked my guts out in those bushes back there at around eight thirty so who knows if anything stayed in my system."

The two of them drove in silence until they reached the turnoff to the ranch. "I thought they were getting better," Coop couldn't stop himself from asking. With each mile they drove in silence, he became even angrier. Maggie kept trying to hide her nightmares, Rowdy was hiding his medical condition, Bryan hid everything. Coop felt like he had completely lost control of his life.

Rowdy forced himself to open his eyes. "They are," he said, glancing at Coop. "I haven't had one in over a month. I think it was just the long drive and the heat. I was feeling dehydrated because I ran out of water a few miles back. I planned to pull off the highway at the next intersection to restock when the car broke down. Do we have to talk about this now?" he asked, clearly not up for a debate.

Mount Haven

Coop wanted to lecture Rowdy on taking care of himself, but deep down he knew it wasn't necessary. He was sure Rowdy had berated himself enough over the situation. He bit his tongue and approached the house in silence. Coop pulled the car to a stop and exited, moving quickly around to help Rowdy into the house. He didn't even have to respond to Rowdy's protests because Maggie was right there to do that for him. Coop closed the bedroom door and grinned. There would be no more arguments about where Rowdy was sleeping tonight. Nobody won an argument with his Maggie, she was a master at getting her way. They all loved her too much to say no on a good day. Right now, Rowdy was in no condition to argue. Coop was halfway down the large flight of stairs before he saw Bryan. His son was standing near the door waiting. Every few seconds he would glance at Rowdy's door and frown. Coop knew his son was worried about his uncle. Coop was worried too, but he had decided to believe his brother. If Rowdy said the headaches were getting better, they were getting better. "He's fine," Coop said immediately when he reached the bottom of the stairs. "Just another headache and his car broke down."

Bryan's head shot to his father. Was he lying? He stood there, motionless for several seconds then relaxed. His dad was telling the truth, Bryan could see it in his eyes. "What do I care?" Bryan said, then wondered why he'd done it. He did care but he didn't know how to deal with all the uncertainty. And he hated being scared all the time.

"I don't know Bryan," Coop said casually. "Do you care?" He opened the door and waited for his son to step out onto the front porch. "I know I care. I care very much and before I found Rowdy I was scared. I was afraid of what could have happened to him. He was traveling alone. I know he had Knight but as talented as that dog is, he can't talk. He couldn't get help if Rowdy was hurt. You saw me leave here in a hurry. That's because I care. That's because

I was afraid," Coop waited but Bryan remained silent. "I think you were afraid, too. It's okay to be scared, Bryan. In fact, I would worry more if I didn't feel that way. Rowdy is my brother, my younger brother. It would be unbearable for me if anything bad happened to him. I know you love him, too. So, I think it's probably scary for you sometimes too and that's okay." Coop watched as Bryan climbed into the car then he started the engine and drove away. He didn't expect Bryan to respond. He just wanted to let his son know fear was not something you needed to run from.

Chapter Three

Bailey pulled out her rag and began cleaning up the liquid mess the obnoxious men left in their wake. She loved this town and usually she loved her job, but sometimes she was surprised by how immature grown men could be. She leaned across the table to wipe the last of the beer when another adolescent smacked her behind. Bailey jumped, knocking over the salt shaker. The lid flew off and salt scattered everywhere. Bailey spun around and glared at the massive man-child that stood grinning from ear to ear. He wasn't looking at her face - of course not. His eyes had instantly moved from her behind to her breasts. So, it was going to be one of those nights then? Well, Bailey could handle it. She'd dealt with worse, but she was not going to think about that. Not now, not ever if she could help it.

Bailey had no idea who the childish guy was. She'd never seen him in the bar before, but she didn't care. Nobody got away with touching the goods, not even a slap on the butt. She moved in and pointed her finger in the guy's chest. "Never, and I mean never, do that again."

The man's smile wavered for just a second then he reached out and grabbed Bailey's wrist. She had to look up but she would not let this guy intimidate her. She whipped her hand away and placed both of her palms on her hips. "You owe me an apology," she insisted.

The man frowned. Clearly this was not going the way he had expected. He was the star quarterback. Women fell at his feet, all he had to do was grin. He would not apologize to this skinny waitress, he wasn't sorry.

"Well?" Bailey asked, continuing to stand her ground. It was at that moment that Max, the bar's owner, stepped from the kitchen. He took one look at the situation and moved in to take control.

"Problem?" he asked, stepping between Bailey and the overconfident jock. Anyone could see the kid was a player and probably used to getting anything he wanted.

"No problem," the guy said, still frowning as he moved to sit with the rest of his teammates.

"And how about you?" Max asked gently as he turned to study Bailey. "Did they hurt you?" He grinned at the fire that sparked at the suggestion. "Maim you for life? Hurt your feelings?" Bailey's eyes narrowed. "Naw, I think it was just your pride," he shrugged. "I can live with that. Yell if you need me." Max turned and walked away. Within seconds he was sliding behind the large wooden counter. As the owner he worked the bar because he wanted to. It was a good way to keep an eye on things and a better way to keep his pulse on the town. If he moved to Manhattan he was going to miss that. But what an opportunity, one he knew he couldn't pass up. Frank had fallen into a sweet deal and Max was looking forward to the challenge. Now, he just had to find someone to buy this place. In such a small town that was going to be difficult.

* * * *

Rowdy sat on the large wrap around porch of the main house. He was relaxed for the first time in a long time and he was enjoying himself. Maggie was entertaining. Not that the movers would agree. She was personally overseeing their every step. He knew Coop would tip them well and so would he. The cash should more than compensate for the trouble. Rowdy had initially argued with Coop when he suggested they gather up the essentials and leave everything else to the professionals. It went against the grain, but he had to admit this move was far easier than Rowdy could have imagined. And he preferred lounging on the porch to dealing with Maggie, hands down. He grinned as Coop stepped past him and pulled up a chair.

"You're enjoying this, aren't you?" Coop said with a scowl.

"Absolutely," Rowdy said, shifting a little to get more comfortable. "My stuff was unloaded and packed nicely into my empty garage in less than an hour." Rowdy checked his watch. "Your stuff…" he glanced at the half empty truck. "Still in the truck. Think they'll get out of here before midnight?"

"That's it," Coop said, clearly at his wits end. "I'm taking charge."

Rowdy laughed. "Sure you are."

Within minutes Coop stormed out of the house, letting the screen door slam behind him.

"Already taking a break, Mr. Incident Commander?" Rowdy nearly bust a gut when his brother slowly raised his arm above his head and flipped him the finger as he continued towards the barn. Rowdy could clearly imagine the scowl that was covering his brother's normally happy face.

Two hours later the truck was unloaded, the movers had been paid and Maggie was singing along to the eighties as she unpacked the kitchen. Coop had returned and the two brothers were now relaxing on the front porch. Bryan was in his game room "made for sissies" and probably wouldn't come down all night. "You in time out or can you leave?" Rowdy asked his brother.

"Funny," Coop said, still annoyed at Maggie. "Where we going?"

"I saw a bar up the road, I thought we could check it out. The Boots and Spurs or something like that. It's not too far from the house so we should probably know what kind of place it is," Rowdy shrugged. He may not have a badge, but he would always think like a cop.

"Give me a minute." Coop stood and disappeared through the front door. Moments later he was back, keys in hand and a smile on his face. "Let's go, I'm driving."

Rowdy stood and slowly walked to the car. His leg wasn't bothering him today. Must have been the two days lag time between arriving and waiting for the movers. His migraine had knocked him out for a full day and a half. The entire time Maggie was there to pamper him and hover until she drove him insane. He needed a break and a trip to the bar; a cold beer and some fresh air was just what the doctor ordered.

Coop watched Rowdy as he walked to the car and slowly slid into the passenger's seat. "No cane?" he finally asked, already knowing the answer.

"Just drive," Rowdy grumbled. When Coop didn't move, Rowdy turned to face him with a scowl. "I thought you were driving."

"I am," Coop said starting the engine.

"Then drive," Rowdy barked.

Coop laughed. "I was just asking, didn't mean to piss you off. I just figured we're in the country. I haven't seen the place, the parking lot could be crap. There could be stairs, what if the place is packed?"

"Shut it, Coop," Rowdy said not willing to give in. There was no way he was going to step foot in that bar supporting himself on a cane. That was not the first impression he wanted to leave in this one horse town.

"Shutting up," Coop said as he pulled onto the highway. Rowdy was right, the place was only a few blocks away and the parking lot was packed. As the new Sheriff, Coop would have to keep an eye on the place until he determined whether it was trouble, or just the only action in town this time of night. He was trying to come up with a way to ask Rowdy if he wanted to be dropped at the door when a slot opened up right near the entrance. Coop swung in and parked. He had to stop himself from hovering as Rowdy cautiously made his way across the dirt parking lot and through the front door. Coop had expected something loud and obnoxious. That was not what he got. The main area was pretty tame, all things considered. There was a backroom and he could see a local college football game playing on several big screen televisions.

"Let's grab that one," Rowdy said, moving in front of Coop to snag a table that had just become vacant.

Coop didn't hear Rowdy at first, he was too busy taking in each and every patron then scouting out the exits. He took a step forward and realized Rowdy was already seated. He moved to the table and sat across from his brother. "Not bad," he finally said, smiling. "However, keep an eye on the table at three o'clock. College kids, and I think they could be trouble."

Rowdy smiled, he'd already spotted the group which is why he'd sat here in the first place. A couple of the kids were harassing their pretty little waitress. If it got any worse, someone would have to step in. Rowdy hoped they had a bouncer, but if not he'd take care of it. "Once a cop always a cop," Rowdy said absently. "You asking as the Sheriff or my brother?"

"Both," Coop said, glancing behind him. "As of eight o'clock this morning, I am officially the top law enforcement official in the area. I don't need trouble my first day on the job."

"Probably true," Rowdy grinned. "Mayor Herlin might regret paying you so much dough if you can't keep the peace here in Podunk."

"Would you stop calling it that?" Coop said, annoyed again. "I thought you said you liked it here?"

"I do," Rowdy agreed. "I just like to annoy you."

Mount Haven

* * * *

Bailey stepped through the swinging doors and froze. Two of the sexiest cowboys she'd seen in her life had just walked through the front door. They moved through the crowd like they owned the place. Every woman in the room watched their tight, Levi clad behinds as they casually took in the place. One of them, the hottest one in Bailey's opinion, walked with a slight limp. Must have been thrown from a bull. She smiled at her own joke, then frowned when he slid onto the bench at one of her tables. His friend continued a slow, methodical survey of the entire room before sliding onto the bench across from his buddy. Probably looking for his next victim. Just what she needed to round off an already stressful night. Wasn't dealing with obnoxious college boys bad enough? Apparently not. Now she had to contend with a couple arrogant men. The two of them were not only hot, but they knew it. Their confidence showed in every cocky step they took.

"Whew-hoo," Theresa said loud enough to be heard across the room. Bailey turned and scowled, the woman could at least pretend to be professional. Theresa shrugged. "It's not every day we get fresh blood in this town and men as fresh as those two…"

Bailey didn't wait to hear how Theresa finished her sentence. She didn't need that kind of image dancing in her head while she dealt with the hotties. And that thought annoyed her even more than Theresa had. She would not be taken in by a pretty face and a hot body and… "Oh, just stop it," she told herself. She stopped at the bar, grabbed two glasses of water and practically stomped to the table. Once there, she plopped the glasses down and waited for the crude remark that never came. The two men just stared at her like she was supposed to say something. What? Did they want an engraved invitation? "Here's the menu." Bailey dropped two plastic covered sheets on the table and disappeared.

Coop furrowed his brow then shook his head. Before he could request a couple beers, the waitress was gone.

Rowdy was watching the sexy vixen as she pushed her way back to the bar. "Friendly town," he finally said then turned his attention back to the college table.

"So," Coop continued. He was still confused by the attitude of the waitress, but whatever. He leaned back and studied his brother. "You are pretty focused on the table in the corner. You're not going to cause trouble are you? I'd hate to have to throw my only brother in jail so soon. I mean, I've been Sheriff less than twenty four hours."

Rowdy's eyes didn't leave the table. He casually flipped Coop off and frowned. One of the men grabbed the waitress's wrist while another one wrapped his large arm around her waist and pulled her into his lap. She began to struggle, clearly trying to get free. The four guys laughed and continued to torment her. Rowdy stood, ready to stop things before they went any further. He had only taken one step when a large man blocked his path. Rowdy scowled, prepared to move the obstacle by force if necessary.

Max held out a hand. "Max Sampson," he said and waited. The stranger took his hand but continued to eye the corner table, not saying a word. Max maneuvered his body, making sure he blocked the man's view. "I'm the owner of this fine establishment. Don't worry about Casey, she can hold her own. And when she can't, either I'll step in or Jase will."

Rowdy shifted in an attempt to check on the girl again. Another man was standing next to the table, scolding the group.

Mount Haven

Must be the bouncer. The bar was too loud for Rowdy to make out the entire conversation, but he caught enough. If they got out of line again they'd not only be tossed out, but they'd never get back in. That was good enough for Rowdy. He moved back to the bench and took his seat.

"I have to say, I don't get much law in here." Max pulled up a chair and sat down. "You two just passing through?"

Coop smiled. "What makes you think we're the law?"

Max threw his head back and laughed, a full out belly laugh. "I can spot a cop a mile away. And the two of you? The minute you walked in, you screamed cops. Oh sure it was subtle but I bet if I asked, you could tell me every escape door in the place as well as where the troublemakers are and who has a weapon."

"You allow guns in a bar?" Rowdy asked, liking the guy instantly.

"No. But you already knew that," Max said, grinning. "I'm talking about the sticking kind. The ones more difficult for me to restrict."

"Okay, you made your point," Coop said, studying the bar owner more closely. "So, what's it to you? Are you trying to tell us cops aren't welcome here?"

"On the contrary," Max said standing. "Just never had one grace me with his presence in this fine little town." Max turned when someone called his name. "Gotta go but all joking aside, straight up, my brother's a cop. If you're eating, it's on me. I appreciate your service."

"Thanks," Coop said, liking Max even more. "But we already ate. We just stopped by for a beer."

"If you leave before I get back tell Bailey to bring your check to me. I'm serious, I don't want you two paying. I know, gratuities and all that but I insist." He turned and pushed his way back to the bar.

"I wonder if he'd feel the same way if he knew you were the new sheriff in town," Rowdy asked, grabbing the now sweating glass of water and chugging down half of it.

"I guess we'll find out soon enough," Coop said with a shrug. "You still want to stay for that beer or you want to head back to the house and grab a cold one. We can sit out on the porch. It's going to be a lot quieter that way."

Rowdy was still considering the question when their waitress returned.

"You decide what you want, boys?" she asked as she impatiently tapped her pen on her pad.

Coop picked up the menus and handed them back. "Thanks, hon, but we're going to pass on food tonight. We'll both take a beer. Whatever's on tap."

"Hon?" Bailey said incredulously as she took the menus. She was still fuming as she pushed through the doors and gathered her next order.

Theresa was right there, drooling. "You want to trade tables?" she asked hopefully. "I don't mind and they seem to annoy you for some reason."

Bailey considered but decided against it. "Not necessary," she said casually as she grabbed three plates and headed to the rowdy college crowd in back. "I've got it under control."

Theresa pouted as she collected her meals and headed back out on the floor.

"Can I run something by you?" Coop finally asked.

"Sure," Rowdy said as he watched their sexy waitress deal with a couple young college guys. She was much friendlier with them than she had been with Coop. He wondered why. Maybe they were friends of hers. She looked close to the same age, so that must be it.

"How do you feel about horses?" Coop asked, watching Rowdy for a reaction.

Rowdy grinned at his brother's question. Great minds must think alike. He'd decided to buy a couple of his own before he even sold his place in Chicago. The more he thought about their new home, the more the idea grew on him. "Don't know any personally. Now we all know Davis was an ass sometimes but I think that's a different species."

"I'm serious," Coop said, scowling. If he started thinking about Davis, he'd need more than one beer to calm him down.

"Okay, fine," Rowdy said, knowing it was time to change the subject before talk of Davis soured the mood. Good thing the ex-cop had moved to Florida immediately after the shooting. With Coop on the warpath, the man didn't stand a chance. Now that they were living in Montana, an entire continent was between them. Even that wasn't enough distance for those two. If Coop had a chance, he would still cause problems for the man. "I was actually thinking of getting a couple horses myself."

"Really?" Coop asked a little surprised.

"Yeah," Rowdy said, trying not to show just how excited he was about the prospect. If it didn't work out, he didn't want his brother to know how disappointed he would be. "I mean I checked out the stables and they're in pretty good shape. It would be a waste to not use them. And I thought it might be good for my leg. I need exercise and variety." He shrugged, not knowing what else to say.

"Would you mind working with Bryan?" Coop asked taking a sip of his water. "I'm going to be working a lot of hours for a while, until I get the hang of things. Maybe you could supervise for me? I think having responsibilities would help him adjust."

"I agree," Rowdy said, sitting back against the bench as their waitress approached. He frowned when she slammed the beer on the table and glared at Coop. What was the woman's problem anyway?

Coop slid a twenty from his billfold and held it out to the waitress. The owner had insisted on buying, but Coop didn't think that was a good idea. Especially since proprietor Max didn't know Coop was his new Sheriff.

Bailey reached for the bill then gave it a forceful tug when the cowboy didn't let go. Whatever he had to say, she didn't want to hear it. She finally made eye contact but regretted it. The guy was smiling as he released the bill, did that usually work for him? What? Was she supposed to swoon all over herself because a good looking man smiled her way? "Will there be anything else?" she grumbled, already turning to leave.

Mount Haven

"Sweetheart, you need to lighten up," Coop commented with a shake of his head. She must be new. Even drunks wouldn't tip all that well if they received this kind of service with an attitude.

"And no doubt you're just the man to help with that?" She braced herself for some obnoxious comeback but it never came. The guy just stared at her like he was confused or something. "Anything else?" she asked again. "Or have you hit your head a few too many times and communicating is beyond your ability?" She glanced at the clock, two more hours before her shift was over. She wasn't sure she was going to make it tonight. She tapped her pad again, wondering what kind of game these two were playing.

Coop glanced at Rowdy in confusion, was this girl whacko or something?

Rowdy sat back and studied the waitress. At first, he thought she was just rude, but then he realized what this was all about. She was used to men coming on to her. She was just arrogant enough to believe that Coop's innocent comment was a prelude to something more suggestive. He was curious to see how it would all play out. When she turned and focused on him, Rowdy just raised an eyebrow and waited.

Bailey started to turn but was stopped by the stranger's commanding voice.

"Ma'am?" Coop called. Sticking around tonight wasn't such a good idea after all. He'd just inform the waitress they were leaving and tell her to give the money to Max. He could put it on their tab or whatever. Chances were good the two of them would venture over again. Hopefully, next time this woman would have the night off.

"Oh pleeease," Bailey said shaking her head. "Now what? Am I supposed to fall all over myself because such a big strong cowboy called me ma'am?"

"What?" Coop asked floored by this woman's aggression.

"Let me guess," Bailey continued. "You call me ma'am and I'm supposed to get all flustered and start to swoon. The sexy cowboy is such a gentleman, my heart is all a flutter. Then what? We head outside to your backseat and have ourselves a quickie?"

Coop's mouth literally fell open. He was so shocked he couldn't speak.

Rowdy couldn't stop himself, he laughed out loud at the absurdity of the woman's assumptions. Sure, the woman was hot, well to be honest she was beautiful but not nearly sexy enough to be that arrogant. And the idea of Coop wanting anything from her was beyond insane.

"What exactly do you find funny about this?" she demanded. She turned on the good looking one but wished she hadn't. Just looking into those deep chocolate eyes had her pulse racing. She would not let him see her attraction. She would die before she gave him the satisfaction. Then she realized the man was actually laughing at her. Of all the... her cheeks flushed and she slammed down the pad she'd been holding. "I'm done here. I've taken about all the arrogance from the two of you I can handle. Theresa would be more than happy to assist you." She glanced back at the first cowboy and couldn't stop herself from adding, "With all your needs."

"What I find funny," Rowdy said calmly, wanting to put the woman in her place before she disappeared, "Is your arrogance."

Mount Haven

"Mine?" Bailey sputtered. Of all the egotistical, condescending, infuriating… "Argh," Bailey growled. Why oh, why did it have to be her?

"Yes yours," Rowdy said raising his eyebrows in challenge. She wouldn't leave, she'd see it as a sign of weakness now. "You see my brother over there is a gentleman through and through, down to the core. He can't help himself. Our mother taught us to respect women, protect them when necessary and always, without exception, call them ma'am. And now that I think back, I believe this all started when Coop called you hon." Rowdy shrugged. "An innocent, polite, term of endearment. Being the arrogant prude that you are that triggered an instant response. It must be difficult, dealing with mere mortal's day after day, night after night, believing you are some kind of Goddess that every man lusts after. Living your life knowing that the mere sight of you would make all us helpless men long for just one 'quickie' from you as you so eloquently put it. But let me fill you in on a little secret." Rowdy leaned in like he was sharing something important. "That thought never once crossed my brother's mind. And your arrogant attitude is rude and insulting," he straightened, giving her a look of utter disgust.

Bailey raised her eyebrows now. "I don't see a crystal ball, cowboy, so how do you know what crossed your brother's mind?"

"Because unfortunately for you, Andy Cooper is a happily married man. Coop is so married, and so in love with his wife, he hasn't so much as looked at another woman since their first date. And I can personally testify that better women than you have tried. So do us all a favor, Bailey is it?"

"How do you know my name?" Bailey said, mortified at herself. If even half of what the cocky cowboy said was true, she'd just made a complete fool of herself. Bailey glanced up when Max stepped to the table, frowning.

"Is there a problem here, Bay?" He could see she was upset, but couldn't imagine the two cops trying anything fishy.

Bailey didn't know how to answer that and was grateful when the man she'd insulted began speaking. His brother, and now that he mentioned it the two of them did look a lot alike, was still watching her intently. She wasn't sure how much longer she could take it.

"No problem," Coop said standing. "Rowdy and I were just leaving."

Max frowned. "But you didn't drink your beer," he said noticing the full mugs on the table.

"Maybe we can take a rain check." He glanced at Bailey then back to Max. "I appreciate your hospitality, but it's getting late. We really do need to get home."

"Home?" Bailey choked out. So they weren't just passing through on their way to the next rodeo? Damn, she was in trouble.

Rowdy smiled when the woman began to squirm. "Yeah, did we forget to mention that?" He slapped his brother on the back. "Meet Sheriff Andy Cooper, Mount Haven's new top cop."

"Well, I'll be," Max said shaking his head. "Sneaky bugger aren't you? So, did I pass the test? I mean now that I know you're the new Sheriff, you had to be checking the place out, cover op and all that."

Mount Haven

Coop and Rowdy looked at Bailey then back to Max. Rowdy noticed the woman had gone sheet white. He'd feel sorry for her, but she deserved her humiliation and he was happy to let her wallow in it.

Bailey was starting to panic. She had just insulted their new Sheriff. The last thing she needed was for the law to start checking into her background. If he did that, she'd be forced to run again. And she didn't want to run. She liked it here. She had loved this place the instant she stepped off the bus. That was just over five months ago. She never stayed anywhere more than six months: a rule she'd set for herself three years ago and had never violated. But she had recently changed her mind about that. She wanted to stay here, in Mount Haven. But with a new sheriff and his too observant brother around, she might have to leave after all. "Excuse me, please," she said softly just before she turned and rushed into the back room. The instant she was out of sight, disappointed tears began to fall.

Max frowned. "Now what in the world has gotten into that girl?"

"Just a little misunderstanding," Coop said, watching their waitress flee. "Don't worry about it. But maybe next time you can guide us to a Bailey-free zone."

"See you around," Rowdy said, slapping Max on the back. He knew the guy was confused, but Bailey could explain it... or not. He followed Cooper out the front door and continued cautiously to the car. He had to admit the woman intrigued him. She was arrogant, but timid, confident and shifty, but self-conscious. She was hiding something, the cop inside Rowdy practically screamed that with certainty. But she wasn't Rowdy's problem. As Sheriff, if there was something shady about the sexy waitress, Coop could figure it out. Rowdy planned to focus on horses.

* * * *

Reese silently stood over the lifeless body. Rage flowing through every particle of his being. He was like a volcano, ready to erupt any minute. He clenched his hands, gritted his teeth and forced air through his nose.

"Seriously, Reese? Get a grip," Cole said happily. He was so pumped he wanted to shout to the world.

Reese spun around so quickly Cole didn't see him coming. His gloved hand fisted around Cole's throat, slamming him against the wall. Cole found himself staring into the eyes of a crazy man. Reese had never scared him before, but in that instant Cole was worried. The fear passed quickly; Cole knew how to handle Reese Weathersby and he would never let his friend see him sweat. He rolled his eyes as he shoved Reese backwards, then he casually walked across the room and leaned against the doorjamb putting distance between them. "You done yet?" he asked with a smirk? "Because I'm in the mood to celebrate."

Reese glared at his partner and oldest friend. *Accident my ass*. The gleam in Cole's eyes and the barely controlled smirk, told Reese Cole had done this on purpose. "Celebrate?" Reese spit out in disgust. "Do you have any idea what you've done?"

Cole shrugged. "So the slut died, who cares? You plan to stay here all night mourning, or can we blow?" Cole smiled at the pun.

Reese took one last scan of the room then stalked to the small window leading to the fire escape. "You're gonna think blow if we've left even one shred of evidence. This isn't a rape investigation

Mount Haven

like the others. This is homicide. Either one of us could have lost a stray hair..." Reese studied his friend. "You didn't drool in your over exuberance did you?"

Cole rolled his eyes again. "Get out of here already. I'll meet you back at the house."

Cole was acting cool, but he was hiding something. Reese hesitated one last second then climbed out the window and slowly made his way down the metal stairs. They had been careful. They were always careful. Nobody even knew he was here and he planned to keep it that way. The two of them had been doing this for years - practice made perfect right? They never arrived together, never left together. They staked out the target and knew every escape route, every neighbor, every schedule. He was safe, but was Cole? There had been something there but what? Reese shrugged it off. Cole had killed that girl on purpose; did he really think he could hide that from his partner? Seriously, they knew each other better than they knew themselves sometimes. That was no accident and Cole was going to hear about it when they were safely ensconced in his private living room. He continued to ponder as he made his way to the dock, climbed into his electric boat and silently made his way home.

The instant Reese pulled into the boat house, he relaxed. It was always like that for him. He thrived for days before a mission. The excitement of outsmarting everyone, planning for every possible contingency, then putting the plan in motion was almost as satisfying as the rape itself. Then, once it was over, he always worried. No matter how close or how far away the target, he stressed over every detail until he finally arrived home. He knew it was up to him to make sure nothing went wrong, Cole was too reckless. He'd proven that tonight in spades, the idiot. Reese slid from the boat, attached the rope then swung the large door into place. As always, the night air remained perfectly quiet. Reese had sanded the door, oiled the hinges and added a thick rubber padding to the bottom. Just another example of his attention to detail. The silence of the boathouse enveloped him and he slowly began to smile. Another successful mission. Adrenaline flowed through him as he lifted the hidden door and slipped into the dark tunnel that led back to his house.

He had a flashlight in his pocket, but he didn't need it. He'd traveled this pathway a million times. He still wondered about the man who had built it. Had old man Perkins used the place for nefarious reasons or just as a convenient shortcut? Everyone knew Perkins loved to fish, but something told Reese there was more to the story. If it was just an innocent escape why all the secrecy? Reese had lived here for years before he located the hidden doorway in the boathouse. And he was certain he never would have found the entrance from the house. No, Mr. Perkins was up to something and Reese admired the guy for it. The old man took his secrets to the grave, just as Reese planned to do.

With each step his mood lightened. By the time he slipped through the hidden panel and stepped into his home, a sense of power and exhilaration had surrounded him. Oh sure, he was still beyond pissed at Cole. He had deviated from the plan. Reese never would have denied Cole the opportunity to snuff the life out of that whore, that wasn't the problem. The woman was insignificant. No, Reese was beyond pissed because Cole hadn't shared his plan. Reese hadn't had time to prepare, hadn't had time to make sure every 'I' was dotted and every 'T' was crossed. And that was simply unacceptable.

By the time Cole stepped into the large den, Reese had calmed down significantly. He eyed the plastic bag tightly secured in Cole's hand then motioned to the fire raging across the room. Cole casually moved in front of the flames and tossed the bag inside. It was only one in a long line of rituals they had developed over the years.

Cole continued to watch as the inferno obliterated the last of the evidence. Well, as far as Reese knew anyway. He needed a second to mask his mistake. A mistake Reese would never know about. It wasn't his fault, not really. He'd been wanting to know what it was like to take a life for months now. Tonight, he'd acted on his need. The power he felt in that moment had been too much. He had been over exuberant just as Reese had said. But he hadn't drooled. No, he'd done something much worse. He'd been so out of control his condom had snapped. There was evidence all right, loads of it inside the body of that worthless slut. But it had been worth it, oh so worth it. He wasn't worried about the evidence. Nobody would ever get his DNA, so no harm no foul. He wouldn't let it dampen his spirit. Cole was still flying. It was a high like no other he had ever experienced and he knew without a doubt... he was going to do it again.

Cole moved to the chair next to Reese and casually lifted the expensive glass to his lips. He knew Reese was watching him, waiting for an explanation, so he'd get one but not until Cole was ready to give it. This too was part of the ritual they called friendship. Each man maneuvering, calculating, hiding in an attempt to best the other. Neither man was willing to back down easily, it was probably the reason they'd remained friends for so long. "Well?" Cole finally said. "Go ahead, spit it out already."

Reese leaned forward, placing his empty glass gently on the table satisfied he'd won that contest. "I'm waiting for an explanation. That was no accident and we both know it."

Cole shrugged. "Fine, it wasn't an accident." He leaned back, pulling the side lever so the chair would recline. "You can't tell me you seriously cared whether that woman lived or died."

"No," Reese admitted. The more he thought about it, the more powerful he felt. It was like playing God. But he intended to be in control, not Cole. "I care that you deviated from the plan. I care that you intended to commit murder all along and never mentioned it. I care that I didn't have time to plan, didn't have time to bring all the necessary materials to ensure we didn't get caught. I care that you were reckless and stupid."

"I wasn't stupid," Cole said, inhaling a long, soothing breath. He had been stupid. Reese was right. If he'd shared his plan, Reese would have been prepared and his DNA would not currently be living, or dying, in the body of their latest victim. Not that he'd ever tell Reese that.

"Okay. I should have told you," he admitted.

"Why didn't you?" Reese asked, truly perplexed. This really wasn't like Cole. They had been partners for years.

"I didn't want to argue about it and I didn't want to wait. I needed this tonight," Cole said, flipping the chair upright with a loud thud. He stood and walked to the window. "I'm getting desperate. Dad asked me about the money for the PI. I tried to play the concerned brother, but he wasn't buying it. He hasn't cut me off, but I know that's coming. I'm not sure he's even worried about Victoria and I don't like it. We're running out of time. Duvall's in Texas, his men aren't any closer to determining the identity of the woman who married the rich oil man and Sissy is driving me crazy with all her wedding plans. Can't I just show up and say I do?" Cole returned to the chair and fell more than sat in the comfortable lounge.

Mount Haven

Aww, Reese understood now and he could empathize. Cole needed to reclaim control of his life. Killing their prey tonight made perfect sense. And Reese could relate. His life was also teetering precariously on a ledge. A ledge that could have unbearable repercussions if he didn't find a solution. The high he had felt tonight in the aftermath of Cole's actions also gave him the strength he needed to carry on. "I've decided to head to Texas myself," he said, considering.

"What?" Cole asked, wide eyed and focused. "You can't. If that woman is Victoria, if she sees you, we'll be back to square one. You know she'll run."

"I'm counting on it," Reese said, smugly. "Little Tory has had the upper hand long enough. I hope she is living in Texas. I hope she does see me. I hope she runs like hell."

Cole grinned. "Right," he agreed. "Vulnerable and on the run, just like we like them."

Both men laughed, content again. Their mission tonight had been more than successful - it had been exhilarating and they finally had a new plan. In no time, Victoria would be back in California where she belonged.

Chapter Four

Rowdy pushed on the door, relieved it was open. He stepped into the empty bar and glanced around. Max was sitting at a table with another man, one Rowdy didn't know but that wasn't a surprise. He'd only been in town a couple days and most of that had been spent in bed with a migraine.

"Rowdy," Max greeted him like he was an old friend. "Come on over and join us."

"I don't want to interrupt, I just had a question and thought you might be able to help me," Rowdy admitted.

Max stood and walked to the bar. "You want a beer or something else?"

"Beer would be great," Rowdy said pulling out a chair.

Mount Haven

Max returned and joined the two men. "This is Trevor Delphin, an old friend of mine. Trevor, this is Rowdy. His brother is our new Sheriff," he studied Rowdy for a minute. "I don't know what you do, will you be one of our Deputies?"

Rowdy scowled. "No," he shifted uncomfortably.

Max nodded. "The leg? You get injured in the line?"

Rowdy didn't want to get into his injuries or relay the story. He'd done that enough to last a lifetime. "Medical retirement. Now I get to figure out what to do with the rest of my life, which is what brings me to you."

"Have any money?" Trevor asked.

Rowdy studied the new addition, trying to get a read on him and his question.

Max scowled at his friend. "Ignore him, he's being impatient. What can I do for you?"

"I'd like to buy a few horses," Rowdy answered. "But I really don't know much about them. Neither does Coop. Any idea where I could find three or four good ones without getting taken to the cleaners?"

"Sure. Missoula has an auction every month, second Saturday I believe," Max said, considering. "So you two live somewhere large enough for horses? I mean three or four of them will need plenty of space."

Rowdy grinned. "I'd say we have plenty of space. We live just up the road a ways."

"The only spread up the road anywhere near here, is Donald Walker's old place. Don't tell me his grandsons finally sold the ranch. Don must be rolling over in his grave." Max frowned, then brightened when he remembered something. "You and Coop are Don's family, ain't ya?"

"You know, it's a little unnerving to show up in a strange town and have all the locals know everything there is to know about your family," Rowdy said, not nearly as annoyed as he thought he should be.

"Don was a great guy," Max said shaking his head. "We all miss him around here," he turned to Trevor. "And he couldn't have been more proud of his family. Good for business too. When one of them - had to be his brother - made sergeant, Don bought a round for everyone in the bar. He wanted to celebrate, but he also wanted everyone to know what amazing grandkids he had. And the two of them were on the SWAT Team in... Chicago was it?"

Rowdy nodded.

"There was another round, first when Rowdy here made the team then again when Coop did. Yeah, good old Donald was great for profits around here." He slapped Rowdy on the back, "I'm glad the two of you finally made it. Donald hoped one of you would get around to seeing the place eventually. He always held out hope you'd love it just like he always did." Max leaned back and studied Rowdy. "So, you want a couple horses to run on that massive spread of yours. I can help you with that. Like I said, the auction's next Saturday. I'll let Bailey know I'll be a little late that night. She's the only one here I'd trust to open the place."

Mount Haven

Rowdy frowned. He wouldn't trust that woman any further than he could throw her. Maybe Max wasn't as observant as he and Coop had originally believed.

"I don't know what happened between the three of you last night, but Bay's okay. She had a rough time with the college boys and I think you two paid the price," Max offered.

Rowdy shrugged. "It doesn't matter. So, we're on for Saturday? What time?"

"We should leave early, maybe seven if we want to get there early enough to check out the stock and settle in," Max turned to Trevor. "You plan to stick around or are you heading back to Manhattan?"

"You don't live here?" Rowdy asked, surprised.

Trevor laughed. "This town is too mellow for my taste," he glanced at Max then continued. "I came out to give Max here a push. He needs to make a decision or the sweet deal I have cooking is going to fall through."

"Sweet deal?" Rowdy asked, looking at Max.

"I'd appreciate it if you kept this to yourself for now," Max said, a little exasperated at his friend. "But Trev fell into an amazing deal on a building in Manhattan. We've always dreamed of starting a club out there and this could be our big break."

"You're leaving?" Rowdy said, disappointed the one guy in town he actually liked planned to pack it in and move to New York.

"Only if I can find the right buyer for this place," Max admitted. "I love it here. I've put my life into this bar for the past fourteen years and I care about my people. I can only sell if I know they'll be okay. If I can find an owner that will care for my baby the way I have." He glanced around the room. "And if I can find someone that will keep Jase and the girls employed. It's a tall order, especially in such a small town. The people here don't have that kind of money."

Rowdy's mind was reeling. Maybe most people didn't, but he did. His house in Chicago had gone for nearly three times what he'd paid for it. It had covered the rest of his mortgage and left him with a handsome nest egg. Rowdy knew Coop had done the same. Running the ranch, even with a few horses, wouldn't put a dent in his income. His medical retirement wasn't much, but it was enough to pay his utilities and care for a few animals. He still needed to find a good truck, but even that would barely make a dent in his savings. If he could swing a good deal from Max, he might just take the guy up on it. He needed a new career and owning a bar and grill might be enough of a challenge to keep him busy.

"See," Trevor said triumphantly. "He's open to it. And you thought I was being rude."

Max continued to study Rowdy. "There is no way you got a good enough payout to afford this place," he finally said.

"Our grandfather left us the ranch. We own the place free and clear," Rowdy explained. "I have a decent medical retirement, just enough to pay the bills but no I didn't get a substantial payout when I left."

"I knew it, they don't pay cops shit when they go down in the line," Max said with disgust.

Rowdy studied his new neighbor. "How do you know?" he finally asked.

Mount Haven

Max sighed. "I was on the job myself," he admitted.

"I knew there was something about you. Sure, you said your brother was a cop but it seemed like more. Nobody picks me and Coop out like you did. Not unless you're on the run or you're a cop yourself."

Max shrugged. "I worked with my brother in New York for a couple years. It wasn't for me. I knew it almost the instant I started, but it took a backstreet ambush in a dark alley to convince me for good."

"Sorry man that blows," Rowdy said, understanding more than he wanted to.

Max shrugged. "I was okay with it, like I said, I was ready for a change. My brother on the other hand, still hasn't forgiven me. He didn't understand how I could throw it all away like that. I didn't just leave, I cashed out my retirement and moved out west. It took me a few months before I landed here, bought this place and never looked back."

"Did your brother ever stop in to see you? Has he seen what you've made of yourself?" Rowdy asked, already knowing the answer from the hurt look on the man's face.

"Nope," Max said, shaking off the hurt. "And I doubt he'll see the place in Manhattan. He doesn't approve. He thinks once a cop, always a cop. What he doesn't know is that I couldn't be on the job if I wanted to. Took a metal pipe to the back of the head. Sneaky bugger, he hid in a doorway while I wrestled with his buddy. Then, at just the right moment, wham the world went black. They must have wailed on me a few times for good measure because in addition to the cracked skull they damaged a nerve in my neck. I can't pass the physical. If you can't pass the physical, you can't be a cop."

"Don't I know it?" Rowdy agreed. "But you clearly love it here. And it looks like you'll be moving onto bigger and better things. It all worked out in the end."

"It did. And it will for you, too. I know what you're going through man. I've been there myself. If you're interested in the place, I'd discuss it. But I can't give it away. I need the cash, the place in Manhattan is going to take more than a little for startup. Think about it then come back. I'm not going anywhere, contrary to Trevor's wishes. You have time, don't jump into something you can't live with forever. This place isn't easy to turn."

"You trying to talk me out of this?" Rowdy asked. "Because I don't remember ever saying I was interested."

"Oh, you're interested," Max said, grinning. "And I think it might be just the right fit. But you need to believe it or the place will fail. I'm just saying think about it, that's all. Now, I have work to do. Feel free to hang out as long as you want," Max stood.

Rowdy stood, too. "Naw, I have unpacking to tackle myself. I'll swing by on Saturday."

"How 'bout I pick you up?" Max suggested, straightening the chair. "I live in town, so if I have to drive out anyway we might as well meet at your place."

"Deal," Rowdy said before he turned and left the bar.

* * * *

Rowdy sat on his front porch contemplated his options. Should he buy the bar? He thought it might actually be a challenge, one he was interested in facing. But what would Coop think? Would his brother be disappointed in him? Coop would never avoid him or stop talking to him no matter what Rowdy did with his life. But his brother might, deep down in his gut, feel like Rowdy had given up. Like he'd taken the easy way out. And would Coop be right? Would giving up on his dream to return to service be taking the easy way out? He hoped not, because Rowdy was beginning to accept his cop days were over for good.

But alcohol and men always created the potential for trouble. Trouble Rowdy would welcome on occasion. It would keep him on his toes. And as a former cop, he knew he could handle a bar fight now and again. So, should he buy the bar? He couldn't stop thinking about the possibilities. Max would insist he keep the staff so he'd agree to that initially. But if Miss Fancy Pants didn't adjust her attitude, she'd be history. He wasn't sure about the rest. The cook he would keep. Rowdy hadn't eaten the food last night but had had noticed how amazing it smelled. It was clearly one of the draws to the bar. The young girl, Max had called her Casey, she'd stay for now. The college kids were drawn to her. The other waitress Rowdy hadn't interacted with but Bailey had mentioned her. Sounded like the woman was a little wild and loose. Not a problem unless she dated the customers. That could cause trouble now and then.

Rowdy jumped when Coop lowered himself into the chair adjacent to his. He hadn't even heard his brother coming. *Note to self, do not get so engrossed in your own thoughts that you ignore your surroundings.* He studied Coop. "Bad day at work?"

Coop sighed and leaned back, teetering the chair on its two back legs. "And at home," he admitted. "I got a call from Bryan's school. He punched a kid in the face this afternoon. Maggie's a mess, she hoped all this would stop once we moved. I guess we both did, but it looks like we're going to have more of the same." Coop leaned forward letting the chair land with a thud then he braced his elbows on his knees and ran his hands through his hair. "I'm at my wits' end with that kid. He doesn't listen, the more I try, the more he just pushes me away. I thought… never mind. How was your day?"

Rowdy felt for his brother and he was just as worried about the kid as his parents were. If he didn't snap out of whatever this funk was, he might lose sight of who he really was. Maybe Rowdy should try to intervene. Once they had the horses, he could spend a little time with his nephew and see if he could get to the bottom of all this violence. "I stopped in and talked to Max. Asked him where to get a few horses without getting hosed."

"Yeah?" Coop asked, curious.

"Yeah," Rowdy said, standing. "I'm gonna grab a beer, want one?"

"Love one," Coop said moving to a nearby lounge chair. He stretched out and forced Bryan and the job from his mind. Something was up with Rowdy, his brother had been so preoccupied he hadn't even heard Coop approach. That was not like Rowdy. The guy was the most alert man Coop knew. No one got the drop on Rowdy Cooper. When his brother reappeared, Coop took a long swig of the cold liquid then balanced his bottle on the armrest. "So, are we buying a horse?" he finally asked.

"Max said the best place to snag a few horses is at the auction. He agreed to take me next Saturday," Rowdy said. Should he mention the bar, or decide on his own?

"I have to work Saturday," Coop frowned.

Mount Haven

"Well, you weren't invited." Rowdy laughed when Coop's frown deepened. He took a deep breath and decided to go for broke. "We also talked about the bar."

"Oh, yeah?" Coop asked, not knowing where this was going. Maybe Rowdy was thinking about being a bouncer. Coop hoped not, he didn't want Rowdy to settle for something like that. His brother could be so much more, but Coop would support him no matter what he decided to do.

"Max wants to sell the place," Rowdy said softly. "It's not public knowledge yet so keep that to yourself… and he wants the owner to keep the staff."

Coop shifted. "Even the haughty waitress, Bailey was it?"

Rowdy nodded. "Especially Bailey, seems Max trusts her. He doesn't know what happened last night, but he said it's unusual and that Bailey was having a difficult night."

"Even more reason to dump her," Coop said, thinking. He wondered if Rowdy would be opposed to going in as partners with Maggie. His wife had always wanted her own café and partnering with Rowdy on a bar and grill might be just what they both needed. He'd have to approach this in the right way, though. Otherwise, Rowdy would think Coop was hovering again.

"I don't know. I think it's a deal breaker," Rowdy admitted. "I could always keep her but have a talk with her. Tell her it was temporary if she couldn't keep her attitude to herself. No matter how sexy those legs of hers are, it doesn't justify the way she treated you."

"So… she had sexy legs, huh?" Coop smiled. Rowdy hadn't been the least bit interested in a woman since the shooting.

"Like you didn't notice," Rowdy said, then smiled. "Of course you didn't. They don't belong to Mags," he shook his head. "You two baffle me sometimes. It's like you're the only two people on the planet."

Coop took another sip of his beer. "That's because we are. Well, she is for me anyway. Why would I look at hot dogs when I have the juiciest, most luscious steak in the world waiting for me at home?"

"Uhhg," Rowdy said, rolling his eyes. "Enough already."

"You're just jealous," Coop said with a grin.

"Sometimes," Rowdy admitted soberly. He wasn't this honest with his brother often, but there was something about tonight. They were both unsettled and a little vulnerable. Rowdy was lost without a job and Coop was lost when it came to Bryan. They were both trying to find their way and it just seemed natural to admit he was sometimes lonely. "You have no idea how lucky you are, Coop."

"Actually I do," Coop said, moving to a sitting position. "But I believe one day you'll be just as lucky. Your girl just hasn't come along yet. I think me, you, Dad… we all inherited a special gene. Dad loved Mom just as much as I love Maggie. He was our example. When the right woman comes along, it will be the same for you. It's just the Cooper way."

"Maybe," Rowdy said, not convinced. He had stopped believing in love a long time ago. Now he was left with short flings and meaningless one night stands. Especially now that he was only half a man.

Mount Haven

Coop could see it was time to change the subject. "So, you seriously thinking about buying the place? Owning a bar might be fun."

Rowdy studied Coop, looking for a catch. When he didn't see what he was looking for he finally asked. "You wouldn't be disappointed in me?"

"Hell no, why would you even ask that?" Coop frowned.

"Max said his brother had a meltdown when he left the job and bought a bar," Rowdy said before taking a long drink of his beer.

"Max used to be a cop? That explains a lot," Coop glanced at Rowdy. "Why'd he leave?"

"Apparently he didn't think being a cop was for him, then he got jumped, injured in the line. He couldn't pass the physical so he bailed."

"And his brother held that against him? So much for love and support. Another example that all families are not like ours Rowdy."

Coop continued, "I would never be disappointed in you. Ever," Coop said emphasizing the last word for effect. "I hate that you can't return to the job. After a few days with my crew you have no idea how much I'd love to hire you as my right-hand man. But that's not going to happen, not right now anyway. Maybe a couple years from now we can look at it, but you can't sit around drinking beer all day and gazing at dragonflies. You need a purpose and even those horses aren't going to give you what you need. If owning a bar will, you should go for it."

Rowdy was watching Coop, waiting for that telltale sign his brother was just humoring him. But it wasn't there. "You mean that, don't you?" he finally asked.

"Every word," Coop said standing. "Now, I have to get back to my wife. You know, the pretty little woman up at the big house that will tan my hide if I spend my one night off with my grumpy brother instead of my beautiful lady." Coop turned to leave then turned back. "I think Dad would be proud of you, Rowdy. I know how hard this has been for you, but the way you've handled yourself, the strength you've shown, I'm proud of you. I know Dad and Mom would have been just as proud. Out of all of us, you are the only one with the strength to go on. Being injured that way would have broken Dad's spirit, just like losing Mom did. We both know that. And I'm just like Dad. I don't know how to be anything but a cop. It doesn't matter where, it's just who I am. I've realized that over the last few months while I considered giving it up."

Rowdy frowned. "So being a cop is in your blood, it was in Dad's blood, but you don't think it's in my blood. Is that what you're saying?" Hearing Coop admit that hurt more than Rowdy ever could have imagined.

Coop was across the porch in two long strides, he dropped to the lounge and fisted his hands around Rowdy's shirt. Once he pulled his brother up so they were nearly nose to nose he spoke slowly, forcing himself to control his words. Coop was beyond pissed. How could Rowdy misread his comments so completely? Unless losing the job made Rowdy feel like he'd lost his identity. Why hadn't Coop seen that coming? That's how he would have felt, of course Rowdy doubted himself. "No," he said before taking another deep breath. "That is not what I'm saying."

Mount Haven

Rowdy tried to shove Coop away, uncomfortable with the look on his brother's face. But Coop had a death grip and wasn't letting go.

"I'm saying I am more proud of the man you are than you could ever imagine. I'm saying I know you have blue running through your veins and not being able to pin on a badge or strap on that belt is hell. A personal hell you face every day, day after day. I'm saying I love you and I would be lost without you. I'm saying that no matter what you decide to do with your life from here on out, I will always be proud of you. If that means training horses, running a bar or driving a garbage truck, I don't care." Coop released Rowdy and stood. "Because you, Rowdy Cooper, have done something nobody else in this family could have done. You survived. And you keep surviving one disappointment after another." With that Coop turned and marched up the trail toward the big house.

Rowdy sat in stunned silence. He was so shocked at what his brother had said, he couldn't even think. Coop was not one to share that way. A lump formed in Rowdy's throat as he remembered each and every word Coop just said. How could his brother be proud of him? He was nothing now. A shell of what he had once been. But out of that entire rant, the only thing Rowdy kept hearing was one sentence. "I'm saying I love you and I would be lost without you." Clearly Coop's day had been worse than Rowdy originally believed. And true to form, he focused on his own problems instead of letting Coop hash out his own.

Rowdy stood and moved silently into his house. He needed a release and he knew just where to find it; his weight room. He'd decide about the bar later. Right now, he just wanted to wear himself out so he could get some sleep.

* * * *

Rowdy woke to the sound of soft knocking and the smell of something wonderful. He climbed out of bed, pulled on his jeans and slowly made his way to the door. He grinned when he saw Maggie impatiently peeking through his window. She jumped when Rowdy opened the door and said "Boo".

"Not funny, Rowdy Cooper," she said pushing past him and setting the plate of goodies on the table. "Did you just get up?" she frowned as she spotted the empty coffee pot.

"Late night," Rowdy admitted. "Give me a minute and I'll make the coffee. I know how you get and I'm sure you've only had what… three… four cups this morning? Not nearly enough."

"Shut up," Maggie said playfully. "I only have two cups, three tops. And this morning I've only had one. I thought we could visit and enjoy the morning together."

Rowdy frowned and studied his favorite woman in the whole world. "What exactly did Coop tell you last night?"

Maggie blushed. Coop had admitted he'd gotten a little sentimental with his brother, but Rowdy didn't need to know that.

"Maggie?" Rowdy pressed. "What's up with Coop anyway? He was clearly not himself last night."

Maggie shrugged. She saw that side of Coop all the time but her husband rarely showed his softer side to anyone else, especially his macho brother. "Nothing really. He's been through a lot this past year, as have you. I think he just wanted to make sure you know how much you mean to him. This thing with Bryan has him frustrated and watching you struggle is hard for him. He's a little lost himself and he loves you Rowdy. The two of you have always been too pig headed to express that, but I know you love Coop too. Almost as much as I do. It wouldn't hurt to tell him that sometimes. I think he might need to hear it."

"So, you're turning my brother into a marshmallow?" Rowdy said, pouring Maggie a large cup of coffee and doctoring it the way she liked it.

"No," she said taking a careful sip of the hot liquid. "I'm helping him become a well-rounded human being. Once I get finished with him, I'll start working on you. I had hoped you'd find your own wife to take care of that, but oh well," she shrugged. "A woman's job is never done."

Rowdy laughed. "Don't waste your time missy, you know I'm a lost cause."

"That's a matter of opinion," Maggie said setting her cup on the table. When she looked into his eyes, her expression was serious.

"Now what?" Rowdy asked, exasperated. Clearly Maggie wanted something.

"I wanted to talk to you about the bar and grill," Maggie said hesitantly.

"Coop told you?" Rowdy sat back and sighed. "I told him that wasn't public knowledge. Does the man not know how to keep a secret?"

"Coop and I don't have secrets," Maggie said, then smiled. "Well, we do but not from each other."

"Don't really want to go there Mags," Rowdy said reaching for the covered plate. "What did you bring me?"

"Banana bread," Maggie said cheerfully. "I know how much you love it."

"And what is it you want?" Rowdy asked suspiciously.

"I want to be your partner," Maggie said seriously. "Please just hear me out. You know I've always wanted to run my own café. In Chicago that wasn't feasible for a number of reasons. But we made a lot of money when we sold our house. Some of it we put into a college fund for Bryan," she frowned. "Not that he's going to make it if he continues on his current path."

"Bryan will sort things out, give the kid some time. He'll figure out violence isn't the answer," Rowdy hoped he was right. Otherwise, Maggie might be right and a college fund was a waste of time.

Maggie swiped her hand, brushing away the topic for now. "Not going there today. We're talking about the bar and grill. I know how bored you've been out here, because I feel the same way. I've about exhausted every chore I can think of. I've cleaned that house so thoroughly even I cringe when I walk through the door. I need something more. I need a hobby, or a career. I haven't seen the bar in person, but Coop told me about it. When he said you were thinking about buying it I asked him a million questions and I'm confident it's perfect. Please Rowdy, let me buy into this place with you. I can't work for you. I need to be on equal footing." She was so excited she was practically bouncing up and down on the chair.

Rowdy couldn't help himself, he laughed. "Mags," he shook his head. "I haven't even decided if I want it yet. Plus, Max said he wasn't giving the place away. He needs the money to open a bigger, more expensive place in Manhattan. We might not be able to afford it, even if we split the cost."

"But if we can, you'll let me in? You'll split it with me, right? With you running the bar and me running the grill it's bound to be a success." She batted her eyes at him, hoping it would work. She wanted this, more than she could put into words. But it was more than that, she needed it probably as much as Rowdy did.

"Did you tell Coop you were interested?" Rowdy asked, wondering if this was his brother's way of protecting him again.

"Sort of," Maggie fibbed.

"Maggie?" Rowdy asked, not sure what to think of her hesitance.

"Okay no," she admitted. "I asked Coop a million question and since he knows me I think he probably figured it out on his own but I wanted to talk to you first. I needed to convince you this is perfect for both of us. Then I'll talk to Andy. He'll support me, I know he will. But you know your brother. Before he agrees to anything he's going to have to check it out, make sure Max isn't ripping us off, he'll probably want to see the books and a ton of other things. Then he'll give me what I want, because this means so much to me and he loves me. So, partners?" she pushed.

Rowdy considered. It could be the perfect solution. He'd been a little worried about running the grill, but the bar he could handle. This way Maggie could deal with Jase and maybe even Bailey and he could handle the bar and the other two waitresses. It was certainly something to consider. "I won't agree to this until Coop does," he finally said. "He's a pain, but he's my brother. And believe it or not, I love him too."

Maggie jumped from her chair and hugged Rowdy. "Thank you," she said, knowing Coop would agree. Last night she had sensed he was telling her because he knew it was perfect. Andy Cooper knew how much she had always wanted to run her own café. Knowing her husband, it had been the first thing he'd thought of when Rowdy mentioned buying the place. But things were strained between these two. If Coop suggested it, Rowdy would have blown him off. Maggie had a sneaking suspicion she and Rowdy had both been played by the clever sheriff. But Maggie didn't care. If in the end she got what she wanted, that was all that mattered. "When do we go talk to Max?"

"Talk to Coop first Magpie," Rowdy insisted. "Max and I are going to the auction tomorrow. Talk to Coop and see if he's okay with you and Bryan joining us. I think Bryan might get a kick out of it. Plus, it will give you and me a chance to talk to Max. If nothing else, we can get an idea of how much he wants for the place. Then we'll go from there."

Maggie did a little dance. "I'm going to get my café. Rowdy, isn't it wonderful? We're going to own our very own bar and grill. I just know it will all work out. This is going to be so much fun." She laughed even harder when Rowdy scowled. "Oh lighten up cowboy, you're in for the adventure of a lifetime."

"That's what worries me," he said following her to the door. He continued to watch as Maggie bounced joyfully up the trail that led back to her house. He had to smile. Going into business with Maggie would be an adventure. And there was no one anywhere he trusted more, except for his brother. Rowdy looked out over the lake. If Coop had manipulated this situation, he hadn't done it for Rowdy. No, this time it was all for his wife. Rowdy knew Coop would do anything for the woman he loved. Rowdy also knew that

Mount Haven

neither of them would stand in the way of Maggie's dream. If the price wasn't too high, Rowdy was going to own a bar.

* * * *

It was Tuesday night, the bar's least busy night of the week so Bailey wondered what had possessed Max to call them all in early. She pushed through the door and walked casually back to the office expecting to see Max alone, working the books behind his desk like he always did on Tuesday evenings. Instead, Bailey spotted a man she had hoped she'd never lay eyes on again. The man she had dreamt about every night for the past week. A man that seemed to be able to see right through her. Living in the same town as this observant cowboy was going to be dangerous. For the hundredth time Bailey wondered if she should just move on. But she refused to let a man run her out of the town she had come to love. For now, she was staying put. She could re-evaluate things later if she needed to.

Bailey was taken by surprise when a lovely woman with beautiful blonde hair stood and walked to the door. She was a tiny little thing, maybe five three, five four and barely a hundred pounds if that. Was this Rowdy's girlfriend? They looked amazing together. Well good, this was good. Then why did she have such a sharp pain in the center of her heart? Get a grip Bailey, she tried to scold herself. The man is trouble with a capital T. He'd never leave such a delicate, graceful woman to hook up with a waitress at a bar. Her brain was telling her she should be relieved. Her cover was safe for now, no worries. But her heart wasn't buying it.

"Hi," the woman held out her hand. "I'm Maggie Cooper."

Rowdy was watching Bailey. Once again he had that feeling that she was hiding from something. And once again he wondered how he was going to spend day after day around the sexy vixen if he didn't trust her. The first test was how she reacted to Maggie.

"Uh…" Bailey said caught off guard. It only took her a minute to regain her composure. She grasped the tiny hand and shook firmly. "Bailey Zander," she shook once then let go and turned to Max. "You said to come in early, where do you want us?"

"Here is fine," Max said, still perplexed. He'd never seen Bailey act like this. She was a nervous wreck and Max wondered why. He just hoped he was doing the right thing by selling to Rowdy and his lovely sister-in-law. No wonder Coop was smitten. Maggie was a rare treat and a beautiful one at that.

"Oh?" Bailey said, confused. "Do you want me to come back later?"

"No. Come in and have a seat," Max said motioning to an empty chair. "I'd like to talk to you first anyway. Well, second. I've already talked to Jase about this."

Bailey's frown deepened. She had a feeling she wasn't going to like what Max had to say. Had Max's strange visitor brought bad news?

"As you know, Trevor stopped by for a visit. He's an old friend of mine." He paused but when Bailey just silently studied him, he continued. "Well, for years we dreamed about opening our own club back east. We thought New York, but Manhattan was also an option. Anyway, Trev fell into an opportunity recently. He bought a building and needs my help to turn it into the hottest club Manhattan has ever seen. I agreed. I'm moving to New York."

Mount Haven

Bailey jumped to her feet. "What about the bar? You can't just close down. What about Jase? What about Casey and Theresa. They need this job." Bailey was furious that Max would just close down without a thought for his employees.

"I didn't hear you mention yourself, Bailey," Max said soberly. "What about you? Don't you need this job?"

Well, no. She actually didn't. What she needed was a place to lie low and avoid her family. What she needed was to live in a place where people didn't ask too many questions. What she needed was for Max to stay here and for things to continue the way they had been for the past five and a half months. "Sure I do," she answered belatedly, kicking herself when she saw the frown on Rowdy's face. Why was he here anyway? Why was Max doing this in the presence of two strangers?

"I thought so," Max said, still wondering what had gotten into Bailey. She was always so confident and sassy. The only other time he'd seen her act this way was when Jase got too close. Was Bailey running from an abusive ex? Did men make her nervous? Max knew she was running, just like he knew Jase was running from something. But hadn't he been running when he landed here fourteen long years ago? The town was therapeutic and he was the last person that was going to pry. "Anyway, the bar won't be closing." He glanced at Rowdy and Maggie. "Meet your new boss." He corrected, "Well, bosses I guess. Maggie and Rowdy are partners."

Bailey swallowed hard. Rowdy now owned The Spurs Bar and Grill?

"Uh…" she struggled for something to say. "Congratulations, I guess." She couldn't muster up any enthusiasm. This was the answer she'd been seeking. She'd asked for a sign to decide if she should stay or go. She couldn't work for Rowdy and she knew it. Not only did she have a secret crush on the man's beautiful body but he was too observant. His brother was the town Sheriff. She couldn't think of a more dangerous scenario to find herself in.

"You don't sound pleased," Rowdy observed.

Maggie was watching Rowdy and the woman who had insulted her husband. There was chemistry there, but both of them were trying to ignore it. There was also distrust and she sensed fear coming from Bailey. "Rowdy, I'm sure Bailey is just surprised. We'll work through it. Max tells us you are his most valued employee. Well, you and Jase. I can see why. I'm sure with your beauty the men go wild for your attention."

Bailey shot to her feet and glared at Rowdy. What had he told his girlfriend about her? Surely the two of them had a good laugh at her expense. So she made a mistake and accused an innocent man of debauchery. She was only human. Anyone could have made that mistake, but Bailey knew they wouldn't have. She'd done exactly what Rowdy had accused her of. She'd been arrogant and haughty. She'd reverted back to her old life, the woman she never wanted to be again. But for some reason, Sheriff Andy Cooper and his sexy brother had brought out the worst in her. Just another reason she had to get out of Dodge. Or Mayberry might be more accurate. The new Sheriff was Andy Cooper for heaven's sake. How much closer could you get?

Rowdy smiled and wondered why he got such pleasure out of making this woman uncomfortable. "I'm sorry," he said as he moved to stand in front of the door; blocking Bailey's escape. "I forgot my manners. Bailey meet Maggie Cooper, Sheriff Andy

Cooper's wife. The one I told you about the other night. As you can see, she's one of a kind."

Maggie frowned at Rowdy; why was he torturing this poor woman? She knew what had happened at the bar, Andy had told her that very night. So the woman had made a mistake. She was still amazed by how oblivious the Cooper brothers were to their sex appeal. Neither one understood the effect they had on women. Maggie understood how Bailey might have misinterpreted her husband's kindness. Not many men treated women the way Coop and Rowdy did. She knew that, but clearly the Coopers didn't. "Do you mind if I have a word alone with Bailey?" She asked the men, but didn't take her eyes off the frightened, embarrassed woman.

"No problem," Max agreed. "I'll just take Rowdy out and introduce him to Theresa. I think I heard her voice. She must be talking to Jase."

Rowdy followed.

Bailey frowned. She didn't want Theresa anywhere near Rowdy. But that was ridiculous. She had no claim on him and never would. The instant the door shut, Bailey turned to face the gorgeous woman. The woman whose husband she had offended. A woman who was probably going to chew her out for making such a stupid assumption.

"They're a little overwhelming," Maggie said, sitting back down in the visitor's chair. She laughed when Bailey just looked at her, clearly confused. "The Cooper brothers."

"I guess," Bailey tentatively agreed. Did she dare take a seat and see what the woman had to say?

"Please join me," Maggie said motioning to the empty chair. She waited while Bailey slowly moved forward and sank into the chair next to Maggie. "Andy told me about your misunderstanding. Sometimes he is so dense, both of them are." She smiled at the surprised look on Bailey's face. "You and I know that men don't act that way nowadays. I think deep down Andy and Rowdy know it too, they just refuse to accept it. They want to believe their fellow men put their best feet forward when it matters," Maggie shrugged. "I wish they did, but I know better. I think you are probably more aware of that than I am. I mean after all, you work in a bar. You see them at their worst, men being obnoxious while they try to show off to their friends. And you have to deal with the alcohol induced stupidity as well. It's not surprising to me that you reacted the way you did to my husband."

"You're not mad?" Bailey asked, truly confused and amazed by this woman.

Maggie laughed. "Not in the least," she shrugged. "Andy Cooper is all mine. I know that with every fiber of my being. I don't know why he chose me, but I have no doubts when it comes to my man's love. The feeling is mutual but I know why I love him. He's the most amazing, sexy, kind hearted man in the world. Rowdy is a close second."

Bailey laughed at that.

"I know, Rowdy has a tough shell, but he's just a big old softy on the inside. Don't tell him I said that. He'll only deny it and do his best to prove to you I'm wrong. But he is, just like his brother. Rowdy just needs the right woman in his life. Someday that will happen. But I'm getting off track. I do know what you did the other night. I know it made Rowdy angry and it baffled my husband. I also know it really wasn't your fault. Max told me you had a rough night. Then the Cooper brothers walk in all cocky and confident." Maggie gave her head a little shake as she laughed. "Do you have any idea how much I enjoy watching that? The two of them walking into a crowded room, completely oblivious to their sex appeal. It's beyond words. And the best part for me is knowing the sexiest one is all mine. I admit I'm a bit small that way."

Bailey had to disagree. The sexiest one was her new boss. Which brought her back to her current problem. "I really don't want to leave you in a bind, but I think it would be best to give you my two weeks' notice right now."

"Well, you could," Maggie said, knowing she had to talk fast. Getting her way with this woman wasn't going to be as easy as it was with Coop or Rowdy. But Maggie was stubborn and tenacious. She had already decided she wanted to keep Bailey as an employee. Max trusted her and Maggie trusted Max for some reason. Now, after seeing the underlying attraction between Bailey and Rowdy, she knew they were meant for each other. She just had to keep Bailey working here long enough for the two of them to realize it. "But I'd rather you didn't. I know things are a little awkward right now with Rowdy. But we talked about this and I thought maybe you would be willing to work for me."

"What do you mean?" Bailey asked, not understanding.

"Well, Rowdy and I are partners like we said. We both bought into the bar and grill. My specialty is food, Rowdy's is… well, he has too many to name. Anyway, Rowdy will be handling the bar side of things. We thought maybe Theresa and Casey could work for him dealing with the bar side, and you could work for me over on the grill side. Both you and Jase would actually work for me. Once we expand, I'm going to need at least one more employee and Rowdy might need one or two more waitresses. In such a small town, I think it's going to be difficult to find the staff we need to run this place the way we want to. I could really use your help and Max trusts you completely. That's good enough for me." Coop had also told Maggie that he thought Bailey was running from something or hiding some kind of secret. If that was true, the woman would be worried. New bosses typically conducted background checks on their employees. Maggie would make sure that didn't happen, not on Bailey or Jase. Both of them seemed to have deep, dark secrets they wanted to keep hidden.

"I don't know," Bailey said, considering. If she didn't have to work for Rowdy, could she stay? She wanted to stay, but the idea of working so close to a man that made her so flustered she couldn't think straight scared her. Plus, it was like he could see right through her. He'd know she was hiding something, if he didn't already. And if he got his brother, the Sheriff, to start looking into her background things were going to blow up in her face. She knew her fake identity wouldn't stand up to scrutiny, which is why she never stayed anywhere very long and never allowed herself to get crossways with the law.

"Let's do this," Maggie said contemplating. This girl was seriously jumpy. "I'm not willing to accept your two weeks' notice. Not right now anyway. Give me and Rowdy a chance. Let's say a week. Then we'll talk. If you still believe you can't work for us, then you can give your two weeks and I won't stand in your way."

Which meant at least three weeks. But she could handle it. She was stronger than she had been years ago. Rowdy Cooper was not going to run her out of a town she loved. "Deal," Bailey said holding out her hand.

Maggie smiled. "Deal," she said, shaking Bailey's hand. "Now," Maggie stood. "Let's go see what the men are up to. Max promised to show us around and let us get a feel for the place before he abandons us. I don't want to miss out on a thing. Rowdy will use that against me and I hate to give him an edge."

Bailey could see just how much Maggie loved her brother–in-law and they were obviously close. She wondered what it would be like to see Maggie and Sheriff Cooper together. If she glowed this much just talking about her husband, it must be downright uncomfortable having them in a room together.

Rowdy smiled when Maggie and Bailey entered the room. Maggie had a way of brightening her surroundings without effort. She'd be good for business, he was sure of it. Now if only he could keep his possessive brother away. He glanced at Bailey and his smile widened. The woman was clearly perplexed. Maggie could do that to a person as well. Before he left the room, Bailey was about to quit. Now, he was pretty sure their little Magpie had talked the woman into staying. Rowdy still didn't know if that was a good thing or a bad thing. Only time would tell. He continued to walk through the bar with Max listening intently as Maggie joined them. He was determined to remember every detail Max was willing to share.

Rowdy wasn't a businessman, he was a cop. Running this place was going to be a challenge. At least he had Maggie. She was a business major with a minor in creative arts. If he were going to be honest, he had to admit he was a little nervous about that part. Maggie was going to redecorate the entire place, no doubt. He just hoped that when she finished it still had the manly appeal a bar needed to succeed. Otherwise, they were going into the restaurant business and maybe he'd occasionally sell a beer now and then on the side. He grunted when Maggie whipped her arm around and collided with his stomach. "What the hell, Mags?"

"I saw that look," she said, laughing.

"What look? I didn't have a look." He tried to scowl but was having a hard time not laughing. "And I've told you a million times, do not use me as your private punching bag. That's what my brother's for. Take your aggression out on him and leave me the hell alone."

"Then stop walking around studying the walls and wondering if I'm going to cover them will frilly roses or some other ghastly motif. I know what I'm doing and you promised to trust me."

Rowdy laughed. Maggie could still surprise him. He hadn't realized he'd been that transparent. "You have my sincere apology, my lady." He gave her a slight bow and lifted her hand to his lips. "Please forgive me."

Maggie laughed and shook her head. Rowdy could be such a ham sometimes. But she was loving it, she hadn't seen him this way since before he got shot. He'd always been so relaxed and fun to be around. Then after that horrible day, he'd retreated into himself and practically stopped living. His only focus was recovery. If this bar brought back the brother she loved, any amount of money was worth it.

Rowdy slung an arm around Maggie. "So, let's talk motif," he said hoping to get Maggie's smile back. Her good mood had sobered instantly. He was sure he didn't want to know what she was thinking.

"Nope," she said cheerfully. "I want to see the kitchen." Rowdy laughed as she pulled him toward the swinging door.

Bailey watched in amazement. If she hadn't seen it herself, she never would have believed it. Maggie was right. Rowdy was just

Mount Haven

a regular guy, one that was funny and goofy around his family. But passionately protective. As she stood there thinking about the first night they'd met, she had an epiphany. Rowdy was protecting his brother, which was just silly. Andy Cooper was the Sheriff after all. He seriously did not need protection. That's when it hit her, was it possible Rowdy was also a cop? But if he was, why didn't he work with his brother? Why had he just purchased a bar? Was he undercover? Had they sent him? Her mind began to wander, confused. If she continued that train of thought, she'd drive herself mad. Rowdy wasn't a cop. Coop just rubbed off on him sometimes. He was a regular guy who just bought a bar and he was going to be her new boss.

Chapter Five

One month later...

Reese slammed the file on the mahogany desk and scowled. He was beyond furious with Cole. They were supposed to be partners and once again, Cole had lied. It was a lie by omission, but still a lie. Why hadn't Cole told him about the mistake that night? Reese could have taken care of things the way he always did. If Reese had known, Cole wouldn't be vulnerable. The cops wouldn't have evidence, the worst kind of evidence. Cole knew that, so what had gotten into his friend lately? First, not telling Reese how he planned to murder the girl, then hiding the mishap with the condom. How was Reese supposed to protect them if he didn't have all the information?

Reese stood and moved to the minibar in the corner of the room. He needed a drink. His life was completely out of control. His friend was hiding things, his father was on the verge of discovering the bad investments Reese had been making with their company funds, and he still hadn't found his woman. He had to find Tori, it was his only hope. If he didn't, he just may tumble over the precarious ledge he'd been teetering the last few months. A ledge he wasn't sure he could come back from. He sighed and threw back his head, opening the back of his throat to swallow the smooth vodka in one fluid motion. As the fiery liquid ran through his system, he closed his eyes and savored the moment.

Reese wasn't sure how long he stood there, eyes closed, head down, thoughts running through his mind. Eventually he opened his eyes and poured himself another glass. He needed a plan. But where to start? This thing with Cole was a ticking time bomb that could erupt at any minute. If only his friend had told him about it sooner. Maybe then Reese could have saved him. But now, it was too late. Their only hope was to make sure that Cole never, ever allowed anyone to collect his DNA. Reese took another sip of vodka and settled into a comfortable lounge chair. Okay, he had to admit the chances of that happening were slim to none. Cole was a wealthy, respectable member of society as far as the community was concerned. So maybe they could contain this, as long as Cole didn't have any further mishaps.

Reese could work with that. He'd research their options later tonight. Clearly using over-the-counter protection from a local drug store had been a mistake. Who knew how long those boxes had been stored on a back shelf. He should have thought of that sooner. He should have thought of it after the crisis with Mandy. He certainly should have taken steps to prevent it after Marnie Montgomery. That thought made him panic momentarily. Someone did have access to Cole's DNA already. But no, Skinner swore he'd destroyed it. The man might be slimy, but he wasn't stupid. All traces of evidence were long gone by now. He had to believe that.

Otherwise, this whole thing had the potential of blowing up in their faces.

* * * *

Several hours later, Cole strolled through the front door and found Reese in the study. His friend looked upset. What now? The man's emotional state had been all over the place for the last month. Being around the guy felt like riding a wild rollercoaster in the middle of a tornado. Reese was trying to maintain control, the way he always did, but Cole saw the cracks forming. He hoped his friend didn't eventually lose it. They made such a perfect team because Cole was willing to take risks and Reese controlled the aftermath. Any shift might disrupt their equilibrium. "Why the long face?" he asked casually.

Reese glanced up then tossed a file onto the coffee table. Cole moved to the couch and relaxed. The instant he read the first page, his heart began to race. He studied his friend, calculating his response. Better to wait this one out. In Reese's current frame of mind it wouldn't take long.

Reese couldn't stand the silence. "If we can't trust each other, I fail to see how we can continue this partnership."

"I agree," Cole said calmly, dropping the file back onto the coffee table. "So, is that the way you demonstrate trust?" He pointed at the file and waited.

Reese glared at his friend, then shrugged. "It wasn't about you. Not initially. I understood why you did it and even why you didn't share the plan with me. You needed the release. You needed to feel like you were in control. Fine. But when you hid something that important from me, it was a lie."

Cole leaned back, settling into the couch as he placed one foot then the other on the coffee table, crossing his legs at the ankle. "So, anytime you failed to disclose the details of your mistakes it was a lie?"

Reese narrowed his eyes at Cole. What did he know? "We're not talking about me. We're talking about you. We're talking about the fact that you let me go into a mission without all the facts. Okay, so you needed to kill the woman. I can live with that. But why not tell me about the condom?"

"Because you were already upset," Cole admitted. "Because it didn't matter. Nobody is going to get my DNA, ever. As long as I'm careful from here on out, I'm safe."

"Somebody already had your DNA," Reese reminded him.

Cole froze; he'd forgotten about that. "Skinner swore he destroyed all the evidence. There is no way that man betrayed us. He has too much to lose."

"On that we do agree," Reese said, standing and moving to the small bar. He poured himself another vodka on ice, threw it back then poured a second. He returned to his chair and slid the glass across the coffee table towards Cole.

Cole relaxed. He'd just received a peace offering. He could reciprocate. "Look, I almost told you. But then it was over and I realized we didn't have anything to worry about. I just need to be careful from now on. I can't make another mistake," he frowned. "Not that I consider Marnie Montgomery a mistake. But I can admit

I wasn't as careful as I should have been on our last mission. It won't happen again."

Reese closed his eyes and let the alcohol sooth him. "I wasn't checking up on you. I know that's what you think. I was just being thorough. It's what I do. You know that. I hadn't prepared for that woman's death. It worried me and I couldn't stop thinking about it. After a couple weeks, I decided the only way to put it behind me was to get the file. I needed to know what the police know. So, I called Rodney. The file arrived today."

"And now?" Cole asked, surprised Reese had already put this behind them.

"I agree with you," Reese said. "We don't have anything to worry about as long as you are careful. Skinner wouldn't dare double cross us, so your DNA on one woman out of..." Reese trailed off, he'd lost track years ago.

Cole smiled. "Too many to count," he provided.

"Yes," Reese smiled back. "One mistake isn't catastrophic. We just need to make sure it never happens again. If you read that file you will see the detective ran the results and came up empty. Your DNA wasn't in the system. I've already done the research and found a new supplier. No more relying on that over-the-counter garbage."

"Is that going to delay our weekend?" Cole hoped not, he needed another adrenalin rush. Plus, Reese was still making noise about heading to Texas. The mysterious woman was not leaving her fortress, which made Cole even more certain it was Victoria.

Mount Haven

"No," Reese assured him. "We're still on for Saturday. The package should arrive on Thursday. However, we will need to make a slight change in the plan."

"What change?" Cole asked. He never liked last minute changes.

"Location," Reese said taking another sip of vodka. "The old woman across the hall has a nephew. He's visiting, apparently deciding if he needs to move in and care for the old hag. His schedule is unpredictable."

"Damn. That apartment was perfect," Cole sighed. "Now what?"

"I found an old cabin," Reese grinned. Then he proceeded to outline the changes he'd come up with. He had to admit this plan might actually be the best one he'd come up with so far. There was only one downside. They would have to travel together. That was something they had never done before and Reese hoped it wouldn't end up being a mistake. The two of them plotted and schemed for the next three hours. Both of them anxious for their next kill.

* * * *

Bailey slid behind the bar and began wiping the counter. Rowdy was in the stock room doing inventory. She didn't think that man ever stopped. He'd been working himself ragged the past week. Bailey smiled, his work, her pleasure. She couldn't help but watch him. He was the sexiest man she had ever met in her life. She knew she couldn't act on the attraction, but there was nothing stopping her from enjoying the show. It had been a long time since she'd been interested in a man. She glanced around the room; it was still empty. She'd be embarrassed if she got caught ogling the boss. Once she was sure the coast was clear, she refocused on the gorgeous man just a few feet away but miles out of her reach. She was glad she'd let Maggie talk her into staying. Working so close to Rowdy still made her nervous, he was far too perceptive. But, it had also reminded her that she was a woman. A young, healthy, albeit lonely woman, but a woman. Plus, it had given her the opportunity to get to know the real Rowdy Cooper. He wasn't cocky and arrogant, okay sometimes he could be. But he was also loyal, protective and entertaining. She suspected Maggie was right, Rowdy Cooper was hard on the outside and a big old softy on the inside. Most of all he was truly a good man.

Rowdy stepped out of sight and Bailey turned just in time. The bell jangled on the front door and a delivery driver stepped into the dimly lit room. "Can I help you?" she asked.

"Yeah," the guy said glancing around. "Got a delivery here for Maggie Cooper."

Rowdy heard the bell and stepped out just in time to hear his delivery had arrived. "Pull around back. It belongs in here," he pointed to the room he had just exited.

Bailey followed Rowdy to the back of the building. She watched as he got into a heated discussion with the driver. A second man joined them, then they both turned and walked across the street. Rowdy moved to the back of the truck, mumbling under his breath. She was pretty sure some of those words weren't meant for mixed company. "What's going on?" she asked when he jumped into the cargo area and began loading the cart. No answer. "Rowdy!"

Mount Haven

Rowdy threw several crates on the cart then slowly lowered the power operated lift. He didn't have time for this. "They said Maggie only paid for delivery. Which is a load of crap but Maggie's at the dentist so I can't call her. Either I unload the truck myself or they take it back to the warehouse."

"No way!" Bailey said, annoyed. "There's too much. You can't unload that by yourself." She stood on her tiptoes to get a better look. "Wow, all that is for us?"

"Yep," he nodded. "So, mind getting out of the way? I have a busier afternoon than I originally thought."

Bailey didn't know what to do. "We both know Maggie paid for delivery and stocking."

Rowdy walked past her so she followed.

"Call their bluff," she suggested.

Rowdy dropped the handcart and began unloading. He glanced at her then shook his head. "Can't afford it. What if they leave? It's Wednesday, it's impossible to get another truck out here before the weekend. We're running on fumes here Bailey. If I let them leave, we're screwed."

They were, but still. Those two men would be screwed if they returned with a truckload of alcohol that was bought and paid for just because they were too lazy to unload the truck. If Jase were here, she could get him to help Rowdy. But, Jase was headed out of town this morning and wouldn't be back until late this afternoon. There was no one she could call. Coop was on duty and she didn't have his number anyway. Rowdy pulled off his shirt and tossed it aside. Bailey's heart did a little happy dance but the rest of her scowled. He was going to wear himself out. He had looked so exhausted last night before he left. On their way to the parking lot she'd noticed his limp was back. She'd watched for it this morning, but he was back to normal. After this ordeal he might not walk for a week. After all this time she still didn't know what had happened to him and she wasn't comfortable enough to ask. She had her secrets, he could keep his.

Bailey continued to watch Rowdy work. She was curious about the man. Why did he limp sometimes? Why hadn't he gone into law enforcement like his brother? What little she knew, told her he would be good at it. He wasn't married, but had he ever been serious? What did he want in a woman? They had developed a casual working friendship over the past few weeks, but Bailey knew if she started asking personal questions he'd pounce on the opportunity to ask her a few of his own. And with a man like that, a little information was way too much. She had to be very cautious about what she said. Other than that, life here in Mount Haven was almost perfect. If only he'd stop calling her that stupid nickname.

An hour later Rowdy was still unloading the truck. Bailey could see he was exhausted. "Let me help," she offered. "I'll load this one, you watch the floor."

Rowdy grunted and kept loading. His leg was killing him and his head was starting to pound. If he got a migraine over this, those two were going to pay dearly. He knew Bailey was just trying to help, but seriously? Was the woman out of her mind? As if he would let a petite thing like her take over and unload this shipment. His mother raised him better than that and anyway, he'd probably have a heart attack. Watching that sexy body lean over and struggle with crates was way more than his mind and body could handle, especially today. "Go back to the floor, Fancy Pants. I got this."

Mount Haven

Bailey scowled and practically stomped back to the bar area. She hated it when he called her that. She knew he was right, it was unlikely that she could unload even one crate off that truck but it still irritated her that he'd dismissed her so callously. She picked up the rag and began taking her aggression out on the counter.

Rowdy loaded the last of the liquor onto the cart and took a deep breath. He glanced at his watch, relieved. Just in time. He'd promised Maggie he'd be at the ranch when Bryan arrived home from school. He might have to cancel their ride today but he'd make sure Jase cooked up something special for an after school snack. Rowdy shoved the last crate of rum onto the shelf and walked up front. Bailey was standing behind the bar, frowning. "I need to head home and meet Bryan. If those two come looking for their cart, it's in the stock room. If not, that's their problem. You okay here alone?" He didn't like leaving Bailey by herself, but he didn't have a choice. Anyway, Jase was due to arrive any minute.

"I'm fine," she said, disappointed when he pulled his shirt back over his gorgeous chest and over those amazing abs. She'd enjoyed watching him work, but he really did look beat. "You need a Coke for the road?" Maybe a cold drink would help.

"No, I'm fine. I'll be back in a while," he strolled out the door and walked to his truck. He would have gone faster, but he was afraid he'd lose his footing and fall flat on his face. Thanks to those deliverymen his leg was killing him. That was never going to happen again. He planned to have a talk with Maggie about that particular distributor. Whoever had made the mistake was going to pay dearly or he'd buy his liquor someplace else.

Rowdy was sitting on the front porch of the big house when Bryan skipped up the drive. At least he'd finally cooled down and the pounding in his head was just a dull ache now. He smiled, it was nice to see his nephew so happy. The kid was starting to come around. Rowdy knew their afternoon rides had contributed to the transformation. They spent an hour nearly every day together talking about whatever came up. Rowdy thought it was helping the kid deal with the uncertainty of the past year. And making him care for the horses seemed to be giving him more confidence. Last week they had finally broached the subject of Rowdy's injuries. Rowdy had assured Bryan he was okay. He just had headaches sometimes. He had also warned the kid one could hit at any minute. He'd taught him what to do if that happened while they were out riding. He hated to disappoint his nephew when he was clearly in a good mood but he wasn't sure his leg was up to a long ride today.

Knight barked a welcome hello and Bryan looked up. He smiled from ear to ear when he spotted Rowdy. "Should I get the horses ready?" he asked immediately.

Rowdy frowned. Knight bolted off the porch and ran for the stables abandoning Toby who was still lazily sunning at Rowdy's feet. How was he going to disappoint both his nephew and his dog? He realized he couldn't. He'd warn Bryan their ride would have to be shorter than usual, then they'd head out. He could handle a half hour on the back of a horse, maybe. Rowdy laughed when Knight darted back and barked twice, that was his cue to get off the porch. Clearly Knight needed this time to explore as much as Bryan did. "Let's take Biscuit and Collie today," Rowdy called out. "It's going to have to be a short one kid, I need to get back to the bar."

Bryan was clearly disappointed but then he shrugged and nodded. Apparently a short ride was better than no ride at all. Rowdy was glad he'd changed his mind. They both needed this time together and sometimes work just had to wait. He could suffer through a little pain if it made his favorite little man happy.

Mount Haven

Bryan was worried. Rowdy hadn't fallen off the horse yet but he was slumped over the saddle and clearly wasn't in control. If the horse realized he was free, would he run away? Rowdy was barely holding on. He wouldn't be able to manage if the horse took off. Bryan moved closer and carefully reached out, grabbing Rowdy's reins. At least the horse couldn't bolt. The two of them slowly made their way towards the house. Bryan chewed his bottom lip in concentration trying not to worry. He glanced at his uncle then back toward the house and finally spotted the barn. Relief flooded through him. Hopefully they would make it. Then he just had to figure out how to get Rowdy out of the saddle and into bed. He knew he couldn't handle that alone. He was going to have to call his father.

He wished he could handle it himself. He'd been awful to his dad lately. He didn't want to be, but sometimes mean things just came out before he could stop them. He'd get scared and it was easy to take it out on his parents. Spending time with Rowdy and the horses helped. He didn't feel so helpless anymore. And today he was going to prove, at least to himself, that he could handle something hard. He wouldn't panic. He'd get Rowdy to the barn, help him off the horse, then call his dad for help. It would be impossible to get his uncle all the way to the cottage alone but with his dad's help they could probably make it.

The instant they entered the stable, Bryan jumped from his horse and led him into a stall, locking the gate behind him. Now for Rowdy. He moved to the side and tried to shake his uncle.

Rowdy felt Bryan shaking him and knew they must be at the barn. He cracked open one eye, relieved they were inside the stables and it was fairly dark. He just had to slide off the horse and stumble to an empty stall. Bryan would handle the horses. The kid was a natural and the horses responded to him. Rowdy usually let Bryan handle the saddling and cleanup anyway so today would be no different. "Bry?" he said then cleared his throat. "I need you to hold the horse steady so I can climb down. Can you do that for me, buddy?"

"I got him Uncle Rowdy," Bryan said confidently. He wasn't about to let Biscuit move even an inch.

Rowdy slid from the saddle then crumpled to the ground. He knew he was probably scaring Bryan, but the left side of his body was completely numb and he couldn't balance his weight. His head felt like it was about to explode from the constant throbbing. He tried to look around to find a corner to crawl into but the light seeping through the door caused his pain to intensify. Rowdy didn't move for several seconds. Now what? He began to open and close his left hand trying to get the pins and needles feeling to dissipate. Sometimes he could shake the feeling by flexing and relaxing but not today, nothing seemed to be working at the moment. Which meant, any minute the nausea was going to start. He didn't want Bryan to see him puke all over the place. Unfortunately, with the horses close by Rowdy wasn't sure he could stop himself. The smell of the stables was making him queasy. When Bryan slammed the gate shut, Rowdy moaned in pain.

"I'm calling Dad," Bryan said, moving to stand next to his uncle. "I can't get you to the house by myself and I can't leave you out here all day."

"That's not..." Rowdy sighed, Bryan was definitely his father's son. "Necessary," he finished quietly to himself, Bryan had already stepped outside and wasn't listening anyway.

Mount Haven

"Dad?" Bryan said softly when his father answered the phone. "Is this a bad time?" He didn't want to interrupt his dad if he was on a call or something.

"Bryan? What's wrong?" Coop said, hearing the stress in his son's voice.

"Me and Rowdy went out for a ride. We were in the back field when Rowdy started to get one of his headaches. I was able to get him back to the stables, but he's scrunched over on the ground and I can't move him. I need your help," Bryan said, speaking faster than usual.

"Shit," Coop said then took a breath. "I'm on my way, but I had a call outside of town. I'm at least forty minutes out, maybe an hour. Can you hang in there for me son? I'll call Mom. At least she can find Rowdy's pills and help make him comfortable until we can get him to his bed."

"Okay," Bryan said swallowing hard. Then with more confidence, "We'll be okay until you get here. If Mom can't come, we'll be okay."

"I know you will. I trust you Bryan. Take care of Rowdy for me until I get home. I'm counting on you." Coop knew Bryan was stressed, but he also knew his son could handle this.

"I will," Bryan said, more confident now. "Hurry okay?"

"I'll be there as fast as I can." The instant he disconnected from Bryan he called the bar. "Hey, Bailey can I talk to Maggie? It's Coop."

"Sorry. She's not here yet," Bailey said casually as she wiped down the last table. "Do you want me to have her call you when she gets back?"

"Do you know where she is?" Coop said a little panicked now. He couldn't leave Bryan alone to deal with Rowdy for long.

"What's wrong?" Bailey asked, straightening.

"There's a little situation at home. I just needed Maggie to head over. I'm on my way, but it's going to take awhile for me to get there."

"Maggie hasn't made it back from the dentist. I can help, Jase can handle things here while I'm gone. What's the situation? I'll go take care of it," Bailey offered, glad Jase had just walked in.

Coop hesitated, but eventually agreed. "Before we moved here, Rowdy was injured. He gets migraines sometimes. Some are fairly mild, some are intense. From what Bryan just described, this one must be intense. They're out in the stables. He and Bryan were out riding. Bryan's handling things, but he's scared and with all he's been going through..."

"Say no more," Bailey said, throwing the rag in the sink. The place was spotless now anyway. "I'll let Jase know what's going on. He can fill Maggie in when she gets here. I'll call if I need anything."

"Thanks Bailey. I hate to ask but things with Bryan are touchy. And be prepared, Rowdy gets a little testy, but it's only because the migraines are so severe. Don't let him hurt your feelings. He doesn't really mean it, whatever he says."

Mount Haven

Bailey laughed. "I can handle Rowdy. See you soon." The instant she hung up, she turned and explained the situation to Jase. "When Maggie gets here, tell her to go home. I might need her help dealing with both Rowdy and Bryan."

"Sure thing," Jase said, glad Bailey was actually talking to him. She'd avoided him completely since she'd arrived.

* * * *

Bailey pulled up outside the stables and shoved her car into park. She was out the door before the engine even stopped. "Bryan," she called, then froze when she heard Rowdy moan.

"Shhh," Bryan said impatiently. "The noise bothers him. If I could get him out of here I would. The horses are making too much noise."

"It's fine," Rowdy forced out, feeling like he was talking in a jumbled mess. Would Bryan even understand what he said?

Bailey was shocked. The scene before her made her insides coil. It was just wrong somehow for her strong, cocky boss to be crumpled on the ground in so much pain. She walked to Bryan and laid a hand on the boy's shoulder. "What can I do to help?" she whispered.

Bryan's eyes watered and he turned away with a shrug. "I don't know," he finally admitted.

Bailey looked around, thinking. If she gave Bryan a job of some kind it might help him feel useful. "How about you run to the house and get your uncle a pillow and a blanket. We can't move him, but your dad is on his way. In the meantime, let's make Rowdy as comfortable as we can."

Bryan's face lit up and Bailey knew she'd made the right decision. "I'll be right back. Don't leave him, okay?"

"I promise," Bailey said, crossing her heart. "I'll stay right here." She smiled as Bryan ran off, determined to do whatever he could to help out his uncle. Bailey turned back to Rowdy. Now what? She moved to his side and knelt down next to his crumpled body. She didn't think, she just reached out and brushed his soft brown hair away from his face. She forced a smile when Rowdy opened one eye then quickly closed it again.

"I'm... fine," he forced out, not wanting Bailey of all people to see him so weak and helpless.

"What can I do to help?" Bailey asked. "Coop said something about medication. If you can tell me where to find it, I'll get it when Bryan gets back."

"Just... take..." Rowdy let out a huge sigh. "Bryan."

"I'll take care of Bryan, but I also want to take care of you," Bailey pressed. "Where's the medication, Rowdy?"

"Bryan," Rowdy insisted.

Bailey knew the headache must be severe if Rowdy couldn't even talk. She didn't know anything about migraines other than what she'd seen on commercials. From what she remembered they could be pretty debilitating. Looking at Rowdy right now, that was an understatement. She glanced up when she heard Bryan approach. He was carrying a large blanket and a pillow tucked under his arm.

Bryan rushed back to the stables and slid to a stop near Rowdy's head. How was he going to get the pillow underneath Rowdy without hurting him? He looked at Bailey for guidance, thankful when she stood and spread out the blanket, coving his uncle's scrunch up body.

"I'm going to lift his head just a little, we have to be gentle. As soon as I do, slide the pillow underneath, okay?" Bailey directed.

Bryan nodded and knelt beside his uncle. While he was down there he watched Rowdy's chest for movement. When he saw his uncle was still breathing, he felt better. Bryan remembered the night they had moved in. Rowdy was like this that night, too. He'd been so worried, but his dad assured him it was only a headache and Rowdy would be fine. His dad had been confident Rowdy would be okay that night. Bryan had to believe this time was the same. He loved his uncle and hated that he got headaches but as long as he wasn't going to die, Bryan could handle this.

Once the pillow and blanket were in place, Bailey felt useless. She didn't know anything about migraines or how to help Rowdy with the pain. And he hadn't been a bit of help when she'd asked about his medication. Would Bryan be okay if she ran to Rowdy's house and searched around? But she'd never been inside Rowdy's house and if it was locked, which it probably was, she'd be leaving Bryan for nothing. She stood and began to pace wishing Coop would get here already.

* * * *

Maggie pulled into the parking lot of The Spurs Bar and Grill, happy to be home at last. She had to admit, she got a special kind of satisfaction out of handling problems all by herself. Her dentist appointment had gone so well, she decided to stop by Iso-Foods and deal with the delayed shipment in person. She hated confrontation but dealing with incompetence was a personal pet peeve. By the time she'd finished, she was glad she had stopped. Their delivery would be here Friday morning, just in time for the weekend rush. She was just reaching for the door when Jase rushed out. Maggie frowned, knowing something else had gone wrong. "What is it, Jase?"

"Bailey's over at your place. Coop called, said something about Rowdy and a headache. Bryan was upset so Bailey headed over to see what she could do. Coop's on his way, but it's going to take him a fair amount of time. He was out at old man Stoddard's again."

"Thanks," Maggie said turning to rush back to her car. "Can you handle things here?"

"Got it covered," Jase said with a cocky wave.

Maggie wasn't sure how long it took her to drive from the bar to the ranch, but she was sure it must have been a record. She came to an abrupt stop, ran into the stables and instantly spotted Rowdy lying on the cold hard ground. She glanced around until she found her son. Bryan was sitting in the corner talking quietly to Bailey, who kept glancing over at Rowdy with a worried look on her face. Maggie took a deep breath then headed over to greet them. "Looks like you two have everything under control," she whispered softly.

"Mom!" Bryan said in a whispered yell and jumped up to hug her. "I wasn't sure what to do, so I called Dad. He should be here soon. I wanted to help Rowdy to his house, but he was too weak to walk."

"We might be able to handle that now," Maggie said, glancing at Bailey for support.

"I had an idea but wasn't sure Bryan and I could handle it alone," Bailey said sheepishly. Was her plan as monumentally stupid as she thought it sounded?

"What's the idea?" Maggie asked, studying Rowdy. He was in bad shape this time. Were the headaches getting worse because they were less frequent? Or were they just getting worse and Rowdy had been hiding them?

"Well, I know it might be dumb but I was thinking if we could load him into that wheelbarrow over there, maybe we could just roll him on home." Bailey blushed, hoping Maggie didn't burst out laughing.

Maggie brightened. "That's perfect," she said, rushing to the corner and grabbing the wheelbarrow. "Let's put the blanket in first then we can load Rowdy and support his head with that pillow."

Bryan stood beside his mom, skeptical. "I don't think the three of us can lift him," he finally said, looking at his mom for help.

"Right," Maggie said, considering.

Rowdy thought the idea was a good one. He had to get out of this barn. The smells were not only making the pain worse, but he'd been fighting intense nausea and knew he was losing the battle. The cramping and vomiting was going to start any minute. He rolled onto his side and tried to stand.

Bailey rushed to Rowdy's side and did her best to steady him. She shot a worried look at Maggie then relaxed a little when Maggie positioned the wheelbarrow in front of Rowdy. "Bryan, go back and hold that pillow in place. We don't want Rowdy hitting his head when we lower him into the wheelbarrow."

Bryan rushed to the side and held the pillow in place. Maggie pushed the handles to the ground hoping Bailey could maneuver Rowdy around her.

Bailey realized what Maggie was doing and slowly took a step forward. She was grateful when Rowdy stepped with her. His weight was almost more than she could handle but somehow they managed to step between the two handles. Bailey held onto Rowdy as he slowly lowered himself into the cart. Once he was settled, Maggie lifted the handles. With Bailey's help they were able to get the wheelbarrow upright. "You doing okay big man?" Maggie asked.

Rowdy reached out and grasped Maggie's hand with his right one. The only one he could use right now, as his left side was still too weak to move. "Thanks Mags," he let out a deep, frustrated breath. "Sorry… for… the… trouble." He was a mess and he knew it. It still bothered him that Bailey was here, witnessing him in such a state, but he had to admit she'd been a big help.

"Let's get you home," Maggie said softly. She was near tears. She hated this. She hated seeing Rowdy so helpless and in pain. But she knew he hated it even more and she was pretty sure given his stubborn independence he was embarrassed that Bailey was here to witness him in this condition. Maggie would need to have a talk with her new friend before 'Rowdy the Bear' surfaced. Maybe if Bailey was prepared, she wouldn't take his reaction the wrong way.

The instant they reached the cottage, Rowdy knew he was going to puke. The bright afternoon sun combined with the constant motion as they moved over the rough terrain was a recipe for disaster. The second Bailey and Maggie lowered the handles, he shifted abruptly. The wheelbarrow tumbled to its side depositing Rowdy with a thud.

Maggie screamed. Bailey rushed to Rowdy's side, trying to help him stand.

Rowdy was doing his best to hold back the nausea, but he wasn't going to last long. He pushed Bailey away and struggled to find Bryan. "Bry?" he called out.

Bryan didn't know what his uncle needed, but he was by his side in an instant. He helped Rowdy stand and waited.

"Bushes," Rowdy said softly, trying to move forward.

Bryan understood. His uncle sometimes got sick when he had headaches. He was surprised Rowdy had wanted his help but maybe he thought the girls would freak out. The two of them slowly made their way the few feet to the bushes and Rowdy lost it.

It didn't take long for Maggie to realize what was coming. She rushed into the house and grabbed a bottle of water. As Rowdy straightened, she raised the bottle to his lips. "Drink then let's get you inside."

Rowdy grabbed the bottle with his right hand and guzzled half of it. Hopefully it would stay down long enough for him to get to his room. His anger increased when Bailey wrapped her arm around his waist on the left as Maggie supported him from the right. He didn't want her here. Why did Bailey have to see him this way? Now the entire bar, and the town, would know Rowdy Cooper was weak. He'd worked so hard to gain their respect and in an instant he was going to lose it.

The three of them made their way into the house, down the hall and finally into Rowdy's bedroom. Bryan led the way, pushing open doors and making sure Knight hadn't left his toys in the way. Rowdy turned to Bryan. "Where's Knight?"

Bryan waited for Rowdy to slowly lower himself to the bed. "I didn't know if he would bite Bailey, so I locked him and Toby inside the barn." He hoped Rowdy didn't get mad at him but he hadn't known what else to do.

"Good job," Rowdy said slowly. He frowned when Maggie shoved the bottle of water back into his hand and held out two of his pills. He glanced up and realized Maggie was scowling. It took him a minute but he finally understood, she was pissed about the pills. If he'd been thinking, he would have insisted Bailey retrieve the prescription. Too late now. Maggie had seen the nearly empty bottle and he would have to explain himself to Coop the instant he recovered. Maybe hiding his condition hadn't been the best idea, but he hated being such a burden to his family. And although the migraines were coming more frequently, they were usually less severe. Rowdy sighed, lifted his head slightly, swallowed the pills then flopped back onto the bed. "Thanks," was all he could choke out. With any luck, the pills would do the trick and he'd be back at the bar tomorrow night.

Bailey watched the small family care for Rowdy and suddenly felt out of place. Bryan was removing Rowdy's boots and Maggie was pulling off his shirt before helping him into bed. Bailey moved backwards, then turned and stepped out of the room. She was about to leave the house and return to the bar but changed her mind. Maggie might still need her help. She lowered herself to the floor, resting her back against the wall and waited. After several seconds, she glanced up and realized Maggie was now removing Rowdy's jeans. She immediately glanced away, suddenly very sad. *What would it be like to have family that cared for you?* A tear ran down her cheek and she impatiently brushed it away. She'd had that once, before her father died. Her father thought his only daughter hung the moon. She glanced back at Rowdy and realized Maggie had him safely tucked into bed and was walking her way.

"Do you mind waiting here for a minute?" Maggie asked. "I want to step out onto the porch and call Coop. He's going to be worried."

"Sure," Bailey said glancing back at Rowdy. She silently watched as Bryan moved to the side of the bed and slowly sat down next to his uncle when Rowdy patted the mattress. She couldn't hear their conversation but the message was clear. Rowdy was proud of his nephew. She continued to watch as Rowdy patted Bryan's stomach and said 'Cooper steel.' Bryan grinned and sat a little straighter on the bed as his uncle continued to praise him. Bailey lowered her head to her knees refusing to cry. She'd had about a million moments like this with her father as a child. But that time in her life was over. She'd never experience another father daughter moment, but she would not feel sorry for herself. Life was tough but she could handle it. She was stronger now. And if she let her memories get out of control she'd be a blubbering mess in no time. She had to think of something else. Her mind settled on Rowdy and began to race, a thousand thoughts running through her head. She felt so bad for her boss and casual friend. He was clearly in a lot of pain. She knew he was going to be embarrassed that she'd witnessed all of this. He was such a strong, independent, stubborn man. Showing any kind of vulnerability would piss him off for sure.

Bailey realized Maggie was standing next to her and wondered how long she'd been daydreaming. She looked up and realized her boss was angry. Had she done something wrong?

"I need Bryan to help me deal with the horses," she whispered. "Do you mind staying with Rowdy until we get back?" She motioned to her son and Bryan immediately stood and walked to his mother. "Coop is only a few minutes out so it shouldn't take us long."

Bailey stood. "I don't mind. I'll be here until you get back." She glanced at Rowdy, wondering how he would feel about her staying. She took a tentative step forward but Rowdy didn't move. Bailey relaxed, maybe he wouldn't realize she was still here.

Bailey watched as Maggie and Bryan slowly left the room. She waited until she heard the front door close then she walked to the side of the bed. Rowdy opened one eye and sighed. She wished she could ask him about his injuries but she knew now wasn't the time and when he was better, he was going to be grumpy and unreasonable about the whole thing. He was a man after all and men like Rowdy didn't like anyone to see they had a weakness. Bailey was so caught up in her thoughts that she didn't see Rowdy reach out to her. She jumped slightly in surprise when Rowdy wrapped his large hand around her fingers.

"Thank you," Rowdy whispered. His speech was better now and the violent thumping was beginning to subside. Escaping the noise and the smells of the stable had done wonders for his condition. "Sorry for the trouble. I'm okay now, you can go back to the bar. I'm afraid I'm not going to make it tonight. You'll do fine without me. Mags will be there I'm sure and if there's trouble tell Jase."

"Rowdy, maybe you could just worry about yourself for the night," Bailey said, a little annoyed at the man. "Maggie, Jase and I will handle the bar. I don't know anything about migraines, but I've seen how you've been pushing yourself the past few days. You unloaded that truck by yourself today," she reminded him. "Your family is worried. Just rest tonight and stop worrying about everything but yourself for a change."

Rowdy was silent for so long Bailey wondered if he'd drifted off to sleep. She turned to leave when he began to speak. "Look, I know they worry which is why I haven't mentioned the migraines."

"So, you've been hiding things from your family?" Bailey asked directly. "Do you have any idea how lucky you are? Your family is so close, they care so much. Not everybody has that." Bailey stopped before she revealed too much.

Rowdy figured Bailey was probably talking about herself. He knew everyone didn't have a close relationship like he did, but that only made his situation worse. "Let me worry about my family. I've burdened them enough already. They don't need the constant reminder. Yeah, I still get migraines, big deal. They have enough to worry about without having to babysit me all the time."

Bailey decided not to press Rowdy any longer. He was clearly agitated and in pain. "I think Bryan is going to stay with you tonight. Are you hungry? I could send something over from the bar."

"No food," Rowdy said immediately. Just the thought of it made him nauseous again. He cracked an eye and glanced at Bailey, she looked so uncomfortable. "Have a seat," he pushed his body backwards to make room for her.

Bailey hesitated then slowly lowered herself onto the bed hoping the movement didn't make Rowdy's condition worse. They sat there in silence for several minutes. Bailey didn't think she'd ever been this awkward in her life. Would it be rude if she left?

Rowdy wondered what was going on in that pretty little head of hers. She looked so sad and lost somehow. He reached out and rested his hand on top of hers.

Bailey jumped again at his touch. After months of keeping their distance, the contact was hard to take. Her reaction impossible to hide, but she had to. The last thing she needed was for Rowdy to know how he affected her.

Rowdy couldn't take his eyes off the enigmatic woman. She was still a mystery to him. He wondered if she always would be. "You going to be okay?" he finally asked.

Bailey sighed. That was so like Rowdy. Here he was miserable, clearly in terrible pain but he was worried about her. How had she ever thought this man selfish and arrogant? His arrogance was just part of the protective shield he put up to keep people out. "I'm fine, Rowdy," she finally answered. "I'm worried about you. I noticed you were limping last night when we closed down. Then you unloaded that entire truck by yourself today. You can't keep pushing yourself like this. You were already beat after cleaning the stock room. I know the Spurs is your bar but you have employees. I'm not incompetent, I could have helped."

Rowdy scowled. "I'm not going to let you do any heavy lifting, Bailey."

"Okay, I agree that I couldn't have unloaded that truck." She considered her next words carefully. "But you shouldn't have done it either," she grinned. "I know you think you're Superman and I

Mount Haven

hate to be the one to shatter your illusion, but you are merely a mortal man. You have limitations just like all the rest of us. Let some of us help you. And stop hiding your headaches from your family."

"You don't know what it's like to be a burden to those you love," Rowdy said quietly. "I'm done with that. Coop and his family have enough problems. They don't need to be saddled with mine."

Bailey understood not wanting to burden anyone. Over the past three years she had become fiercely independent. But that was out of necessity, not choice. How could Rowdy believe his family felt anything but love for him? "Love is never a burden," she said softly. Before she could continue, Bailey heard the front door close. She stood, knowing this conversation was over. It was time to head back to the bar. With family in the house, Rowdy would shut down completely.

"Okay, see you around, cowboy." Bailey tried for light and friendly but was pretty sure she'd missed the mark. As she turned toward the door, she spotted Maggie darting down the hallway. Bailey followed, wondering how long she'd been there. The instant Bailey stepped foot outside she knew. Maggie was crying, her face resting against Coop's broad chest.

"He's hiding them again," she whispered softly into Coop's shirt.

Coop rubbed Maggie's back. "I figured as much when I stepped into the barn and saw your face."

"That night we arrived here, when you had to go find him on the side of the road, there was half a bottle of pills left. Today, it's almost empty. Do you think there's something wrong? Do we need to force him to see a doctor?"

"I don't know," Coop admitted. "But we both know we can't force Rowdy to do anything he doesn't want to do." He leaned down and gently kissed Maggie's forehead then realized Bailey was standing in the doorway. "I have to get back to work. Do you think you can handle it from here? Bryan took the bedding back up to the house. I want to talk to him before I leave but he offered to sit with Rowdy until one of us gets home tonight. I think that might be good for him."

"He was great today," Maggie said, proud of her son. "He didn't panic and he didn't turn into alter ego Bryan. I'm so proud of him."

"Me too," Coop said, hesitating. "I'm optimistic that things might be getting better."

"I hope so," Maggie said stepping back.

"I'll get off as soon as I can." Coop gave Maggie a gentle kiss. "I'll stop in at the bar and grab whatever special Jase is making for dinner. I don't like you girls dealing with the place alone. Once I bring Bryan dinner and check on him I might come back and hang around until closing."

"Not if you plan to scare away the customers," Maggie said, stepping back to glare at her husband. "I will not have you loitering around, intimidating any man that has the gall to say hello to your precious wife."

Coop smiled. "You are pretty precious." He leaned down and gave her another kiss. "I'll be on my best behavior. I promise," he was still smiling as he crossed his heart with his right hand. "Now, I need to talk to my son before I head back to the station and deal with paperwork."

Mount Haven

Coop strolled up the walkway, determined to speak to his son before he left. He found Bryan sitting on their front porch. "Thanks for taking care of things out here today. Rowdy would have been lost without you."

Bryan shrugged, not sure how to take his father's praise. "I was scared at first," he admitted. His dad said it was okay to be afraid; maybe it was time to admit how he felt. "But Rowdy helped and then Bailey got here. As long as I could see Rowdy was still breathing, I knew it was going to be okay."

Coop moved silently to the wooden porch swing and sat down. He waited until Bryan stepped forward and sat down next to him. "I know it's sometimes hard, but I want you to know that Rowdy is going to be okay. He still gets headaches and he probably always will. But his leg is better and he's doing okay. You know that, right?"

Bryan nodded. "I guess," he finally said.

Coop reached out and ruffled his son's hair. "He's stubborn and pigheaded and probably won't ask for help but as long as we're here for him when he needs us, your Uncle Rowdy is going to be fine."

Bryan moved forward and hugged his dad. "I'm sorry I've been so much trouble," he said softly as he sat back in his chair. "I'm trying to do better."

"I know," Coop said, blinking rapidly as he ran a hand through his hair. It was the first time Bryan had shown any kind of affection since the shooting took place. Coop wasn't really sure what to do here. There were so many things he wanted to say, but he was afraid of pushing Bryan away again. "We're all trying and things are getting better." He looked at Bryan. "Are we okay now?"

Bryan nodded again. Being the only one here to take care of Rowdy had helped him to see his uncle wasn't going to die. It had been scary. Until Bailey got there and helped, Bryan wasn't sure what to do or how bad Rowdy was going to get, but now he knew. Rowdy's headaches were bad and Bryan didn't like seeing his uncle like that, but he wasn't going to die. Bryan felt calm for the first time in a very long time. "It's okay if you have to go back to work, Dad," Bryan said, turning to look his father in the eye. "I'm better now and I can watch Rowdy. Mom and Bailey are just up the road. If I need anything I'll call, I promise." Bryan stood.

Coop smiled. "I think you are okay now, Bry. Come here." He held out his arms and Bryan moved into them. Coop gave his son a bear hug, then he kissed the top of Bryan's head and released him. "I love you, kid. Always will. I hope you remember that."

"Love you too," Bryan said uncomfortable voicing his feelings. It had been a long time since he'd said that to either one of his parents. He kept telling himself he was too old for kids' stuff like that, but if his dad could say it, Bryan could right? "I'll tell Mom it's okay to leave." Things were getting too serious on the porch and Bryan wanted an escape.

Coop laughed, stood and headed for the car. He watched as Bryan darted through the trees, escaping to the safety of his uncle's cottage.

* * * *

"He looks a little better," Bailey said, not really knowing how to approach the topic.

Mount Haven

"The pills help him. If he can get to them soon enough, it doesn't get this bad." Maggie tried to smile but didn't succeed.

"How long has this been going on?" Bailey asked as she sat next to Maggie in one of Rowdy's lounge chairs.

"I probably shouldn't tell you this. Rowdy is going to be livid when he finds out but right now I'm beyond angry with him, so I'm finding it hard to care. He's so stubborn and independent. Will you please keep his secret? In light of what happened today I think you have a right to know, but Rowdy's a private person. He doesn't want to be seen as having any kind of disability."

"I promise," Bailey said, not liking how this was going.

"Rowdy was shot, three times." Maggie inhaled sharply, hoping she could get through this without making a complete fool of herself. She was already near tears and wanted to strangle the fool lying inside.

Bailey's mind was reeling. What did being shot have to do with headaches?

"The first shot was high on his thigh," Maggie continued. "He lost a lot of blood and the bullet did a lot of damage. That hit alone could have killed him. Then he was struck in the chest, of course he was wearing a vest so he only had a couple broken ribs and a lot of bruising from that one. The last bullet hit Rowdy in the side of the head." Maggie shuddered and wiped away the tears that insisted on falling. "We all thought we'd lost him. He was in a coma for almost three weeks."

"Rowdy was a cop?" Bailey asked, everything falling into place now. She had wondered why someone as perceptive as Rowdy hadn't joined the force like his brother. It also explained his reluctance to talk about his injury. Bailey considered the possibility of what could have happened. Rowdy was shot in the head. He could have died and she never would have met him. Somehow she couldn't imagine a world without Rowdy in it. And that was just ridiculous, she barely knew the man. Sure, they had finally become friends, but that is all they would ever be.

"Yes," Maggie admitted. "Coop and Rowdy were two peas in a pod. Well, to be honest there were three. Their father was also a cop. The boys take after Pappy, more than they do their mother. They were both good at it. When Andy decided to join SWAT, I really didn't worry because Rowdy was already on the team. They protect each other, respect each other, understand each other in a way none of the rest of us ever could. Loosing that has been hard on Rowdy, but it's also hard on Coop. He feels guilty that he can still work while Rowdy has to find a new way. I thought the bar was helping, now I don't know. I heard you say Rowdy's been overdoing it. Why didn't I know that? I'm a terrible sister."

"You didn't know because Rowdy has been hiding it," Bailey corrected. "You should know those guys that brought the delivery today ditched for hours. Rowdy unloaded the entire truck himself. I told him you paid for delivery and stocking but the guys drew a hard line. Rowdy decided to take care of it himself, he said he couldn't wait. He couldn't risk them driving away like they said they would. I know he was right. We couldn't have managed without alcohol this weekend, but it still infuriates me. I didn't know how to contact the company or I would have. I told him he needed to tell you but he said he was going to take care of it himself."

"No wonder he collapsed today," Maggie said, considering. She was pissed at the delivery men and would handle that situation herself. They had paid for stocking and their boss was going to hear about it. But right now she had more important things to deal with.

Mount Haven

Maybe her waitress could help. "Bailey I'm going to ask a favor. One that might be difficult but it's important."

"I'm not going to like this am I?" Bailey asked, narrowing her eyes at Maggie.

Maggie laughed. "It's not bad, but Rowdy feels like he's a burden. That's the most idiotic thing that's come out of that man's mouth but I guess I see why he feels that way. Because of that, he's going to continue to hide things from me and Coop."

"No way," Bailey refused, shaking her head. "I will not spy on Rowdy for you. We have finally developed a comfortable friendship. I won't jeopardize that to rat him out so you two can feel better."

Maggie smiled. They had developed more than a comfortable friendship. "I'm not asking you for that. What I'm asking is for you to continue to be Rowdy's friend. Be there for him if he needs you. I can help you to understand what kind of things seem to trigger his migraines. Just help him. Support him. If I try, he feels like I'm hovering which is why I've taken a step back. If he tries to unload another truck himself, ask Jase to help. Or call me and I'll find someone to come do it. If he seems dehydrated set a glass of water close by. Rowdy won't stop working to take care of himself but if the glass is right there, he'll take advantage of it. That's all I'm asking."

"And then he'll start resenting me and thinking I'm hovering." Bailey still wasn't convinced this was a good idea. She spent entirely too much time thinking about Rowdy Cooper. If she agreed to this, she'd be having those thoughts 24/7.

"No, he won't because you won't be hovering. And you shouldn't. Rowdy needs to figure this out on his own. I'm going to

150

take a step back for a while and I'm going to make sure Coop does the same. It might kill my husband to do it, but we will. It will be easier if we know we can count on you."

Maggie made her request seem so reasonable and Bailey did care about Rowdy. If Maggie and Coop were going to step back and let him figure this out on his own, it wouldn't hurt to have a friend watching out for trouble. "I'll do my best," Bailey finally agreed. "Just remember, I have my own problems to deal with though. I might not be the right person for the job."

"Of course you are. Thanks," Maggie said, standing. "Now we need to get back to the bar and I need to tell my son goodbye. He's pretty proud of himself and I want him to know I'm just as proud."

"He did good," Bailey said, standing. "I'll see you in a few. I'm heading back over now." She slowly walked to her car and headed back to work. It was sure to be a long night without Rowdy to tend bar. At least it was a weeknight. Between herself, Maggie and Jase they could handle it. They had to.

* * * *

Bailey glanced at Rowdy for the hundredth time tonight. Something had changed between them. She knew he was just embarrassed that she'd seen him so vulnerable but seriously the man needed to get over it already. When he noticed her watching him he grunted, actually grunted, and walked into the backroom.

"Okay, it's now or never," Bailey said under her breath. She was nervous and still questioned whether this was a good idea or not, but they needed to get back to the way things were before. The only solution she could think of to do that, was to show Rowdy her own vulnerabilities. Before she could chicken out, Bailey pushed through the back door and strolled into Rowdy's office. She didn't even knock, she just stepped inside, shut the door and locked it behind her.

"What are you doing?" Rowdy asked, even less comfortable with the woman than he'd been all evening.

"We need to talk," Bailey said moving to the visitor's chair and taking a seat.

"It will have to wait," Rowdy said standing. "I have a lot to get through before I leave. As you well know, I had an unscheduled night off." He studied her, waiting for that telltale sign of pity before she masked it. Rowdy was surprised when it never came.

"That's what we need to talk about." Bailey wasn't going to budge. Now that she'd made up her mind Rowdy was going to listen. "Here's how I see it," Bailey continued, hoping Rowdy didn't just up and leave the room. "You feel awkward because I saw your human side yesterday." She grinned at the scowl Rowdy wasn't even trying to hide. "I know, I was shocked too. Rowdy Cooper is actually human, call the Times."

"Funny Zander. Get to the point already." He hated the reaction he always had to this feisty little firecracker. But he would not smile, if he did he'd never get the anger back. And that would just leave him with humiliation.

Bailey's smiled widened. She was getting to him. "So, the way I see it, we're not going to get back to normal until you see my human side. Until I admit one of my vulnerabilities."

"Is that how you see it?" Rowdy said, intrigued more than he cared to be. He returned to his chair and sat behind the desk, studying Bailey Zander intently. Any twitch, one wrong blink and he'd catch it.

"Yeah," she let out a long difficult breath. "If I open up a little, can we put it all behind us and move forward, Rowdy? We work together. It can't be the way it was today. I can't take that day after day with you."

"So, you saw me at my worst. Witnessed my deepest secret firsthand. Are you're telling me you are willing to share your deepest, darkest secret with me?" Rowdy challenged.

Not likely, Bailey thought. "Well, first of all I witnessed the invincible Rowdy Cooper with a migraine. That hardly seems like your deepest, darkest secret. Now, if you were to explain why they are such a big deal, I might be willing to reciprocate."

Rowdy pushed back in his chair, debating. On the one hand if he just got it out there, he wouldn't have to hide his condition from Bailey. And Max had been right, she was a wiz at this business stuff. He actually wanted to promote her to manager but he and Maggie weren't ready for that step yet. If he did promote her, they would be working together even more closely. He wasn't sure he could handle that but if he had another episode, he'd need someone he could rely on. He knew that someone could be Bailey. On the other hand, telling her would mean reliving the nightmare. "How do I know the exchange is a fair one? I mean, you saw me at my worst already. Now you want to know all the dirty little details about my history. Once you get what you want, you may just say something stupid like 'I'm afraid of spiders'."

Mount Haven

Bailey had to admit Rowdy was right. She was asking him to be completely vulnerable before she shared a thing. Maybe she should tackle this in reverse. "You have a point. So, how about we make a deal? I'll share something with you, something personal, a secret so to speak and then you share with me. I want to know why you get such terrible headaches." She wanted Rowdy to tell her he'd been a cop and was wounded while on the job. It was something she wouldn't be able to hide knowing and she didn't want him to be mad at Maggie for telling her.

Rowdy could live with that. "Deal," he held out his hand and they shook on it.

"Okay," Bailey said, trusting Rowdy. She knew he was a man of his word. "I know you have figured out that I'm running from something," she began. Rowdy hadn't trusted her from the moment they'd met. "I am." She took a moment to decide how much she would share. "I'm running from my extended family. Well, more specifically one of my relatives and his creepy friend."

Rowdy sat up straight. He never in a million years would have guessed this was the secret Bailey would share.

"I'm not running from the law. I've never done anything even close to illegal. But the men I am hiding from are bad news. They are creepy and sadistic. If they find me..." Bailey's body gave an involuntary shudder.

"How sadistic?" Rowdy needed to know. He'd come face to face with evil and sadistic on the job more than once. If Bailey's relatives were anything like some of the men he'd arrested, she was in trouble.

"Let's just say any encounter with them would not be a happy reunion," Bailey hesitated.

"Not enough," Rowdy pressed. "Did they hurt you, Bailey?" If anyone had laid a hand on this woman they would answer to him.

Bailey studied Rowdy, this wasn't going exactly how she'd planned. Somehow Rowdy always got her to talk more than she should. "They tried, can we just leave it at that Rowdy?"

Rowdy studied Bailey. He didn't want to leave it at that, but he knew her well enough to see she was done sharing. "Okay, on one condition."

"What?" Bailey asked reluctantly.

"If you see anyone that makes you nervous, anyone that you think might be connected to your family or that friend, you tell me immediately. If you feel like you're in danger, I need to know," Rowdy continued to study Bailey. "No matter how small it might seem. I assume you are probably using a fake name and that's okay. But because of that, I'm not going to recognize them. I won't make the connection myself. I'm going to need you to fill in the blanks."

"Okay," Bailey agreed immediately. She didn't have a problem with that in the least. Knowing she could go to Rowdy made her feel safer somehow. "Anyway, that's my only secret. I'm on the run. I have changed my name but I'm not comfortable sharing my real name with you yet. I've been running, hiding out, for just over three years now. And as much as it scares me, one day soon I'm going to have to surface again. Until then, I could really use a friend. Which is why I have no problem taking you up on your offer to help." She studied Rowdy; he wanted more she could tell, but she wasn't ready to provide additional details. She wasn't ready to be that vulnerable again, not even with Rowdy Cooper. "So, it's your turn now. Spill the dirty details as you put it, then we can get back to comfortably tolerating each other."

Mount Haven

Rowdy did smile now. "Fair enough." She might think he just tolerated her, but if he was going to be honest it was much more than that. He truly considered Bailey a friend. She was easy to be around, and definitely easy on the eyes. He wanted her more than he'd ever wanted a woman in his life. He also knew that while she was hiding, while she was running, was not the time to start something they could never finish. So he'd settle for friends and hope the need growing stronger and stronger inside him with each passing day would eventually subside. If not, being around this woman was going to finally push him over the edge into the dark abyss of insanity.

"Your headaches?" Bailey asked, raising her eyebrows. What exactly was Rowdy thinking?

"Right," Rowdy said, taking a deep breath to clear his head. "Just over a year ago, I was on the job." He glanced up and saw Bailey wasn't surprised to learn he was a cop. Maybe she didn't understand what he was saying. Someone on the run should be more on edge knowing she'd just told an ex-cop she was hiding from the world. "I was a cop."

"I realized that yesterday," Bailey admitted. "Maggie said something about it being hard on all of you that Coop could still work and you had to reinvent yourself."

Coop wondered what else Maggie had said, but realized it didn't matter. He trusted Bailey and was going to tell her everything. "So, I was patrolling one night, looking for some burglars that had been wreaking havoc in the area. Knight was with me and as we came around the corner of an industrial area, Knight went nuts. I pulled behind a truck loaded with high end electronics, positive I'd found the guys we'd been chasing for weeks."

That's how Rowdy got shot? Chasing stupid burglars? What a waste.

"I blocked in the car and stepped out. I knew I had to get Knight free, so I moved to the back of the truck and released the cage. I don't know if the guy had already taken aim, or if the noise drew him to me. But as Knight flew from the truck I was shot in the leg." He glanced down with disgust.

"So that's why you have a slight limp when you're tired?" Bailey asked, she would not let Rowdy know Maggie had already told her this. She smiled, thinking back to the first night she'd seen him and her image of him getting thrown by a bull.

"Yes," Rowdy said, annoyed Bailey thought that was funny.

Bailey realized her mistake and immediately corrected it. "That first night you and Coop came in here, the night I was beyond rude to your brother, I saw you walk in. I had no idea the two of you were cops. From my first impression I thought you were cowboys, passing through on your way to the next rodeo. I pegged you for a bull rider and told myself you had just been thrown from a nasty bull, which was why you walked with a limp."

Rowdy smiled. "You do realize Coop and I were city slickers back then. We couldn't have been further away from being cowboys if we'd tried."

"I know that now," Bailey said with a shrug, "But at the time it seemed like a good explanation. And as cocky as you two were, I enjoyed the visual. The thought of some big, bad bull throwing the cocky man taking up space in my booth across a dusty arena... made my night."

Mount Haven

"I'm still not sure what we ever did to you, but whatever works," Rowdy said with a grin. "Anyway I got shot in the leg. I fired back once and was sure I hit my target but the guy kept coming. He shot me in the chest, but I had on a vest. It hurt like a bugger but I aimed and fired again. I got him that time, but he also got me. His bullet grazed my head. Now, I'm plagued with migraines, the doctors say probably forever."

"And by 'grazed' you mean someone shot you in the head," Bailey corrected softly. It was difficult to say out loud. It made the nightmare even more real. It hit her again, Rowdy could have been killed. The thought made Bailey physically ill.

"I said grazed," Rowdy repeated stubbornly, trying to downplay the severity of his injury

"So, did you just head on over to the ER and get stitches or did they have to go in and remove the bullet?" Bailey pushed. She wasn't going to let him get away with minimizing his injury.

"I had surgery to remove the bullet. Well, bullets. First they got the one lodged in my head then while I was out with that one, they took the one out of my leg." Rowdy stood and moved to the window. He hadn't intended to tell her that much, but it was out now. How would Bailey react?

"No wonder you have migraines," she realized softly. "Do you have any warning or do they just hit you out of the blue?"

Rowdy turned, again expecting pity. But he only saw compassion and understanding. "Both, sort of," Rowdy said returning to his chair. "I usually have a little warning, but not much. If I overexert myself or let myself become dehydrated that can bring one of them on. Excessive stress will also take a toll."

"Like when you insisted on unloading that stupid truck all by yourself? Something like that?" Bailey accused.

Rowdy smiled. "Yeah, something like that."

"Well then, moron, I suggest in the future you insist lazy, no good drivers unload their own trucks. Especially when it's in their contract and they're getting paid to do exactly that."

"Funny. I thought you worked for me, not the other way around," Rowdy countered.

"Actually, I technically work for Maggie," Bailey pointed out with a smile. "And if you won't listen to me maybe you'll listen to her. I tried to reason with you yesterday. Had I known you were being reckless with your health I would have reported you."

Rowdy frowned. "Are you seriously sitting in my office telling me you plan to tattle to your boss when I do something you believe is unhealthy?"

"No," Bailey said immediately. If Rowdy believed that, their friendship would be over for sure. "I'm telling you that I intend to read up on migraines. And if you do something stupid in the future, I'm going to suggest you stop. If you don't listen to my educated suggestions, I will be forced to bring in reinforcements."

Rowdy could live with that. As long as Bailey came to him first, he was sure he could handle the sexy little do-gooder. He also knew he was stubborn and reckless with his health sometimes. Which was probably the reason he'd been having so many migraines lately. He studied Bailey. Her admission that someone was after her had him on edge. Well, Rowdy believed in tit for tat. If she was going to keep an eye on him, he would do the same. But he was going to go one further, he'd enlist Coop and Jase to help. Bailey

Mount Haven

Zander AKA whoever she was, would be safe as long as she lived in Mount Haven.

"Are we good now?" Bailey asked seriously.

"I think so," Rowdy agreed. It did feel better, more comfortable now that Bailey knew he had limitations. He hated being a burden to anyone but Bailey acted like his injuries were no big deal

"Thank you, Rowdy," Bailey said as she stood. "You didn't have to tell me any of that. I'm sorry you got shot. But I'm also selfish enough to admit fate did us a favor around here. Coop's perfect for this town, and you and Maggie and this place? Well, anyway..." Bailey shrugged. "What I'm trying to say is that fate may have set you back some, but Mount Haven came out ahead." She was a little embarrassed and extremely self-conscious about her admission so she rushed for the door.

"You better be careful Fancy Pants. If you're not careful, I might take that as a compliment." Rowdy grinned, but sobered when Bailey turned back to him.

Bailey hated that nickname. It reminded her too much of the woman she used to be. "Would you do me a favor, Rowdy?"

"What did I do?" he asked quickly.

"Will you stop calling me that? It makes me uncomfortable," Bailey said looking at the ground. She really didn't want to explain why it bothered her so much but she would if necessary. Technically, Rowdy had shared more than she had and she owed it to him to be honest.

"Bailey," Rowdy said softly. He waited until she finally raised her head and looked at him. "I'm sorry." He moved to stand in front of her. "You should have told me that sooner. At first I thought it bugged you, which is why I kept using it. But then, you seemed to warm up to it. I had no idea it… well, I assume something about it reminds you of your past."

Rowdy Cooper was way too observant. Bailey was going to have to watch what she said from now on. Now that he knew a little, she was sure he would pick up on more. She was terrible at hiding things and couldn't lie if her life depended on it, which it did.

"Thanks," Bailey said realizing she should have said something weeks ago. Rowdy cared about people and would never do anything that made them uncomfortable. "Uh… why don't you take care of whatever it was you needed to do in here? I'll go stock the bar so we're ready for the rush." Then she turned and flew out the door.

Rowdy watched Bailey escape. That was exactly what she was doing, escaping. He'd messed up with her again. He never would have called her Fancy Pants if he'd known it bothered her. Well, okay that wasn't exactly true. He had known it bothered her in the beginning, which had been half the fun. But later, it had actually been a term of endearment. A nickname one friend had for another friend. He momentarily wondered if he'd lost his touch. Back in Chicago he would have known if he was offending a woman. Here, he was so wrapped up in his own problems he wasn't paying attention to those around him. Well, that stopped tonight. He would need to be on alert if he was going to protect Bailey from whoever wanted to hurt her. And he would protect her, she was his now. He ran his fingers through his hair in frustration. No. He couldn't think of her that way, she couldn't be his. She was on the run and eventually she was going to leave. But she was his friend and he would make sure she was safe for as long as she remained a part of his world.

Chapter Six

Reese stood, smiling. He couldn't help it. He felt powerful. Taking a life was the most exhilarating thing he had ever experienced. He glanced up at Cole as he slid the condom into the plastic baggie and wondered why his friend was frowning. He was so focused on his companion that he didn't realize the rubber shield grazed the side of the outer plastic before falling into the bottom of the bag. The instant the item landed on top of the other evidence, Cole turned away. Reese was perplexed but decided not to address his friend's mood change at the moment. They had work to do. It was important to ensure nothing could lead the police to either man. After surveying the lifeless body, Reese began moving around the room. He knew there were no fingerprints, both of them had worn gloves. But he needed to make sure nothing else connecting the two of them to this body could be found.

Once he was positive they would leave no trace of themselves, he motioned to the closed door. Cole nodded, retrieved the bag from

Mount Haven

the table where he had set it while he waited for Reese to conduct his ritual sweep, and stepped outside. Reese followed a few steps behind. He was confident the body wouldn't be discovered for months, if it was discovered at all. And by that time the girl would be so decomposed nobody would recognize her. The slut would be just another drifter lost in the wind. Reese continued to survey the area as they slowly walked to the car.

Cole exited the small cabin, frowning. He felt so unsatisfied. Taking the life of the last woman had put him on a high for days. Tonight, he just felt cheated. He knew it was irrational to be angry with Reese, but he was. His partner had stolen his release. This entire incident had left him frustrated, rather than fulfilled as usual. He was already itching for another mark. He slid into the passenger's seat and waited for his friend to join him. It was the first time in years they would be leaving the scene together. Cole wished they hadn't deviated from their normal routine. He needed a few minutes alone before he faced Reese again. Just another irritation to deal with in an already frustrating evening.

The two men rode in silence, each one deep in thought. Reese was on a high. He was so engrossed in his euphoria he didn't realize how upset his friend actually was. Cole on the other hand was depressed. He knew he was pouting, but he'd been cheated. He'd been the one to find the girl, track her, lure her and then Reese had stolen all his fun. This arrangement was not going to work. In the future they would need two women. Each man would need his own girl if Reese wanted to participate in the final act of dominance. Two would be just as easy to snatch as one. And both men were confident that they would never be caught. They were smarter than the cops, and they were careful. Little did they know just a few more minutes at the cabin and their lives would have changed forever. They were so wrapped up in their own thoughts, neither man noticed the police cruiser take the corner a little too fast as it sped away from the upper class neighborhood, headed away from the city.

Detective Kyle Lloyd traveled the last few yards to the turn off. He was afraid of what he was going to find tonight, afraid of how Kathy's mother was going to take the news. Tina Langley was a devoted, overprotective mother who loved her daughter dearly. She was also wrong. Tina was sure Dusty Freeman was responsible for her daughter's recent behavior and current absence in her life. Unfortunately, Dusty had pulled the plug on that relationship weeks ago. He was too self-absorbed and impatient for his fling with Kathy to last. The guy had dumped the perky brunette because in his words 'I ain't got time for a chick that won't put out.' Even with all that class, Dusty would have remained on the short list if he hadn't had an ironclad alibi. It would have been impossible for the kid to slip out undetected by his brute of an uncle. No, Dusty had been at work since four that afternoon. So, who was Kathy with out in the deserted cabin on the outskirts of town? Lloyd could only think of two options, a new boyfriend or a stranger.

After their initial discussion with Tina, Lloyd's partner returned to the office to try to track Kathy's phone while Lloyd drove out to interrogate Dusty Freeman. That interaction had been a waste of time but when he called his partner for an update, Detective Crowther had good news. He was able to ping Kathy's cellphone and track the signal to the forest just outside of town. There was only one cabin still habitable in that area and it was seasonal. Lloyd had done a little checking and the family who owned the place hadn't visited for months. He just hoped Kathy had met up with another kid who knew the area and wasn't worried about a little B&E, maybe someone who fished the nearby lake. Unfortunately, his gut told him this was not going to end well. Especially since none of Kathy's friends could finger a new local boyfriend. This smelled of a recent hookup with a stranger.

Mount Haven

He finally spotted the old cabin and pulled to the side of the road. If this turned out the way his gut told him it would, he didn't want to spoil any evidence. Detective Lloyd grabbed his flashlight and exited his vehicle. He walked slowly, studying the ground as he went. There were fresh tire tracks on the dirt drive that led to the main roadway, but nothing else. As he continued toward the cabin, he spotted footprints. Crouching down, he studied the prints carefully using his flashlight to illuminate the ground between the first set of prints and the cabin. As he walked the short distance, he realized there had been two men not one. He closed his eyes and sighed before ascending the two short steps that led to the front porch. He walked the area looking for clues but didn't see a thing. As he returned to the small, dirty window he shut off his light. It was difficult to see inside, but within seconds he knew. The lumpy blanket lying on the floor inside was in all likelihood Kathy Langley. Lloyd walked the surrounding area. Nothing. Whoever had done this had experience. He was sure the duo had left the cabin through the front so Lloyd pushed through a rusty door located on the right side of the building. He stepped inside and crouched near the body. The girl was still warm, but clearly deceased. He relayed the information to dispatch as he exited the building. He'd wait by his car and ensure nobody messed with what little evidence he had. This was definitely going to be a long night; not only would processing the scene take time but he'd need to head back over to the Langleys' and break the news to the family.

* * * *

Reese pushed open the door to his residence and headed straight for the study. He'd go through their usual ritual tonight because rituals were important. But he didn't need alcohol this time. In all honesty, he didn't really want it. Vodka would sooth him and he wasn't ready for calm. He wanted to revel in the high for a little while longer. Once the fire was started, Reese poured two glasses and moved to sit in his usual chair. He watched as Cole flung the evidence into the hot flames. His friend wasn't himself tonight. "What's wrong?" Reese finally asked.

"I think we need two women from now on," Cole announced as he dropped onto the comfortable couch.

Reese furrowed his brow and tried to relate. Cole was upset because Reese had taken the girl out? Okay, now that he knew what it felt like, he could understand that. He realized that if they took turns, the next event would not be as pleasurable as this one. In fact, it would be downright annoying. He could understand Cole's mood. "I agree," he said without hesitation. "But they cannot have a connection. We're going to have to work on a plan. We'll have to be very careful. We'll need…"

"Let's head to Mexico," Cole interrupted. "If anything goes wrong we can pay off the cops. This is going to be risky and we need contingencies. We can test it out there, then move back home once we're sure we've thought of everything."

Reese pondered for a long moment. "Maybe," he finally conceded, then smiled. "Maybe we will head to Mexico by way of Texas. How do you feel about sailing? We can take the yacht."

Cole smiled; finally they were going to get some answers about that devious woman who married the oil tycoon. This trip was going to be productive and with any luck a turning point for both of them.

* * * *

Mount Haven

Rowdy entered his office to find Bailey at his computer, again. He realized this had become a habit since she'd discovered his migraines. Well, the woman had warned him she'd be doing research. Apparently when Bailey delved into something she was thorough. He watched her silently, wondering why this was all so important to her. He must have made a noise because Bailey suddenly looked up. Their eyes met and held for the slightest moment then she jumped from the chair and hurried out the door. She slid past him and mumbled a quick apology. Rowdy reached out and grabbed her elbow.

"Bay, don't apologize. You can use the computer any time." He was annoyed she wouldn't look at him so he waited. Finally she glanced up and swallowed hard. "I appreciate all the work you are doing but it's really not necessary. I'm working on my health and pacing myself. What happened last week won't happen again," he promised, not knowing what else to say. "Anyway, the computer's yours as long as I don't need it." He frowned. "Unfortunately, if I don't catch up on the accounts today, someone is going to have to save me from paperwork hell tomorrow."

Bailey smiled. "Thanks." She placed a hand on Rowdy's arm forcing her body not to react to the chemistry they both shared. "I'm about finished anyway. It's been interesting. I never knew how debilitating migraines could be. I really didn't know anything about them before. I'm sorry you have to go through that. It must be challenging." Her smile widened. "For a tough guy like yourself, it must be disappointing to have problems like all the rest of us." She faked a shudder. "Being normal is such a burden."

Rowdy grinned. "Who said I was normal?" He released his grip and stepped into the room. Another minute in that doorway and he might actually act on the intense attraction he felt for the woman.

It was getting harder with each passing day to convince himself being her friend was enough. He wanted more but was crystal clear that was never going to happen.

Bailey turned and practically ran down the hallway. She had to escape before she did something stupid. Kissing Rowdy would be bad. Well, scratch that. She was pretty sure it would be amazing. Hot, sexy, delicious and out of this world. Which is why she could never allow it to happen. She couldn't stay here much longer. She wouldn't risk Rowdy or his family's safety that way. If her family ever found her... no, she couldn't even finish that thought. The result would be far too devastating to consider.

Rowdy slid into his chair and sighed. *An afternoon going over the books, yay! Not.* He hated this part of the job. He ran a frustrated hand through his hair; he had to talk to Maggie soon. She was the fancy college grad, not him. It was only fair she share in the tedious bookwork. Okay so she hated it, so did he. They were partners. He was just going to have to put his foot down. He hit the spacebar a little too hard then grumpily clicked open the spreadsheet. His brows furrowed and he straightened in his chair, confused. Was this possible? He scrolled through the database, amazed. Had Maggie done this? When? A genuine smile spread across his face. The woman was a genius. The changes she'd made to the records would make his job a hundred times easier. He clicked on the last tab and whistled. Maggie was a fraud. The girl had used complicated formulas to streamline every aspect of their operation. From this point on, all Rowdy would need to do was document purchases and record profits. He clicked the inventory tab and let out a soft 'yes'. Tracking what they had and what they needed was going to be a snap now. Rowdy frowned, leaned back in his chair and considered. Was it possible Maggie had done all this? Or could Bailey have been the one? The girl had been spending a lot of time in front of his computer lately.

Mount Haven

He immediately switched the screen to the internet and scrolled through the history. Okay, that all checked out. Bailey had been using the internet. So that left Maggie, as unlikely as it seemed. Now that he was here, he was curious. As he scrolled through listing after listing a title caught his attention. He sighed. So she hadn't just been researching migraines, she'd been researching him. He clicked through line after line. Bailey must have found every article ever written on his incident in Chicago. Why did she care? The last article caught his attention. It was a follow up written two, maybe three weeks after he'd been released from the hospital. He barely recognized himself in the large photo prominently positioned beneath the caption. "Cop injured, but his K9 partner is the one to suffer." The journalist had hounded him for days, trying to interact with Knight and snap a photo of the loveable mutt. Rowdy had refused. He knew his own depression was impacting his dog and he would not let a biased reporter cause problems for his unit. Every working dog they had loved the job as much as their handler. For them it was a game, one they were allowed to play ten hours a day, four days a week. It wasn't the first time some animal activist tried to twist the truth and make the job sound brutal and heartless somehow.

His mind drifted back to that time in his life. He hadn't looked at these articles in months. He'd actually avoided them. Dealing with his recovery on top of the knowledge that he'd had to kill that kid was just too much to take. Then there had been the threat of a lawsuit. Both kids' parents were threatening him, the office and the county. The first one because their son was dead, the second because they claimed Knight had traumatized the kid so badly he'd never go near a dog again. Rowdy smiled, Knight did tend to have that effect on people. Especially the ones he bit. He shut down the computer and walked out of the room. He had to stop that train of thought immediately. Remembering that night always made him anxious.

He knew he hadn't had a choice, but that didn't change the fact that he had taken another man's life. Living with that fact wasn't always easy. He knew what it was like to lose someone you loved. He and Coop had been laughing and joking with their father one night and the following morning he was gone. In a way, it was easier when his mother went. They all knew she'd been sick and they'd had time to accept the inevitable. Sudden, unexpected death… that was harder to take. And that was exactly what that kid's parents had to live with. So yeah, he felt bad about the whole messed up situation but he would never feel guilty. If he hadn't shot that kid, he had no doubt he'd be the one that was dead. He was completely lost in his thoughts when he rounded the corner and collided with Bailey.

Bailey was doing her best to focus on restocking the bar. She had to get her sexy boss out of her head. They had a busy night ahead of them, she couldn't afford to be distracted. It was the weekend, so she knew it was going to be crazy. On top of the usual crowd, the college team one town over had a big game tonight. That always brought in the young obnoxious patrons. She pushed herself up on her tip toes and barely reached the nearly empty container of Jack. As she lowered herself and took a step back, the bottle slipped from her hands. She was fumbling with the thing, trying to get a grip before the bottle splattered on the floor when she collided with something solid. The bottle went flying, then collided with the hardwood floor making a loud thud before it shattered into a million pieces. Jack Daniels now covered the decorative redwood cabinets and glass shards speckled the freshly mopped floor. Bailey groaned, frustrated at the mess she'd just made. At the same time she lost her footing and began to fall.

Rowdy realized what was happening a second too late. He couldn't save the bottle, but he could save the woman. He reached out, wrapping his arms around Bailey's tiny waist. Her hands settled against his chest and he inhaled sharply. He finally had her in his arms, exactly where she belonged. Rowdy closed his eyes and inhaled deeply, taking in Bailey's amazing scent. The woman was intoxicating and far too tempting... he needed to escape. He was about to push her away when their eyes met and he was trapped. Normally a soft shade of blue, Bailey's eyes seemed darker somehow. It was as if he had found a portal to her soul. The emotion swirling behind her lids made the sapphire spheres come alive, like a raging tempest that drew him in. He couldn't look away no matter how hard he tried. What was he thinking, raging tempest? Seriously? He wasn't a damn poet. Just when he was about to take a step to the side Bailey's mouth settled softly against his lips and he was lost.

Bailey's insides were on fire starting from her hips where Rowdy's strong arms held her upright and cascading out to every tingling inch of her body. She was surrounded by sexy, masculine man and she loved it. Four of her five senses were heightened but somehow her brain seemed to dissolve into a worthless pile of goo. She knew this was bad. She knew she needed to step away, somewhere in her fuzzy head she could almost remember why. But her body refused. Instead of turning away from Rowdy, that fifth sense demanded attention. She had to taste him. Their eyes were locked on each other, his a creamy chocolate sensation she couldn't resist. All logical thought escaped her as she gently pressed her mouth to his.

At first, the kiss was soft and gentle but suddenly Rowdy deepened the kiss and the two of them erupted into a frenzy of need. Months of watching, waiting, wanting suddenly made them both desperate for more. Rowdy pushed away the hem of her shirt and ran his right hand up the center of her bare back pulling her even tighter against his raging body. He couldn't get enough of this woman. His left hand slowly slid lower and as it rested on the curve of her buttocks a noise cut through his lustful haze and suddenly brought him back to reality. Maggie was here. Rowdy dropped Bailey like a hot potato and took an enormous step backwards, then another one. What had he done? How had he let that happen? He was her boss and this was beyond unprofessional.

"Rowdy?" Bailey questioned, then nervously glanced outside at the sound of Maggie's laughter getting closer.

"I'm sorry," Rowdy finally said flatly. "That never should have happened. I'm sorry, don't worry, it won't happen again." Then he turned and made a beeline for his office.

Bailey was stunned. She felt off balance and couldn't organize her thoughts. That kiss had been the best, most amazing kiss of her life. She craved more with every fiber of her being. But clearly Rowdy did not feel the same. There was no question in her mind he had been serious. The look on his face had said it all. He was horrified at what they had done. Had she read him wrong? Had she been seeing interest where there wasn't any because it was what she wanted? She lowered herself onto a stool and considered. No, Rowdy was interested. But like her, he was resisting. Why? She knew what was driving her, the need to protect him and his wonderful family. What was his excuse? Could they overcome it? Should she even try? Her thoughts were interrupted when Maggie and Jase strolled happily through the front door.

"Hey, Bailey," Maggie called. "Jase and I are going to try out a new special tonight. For appetizers we are going to have Beer-Battered Asparagus or Guacamole Bruschetta. Of course we'll still have the standards; buffalo wings and candied onions."

"Sounds great," Bailey said, trying to force some enthusiasm into her tone. It was difficult because the only thing her body seemed to find interesting was Rowdy.

Mount Haven

"He's also going to make some fancy seafood linguini and for the diehard beef fans some kind of spicy prime rib. He promised it would be yummy. I can't wait!" Maggie said clearly pumped about the new menu choices. "Of course we'll still offer burgers and Jase's famous meatloaf." When she didn't get an enthusiastic response from Bailey, she frowned and walked over to take a seat next to her new friend. "What's wrong?"

"Nothing," Bailey said, suddenly regretting the last ten minutes of her life. "Just a lot on my mind I guess," she added, hoping Maggie would drop it. She couldn't admit what had just happened with Rowdy.

"Okay," Maggie said, realizing Bailey didn't want to talk. "What brings you in so early anyway? Your shift doesn't start for another hour."

"I wanted to do some more research on the computer," Bailey said absently.

"Then why are you out here instead of back in the office?" Maggie inquired.

"Oh, I finished up and Rowdy had some paperwork he needed to handle." Bailey slid off the stool and turned to Maggie. "Sorry, I have a couple things I need to do before the rush."

"No problem," Maggie said, confused. She glanced at Jase but instantly knew she would not be welcome in his kitchen. Instead, she headed down the hall and straight for Rowdy.

Rowdy glanced up as Maggie entered the room. He had been expecting her, but still wasn't ready. He could not let her see how rattled he was. That kiss he shared with Bailey was mind-blowing and memorable. How could he hide that from the woman who noticed everything? "Hey Mags, what's up?" He wanted to thank her for all the work she'd done to make the paperwork easier but he didn't dare. The instant he looked in her eyes, she'd know something was wrong. Instead, he stayed focused on the task of entering receipts.

Maggie settled into the comfortable visitor's chair and began to tell Rowdy about the new menu. At least he was happy about the changes. She knew he was distracted and was careful not to be too much of a pest. She hated paperwork, as long as Rowdy was willing to do it, she planned to let him. It wasn't long before she stood and left him to it, still wondering what had happened with Bailey.

* * * *

Rowdy glanced up expecting Bailey to enter the bar but instead he saw Jase. It had been three long days since that kiss. That monumental kiss that had him dreaming about not only kissing Bailey Zander, but taking more. Having it all. He wasn't sure what to do about it, either. This was so unlike him. Women didn't get under his skin this way. He could take them or leave them and for the last year he'd opted for leaving them the hell alone. A woman that wanted more was the last thing he needed while he sorted out his pathetic life. So why did he crave the one woman he knew he could never have? She had secrets, she was on the run. She was a complication, nothing more. His mind immediately rejected that theory. She was so much more and he wanted it all. But she would be leaving, hadn't she told him as much? Giving in to the attraction they both obviously shared would be a disaster. Unfortunately, with each passing day he was finding it harder to care about the consequences. He wanted her... now.

Mount Haven

"Need any help?" Jase asked as he settled into a comfortable bar stool. "The menu's all set for tonight so I've got a little time."

"Naw, I'm good," Rowdy said as he slid the last bottle into place. "But I would like to talk to you about something if you don't mind." Rowdy had meant to have this conversation earlier but somehow he could never get Jase alone.

"Sure, what's up?" Jase asked, curious about what was on Rowdy's mind; he was obviously preoccupied.

"It's about Bailey," Rowdy said hesitantly. He didn't want to betray a trust, but he would make sure the girl was safe.

"What about her?" Jase said reluctantly. He knew far more than anyone realized about the complicated woman. He was sure Bailey sensed that, which was why she'd kept her distance from the start.

"I know you guys aren't exactly friends. I'm not going to ask why. But I need your help," Rowdy continued. "I'm a former cop, I know the two of you are running from something. I knew it the first time I met you. I've never cared what, that's your business. You can keep your secrets as long as you work hard and stay out of trouble, which you have. You're solid Jase, whatever hounds you won't cause you problems here. Do you understand?"

"Thanks," Jase said humbled. He respected Rowdy, his brother and his firecracker of a sister-in-law. The family was genuine and unique. "So what do you need? I've worked here almost four years. I was here when Bailey first started. She's never been comfortable around me. I really don't think she ever will be." Because he knew her secret and he was pretty sure she sensed it. That alone would worry a girl on the run.

"Bailey admitted to me that she is on the run, too," Rowdy said softly, looking around to make sure they wouldn't be overheard by anyone. "She's scared and alone. I can't be specific, but she could be in danger. All I'm asking is that you stay alert, keep an eye out. Watch for strangers that get to close to her, anyone that seems to make her uncomfortable. Let me know if you sense danger. You can do that from a distance. I'm just asking for your eyes and ears, and your gut. You're solid, I know that. Your instincts are good. Just be my eyes and ears when I can't do it myself. I'm not asking for anything more. Coop is also going to keep an eye on the place. Can you help us out here?"

"Of course," Jase promised with a solemn nod. He wondered what Bailey had told Rowdy. Was it possible her family was headed this way? If so, Bailey wasn't the only one in trouble. Jase would stay alert, not for Bailey but for himself. If that helped the girl out, so be it.

"Thanks," Rowdy said, relieved. "I owe you one. I also need to warn you, I'm going to start bringing Knight with me to the bar from now on. I'll keep him away from the kitchen, but he's going to be around."

Jase frowned inwardly; whatever Bailey told Rowdy must have been disturbing, the man was extremely tense and overly cautious, now.

"If there is ever anything I can do for you man, just ask," Rowdy said seriously, noticing Jase's mood change. His cook was still skittish and guarded with his secrets.

Jase gave a silent nod then disappeared into the kitchen. Rowdy's offer was thoughtful and completely out of the question. He would never put an honorable man like that in a tight position.

Mount Haven

Working here was bad enough. Asking for help was simply out of the question.

Chapter Seven

Cole stepped from the air conditioned building into the stifling Florida heat. He wished he was back in San Diego. The temperatures were far less drastic on the west coast. He reached up to loosen his tie as he casually strolled to his rental. Ideas were running through his mind a mile a minute. He had dreaded this trip for weeks but now that he'd finished his last meeting, he was glad he had come. Oh, his father would be pissed if the old man knew what Cole planned. But screw his father. The guy had no imagination. Of course, if he got caught, the company would be in a world of hurt but Cole wasn't worried about that in the least. Cole Hughes never got caught. He was above the law and had been for decades. Anyway, the tip he'd just been given was going to fix every bad investment he'd made over the past three years. He would never pass up such a lucrative opportunity.

He slid into the driver's seat, turned the key and adjusted the air. Life had just gotten a whole lot better. Even Miami traffic

Mount Haven

couldn't dampen his mood. Cole glanced over his shoulder and pulled onto the busy street wondering if he should share his good fortune with his closest friend. Reese was beyond stressed these days. A little windfall would do wonders to settle the man's nerves. Of course he'd share. That's what friends were for, right? They took care of each other and heaven only knew how many times Reese Weathersby had stepped up and taken care of Cole. Yes, things were finally looking up. If they could only find Victoria, life would be perfect.

Several hours later, Cole slowly pulled into the parking lot of the rundown motel on Okeechobee Road. He knew he was taking a risk, but it was a calculated one. He'd dealt with this guy for years over the internet. Meeting him in person was risky, but relatively safe. Malik Arenas knew better than to cross Cole Hughes, everyone in this elite internet group did. The wrath they would suffer for their betrayal was far worse than anything a cop could inflict. Plus, the group was beyond paranoid, which was why Cole had joined in the first place. The lengths they went to in order to safeguard against law enforcement intrusion was impressive. It was even more convenient that no money would be exchanged - not at this meeting anyway. Dealing with obsessed, distrustful people had its perks. Cole had cashed in his chips during lunch at that obscure internet cafe without incident. His merchandise was already bought and paid for. No, this meeting would be safe and it was a good thing because Cole desperately needed the release. He glanced around one more time, careful not to draw attention to himself. It was easy to blend into Hialeah, Florida. Not as a resident, they were mostly Cubans, but as a wealthy businessman just passing through. It was beyond convenient that his urgent business meeting had brought him to Miami and his internet pal, who just happened to deal in human trafficking. Cole could purchase a woman, use her to get his much needed release and sleep like a baby for the first time in weeks. He grinned like a child at Christmastime, adrenaline was already coursing through his body in anticipation. Yes, today was turning out to be a perfect day.

* * * *

Agent Skeet Perkins shut down his computer in frustration. Once again he'd hit a dead end. He was fairly confident that Cole Hughes was Slick GlozzomCreeper but once again trying to track the chips back to Hughes was impossible. The instant it hit the Caymans, the trace went cold. If he had more time in that perverted chat room he was sure he'd hit on something that would lead back to the nefarious businessman. But the kinky pricks running this conglomerate were also paranoid, crafty and shrewd. He had to be extra careful or his backdoor into the system would be discovered and shut down for good. He couldn't risk that, not even to catch Cole Hughes.

Perkins stood, locked up and headed out of the office. His wife needed him. The moment he stepped from the building he realized it was later than he originally believed. Darkness had already settled in. He immediately reached for his phone and dialed home. Angie had nearly recovered from her kidnapping but the dark still bothered her. Skeet suspected it always would. He would never be able to repay Andy Cooper for saving the love of his life but he'd never stop trying. Skeet smiled as he climbed into his sleek black Audi. It was hard to picture Detective Andy Cooper, Coop to his friends, as a small town police chief. He hoped his friend was happy. The Cooper brothers had suffered more than their share of hardships over the past few years. They deserved a little solitude for a change.

Mount Haven

* * * *

Cole sat in the driver's seat, fuming. He knew Malik was a sick bastard but apparently he hadn't known just how sick. He glanced at the woman sitting quietly beside him. Somehow he was going to make Malik pay. The girl was perfect. Cole should be flying high in anticipation of what was to come, but instead he was driving down a dark roadway trying to get control of his anger. If he touched the girl in his current state of mind, the fun would be over almost as soon as it began. No, he had to calm down. He had to think. Developing a clever but untraceable plan to pay the man back was the only way he would be able to salvage the evening.

So, what was important to Malik? His hotel and his property. That thought brought the anger back to the surface. The man had nerve. Cole had known the guy was into trafficking, but he had no idea how young those kids were. He had barely been able to contain himself when Malik had tried to blackmail him into buying the timid ten year old boy. What the hell would he do with a ten year old kid? Oh, he knew what Malik had in mind but that was never going to happen. Nobody… nobody tried to blackmail a Hughes. So, how to make Malik pay for his bad behavior. Hit him where it hurts. The locals knew about the shady motel, they had to. The place rented rooms, not by the night but in three hour blocks. Cole shuddered at the thought of using a child in Malik's "love chair". Okay sure, having a chair that allowed you to maneuver into a variety of positions might be fun with a willing adult. Or even with a non-willing adult. But with a child? Never. For an instant his mind was sidetracked… would Sissy be willing to experiment that way? Probably not. The girl was the epitome of naïve, which was one of the main reasons he was marrying her. She was the perfect trophy wife: timid, beautiful and submissive… everything Cole wanted in a woman. Well, his main, public woman anyway. However, his extracurricular activities would continue after the honeymoon. A man could only take so much vanilla before he needed a little kink.

Cole sighed and glanced at the woman he had just purchased. Yes, he definitely needed some kink tonight. But first, he had to deal with the Malik problem. Cole took the next right and headed back to Hialeah. He'd stop at the Westland Mall, find a throwaway phone and make an anonymous call. Better yet, he'd make the girl do it. She'd cooperate if she believed she was helping the others. Malik would never suspect the tip came from him. The man was an idiot. He'd never consider the possibility that Cole would interrupt his night of fun to plot revenge. The plan was perfect. He'd feel better once he knew Malik was behind bars and he could get back to the pleasant evening he had planned. Once this unexpected side-mission was complete he could head back out on Highway 27, find a secluded area in the Everglade wilderness and have a little fun. If he was lucky he might even see the police hit the motel on his way back out, now wouldn't that be amusing? The instant the car re-entered the city, Cole felt his body relax. He sighed in relief. He was feeling better already. The anticipation was starting to build again and ideas fluttered through his mind. Tonight was going to be cathartic.

* * * *

Cole gripped the handcuffs and yanked the girl forward. He hadn't wanted to cuff and gag her already but she was a feisty one. She'd been more than happy to make the call to the police, but the closer they got to the old motel the more she had fidgeted. It was obvious she had something planned. Cole reacted immediately, the girl didn't stand a chance. Once she was cuffed and gagged, he had placed her on the passenger floor and secured her wrists to the seat lever. It had worked perfectly. Cole drove right past Malik's hotel paradise, which was now lit up with red and blues, smiling all the way. He was still smiling. The girl on the other hand… not so much. She was sobbing and stumbling as they made their way closer to their destination, which only heightened Cole's excitement. Just a few more minutes and the fun could begin. The tall grass would keep them hidden, not that anyone would see them. The place was deserted. He could play for hours without a worry, which is exactly what he planned to do. He paid good money for this one so he intended to get his fill before he finished her off and left her body to the alligators. This time he wouldn't even need a condom. His new toy would never be found.

Hours later Cole stood on the edge of the swamp and watched as a momma alligator tore the woman's body apart piece by piece. Once he was sure nothing identifiable remained, he turned and strolled back to his rental. His mood was difficult to describe. He felt at peace, a feeling he hadn't experienced since his last kill, but he was also flying high. A high that couldn't be achieved through alcohol, drugs or all the money in the world. A rare and distinct euphoria that could only be obtained by taking another life. And in that moment he knew… he was addicted. He would never tire of this game. It would become his lifelong passion whether Reese continued or not. He couldn't survive without his next fix.

Cole climbed into his car, started the engine and made his way back to the casino. He'd sleep well tonight and tomorrow he'd spend the day gambling, another favorite hobby. He had his entire day planned out. First he'd sleep in; he deserved it after such a long night. Then, he'd head down to the casino and play a little poker while he waited for the races to start. Watching the jockey's control their horses while they barreled down the track at high speeds was almost as orgasmic as riding a woman. His mind returned to the last few hours, replaying each and every erotic act until he reached the crescendo: the girl's death. He was a little surprised when his body responded. Cole grinned, he'd take care of that once he returned to the hotel. After what he'd just done, a little vanilla with the perky desk clerk might round off the evening nicely.

* * * *

Bailey was studying Rowdy. It had been two full weeks since that amazing, stupid kiss. She craved him like a man stranded in the desert craved water. Too bad he was off limits. Rowdy had made that perfectly clear over the past few days. He was such a contradiction. She knew the dog was there for her protection. Before her revelation, Knight was not allowed within a mile of the place. Now, he was a constant mascot. Bailey smiled as the gentle Shepherd moved in beside her and rubbed against her leg. He wanted attention again. She reached over and slipped a strip of bacon from her burger, casually offering it to her new friend. If Rowdy saw her he'd go ballistic, but she didn't care. The loyal pooch deserved a treat and she was just the woman to provide it. It was hard for her to imagine this dog as a vicious cop, he was far too friendly.

"I saw that," Rowdy grumbled and barely stifled a laugh when Bailey jumped, then scowled at him. He had to turn away before he smiled. If he didn't keep up the appearance of annoyance, Knight would weigh two hundred pounds by next month. Little did they all know, Rowdy spoiled that mutt rotten. He just did it in the privacy of his own home. When Rowdy had steak, the dog had steak. When he barbequed burgers, Knight had his own generous patty. But a special treat each night was one thing, constant garbage from his family and every one of his employees was entirely different. Rowdy watched as Bailey crouched down and began to rub Knight's

Mount Haven

belly. The dog clearly did not have one ounce of self-respect. He'd been taken in by the sexy vixen and didn't care what the world thought. Well, Rowdy could relate. What he wouldn't give for a little belly rub from that particular woman. Well... belly, chest, biceps and a few other places Rowdy refused to allow inside his head. He ran his hand through his hair in frustration. How was he going to handle working with her? It had been two weeks since that damn kiss and he wasn't any closer to putting it behind him. Every time Bailey Zander walked into the room, Rowdy had to fight the urge to pick up where they had left off. The whole situation was one messed up conundrum. Well, he'd just have to deal with it. As long as Bailey was in danger, Rowdy needed to keep her close. And as long as she was on the run, she was off limits. His body would just have to find a way to cope.

Bailey stood and caught Rowdy watching her. The raw desire she saw on his face before he masked his feelings gave her hope. Maybe Rowdy was more affected by that kiss than he wanted to admit. Maybe he wanted her as much as she wanted him. A girl could hope, right?

* * * *

Reese tried to relax, but it was impossible. He needed something and he knew what it was, but planning another mission this soon was out of the question. Especially now that they would have to take two girls instead of one. Cole's plan to head to Mexico was looking better and better with each passing hour. Reese frowned; something was up with his good friend Cole. The man had been antsy and moody ever since that night in the cabin. Now, after spending a few days in Florida the guy was annoyingly happy. Was it possible Cole had ventured out alone? No, the idea was preposterous. Cole needed Reese. He was the only one that could plan a mission to perfection. Maybe it was just the stock tip he'd gotten from the too friendly, too talkative client. That tip had yielded a profit already. Reese was almost out of the red with this last windfall. Another week, two tops, and Reese would be free of the worry. His father would bluster and bellow if they were doing poorly because of a bad investment but he would quietly sit back and reap the rewards if Reese hit it big. And thanks to Cole, he had won the jackpot on this one.

Reese heard the door open and close seconds before Cole stepped into the room. He immediately began to outline his plan to head to Mexico. Once they were established in a room in Cabo with their yacht safely moored in a nearby strip, they could venture up to Texas and retrieve Victoria. They were both fairly confident the elusive woman was Cole's long lost sister. Once they returned to the ship and began the long journey home they would have all the time in the world to punish her for such bad behavior. Then, upon their return to San Diego, Piper Hughes could start planning a wedding. Reese couldn't wait. He would never have to plan a dangerous mission again. He'd have to talk to Cole about that. He wasn't entirely sure his friend could stop. Especially now that he was marrying a weak, boring woman. At least Reese would have Tory. He didn't know a woman more feisty and strong willed than Victoria Hughes. Married life was going to agree with him, he was sure of it. Right now, that was the only thing he was really sure of. He couldn't wait to get started. Three years was long enough for Tory to have her freedom. It was time she began her life as his submissive and Reese was looking forward to her upcoming training.

* * * *

Mount Haven

Maggie stepped through the doors and blinked a few times until her eyes adjusted to her dim surroundings. It was such a nice, bright day outside and she hated spending the afternoon inside but she would not complain. Finally owning her own café was a dream come true. Now she just had to convince Rowdy it was worth the expense to expand. She grinned when she spotted Bailey with Knight. They were both sprawled out on the floor and Bailey was rubbing the mutt's stomach. Maggie never would have believed that dog would latch on to anyone but Rowdy that way. But Knight had surprised them all. He had grown to love his new friend immensely in a very short period of time. Maggie's smile widened, *just like his owner had*. Too bad Rowdy wasn't as open and affectionate as his dog. She pushed open the door to the office. Rowdy looked almost happy, which was unheard of while he dealt with paperwork. What was up with him anyway? "Mind if I come in?"

Rowdy glanced up and gave Maggie a genuine smile. "You're amazing, Mags." He stood and moved to the small refrigerator to grab a bottle of water. "Want one?" he asked, glancing over his shoulder.

"Sure," she answered still perplexed. She waited while he handed her the bottle then returned to his chair. "Not that I'm complaining, but exactly why am I amazing?"

"I can't believe what you've done with this database." He pushed back his chair and casually raised his legs onto the desk, reclining slightly as he studied his sister-in-law. When he saw her face, he frowned. "You did work on the books, right?"

"Nope," Maggie admitted. It took her a minute, but she was sure she knew who the amazing woman was: Bailey.

"Then who?" Rowdy began then stopped. "Bailey?"

"That would be my guess," Maggie shrugged.

"We need to compensate her for this work," Rowdy insisted. "We talked about making her a manager. I'm ready for that step if you are."

Maggie considered. She knew she would have to promote Bailey eventually, but she wasn't sure she was ready yet. Once they made her manager, Bailey would no longer be available to help out. Maggie was going to miss that. They had become fast friends and Maggie was worried any change in their arrangement would disrupt their easy camaraderie.

"Maggie," Rowdy pressed. "It's time."

"I know," Maggie relented. "I'm just going to miss her."

Rowdy scowled. "What do you mean by that? If we promote her, you are going to have to spend more time together, not less."

Maggie sat up, intrigued by Rowdy's comment. "Why? What do you mean by that?"

"Well, as manager, Bailey will have to learn how to run the place. We both agreed that eventually we would want someone that could step in if we both had something come up. There needs to be someone that can run the bar and grill in our absence. That job goes to a manager. I'd recommend you take Bay into town the next time you do an order. Show her the ropes, let her learn this job inside and out. We don't have anything to hide and she's already proven she can handle the financial end of things. This database is amazing. She's streamlined everything. Now, even you can do your share of the paperwork without going crazy." Rowdy smiled. He should have known Maggie hadn't been working on their financials, but he'd made the assumption because she'd been secretly trying so hard to make his life easier.

"Funny," Maggie narrowed her eyes at him. "Not. But I like your idea of taking Bailey with me to town. Those trips into Missoula are long and boring. Having Bay with me will make them more tolerable. Can you handle things here without her tomorrow?"

"Sure," Rowdy said, grinning. He knew he could bring Maggie around to his way of thinking, he just had to pick the right approach.

Maggie sobered. "Uh, Rowdy?" she said hesitantly.

"What's up Magpie?" Rowdy asked. He was concerned with her abrupt mood change.

"I need to ask a favor and I'm not sure how to do it," Maggie admitted. If she got her way, they would be spending an awful lot of money and she still wasn't sure the added space would justify the expense.

"Tell me," Rowdy demanded.

"Well, I was talking to Bailey the other day and we kind of got carried away. I mean we were talking about expanding the café." She paused to study Rowdy, he seemed okay so far. "I mean with summer coming and all, we thought it would be nice to have a place for people to sit outside and enjoy the afternoon. Then..."

"Yes," Rowdy pushed when Maggie hesitated.

"Well, there's that door to the side and we thought... I mean I thought it would be nice if we moved the jukebox so it wasn't blocking that doorway and make an entrance for families. You know we can't allow anyone under eighteen into the bar after eight. That means we have to close down the café to comply with city regs. But… if we moved the jukebox and made that side door an entrance to the café, we could still allow families in after eight. We'd probably have to modify the walkway between the bar and the grill area but that shouldn't be too much work."

Rowdy sat up, letting his legs drop with a thud. He leaned forward and waited until Maggie looked up at him. "Mags, what's going on? This is so out of character for you, I don't even know what to say. Normally you would just be telling me what we are going to do, not asking. And certainly not acting all nervous and fidgety."

Maggie let out a long, deep sigh. "I know," she finally said before she sighed again. "I guess I'm just not sure about it. I mean I love the idea and when I start to think about the possibilities I get all excited and can't wait for it to be completed."

"But?" Rowdy encouraged.

"But I'm just not sure. I mean we just bought this place. Sure, it's doing well, but it's the only show in town. What if Joe Clayton finally decides to sell and we suddenly have competition? Jase is good but we both know he's running from something and could leave any day. I'm just not sure if sinking that kind of money into this place so quickly is such a good idea."

"Well, you're probably right." Rowdy laughed when Maggie's expression turned into a pout. "But…" he smiled. "Who says we have to spend a lot of money on the project?"

"Rowdy, the kind of expansion I'm talking about is going to cost money. I want a large patio and a garden area. Maybe even a fountain. We'd have to start with a construction crew and once that's done, bring in a landscaper. In a town this size we might not be able to find someone qualified. If we have to hire out of Missoula the travel cost alone is going to break the bank."

Rowdy laughed. "Oh Maggie, you can be so dramatic sometimes."

Maggie stood, sorry she'd started this conversation in the first place. If Rowdy was going to make fun of her she'd just get back to work.

Rowdy was out of his chair and around the desk in seconds. He gripped Maggie's shoulders so she couldn't escape. "I'm not making fun of you. We both know Coop would kick my butt if I even hinted at making fun of you."

"I never said you were," Maggie said resting her forehead on his shoulder. "This is my dream, Rowdy. I want to succeed. I just keep wondering if my next decision is going to be the one that ruins it all. It just seems too good to be true."

Rowdy wrapped his arms around Maggie and pulled her into a brotherly hug. "You're not going to mess anything up. And we are going to work on that expansion because once again, it's a great idea. And…"

"Maybe we could wait…" Maggie interrupted.

"And…" Rowdy continued. "The fact that you and Bailey thought this up only goes to prove my point. It's time to promote that woman."

"I know," Maggie relented. "But how are we going to afford the add on? Should we just do a little at a time, like maybe work on the inside so we can accommodate families at night?"

"No," Rowdy shook his head then pushed Maggie's shoulder back so he could see her face. "We are going to go all out and renovate the way you want. Only we're not going to hire out the work. I'm going to con Coop into helping me. You do remember the amazing patio he and I constructed at my old place don't you?"

Maggie's eyes brightened. She had forgotten about Rowdy's party pad. The thing was amazing and Coop and Rowdy had built it all themselves.

"I'll take that as a no. I can't believe you, Mags. I'm hurt. How could you forget that amazing patio?" Rowdy joked.

"Because I was married. Coop and I weren't exactly invited to all those bachelor parties were we?" she laughed. "I've told Andy about a million times your parents knew what they were doing when they named you Rowdy. I can't believe I forgot about your construction skills. I guess they got lost in all your other more domineering qualities."

"I'm not even going to get offended," Rowdy returned to his chair and sat down. "And as for your other concern, the one about Joe selling to someone better? That is just ridiculous. You're amazing at what you do Maggie. Stop doubting yourself. That's the only time you make mistakes. Plus, I've been talking to Skip. The kid's okay, just terrible at making a real meal."

"What did you talk to Skip about?" Maggie asked returning to her seat.

Mount Haven

"Well, Gracie's been making pies for years. That first day we arrived Coop and I stopped by the café and Joe made a comment about Gracie's arthritis. Yet, every day there are still fresh pies. Lately, there's been other desserts as well. I finally asked Skip about it. He reluctantly told me that he'd been working with Gracie to learn her recipes. He's got the pies down so he's been experimenting with other stuff. I would die a happy man if I had a dozen of his eclairs delivered to my doorstep every day."

Maggie laughed. Rowdy was the pickiest man she knew when it came to diet. He'd always been that way but since the shooting he'd been almost fanatical about it. "Somehow I doubt that."

"Okay, you're right. But even I have a hard time resisting one of Skip's eclairs. I don't know what he uses in those things but it's like a drug. Maybe it is a drug, I wonder if I should have Coop start up an investigation."

"Not funny Rowdy," Maggie scowled. "Don't even mention that in jest. Coop is dying for some real police work. I think he's going to go mad if he has to referee the Haverson brothers again. Those four get drunk and unruly more than anyone I know."

Rowdy laughed. "So, let's get started on those plans."

"Hold on; you still haven't told me what you've been talking to Skip about."

Rowdy smiled. "A contract."

"What kind of contract," Maggie considered.

"I didn't want to say anything yet, but he's interested in supplying your café with desserts. He wants to continue to operate out of town and sell some of his fancier products out of the café but

194

he'd make it more of a coffee shop I think. Most of his products would be geared towards the coffee and pastry crowd. Then we could contract with him for some suitable desserts for our bar and grill."

Maggie jumped up and rushed around the desk. She threw her arms around Rowdy in a huge hug just as the door swung open and Coop walked in.

"How many times do I have to tell you she's my wife? Keep your grubby hands off my woman," Coop said calmly.

Maggie planted a huge sloppy kiss on Rowdy's mouth for show then stood and casually moved to stand in front of her husband. "I'm pretty sure it was my hands that were planted on your brother, Coop. Are you going to tell me to keep my grubby hands off Rowdy?"

Coop reached out and took both of Maggie's tiny hands in his own. Then, he raised them one after the other and placed a gentle kiss on her knuckles. "These hands are delicate and petite. They could never be mistaken for grubby, baby."

Rowdy rolled his eyes, his brother was such a sap when it came to his wife.

"So, what did I miss?" Coop asked letting go of one of Maggie's hands and leading her to the visitors chair where he sat down and then pulled her onto his lap.

"Maggie and I are going to expand," Rowdy answered immediately. He didn't want Maggie giving off any of her nervous uncertain vibes. He needed Coop to be on board with this and he needed his brother's help. "I was hoping the two of us could handle most of it. It's going to save money and we both know being Chief of Police in Mayberry isn't keeping you nearly busy enough. If you're going to stop by every hour on the hour to check on your beautiful wife, you might as well make yourself useful."

Coop considered. He wasn't going to discuss Rowdy's attempt to taunt him about living in Mayberry or his habit of popping in to check on Maggie. She was his wife and this was a bar. But expanding wasn't a bad idea if they could do the work themselves. He'd have to talk to the mayor, but he was sure that Herlin wouldn't mind as long as he was available to take a call when needed. The only calls Matthew couldn't handle on his own were the Haversons. And if that family got into another knockdown, drag out brawl they were all going to spend the night in jail. "Let me talk to Jon but I don't think that's going to be a problem."

"Then it's settled," Rowdy stood. "I'll leave the two of you alone. A man can only take so much of you at one time. Mags, we'll talk expansion later if that's okay. I actually have a couple ideas myself."

The instant Rowdy was out the door Maggie turned and wrapped her arms around her husband's neck. "Thank you, babe."

"You know I'd do anything for you, baby," Coop answered as he pulled Maggie in tighter. "I love you more than life itself." He sobered. "It doesn't bother you that I stop by sometimes, does it?"

Maggie laughed. "You know you only get into trouble with me when you scare off the customers. Lately, you've been behaving so you can stop by as often as you like. I kind of like it when you drop by and surprise me. I love you, too. You know that. Now, come out back so I can tell you what I had in mind." The two of them walked hand in hand out the back door. It was going to take a lot of work to spruce the place up, but Maggie was excited for the new challenge. And, she was pretty good at landscaping herself. Maybe if Jase helped they could manage that part of the remodeling project as well.

* * * *

Reese was fuming! He was beginning to think Cole's habit of throwing things might be the way to go. They had traveled over nine hundred miles of open ocean in a damn yacht to dock on the beaches of Cabo San Lucas. Not for a relaxing vacation, for a snatch and grab mission. Once the yacht was secure, they'd immediately taken a chopper to Texas. If the incompetent Flint Duvall actually believed that woman could be Victoria, Cole should demand his money back! The man was inept. Seriously, the woman was thirty pounds overweight and had a nose the size of Pinocchio. You couldn't get more homely than Alexia Torrin. All the work, the time, the anticipation, only to discover a homely gold digger on the run from an ex-lover who knocked her around a few times. Well, what did she expect? The guy must have been drunk to date her in the first place. Seriously, the woman had fallen from the ugly tree and hit every branch on the way down. She was reclusive alright. Her husband probably demanded it. How that woman had wormed her way into the heart of any man was beyond him.

Reese sighed and dropped into the nearby chair. Cole was still on deck chewing out the incompetent PI. Once he returned, Reese knew his friend would want to start planning their next mission. At least while they were here they could both get the release they desperately needed before heading back home. The return trip would take longer than two days, it was uphill in the open Pacific. The weather forecast was sunny and clear but you just never knew what might come up. They'd have to prepare for the worst and allow extra time just to be safe. Reese decided to focus on their return trip rather than the debacle in Texas. His blood pressure couldn't handle the stress of reliving that nightmare.

Several hours later, Reese and Cole sat on the deck of the ship, sipping vodka. They had a solid plan in place, now they just needed the women. Reese would need a couple days to plan for disposal and shop for the necessary supplies. That would give them both time to hang out on the beach, hop a couple bars and make themselves visible. If anything went wrong and the authorities started sniffing around, they wanted to be remembered as a couple of rich guys out having a good time. Not suspects. In the event they were cornered, they could just buy their way out of the mess. But, Reese was hoping to avoid that. Plus, bar hopping would be a great way to select their targets. This was almost too easy, like shooting fish in a barrel. Both men were grateful for that.

After almost getting arrested in Texas, easy was a welcome reprieve. They had ignored every 'No trespassing' sign littering the tycoon's large estate, boldly knocked on the front door and demanded to see Alexia. It was at that moment they had been tackled and held at gunpoint until the authorities arrived. Surprisingly it was Cole who had saved them by telling the truth, no less. Well, a filtered version of the truth anyway. He had simply told the cops who he was and explained that he was searching for his sister. The Hughes had filed a missing person report a few months after Tory left so the story was easy to verify. Cole had acted insulted, told the cops he intended to check out every lead that came his way and demanded an apology from the tycoon. The guy was visibly suspicious and refused to apologize but agreed to let the situation go. The cops had even convinced the guy to drop all trespassing charges. If they had been arrested, things could have gotten a lot worse for both of them. Cole's DNA was now in the system and Reese had his own mistake he had to dodge. One not even Cole knew about. But they didn't need to worry about that now. At least that was something, no legal mess to worm their way out of. They could focus on the mission and return home, regroup and decide their next move. He would find Tory somehow. Nobody ran from Reese Weathersby for long.

* * * *

Three days later Cole and Reese had a solid plan they both agreed on. They had selected their targets and even agreed on the location of each abduction. What they couldn't agree on was disposal. Reese had planned their escape and subsequent disposal of the bodies down to the tiniest detail. Cole on the other hand, wanted to ship out immediately and dump the bodies in the ocean. Reese would not budge on this one. Too many bodies were discovered when they surfaced weeks later. And dead bodies always surfaced. No, his plan was better. Cole would just have to give in. There was no way around it.

"Okay," Cole said as he gritted his teeth. "I agree that there are some advantages to splitting up. However," he continued when Reese was about to interrupt, "We have spent day after day flirting with mindless airheads in an attempt to show the masses we are a couple of playboy tourists out having a good time. What if you're stopped on the way out of town? What if I am? It's going to be hard to explain the separation."

"No Cole, it won't," Reese said, trying to remain patient. "You solved that problem for us. I thought you were crazy when you gave your real name back in Texas but it was brilliant. You set up our cover. We just stick to the story and we'll be fine. You received a lead on Victoria. We both headed down to try to find her.

Mount Haven

Once we realized it wasn't her, we stuck around to let off some steam. Unfortunately, I was completely crushed that I still hadn't found the woman I love and plan to marry. So rather than return with you on the yacht, I decided to rent a car and take a long drive. I've always wanted to see Yellowstone and Glacier National Parks. I decided to rent a car and take a drive to stave off my growing depression. You needed to get back home and deal with business, so we split up."

"But that doesn't make sense," Cole insisted. "Why wouldn't you just head back to San Diego with me then take off on a road trip from there?"

"Okay, you have a point." Reese considered their options. If he initially set out with Cole it would resolve one big problem, the border crossing. He was still worried about transporting two dead bodies over the border. "So, we stash the bodies and make the trip back to San Diego on the yacht. We aren't using the walk-in freezer so we just hide them in there. Just north of Tijuana there's that wildlife refuge area. You can drop me there. Nobody will know we didn't make it all the way to the port before I ditched. Just pull into The Club and dock. That worthless Bobby should be able to help you."

"Are you sure that's wise? He'll know I was alone," Cole argued.

"You pay the man enough, can't you buy his silence?" Reese stood and walked to the edge of the deck. He really did need some time alone.

"I'd rather use Flint," Cole disagreed.

"I need Flint to head back and rent an SUV. It needs to be waiting for us when we cross the border. Have him get something comfortable but not flashy. I don't want to draw attention to the vehicle as I leave the wilderness area." Reese turned to study his friend. "This is the best way, Cole. Just dumping the bodies at sea is too risky. There are too many boats passing through that way. Any one of them could see us. If they make a report and divers find the bodies we're screwed."

Cole ran his hand through his hair in frustration. He knew Reese was right, but it made him more than a little nervous to have his friend transporting two dead women across several state lines just to dump them in the Nevada desert. But if Reese wanted to risk it, who was Cole to stop him. "Okay, but I'm not using Bobby. I don't trust him, not completely."

"Then why does the man still work for you?" Reese wondered.

"He doesn't," Cole said absently. "He works for my old man and Piper. They trust him, which is why I don't."

"Sound wisdom." Reese grinned. "So are we in agreement?"

"Not exactly, but we'll go with it. You want to risk getting caught, why would I stand in your way?" Cole grinned back.

"Who will you get to help you dock the ship?" Reese couldn't think of anyone they could trust.

"I'd rather use Dalton Finley. I can control him," Cole insisted.

Reese laughed. "I hadn't thought of that. Finley is perfect. He would never betray us, no matter how much pressure the police try to exert." Reese poured them both another drink and the two of them began to go over the plan for the final time. This was going to work out. The plan was perfect. And both men were past due for another release. Reese was a little worried about how quickly he needed this. When he got Tory back for good, he would no longer be participating in these activities. Could he give up the killing already? They had only just started and he was afraid he was becoming addicted to the high. Playing God was exhilarating.

* * * *

Bailey arrived early for her shift. She wanted to talk to Rowdy. Things had been so awkward between them since that kiss. She couldn't stand it any longer. He would just have to get over it. But could she? If she were honest, her behavior had changed just as much as Rowdy's had. Well, they both needed to get over it. She pushed open the door and was surprised to see Maggie sitting at the desk. "Oh," Bailey let out a startled gasp.

"Hey Bay," Maggie said looking up. "You're early." She stood. "Good, I was hoping you'd join me this afternoon. I have to head into Missoula again and I could use backup."

Bailey frowned. "That doesn't sound good."

"I'm getting the runaround again from Iso-Foods. I thought I had everything worked out, but I just received the bill and they have so many fake charges it's not even funny. I've already called them twice, but the manager is dodging me. I'm going down in person and if they blow me off, we're finding a new supplier."

"Okay, I just need a minute with Rowdy before we go. Do you know where he is?" Bailey asked, still surprised to find Maggie in the office.

"He won't be in today," Maggie glanced up. "He's taking the day off."

"Is he sick? Another migraine? He's been doing so well lately. Maybe we've been pushing him too hard on the expansion."

"We have been pushing too hard, but he doesn't have a migraine. Thank goodness for that. In fact, now that you mention it I think it's been almost a month since he had his last episode." Maggie smiled realizing that was the best news she'd had all day.

"Oh, then what's going on?" Now Bailey was worried. Rowdy didn't just take a day off for no reason. He was a workaholic and always pushed himself beyond his abilities.

Maggie sighed. "He was working on the patio out back last night with Coop and he injured his leg. He insists it's nothing but Coop practically had to carry him to the truck. Rowdy is the most stubborn, bullheaded man I know. I stopped by this morning to bring him breakfast, and he was sprawled out in the hallway. He collapsed but was determined to go to work if it killed him."

"What did you do?" Bailey asked, worried.

"I helped him back to bed and stole his truck keys." Maggie grinned as she dangled Rowdy's keys from her middle finger. "He's not going anywhere. Now, is there something I can help you with or are you ready to go?"

"No, I'm good. I need to talk to Rowdy but it will keep." Bailey shrugged and followed Maggie out the door. An afternoon on the road was better than a night dodging Rowdy and his annoying, sexy laughter aimed at anyone but her. She hated that he had started to ignore her. She missed his friendship. She missed him. And now thanks to her and her brilliant idea to expand the grill,

Mount Haven

Rowdy was injured. She'd have to do something to make it up to him. But what? She could bake him brownies. That was the only treat she knew how to make but her brownies were amazing. The recipe had been her father's and she'd been making them since she could walk. Daddy had gotten the recipe from his mother and she'd gotten it from her mother. Nobody knew how far back it went, but they were definitely to die for. That's what she would do, make Rowdy brownies and force him to talk to her. If they just sat down and discussed the situation, she was sure they could work through this. They'd done it before, this time would be no different. The conversation would have to happen tonight. That put her on a tight schedule. Once they got back from Missoula she'd have to rush back to her apartment, make the brownies and then stop in at Rowdy's house. But this couldn't wait. If she knew Rowdy, he'd show up at the bar tomorrow if it killed him and getting time alone at work was proving impossible.

Maggie brought Bailey out of her thoughts as she pulled onto the highway and began to discuss the problem with Iso-Foods. Bailey was grateful for the distraction. This was a topic she could help with. She'd watched her father deal with hard-nosed managers a million times. After his death, she'd watched Peter handle them in almost the same manner. Maggie would only need a few tips and she'd be a pro.

Several hours later the two women pulled back into town. Their trip had been a success. Iso-Foods was scrambling to make Maggie happy, fearful they would lose the bar as a customer if they didn't deliver. Bailey had loved watching Maggie at work. The woman was a natural negotiator. Once they had finished their business, Bailey expected to return to town immediately but Maggie had other ideas. She insisted they needed some girl time. Bailey resisted at first, but spending the day with Maggie was a blast. She hadn't had a real girlfriend for years and she realized she missed it.

The two women had shopped, joked and eaten until they were sick before they finally headed home. Bailey didn't think she had ever laughed that much in her life.

Maggie pulled the car to a stop and waited for Bailey to gather her things from the back seat. "See you tomorrow and thanks for today. I love my men dearly, but sometimes a girl just needs to get away and hang with another woman. We will definitely do this again, soon."

Bailey grinned as she shut the back door. "Okay, you're right. I know I was reluctant at first and I swear, I will pay you back. I know you said this was a gift, but it's one I can't accept."

"Nonsense," Maggie said shaking her head. "You needed something to make you feel sexy and I owe you. Your advice was amazing. Without you, we never would have sorted this thing out with Iso. It's a gift. Accept it and use it wisely," Maggie said, grinning as she maneuvered her car out of the parking lot.

Bailey smiled too. Maggie was one of a kind. She never would have guessed they'd become such good friends. She wondered if it was wise in light of her current situation but she was tired of being lonely. While she was here in Mount Haven, she was going to enjoy the company. Could that include Rowdy, too? She really didn't know, but she got the feeling she had Maggie's blessing if she chose to act on her attraction. The woman hadn't exactly been subtle this afternoon. Oh sure, Bailey knew Maggie truly wanted to buy that sexy black chiffon and the two piece teddy for Coop. But Maggie's ultimate goal was to purchase something for Bailey. She slid the key in the lock and fumbled to open her door. Once inside, she went straight to her room. She might never have the opportunity to wear the silk and lace chemise for the man that haunted her dreams but she could admire the way she looked in it tonight, in the privacy of

Mount Haven

her own room. A girl could dream, couldn't she? And a harmless fantasy about Rowdy Cooper was just what the doctor ordered.

* * * *

Reese stood in the shadows, watching as Cole enticed the young female onto the ship. He was curious about the woman his friend had selected for him. It was always like this, the anticipation, the buildup before the final reveal. Reese preferred it this way. Cole selected the women and Reese made sure they could never get caught. They each had their strengths, their own personal roles in this partnership. Reese was meticulous and Cole always chose the perfect target. He'd been tempted, more than once to sneak a peek at the woman's photo but he forced himself to refrain. He could gather data without actually seeing a photo of the next mark. It made the evening that much more enjoyable for him, like unwrapping a special present. The anticipation heightened the ecstasy.

Cole lured the woman into the bedroom then expertly locked her inside. He slowly turned to face his friend. "One down, one to go. You agreed to wait until I return before you start."

"And I will," Reese promised. "Once the second girl is locked in your room, we'll head to the tiny cove I located and then we can begin." For the past several days, while Cole scoured the beach and the open bars for two targets, Reese had been sailing. Oh, he ventured out at night for a few hours to ensure he was seen but most of his time was spent plotting. He'd located the perfect area his first day out. The tiny cove was close enough to shore, but secluded enough for privacy. The last thing they needed was for some do-gooder to hear the screams and rush in to help, or worse call the authorities. No, the cove was perfect. He'd checked on it several days in a row and it was rarely visited by anyone. There were divers in the area occasionally in the early morning, then nothing. Probably because the shoreline had jagged rocks rather than a sandy beach. Reese grinned again; it was perfect. His plans always were, that was why they had been so successful all these years. Lesser men had played this dangerous game, but they were eventually apprehended. Not Reese, he was too smart to leave evidence lying around. Too smart to give the police the slightest edge. Which is why he had been so angry with Cole over the broken condom. Oh, well. No need to recap that mistake, it was in the past and it would never happen again.

Reese continued to gaze into the darkness, growing more and more anxious by the second. Cole wouldn't be long now and the wait would only make that final moment better. He was looking forward to this experience. For years the two of them had shared one woman, tonight they would each have their own. Tonight, the pleasure, the control, the amazing moment when they each took a life would be shared by the two of them but also enjoyed individually. It was going to be a night like no other, the beginning of something new. Reese moved to the bow of the ship and studied the night sky. Would he be able to stop? Once he had Tory back in his life where she rightfully belonged, could he give this up? He was beginning to wonder. He would never allow himself to lose control with his wife, not to the point he killed her. Then how would he get the amazing high he'd grown to crave, unless he and Cole remained partners. The idea was growing on him, more and more with each passing day. He'd always believed he could stop, that he would stop the instant he achieved his ultimate goal. Now, he had doubts.

They would have to be very careful. But they were always careful, weren't they? Sure, each one of them had made mistakes. Cole's DNA was on file now and Reese, well that little mistake was so insignificant the police probably hadn't even found it. He had to believe that, the alternative was unacceptable. But did it matter, really? He had outsmarted the police for years. Even if they had found his blood, they couldn't trace it back to him. No, he was perfectly safe and he planned to remain that way. He smiled a wicked, knowing smile when Cole ascended the stairs, guiding the second woman onto the ship. Showtime!

* * * *

Cheyenne Dempsey paced the room again, looking for an escape route but knowing she wouldn't find one. At first she'd believed the sexy gentleman was just playing a silly game. He'd been so charming the night before. But now her gut told her she was in trouble. With each passing second she became more and more certain she would not make it out of this alive. She had to think. If she could fight her way free she would but that was unlikely. The guy was masculine and arrogant. His arrogance might be her only hope. A tear slid down her cheek and she hastily brushed it away. She might not live to see the morning but she didn't have to make this easy. She was a fighter, she would fight. But if that failed, she needed to somehow give the police a clue.

Her eyes darted from the closet to the bathroom, back to the bed. What could she take and where could she hide it? Whatever she did, she would need to act now. She was positive that guy wouldn't leave her in here for long. She rushed to the side of the bed and pulled out the nightstand drawer, empty. Next she looked under the bed, no luck there either. As she slowly pulled open the closet door she realized it was full of men's clothing. Cheyenne frantically reached in the pocket of every suit coat and every pair of slacks. Seriously? The guy was supposed to be on vacation. Where were his cargos? Where were the t-shirts?

She glanced nervously at the door again, defeated and ready to give up when her fingers touched some kind of paper. Palming the item just in case her captor instantly came through the door, she rushed to the bed and sat on the edge with her back to the entrance. That might give her more time to hide whatever she'd found. As she looked over the crumpled paper, she realized it was a gas receipt and whoever it belonged to had used a credit card. Jackpot! Cheyenne knew she was running out of time but she had to try something. She hastily shoved off her shoe and then pulled down her sock, placing the folded receipt between her toes. Then she shoved her sock back in place and had barely replaced her shoe when the door knob began to turn.

Reese cautiously slid the door open, expecting the woman to attempt an ambush. He wasn't disappointed. The instant he stepped into the room, the girl rushed him, launching her body aggressively toward his midsection. Reese was ready for it. He pivoted, turned and slammed her head against the door, closing it securely behind him. The girl slumped to the floor, dazed. Reese used his key to lock both of them inside, a little security measure he had installed in preparation for this mission. The room Cole was using had one, too. Neither woman had the slightest chance of escaping but they didn't know that yet. He slid open a small box he'd installed on the wall and quickly secured the key inside. The lock engaged as he pushed the door closed. The key was safely hidden and only he had the combination. He couldn't be expected to keep track of a key while he was naked and preoccupied. He mentally checked the first box on his list. Security was now in place. It was time to start the fun.

Cheyenne studied the stranger, this was not the same guy that had lured her here but that didn't mean she wasn't in trouble. This guy was even scarier than the first one had been. This one had dead, evil eyes and they were staring at her with sadistic intent. This was going to be bad, she just hoped it would be over soon.

Mount Haven

"Cheyenne, is it?" the stranger asked. Cheyenne remained silent. She knew if she tried to answer her voice would shake and the man would know just how terrified she really was. She refused to give him the satisfaction.

Reese laughed. Oh, yes. This was going to be exciting. Cole had chosen well tonight. Little Miss Cheyenne had spunk. He watched as the girl slowly backed away from him. As if that was going to matter. He'd let her believe she was in control, for a little while. The moment her back hit the wall, Reese made his move. He casually walked to the bed and began removing his clothing. His body surged to life when her eyes widened and she began to scream.

* * * *

Cole knocked twice on the door then slowly slid the key in the lock and pushed open the door. He froze at the sight of the girl sprawled out on the bed, battered and bruised. Steam flowed from the opened door of the bathroom and Cole could hear the spray of the water as it hit the shower wall. Had Reese only just finished? Why had it taken so long? He glanced back at the woman's lifeless body. She was completely naked, except her shoes. For some reason, Cole found that humorous. He began to laugh then turned when the door opened and Reese stepped into the room. His friend was practically glowing with happiness. "Well?" he prompted.

A smile spread across Reese's face as he strolled naked across the room. He didn't speak for several minutes, just casually dressed then turned to his friend. "I couldn't have chosen better myself. It was amazing, freaking amazing Cole. She was feisty and terrified and absolutely perfect. What about yours? Was Biannca all you had hoped for?"

Cole grinned. "And more." He was flying higher than he ever had in his life. Tonight was even better than Florida, not that Reese would ever know about that. So perfect in fact, he'd wished he'd taken a little more time with Biannca before he wrung her feisty little neck. Obviously Reese had done just that with Cheyenne. Glancing at the bed, it was obvious his friend had completely let loose on the girl before he snuffed out her life. He'd seen Reese like this before. The man was an animal sometimes. It was a pleasure to behold. For the slightest second, Cole regretted not being in the room. But the feeling didn't last. The only way that was possible was if they only took one girl. He remembered the feeling of loss, the frustration, the aggravation the night his friend had deprived him of the kill. No, this was much better. This was the way it had to be from now on. But maybe… next time he might suggest they use one room instead of two. That way he could watch his friend in action, the way he always had. He knew he could never admit it to anyone but seeing Reese as he took a victim was part of what made Cole's experience so fulfilling. He wasn't gay; no he definitely liked women, but for some reason watching Reese in action, sharing a woman with his friend, always got to Cole. It made each experience even more fulfilling. He wasn't sure what that meant and he really didn't care. All he cared about right now was celebrating. "You want to head back to the beach? Maybe snag a couple sluts and set ourselves up with a solid alibi?"

Reese laughed out loud. "You, my friend, are amazing."

Cole shrugged.

"I'm game," Reese finally said, glancing back at the bed. "I just need to clean up this mess and we can head out. Let's stash the bodies in the freezer. It should only take a minute."

Mount Haven

Cole moved to the bed and silently began wrapping the woman in Reese's bedding. "Biannca is already down there. I guess I'm not nearly as methodical as you are buddy. Wham, bam and oh yeah, thank you ma'am. Maybe that's why I'm in the mood for another round, even if I have to tone it down a bit for the encore."

Reese shook his head and grabbed Cheyenne's clothing. He'd put the skirt and blouse back on before they pulled out in the morning. Right now he wanted a drink, and a cool down might be nice. He'd have to get used to shifting gears once Tory was back anyway. After tonight he knew he couldn't stop, not even with someone as gorgeous and lively as Victoria in his bed. He'd just continue his partnership with Cole then head on home to his wife. Tory could be his encore for the rest of his life. Once he found the elusive woman, his life was going to be perfect. He just knew it.

* * * *

Cole pulled the yacht as close to the shoreline as he dared. He had to admit the area was perfect for offloading a couple bodies. At the moment, they were the only yacht in sight but that could change in an instant. They would need to work fast if they wanted to remain undetected. He glanced at the shoreline and confirmed the wilderness area was also deserted. Too bad they couldn't just sink the women out here and call it good. But even Cole knew that was too risky. This stretch of ocean was heavily traveled all season long. If the bodies surfaced, they would definitely be discovered. There would be a record proving he and Reese were in the area during this time. It might seem like an insignificant detail, but paying attention to details was what had kept them ahead of the game for years. He wasn't willing to deviate any more than Reese was on that one.

They were just north of the border near a state park. Cole was sure the place would be swarming later in the season but right now the coast was clear. Reese could depart through the park and connect with I-5. Cole would head back to the yacht and dock at The Club. He just hoped nothing went wrong. If Reese got caught with not one but two dead bodies in the back of the car, they would be in real trouble. He still didn't understand why his friend insisted on traveling so far to dispose of the evidence. Okay, sure the desert was vast and secluded but there were other ways to accomplish the same thing. If it were up to him, he'd just tie something heavy to the things and dump them in the ocean. The sea life would eat the evidence in no time at all. Okay, he agreed with Reese that there was a lot of traffic along this section of the ocean but they could head out further, out to sea where nobody could see them and dispose of the girls in a few seconds. Instead, Reese wanted to travel to the Nevada desert and ditch the women out in the middle of BFE. He shook his head and opened the freezer. There was no use having this conversation again, Reese was determined to do things his way no matter what Cole said. He picked up Biannca's frozen corpse and draped it across the serving cart. It was just a good thing Reese had an elevator in this thing. Otherwise the bodies would be impossible to move.

The electric boat silently moved through the choppy water as they approached the jagged shore. The two men remained silent as they spotted the rental and secured the raft. It was fairly easy to transfer the cargo from the boat to the waiting vehicle. Once the car was loaded and a blanket was draped over the bodies, Cole gave his friend one last glance. "You're absolutely sure about this?"

"We've been over this a hundred times, Cole. It's the best way. Trying to dump the bodies with the yacht races going on is too dangerous. That stretch of waterway is busy and congested. It's too risky. What if someone saw us dropping the cargo overboard?

Mount Haven

They'd have divers in the area within an hour. My way is better. This car has all-wheel drive. The bodies will be locked in the trunk and out of sight. I'm only vulnerable until I reach Nevada. As long as I make sure I don't do anything to draw attention to myself, I'll be fine. This way I can find a desolate stretch of desert, drive off the road and dump them a few hundred yards out. It's going to be dark and I can just roll them out, cut an opening in the sheets and drive away. Nobody will ever find the bodies and the coyotes will devour them in no time at all. It's a perfect means of disposal. Trust me on this. You have nothing to worry about. Now get back to the boat and push off before the yacht is spotted. You need to be home before nightfall and Finley is waiting for you."

Cole stepped forward and gave his friend a hug, patting his back in a manly, friendly way before he stepped back. "Be careful. I'll see you in a week or so." Then he turned and headed back to the raft.

Reese watched as Cole pushed off and started the small motor on the electric boat. Once Cole was halfway to the yacht he climbed behind the wheel and headed out. He figured it would take him at least ten hours to get to the desert area he had selected after studying the terrain on Google Maps. By that time it would be nice and dark. Once he dropped off his cargo, he'd head to Salt Lake for the night. First thing in the morning he'd pass through Evanston to Jackson and into Yellowstone National Park. He could then cross Montana into Glacier and loop back down through Washington and continue on home to San Diego. It was going to be a long trip, but it was worth it. Disposing of the bodies with wild animals was a sure way to eliminate any evidence. He was so confident the bodies would completely disappear that he almost didn't wear a condom this time. He'd been fantasizing about that, wondering what it would be like but his meticulous side had won out. He wasn't ready to be that reckless, not yet anyway. Someday… maybe.

Chapter Eight

Rowdy stood behind the bar watching Bailey deal with the strangers. His gut told him the guys were trouble but so far they hadn't done anything to get ejected. He glanced at Knight and realized his dog was just as on edge as he was. Rowdy furrowed his brows, was Knight mirroring his reaction or was he responding on his own? It was impossible to tell. He looked up when one of the men grabbed Bailey's arm and forcefully pulled her against his side. The second man slammed his mug onto the table shattering it on impact. They were clearly competing for Bailey's attention. And they were drunk.

Rowdy was around the bar and across the room in seconds. He immediately had the aggressor out of his seat with his arm twisted behind his back as he perp walked him to the door. Before he tossed the guy out, he heard Knight begin to growl. He glanced back just in time to see Bailey elbow the remaining drunk in the stomach. The guy reacted. He backhanded Bailey, striking her across her left cheekbone. Bailey fell forward, her hands landing flat on the table lodging a large chard of glass in her palm. At just that moment Coop walked through the door. He took one look at the scene before him and relieved Rowdy of his suspect.

Rowdy darted across the room and secured Knight on a leash he always strapped around his waist. He then helped Bailey to her feet as Coop returned and cuffed the second guy. What happened to his friend? Probably cuffed and secured in the back seat of Coop's police car. Rowdy wrapped an arm around Bailey and maneuvered her into his office and closed the door securely behind them, releasing the leash so Knight could roam freely around the room. The dog had finally settled down, but he remained focused and alert. After several seconds of pacing the small space, Knight moved back beside the door and settled onto his stomach, his eyes continued to dart between his owner and the closed door.

"I'm okay," Bailey finally insisted. She had to admit, the entire episode had been a little unnerving. For the first time in years she'd had flashbacks to her previous life, to the night she'd escaped. She'd felt just as helpless as she had that night, and she hated it.

Rowdy ignored her protest and yanked a medical kit from the top shelf of his bookcase. He gently settled Bailey in his chair then pulled one of the guest chairs around and began to doctor her wound. "This is pretty deep. You might need stitches. We should take you to the hospital."

"No way," Bailey objected at once. She would not go to the hospital. For one thing, she couldn't afford to pay an ER bill on her salary and she certainly couldn't dip into her family trust to cover the expense. For another, Rowdy and Coop might accept the fake identity she'd created but she couldn't risk dealing with a strange cop in a strange town. Plus, medical procedures were recorded.

They were computerized and her brother was a master with computers. It was too risky. She'd just have to deal with a scar and hope the wound didn't get infected.

"Bay," Rowdy pressed. "Trust me, this is going to scar if you don't get it fixed right away."

"Do you honestly think I care if I have a scar on the palm of my hand?" She was insulted that his tone and the look on his face clearly said he did believe the deformity would bother her.

She shrugged. "So, I guess I'll never get a date again. Oh, well. Having a man in your life is highly overrated." She looked away. She couldn't look into Rowdy's deep, knowing eyes and tell a big fat lie.

Rowdy grinned. "I'm pretty sure this…" he took her palm in his and gently kissed the bandage, "…is not going to stop any man from falling head over heels in love with you. I just think you need stitches and probably a tetanus shot. When was the last time you had one of those anyway?"

Bailey's heart was racing and she couldn't think. Why was Rowdy being so nice? He'd avoided her for weeks and now this? She truly could not keep up with this complex, frustrating man.

"If it's been that long, we are definitely going to the hospital." Rowdy stood, pushing the chair out of the way as he held out a hand for Bailey.

"What?" She'd missed something. "Oh, the shot. No, I'm fine. I uh… well, I stepped on a nail less than a year ago. My employer insisted I go to the on-site clinic and they gave me a tetanus shot then. I'm fine, really. Thank you for coming to my aid tonight." She smiled, remembering how quickly Rowdy had darted from the bar to the table. In that moment she clearly saw the cop in him. And any criminal that went up against Rowdy Cooper was doomed for sure. Her smile faltered when she realized what he had given up. What a drugged out criminal had taken from this wonderful, thoughtful, selfless man. She forced herself to keep her feelings hidden. Rowdy would not want her sympathy.

Rowdy pulled Bailey to her feet. Once she was standing he began to massage her elbow, looking for bruising.

At first Bailey was confused, what was Rowdy doing? Then it hit her. He was searching for damage because she had elbowed the idiot. Her elbow was fine; it was her face and her hand that were radiating pain.

Once Rowdy was sure there was no damage to Bailey's arm, he reached into his small fridge and pulled ice from the compact freezer. Within seconds he had several large cubes wrapped in a fresh rag and was placing it on Bailey's cheek. "You do realize you're going to have one mother of a bruise tomorrow don't you?"

Bailey lifted her hand to her face and brushed Rowdy's knuckles. The contact was electrifying. Tingles shot through her body instantly and she inhaled sharply.

Rowdy misread her reaction. "I'm sorry. I'll try to be more gentle," he said as he brushed her hair away from her face. "There's not much you can do for the black eye you are sure to have but the ice pack should reduce the swelling. Why don't you head home? Theresa and Jase are here and the three of us can handle things until closing. We're really not that busy anyway. I have to warn you, Coop is going to need to talk to you. He'll need a statement to support the arrests."

"Oh," Bailey said, panicked once again.

"Hey," Rowdy said softly as he gently wrapped his strong arms around her and pulled her against his chest. "It's going to be fine. Coop knows you're on the run. He's okay with it. He just needs you to tell him what happened. We'll take care of the rest."

"But that will be lying. I can't give false information to a police officer. It's against the law," she argued.

"Then I will," Rowdy decided.

"What? No," Bailey objected, worried what the man had in mind.

"I'm going to pull Max's employment file and give a copy of your app to Coop. There's no law against lying to your employer and there is no law against me providing the file to the police. You won't be breaking the law, I won't be breaking the law and Coop won't be breaking the law. He'll have what he needs for the report and we can focus on the details." Rowdy moved to the door and opened it. Seconds later Coop entered the room.

"Bailey," he studied her face for a moment then turned to Rowdy. "Maybe I should handle this alone."

Rowdy shook his head and settled into a guest chair.

Coop sighed and moved to settle in next to his brother. "Okay, tell me what happened."

Bailey walked the two of them through the incident then Rowdy also gave a statement and told Coop to make sure he talked to Theresa and Jase. Both of them had also witnessed the attack. When he was finished Coop stood. "Rowdy, walk with me out to the car."

Mount Haven

Rowdy glanced at Bailey then nodded and stood. The two brothers strolled confidently out the door and into the dimly lit bar. Once they stepped onto the outside wrap around porch, Rowdy moved to the railing and Coop leaned against the outer wall. They stood there, silent for several minutes before Coop spoke. "She probably needs a doctor."

"She won't go," Rowdy said as he turned to face his brother. "And I understand why. Hospitals have records. She's on the run. We know she's changed her name but whoever is looking for her is probably watching descriptions as well. I wish she trusted me enough to tell me who they are, but until she does we have to do things her way. And her way is taking care of this herself. I'll make sure the cut doesn't get infected. We both know there's nothing that can be done for the black eye. She'll be fine. I'll make sure of it."

"I have to ask," Coop started, "Do you think those two have anything to do with what she's running from?"

"Not a chance," Rowdy said instantly. "She wasn't afraid of them. Not at first. She was just annoyed. They were just two guys who got drunk and stupid and took it out on a pretty girl."

Coop grinned. "So, you think Bailey's pretty?"

"Shut up," Rowdy grumbled. "We both know what I think doesn't matter. The woman is on the run. She's temporary. Nothing is going to keep her here for long. I'm going to show up to work one day and find out Bailey has disappeared."

"As long as you remember that," Coop said placing a hand on Rowdy's shoulder. "I'm sorry. I know you're attracted. I wish things could be easier for you. Looking back, it was so simple for me and Maggie. The instant I met her I just knew no woman would ever take her place."

"I've got work," Rowdy said turning back toward the door. He didn't want to hear how blissfully happy his brother was. He didn't want to remember how everything had just fallen into place with Andy and Maggie. He didn't want to consider what he was missing out on because Bailey was a complete mystery that he would never be able to solve.

"Yeah," Coop agreed. "I'll be at the station booking our suspects if you need anything. I had Mike take them in, but I want to have a personal chat with them before they pass out for the night. Depending on how it goes, I'll probably need to have another one first thing in the morning. I'm looking forward to having a little discussion with those two while they are hung over and miserable."

Rowdy laughed, then let the door swing shut behind him. Yeah, Coop would have a great time interrogating the duo. A wave of jealousy hit from nowhere. Well, not nowhere. Rowdy knew where it came from. He would never conduct an interrogation again. He'd never have the chance to pressure another perp for information. He'd never have the satisfaction of throwing a criminal in jail, knowing he'd be miserable for the next several hours of his life. He continued to scowl as he took his place behind the bar and began serving his patrons.

* * * *

The following afternoon Rowdy paced anxiously around the empty bar and grill. They were opening late today. Maggie had put her foot down after the scene last night. She thought all the employees needed the break. Theresa and Jase would be arriving any minute. Would Bailey arrive first? Rowdy hoped so, but at the same time he wasn't sure what to say to her. He had tried to call her,

Mount Haven

she shouldn't work tonight. He knew from experience she was going to be sore. She'd definitely have a black eye and from the look of her cheekbone it was going to be swollen and tender. They could manage one short, but Bailey had ignored his calls. Knowing her, it was on purpose. The woman was nearly as stubborn as he was.

The door opened and Bailey stepped inside the dimly lit room. Rowdy studied her closely, if he saw the slightest sign of pain or discomfort she was out of here.

Bailey strolled to the bar and dropped her bag on the counter. Rowdy was scrutinizing her like she was an alien or something. She wondered if he was angry. She had avoided him like the plague today. She absolutely was not bailing tonight. She needed to work. Her car tires were nearly worn bald and hanging out alone in that apartment was driving her insane. All she could think about was Rowdy Cooper and how kind he had been the night before.

"You okay?" Rowdy finally asked.

"I'm good, Rowdy. Please don't hover tonight," Bailey requested. "I'd just like to forget what happened and get to work."

Rowdy laughed. "Sorry, Bay but that is not going to be possible. Have you looked in the mirror? You are going to get about a hundred questions about that black eye before the night is over. You sure you can take it? I mean, you seem a little touchy with me and I was the first one to ask."

Bailey sighed. "Yes, I can handle it. And I know people are going to be curious. I doubt I'm going to get that many questions, though. Seriously, how long have you lived here? Mount Haven is a small town, news travels fast. Nobody is going to ask what happened, they already know."

Rowdy grinned. "True." He dropped the rag he was using to wipe down the counter in the sink and headed into the back room. The woman was stubborn and beautiful, even with that shiner and too damn tempting. All he wanted to do was pull her into his arms and hold onto her. He kept telling tell himself it was to give her strength, but deep down he knew his desire to hold her and comfort her was as much for himself as it was for Bailey.

* * * *

Reese swore again as he rolled down the back windows and pulled onto the paved road. Mission accomplished. The bodies were dumped and he would be on the highway within minutes. State Road 318 would hook back up with 93 and take him directly to I-80. From there, it was an easy shot into Wendover. He might just layover there instead of pushing on into Salt Lake tonight. He was so tired and he had to get out of this car. He could admit he'd misjudged the time. He mistakenly believed the bodies would take longer to thaw. But, he was traveling across the desert and the heat was stifling without air conditioning. What idiot thought it was okay to rent a vehicle without air? The smell had gotten so horrendous he had prematurely pulled off on the first dirt road he saw. Now, he was back on the highway minus two putrid, reeking corpses. Unfortunately, the smell was still lingering. He wasn't sure if that was his imagination or if the rental was saturated and would carry the awful smell permanently. He glanced at his gloves lying across the passenger seat. Did they smell now, too? He'd have to destroy them later. He was too tired to think about that now.

Reese fumbled in his bag, trying desperately to find something to distract him from the memory of that smell. He was sure he had a tin full of breath mints somewhere in the pocket. He glanced down for several seconds and panicked when the car jerked and swerved as the passenger tires rolled over something lying in the roadway. Reese slammed on the brakes then slowly pulled to the shoulder wondering what else could go wrong. He was in the middle of nowhere. What the hell could be sprawled out across the damn highway? The instant the car stopped moving he shoved it into park and flung open his door. Well, at least he could get a breath of fresh air while he sorted out this mess. He would never admit that Cole had been right, but after the day he had… maybe dumping the garbage in the ocean was the better option.

No, he would not second guess himself. He was right, he was always right. Disposing of the remains in the desert was brilliant. He just needed to adjust, re-evaluate his current situation and adapt. Reese slammed the door shut and made his way to the debris in the road. The instant he stood over the dead animal, it hit him. He wasn't smelling remnants of the women, he was smelling roadkill. Or… at least that was partially true. He moved back to his car and opened the trunk. The smell hit him immediately. No, the car was contaminated too. He needed a plan. Could he use the animal to get him out of this mess? He closed the hatch and considered. How could he use that dead thing back there to his advantage? Once again, he surveyed the area making sure he was alone. After several minutes he relaxed. There wasn't another soul for miles.

Well, there was no time like the present to destroy evidence. He reached into the car and pulled out the contaminated gloves and his lighter. It took a couple tries but the material finally began to smolder then flames kicked up and the glove was completely engulfed. He threw the second glove on top of the first one and watched as the last of the evidence was destroyed. Now, what to do about the smell inside the vehicle.

Reese walked to the side of the road and crouched down, surveying the underside of the car. What if he shoved the animal up under a tire or maybe that long metal pole thing? Would the rental agency believe he'd run over the animal and it got lodged up there itself? He could just pull into Wendover and insist they switch out the vehicle for a more comfortable ride. They could deal with the mess and he'd be on his way. The plan was fool proof. The idiots at the rental place wouldn't know any better and he'd be long gone before they could change their minds. Now he just needed to find a way to shove that thing up there and secure it.

Twenty minutes later Reese was back on the road. The smell might kill him before he made the switch but at least he wouldn't have to answer difficult questions. If he wasn't out here in the middle of backwater hell he'd just pull over and call a cab. The rental company could retrieve their vehicle and he'd be happily on his way. He glanced at the GPS and moaned. He had at least six hours before he would reach Salt Lake, four if he decided to stay in Wendover. He might be able to handle four. *Wendover it is.*

* * * *

A week later, Reese had left Yellowstone National Park in his dust. He hated the place. Seriously, people actually went out of their way to visit such a remote stretch of nothing? Drivers were idiots. They just stopped for no reason in the middle of the road to take a picture of a large ugly animal standing there munching on a patch of weeds. And heaven forbid the car in front of you decides to pull off to grab a snack or something. Traffic grinds to an immediate halt. It's worse than rush hour traffic in California. No, thank you. He'd originally planned to stay inside the park, it would be great proof he'd truly been vacationing there. The instant he realized the

Mount Haven

hotels were a hundred years old and the beds were built decades ago he changed his mind. Instead, he'd found a decent room in West Yellowstone. Now he was headed north through Montana to another hole in the wall that probably wouldn't be much better. The sooner he reached home, the better.

He'd planned to get an early start out but even that hadn't gone according to plan. The morning was cool and as he slid the key into the ignition and attempted to start the engine the 'Check Engine' light flashed. He waited a few seconds, then tried again. The light flashed then stayed solid. Reese decided to walk across the street and have a large breakfast instead. The diner was busy and it took forever to be served. The waitress had paid the price for that mistake. He didn't even leave a tip. Upon returning to his room he tracked down another rental agency, prepared to turn in yet another vehicle and try again. But, luck was on his side. He slid into the driver's seat, started the vehicle and grinned. No warning light. Must have been a fluke, maybe a malfunction because of the cold weather. Now, he was headed up US 287 in backwoods Montana on his way to Glacier. The sooner he could check that one off his to do list the sooner he could be home in a comfortable bed, living his comfortable life. Reese pushed a little harder on the gas pedal determined to go faster. Instead, the car sputtered. The 'Check Engine' light flashed and an annoying ticking sound started. Reese pushed harder on the gas but the car jerked, stalled then jerked again before slowly accelerating. "Shit," Reese grumbled. "Another delay."

He slammed his hand against the steering wheel as he took the next exit and entered the Twilight Zone. If he thought Yellowstone was bad, he'd just entered Mayberry. The vehicle continued to sputter and jerk but luckily the town was so small that once he hit the main roadway, he could see a small garage up ahead. He started to make the left turn into the parking lot when the car died completely. Reese shifted into neutral and let the hunk of junk coast to a stop. He slammed the door behind him as he practically stomped into the office. Yep, Mayberry. Gomer Pyle himself stepped through the door and smiled a cheesy grin in welcome. Reese gritted his teeth and ignored the grease stains running up the man's arms and the black fingernails that hadn't been groomed... probably ever.

"Looks like engine trouble," the man observed as he stepped behind the counter and plopped down on a worn metal stool.

"Can I just leave it here and have the rental agency deal with it?" Reese inquired.

Mike Williams studied the stranger and frowned. The guy clearly had money and thought he was something special. Well, not in this town he wasn't. He waited an extra second before answering the guy's question. If that didn't piss him off, Mike's answer was going to. "Only rental place in these parts is about a hundred miles northwest of here. You can leave it, but it's after five. Pete's gonna be gone by now. You'll have to hunker down for the night and call first thing tomorrow." He watched while the stranger digested what he was saying. Mike shrugged. "While it's here, I might as well take a look. Fifty bucks for a diagnostic, might be able to get you on the road sooner than Pete can get another car out here. He only has two and it's tourist season around here."

Reese stared at the man, not sure what the guy was trying to tell him. "I don't understand," he finally said.

Mike smiled. "Well, then let me spell it out for you. Old Pete has two rentals. He issues them out first come, first served. I know he had a couple that broke down last week who was headed out to Rapid City. Couldn't say if he has that there Tahoe back in service

Mount Haven

yet. Which means, Pete has one car that can be rented. Even if there's nobody waiting, I ain't sure Pete would be willing to let both them cars go across state lines at the same time."

"You've got to be shitting me," Reese growled. A cacophony of expletives ran through his mind. That's it. The final straw. This trip is over. Reese pulled out his cellphone and barely stopped himself from hurling it across the room. No service. Fine, he'd get the snarky mechanic to point him towards the Timbuktu Motel and use their phone. He'd just call Barney and have him head out in the morning and pick him up in the company chopper. He couldn't care less what Gomer here did with the rental. "I assume you do have a motel here in town?"

"Sure," Mike had to bite his tongue. The guy was an eruption waiting to happen. "Two blocks down on the left. Go ahead and tell Betty I sent you. She'll take good care of you. Betty's great that way. What about the car? You want me to take a look just in case?"

"No," Reese barked. "I don't. You can call the rental agency and tell them where they can shove it for all I care. It's their problem now. You want to charge them for space, be my guest." He shoved through the door and stomped across the parking lot. Once he reached the rental, he flung the door open, pulled out his bag and marched up the sidewalk headed for the sorriest looking motel he'd ever run across. Sure, Betty would take care of him. Unless the woman was offering sexual favors, her kind of pampering wasn't nearly enough to compensate for the day he'd had.

* * * *

Timothy Johnson climbed from his horse and sighed. That mangy mutt was pushing it this time. Molly couldn't round up the cattle on her own. She needed Rosko's help. And Rosko was nowhere to be found. If that dog was off marking territory again, he was done. Tim removed his cowboy hat and ran his fingers through his damp hair. The heat was gonna kill them all if he didn't get this job done.

"Rosko," he called again then grabbed his reins and led the horse in the direction he'd last seen his newest herding dog. Tim crested a hill and surveyed the area. Still no sign of the deserter. "Rosko, if you don't get back here right this instant, Molly is going to have herself a new playmate. Your romping days are over my friend. This is no way to impress the ladies. Get your mangy butt back here this instant."

Tim stopped and listened, he was sure he'd heard some kind of rustling. "Rosko! Come," he called out one more time. Seconds later the rambunctious Aussie came running. He was a few feet away when Timothy smelled it. "Aw, man. We lost another one?" He reached out and patted the dogs head. "Good boy," he relented. The dog had been trained to find all the cattle, dead or alive. He was just doing his job. Maybe he was catching on after all. Timothy tied the horse to a nearby cedar and headed back the way Rosko had come. If he'd lost another calf to coyotes, that would make three this year. It might be time to find another location. He couldn't afford to have his calves killed months after they were born.

Rosko darted ahead then came to an abrupt stop and began to bark. Timothy casually moved around the bend and stopped. That was no calf. "Rosko come," he demanded. The dog glanced at the two large lumps then headed for his owner. Timothy's stomach fell at the sight. Two large objects wrapped in sheets and left in the desert could only mean one thing. He needed to get back into phone range. The cows were going to have to wait. He slowly returned to his horse, mounted and gave the mare a gentle kick. At least the dogs would get their exercise today. Molly and Rosko ran past Timothy barking and nipping at each other all along the way. They knew where the truck was and this was a game for them. It definitely wasn't for him... or those two bodies back there. "Live it up you two," he called out. "Because this is going to be a very long night."

* * * *

Sheriff Andy Cooper pulled into the narrow parking lot of the Mount Haven Motel and strolled toward the office. Betty had called but refused to say what the problem was over the phone. That could only mean one thing... a couple high school kids were messing around again. The instant he stepped through the door his cop senses went on alert. Betty was dealing with a stranger and the guy screamed money and trouble. Coop moved forward, crowding the counter just enough to alert the man to his presence.

Betty was flustered. The man was rude and insulting but he was a paying customer so she had to bite her tongue. The sooner she got him a room, the sooner he would leave. She glanced up when the door closed and spotted Sheriff Cooper. Thank heavens! She'd completely forgotten about the kids once the man had walked in. She relaxed even more when her favorite town cop moved forward and crowded the abusive snob as he signed the credit card slip.

Cooper stood, completely silent as the man finished up his business with Betty. The instant he stepped back Coop acted. He moved into the man's pathway and held out a hand. "Sheriff Cooper." He waited. The guy straightened his shoulders and looked down his nose at Coop for several seconds before picking up his luggage and moving to the right. "Do you have business here?" Coop persisted.

"No," the man replied. "Not exactly. My rental broke down. I'll just be here for the night. I have a ride coming in first thing tomorrow. Now, if you'll excuse me… it's been a long day."

Coop watched as the man wheeled a small suitcase down the hall and disappeared into the last door on the right. He turned to Betty. "You called? What seems to be the trouble here?"

"Oh," Betty relaxed. "Well, Sheriff it's like this… Kenny and Joey Stillwater rented a room for the night, which is okay with me. I don't give no never mind what they do with their cash."

"Then why am I here, Betty?" Coop pressed.

"Well, because, Sheriff Cooper, I saw them sneak a case of beer into their room and then not fifteen minutes later Kerstin Jones and Amanda Willingham snuck around back and climbed into their window. I ain't got no problem renting to teenagers mind you, but when they bring booze and girls into the mix… that's where I draw the line."

"I'll take care of it," Coop promised. "You go on back to the desk and I'll handle things. Did that stranger give you any trouble?"

Betty hesitated. "No. No trouble, he was a little rude and put out a bit that he had to spend the night here in town but nothing that needs attention from the Sheriff. Now those kids… that's another story."

"I'm on it." Coop gave her a backhanded wave as he strolled to the room three doors down. He knocked and shook his head when Joey slowly slid open the hallway door. "Joey," Coop said casually.

Mount Haven

"Oh, hi, Sheriff." Joey glanced backwards then stepped aside when Kenny moved into view.

"You two mind if I come in?" Cooper asked putting the palm of his hand on the door so they couldn't shut him out.

"Uh…" Kenny hesitated. "What for? We weren't being loud or nothing."

"Amanda, Kerstin? You two girls come on out here now," Cooper called through the door. Several seconds passed before the two girls peeked their heads out of the bathroom door. "You're not in trouble. Not yet, anyway. If you don't do what I say, then that's a different story. Come on out here, all four of you. We can do this in the hallway or you can invite me into your room. It's your call, boys."

Joey pushed Kenny out of the way and opened the door wider. "Come on in, Sheriff."

Thirty minutes later, four sets of parents were ushering their delinquents to their cars. Coop waited until the last vehicle pulled away before he let out a laugh. He felt a little bad for the bunch. They were all good kids, really. And they weren't doing anything he and Rowdy hadn't done a hundred times when they were teens. Unfortunately, these kids had Cooper for a Sheriff. He smiled all the way to the bar thinking about his childhood. He and Rowdy had it just as bad. They had Pappy Cooper for a father. You never could pull one over on their father, or their mother for that matter. It was like those two had some kind of troublemaker radar.

He stopped the car outside the bar and took a minute to glance around. All quiet on the home front, just as he liked it. The stranger he'd seen at the motel came back to mind and Cooper frowned. He wondered if the guy would just head straight to bed of if he'd venture out and about tonight. The only place to go would be the bar and Cooper didn't like knowing a man that instantly hit a ten on the Cooper crime-o-meter was anywhere near his lovely wife. Maybe he'd just hang out until closing and escort the lovely Mrs. Cooper home tonight. He'd head back to Betty's and make sure the guy really did check out and leave first thing tomorrow.

The instant Cooper stepped through the door he was glad he'd stopped in. There was a large, boisterous crowd tonight. The kind that could easily get out of hand once they had a few too many. He'd just sit it out and watch. It never hurt to have a cop around at closing time. Rowdy could handle things, but why go it alone when you had a big brother that could help. He slipped onto a stool and waited for Rowdy to notice him.

Rowdy spotted his brother the second he walked in the room. To be honest, he was grateful he had backup. The boys up north lost tonight and the crowd wasn't taking it all that well. He'd already thrown two college kids out and a couple more were pushing it. One more outburst and they'd be gone, too. He slid a Coke in front of Coop and went back to the paying customers. He couldn't have a conversation if he wanted to. The jukebox was blaring and the place was packed. Good for business but it was going to be touch and go for the next hour until he shut the place down.

* * * *

Reese tried to sleep, but he was too angry to settle. This entire trip had been a disaster, starting with the detour to Texas. He smiled, well not the entire trip. Mexico had been fun and that little mission had solidified his commitment to the extracurricular activities he and Cole participated in on the side. Even when he found Tory, those outings were going to continue. He was sure Cole was on board and now that things had escalated, Reese was in one hundred and ten percent.

Now he just needed to get some rest and blow this town. He couldn't get back to San Diego fast enough. Barney would be here by tomorrow afternoon and by early evening he'd be relaxing beside his private pool. No more detours to out of the way hellholes. Next time they would have to find a quicker way to dispose of the women. Maybe he could find an old mortuary close by. They could just incinerate the corpses and toss the ashes. Reese smiled as the idea began to take form.

Even with a new plan to consider, Reese couldn't sleep. He finally climbed from the bed, got dressed and headed out the door. He'd go for a long walk. The air was cool and crisp but pleasant. He'd just make a loop around town then return to his room. That should be enough to settle his nerves. If he was lucky he'd find a bar or a liquor store along the way. A nightcap, a long walk and fresh air. That was all he needed to relax.

* * * *

Bailey stepped around the side of the building and moved cautiously to her old, plain vehicle. She'd bought it that way on purpose. The thing had been reliable enough and it allowed her to blend in to her surroundings. The last thing she wanted to do was stand out. It had been a long night. The crowd was larger and more unruly than usual. She slid behind the wheel and closed the door quickly, locking it the instant the latch sounded. She knew she was being paranoid but something about tonight made her uneasy. Her senses were on high alert and all she wanted to do was rush into her apartment and lock the door securely behind her. Once inside she could relax. She knew she was safe inside that small, run-down place. She'd fortified the doors with extra locks and secured all the windows. Her landlord thought she was crazy, but she didn't care. Being crazy and paranoid had kept her safe the past three years. She could live with crazy. What she couldn't live with was captivity.

Bailey slowly pulled away from the bar and made her way into town. It would be a nice night if she wasn't so on edge. Why tonight? Was it just the crowd and the tension or something else? No, they were all on alert tonight. She'd sensed it in Rowdy and Coop. Maggie was a nervous wreck, but she always was when Coop was around, acting all macho caveman on her. It must be the stress of dealing with a bunch of drunken college kids. She just needed to get home, slide into a nice hot bath and then sink into bed. Tomorrow would be better.

* * * *

Bailey stepped onto the landing and frowned. "Really?!" she yelled as she darted down the large flight of stairs. The instant she reached her car, anger engulfed her. She kicked the flat tire then slammed her hands on the hood of the car, lowing her head into her hands as she leaned onto the hot surface. "Whoever did this, I swear I'll find you. I'll find you and make you pay… mark my words." She straightened and moved to the other side, studying the damage. All four tires had been slashed. They were crap anyway. She'd been running on baldies for months but still… she hated knowing someone had deliberately attacked her using her vehicle. Her mind began to race with possibilities. It could have been the two guys from a few weeks back. The ones Coop arrested after they'd assaulted her. Or… it could have been any number of guys from last

Mount Haven

night. She'd shot several of them down and college guys didn't always react rationally when they were rejected. Had one of them followed her home and retaliated? That thought made her more nervous than the knowledge that someone had deliberately vandalized her car. She didn't want anyone knowing where she lived. She had always felt safe in her little apartment. She didn't want that to change.

Bailey took a deep breath and slowly ascended the stairs. She'd need to call Maggie and let her know she was going to be late. And, she needed to change shoes. She had a long walk ahead of her and she was not going to do it in these boots. They were made for style, not comfort. It was one thing to move around the bar all night in them, it was completely different to walk two miles in the dirt and gravel then move around the bar all night. No, today she was doomed to wear sneakers. Not the greatest fashion statement, but it would have to do.

* * * *

Rowdy stepped from the office and headed out to the new covered patio. He knew that was where he'd find Maggie. He hadn't realized Bailey was there, too. Things were a little more comfortable between them but only because he limited their interaction. He wasn't sure what was wrong with him, but the instant she walked into the room, Rowdy wanted her. He wanted her with an intensity that scared him. He tried to tell himself the draw was the fact that she was off limits but he knew better. He was just drawn to her, plain and simple. He wished she'd stick around, but deep down he knew with certainty she'd be leaving. Whatever she was running from would either catch up to her or she'd feel strong enough to face it head on. And when that happened, Rowdy would lose her. It was better to not have her in the first place. So why did that feel so wrong?

"Hey Rowdy," Maggie greeted as she dropped her legs from the chair next to her and motioned for him to join them. "I absolutely love it out here."

Rowdy smiled. "Yeah, it did turn out pretty great, didn't it?"

Maggie poured Rowdy a glass of lemonade and relaxed back into her chair. "Coop was a mess last night. I hope we don't have another home game for a few weeks. I don't think I can take that kind of stress again before then."

Rowdy shrugged. It had been intense but nothing he wasn't used to. He actually enjoyed the challenge and wondered how often they would be dealing with the college boys. Once basketball was over, did they move onto baseball? Then football? He just didn't know how each season impacted this sleepy little town.

"These guys are seriously into basketball. That's why things went haywire last night. They're college kids and their team lost. It gets really interesting when the rodeo comes through. These guys are country through and through. And those traveling cowboys... well, let's just say they are rough and ready if you know what I mean. Things can get a little edgy, especially if the college boys show up. There's something about men and booze and the size of their..."

Rowdy cleared his throat. "Really? You do remember I'm here, right?"

Maggie giggled. "Yeah, but you're just one of the girls, Rowdy. I can talk to you about anything."

Mount Haven

Rowdy glanced at Bailey; she clearly disagreed. Her cheeks had turned a cute little shade of red. Obviously she had forgotten who she was talking to. He'd give anything to reach out and slide a finger over those colorful blotches. He was sure they'd be warm and so inviting. He stood abruptly. "I need to enter the receipts before we get busy. See you two later."

Maggie laughed as she watched her studly brother-in-law practically run through the door. "Guess he's not comfortable being one of the girls."

"Sorry," Bailey said just before she too began to laugh. "I completely forgot he was sitting there. How I did that, I have no idea but I never would have…"

"Bailey Zander, you're blushing a bright scarlet shade of red." Maggie laughed again. She wondered just how much longer it was going to be before the two of them finally gave into their basic needs. They were fighting a losing battle and Maggie hoped they'd come to their senses sooner rather than later. They were perfect for each other and Rowdy needed a woman like Bailey in his life. Come to think of it, Bailey probably needed Rowdy just as much.

"You are so not funny Maggie. I have to wipe down the tables and fill the salt shakers before today's rush begins." Bailey stood and escaped into the building just as quickly as Rowdy had.

"Yep, two peas in a pod." Maggie grinned and took another sip of lemonade. She'd be willing to bet the wait was almost over.

* * * *

Coop stepped through the door and spotted Betty immediately. She was teetering on an old chair, trying to reach something off a high shelf. He rushed to her side and wrapped his hand around her skinny arm. "Betty Daniels, are you trying to get yourself killed?"

"Oh, thank you, son." She finally reached the vase and slipped it off the shelf and into her left hand. "Maybe you could just help me down from here. Not that I need it mind you, but since you're here…"

"Of course," Cooper said shaking his head as he wrapped an arm around the elderly woman's waist and helped her off the chair. "Do me a favor Betty, next time call me. I drive past this place about a dozen times every day. I'd be happy to help you out. Much happier than I'd be if I drove by and found you lying unconscious on the floor because you just had to have an old vase off a high shelf."

"Oh fiddlesticks. Don't you worry your gorgeous little head over this. I rarely need to reach back there these days. But Vern stopped by and picked those sweet flowers over there. I couldn't let them go to waste now could I?"

"I don't suppose you could," Coop agreed. "However, now that you got that vase, how about you put it somewhere easier to get to. You never know, Vern might just bring you another dozen of those beauties and I can't have you teetering on that rickety old chair when I'm not around. Would you do that for me? Please?" He flashed her his best smile and waited.

"Okay, sure. Sheriff Cooper, you are a rascal but I certainly wouldn't want you to worry about me or my safety and it is possible that Vern might decide to bring over a few more flowers someday. So, it wouldn't hurt to have the vase handy now would it?" Betty blushed and turned away. "I didn't call, so what brings you in today, Sheriff?"

"I just wanted to check on that stranger you had in here last night. He said he was leaving. Did his ride show?" Cooper asked, trying to sound nonchalant about it.

Betty narrowed her eyes at the young man standing before her. He wasn't nearly as clever as he thought he was. She knew the lawman didn't like the stranger any more than she had. "He checked out alright. Took off this morning with another extravagant businessman in a fancy silver BMW. I checked, it was one of those four-wheel-drive things."

"An SUV?" Coop asked.

"Yeah, one of those," Betty said absently. "Anyhow he took off this morning around ten or so. Can't say I was sad to see him go, but he paid the bill so I'm not complaining."

"Good," Coop said, relieved. He was happy the guy would be someone else's problem. Now he had to head back out to the Stoddards' farm and take another trespassing report. The guy was diabolical but if he sent Matthew, his deputy would just enrage the old man and Coop would end up driving out anyway. It was easier to just handle this one himself.

* * * *

Bailey climbed the last stair and moved in front of her weathered door. She frowned as something crunched underneath her feet. She glanced down and realized it was glass but it was too dark to see clearly. Why was it dark? She looked up and realized the glass was from her patio light. She glanced around nervously then opened her door and rushed inside. The instant she closed the door she began fastening the locks. She grabbed the baseball bat leaning against the small table and began to slowly make her way through the small space. Once she'd checked every possible nook and cranny, she relaxed onto the couch. Was it a coincidence? Was somebody messing with her on purpose? Or had the kids been out playing baseball again? This wasn't the first time her light had been shattered. It just made her nervous because of the tires. She was being silly. She'd pissed off a college kid who had followed her home and taken his frustration out on her car. Then he'd left town and gone back to school. The broken light had nothing to do with her slashed tires. So why wasn't that panicked feeling going away? Maybe she should call Rowdy?

"Urggg," Bailey growled in frustration. She hated this. She would not call Rowdy. What would she say? *I'm scared because someone broke out my porch light, come save me from myself?* No. She would not let her imagination rule her life. And if she didn't get a grip on her emotions that's exactly what was going to happen. Before she knew it, she'd be packing her stuff and fleeing again. She loved it here. She had friends. She was not going to spook herself and bolt. She would just check all the windows and then go to bed. She was exhausted tonight and tomorrow she was going to need to do something about her car. If Rowdy or Maggie knew she had walked home after midnight, she would definitely be in trouble. Plus, walking to and from the bar after a long night on her feet was not going to last. She'd wear herself out. She would just have to figure out a way to buy new tires and get them mounted. And for that she needed rest.

Bailey slid silently into her comfortable bed and closed her eyes. It was over an hour later when sleep finally came. Once it did, the nightmares returned.

Mount Haven

* * * *

Cole and Reese sat silently in the shiny new BMW, each lost in their own thoughts. "I still can't believe it," Cole finally whispered. "I'm seeing it, but I can't believe it."

"She is a clever little wench, isn't she?" Reese answered amazed. Fate had once again intervened. If his POS car hadn't broken down at that exact moment he never would have found her. If he hadn't been restless that night and decided to go for a walk, he never would have spotted the woman leaving the bar. Everything had just fallen into place. Now, they just needed a closer headquarters and they could snatch up Tory and head home. "Did you find a place for us to stay yet? You know we can't drive a hundred miles every day just to get a glimpse."

"Actually, I think I did." Cole grinned. "But it's pricey and they won't rent. They insist on selling. I don't have that kind of cash, but Tory does. I'm thinking we'll just dip into that sweet little trust fund and buy a little property."

Reese swung around and faced Cole. "How much?" He didn't want Cole wasting his money on some crappy backwoods property.

"One point five million," Cole said with a shrug. "Pocket change compared to the balance of that trust of hers. Plus, it's the only place nearby that fits our needs."

Reese wasn't convinced. What was he going to do with some isolated cabin out in Podunk once he and Tory were married? "I need to see it first. If it isn't perfect, you keep looking."

Cole shrugged. He didn't care if Reese wanted to check the place out. He'd already gotten a virtual tour and knew the cabin was ideal. Plus, it sounded like there were two other buyers waiting in the wings. Reese wouldn't need to keep the place. He could re-list and sell the instant they were finished.

Reese slowly backed the SUV and disappeared into the trees. They were lucky to find the old dirt road. It was the perfect place to park and watch Tory as she went absently about her business. Once he had a place to take her and he got a feel for her routine, she was his. The wait would be over. Snatch her, hide her in the cabin for a few days, then his pilot, Barry would fly them all home and he'd have the private ceremony he'd planned three years ago. Later on, Piper could have her extravagant public celebration. As long as Tory was his, he didn't really care what the two of them did for fun.

Cole pulled the SUV to a stop in front of the cabin. Reese was more quiet than usual and it was making Cole nervous. This place was perfect, but would Reese agree? Lately he seemed to find fault in everything Cole did. The two men slid from the car and began walking casually around the property. Finally, Cole couldn't stand it any longer. He veered off toward the outbuilding as Reese ascended the steps to the front porch.

Cole exited the small storage shed grinning from ear to ear. He spotted Reese relaxing on a lounge just outside the front door. The moment he reached the cabin, excitement overcame him. "You will never guess what I just found in that storage unit over there."

Reese studied his friend closely. He had to admit Cole had hit the jackpot with this place. It was isolated and remote yet from the looks of things comfortable. He smiled and shook his head. "Well... spill it already, before you burst."

Mount Haven

Cole laughed. "You'd be bursting too, my friend. Whoever owns this place must have been a doctor or something. Maybe a vet. There's a bottle of chloroform in the shed. Should we grab it? Store it in the car until the sale is final just to make sure? We've been searching for a way to grab Victoria quietly and I think we just found the perfect solution."

Reese considered. They would be dealing with a realtor, not the actual owners, so the woman, in all likelihood, would not even know the chemical was out here. On the other hand, did they really want to take a chance? "Grab it. We'll stash it at the hotel until we finalize everything. We can stop at that general store on our way back to Missoula and grab a couple rags. I want to study Tory for at least one more day before we make our move."

"Does that mean you're in? Are we buying the place? I'll need to make the call and I want to fast track the sale as quickly as possible. Frank will have to transfer the funds. I don't want Dad knowing about this," Cole mused.

"Can you pull it off?" Reese questioned. "Can you tap into Tory's trust without the family knowing? We can't have interference from Peter or Piper on this. Especially considering what you plan to do to my wife once we have her at our disposal." Reese wasn't planning on forcing the issue of intimacy with Tory until after the wedding but now that he was so close to the end game, he wasn't sure he could wait. It still bothered him that Cole would have time with her but that couldn't be helped. He might just have to lay a few ground rules beforehand. Convince Cole that he needed to go a little easy on her just like he would have to go easy on Sissy. That woman was still his ace in the hole and he planned to use her to his advantage at every turn.

"No problem," Cole assured him. "Frank has his own dirty little secret. He'll do as I say, no worries there."

"Then let's move forward. The place will work and I'll just have to do my best to off load it once we no longer have a need," Reese said quietly.

"That's it?" Cole asked, annoyed. "The place will work? Would it kill you to actually give me a compliment? You know as well as I do this place is perfect. I have no problem expressing my pleasure when you get something right. Why is it so hard for you to reciprocate? I get that your old man did a number on you Reese, but seriously? Do you have to act like him all the damn time?"

Reese cringed at that. He was acting like his father. Somehow, those old lessons were impossible to abandon. "Sorry, you're right. Not about my father, but about the property. It is perfect and I should have said so. I'm not acting like my father, Cole. I just have a lot on my mind." He would never admit the truth about that. His father still had far too much influence on Reese's actions. He viewed that as a weakness, one he would never admit... not even to Cole. "This is our one shot at getting Tory back. We can't make any mistakes. She's outmaneuvered us for three years. I never would have believed she'd move to a small town and take up work as a waitress. I'm still floored by that revelation. If she's able to manage that, what else is she capable of? I'm just a little too focused on the mission and took the details for granted," he smiled. "Maybe because you're so good at handling your end of the deal. We are like a well-oiled machine when it comes to planning the perfect snatch and grab. Years of experience, I suppose. I just get a little caught up, that's all."

"Better, that's all I wanted my friend." Cole turned and headed for the car. That was the highest praise the guy was capable

Mount Haven

of giving. Reese would deny, to his dying day, that he emulated his father in any way. Unfortunately for Reese, Cole knew the man. And Reese subconsciously mirrored the guy more than he would care to admit. His friend just had a better avenue of relieving his tension than the old man did. Raping and killing sluts was a far better release than brow beating your own son. That should be obvious to anyone. Cole never could understand why people abused their own family when there were plenty of mindless strangers to satisfy that need.

The two men drove silently up the dirt road, each plotting their next move. Finally, Reese turned to Cole with a grin. "I want to stop by Tory's place one more time before we head out tonight. The tires and the broken glass have her on edge. I think she needs one more prank to keep her off balance. Then we strike. See what you can do to get access to the place by tomorrow. If it's impossible, we'll wait but I want to act fast on this one. Tory could bolt at any minute."

Cole pulled out his phone and studied the display. Two bars, that should be enough. "On it," he said casually as he tapped out a text to Frank with instructions. "I can't meet with the realtor until we get back to Missoula but Frank should have the transfer ready to go on my say so."

Reese was now on the paved highway, headed back towards Mount Haven. The drive was long and arduous but well worth it if this all worked out the way he hoped. He drove by another dirt road and slammed on the brakes.

Cole wasn't ready for the sudden stop. He was just grateful he'd fastened the seatbelt before they left. "What the…"

"Grab the map," Reese ordered. "I want to know where that road goes. We happened onto that shortcut in the trees near the apartments, this could be a shortcut back to the cabin. Once we grab

246

Tory, we're going to need a plan. One that doesn't include driving through the borough with small town busybodies on our tail."

Cole snatched up the map and began to study it closely. "It looks like it might wind around and eventually lead back to the cabin." He smiled. "And, I think there's an entrance further out, not too far from the bar. Let's head back to Missoula now so I can hook up with the realtor, then tomorrow morning we can spend some time exploring our options. I think we just caught another break. If this map is correct, there are dozens of dirt roads out there. Even if someone tried to follow, we could lose them for sure."

Reese nodded and grinned as he pulled back onto the roadway. He loved it when a plan came together and this plan was coming together nicely.

Chapter Nine

Bailey stepped through the back door and moved into the darkness. Another night behind her and she still didn't have a vehicle. She'd almost confessed her dilemma to Rowdy a dozen times. Almost. But she just couldn't do it. He was clearly exhausted and if she'd let on that she didn't have a ride home he would have driven her back to the apartment himself. There were more things wrong with that scenario than she could count. First and foremost was the fact that she would probably embarrass herself by inviting him in. Nope, not gonna happen.

Once she'd crossed Rowdy off her list of possibilities she'd actually considered asking Jase for a ride, she was that desperate. But something about him still made her nervous. So, here she was, faced with another long walk into town, alone. The morning was quiet; it was now after one o'clock so it should be peaceful. But Bailey knew all too well that bad things could happen during the most peaceful of moments. In fact, those occasions usually turned out the most deadly; the times when you let your guard down. Bailey had learned her lesson the hard way. These days she was always on edge, always alert, always prepared. It was a matter of survival.

She moved through the shadows, careful to hide her progress from the bar's patrons slowly making their way home. She was sure some of the cars had drunk drivers behind the wheel, but that wasn't her problem. No, her problem was making the two mile walk back to her apartment without being noticed. Once Bailey reached the end of the parking lot, she casually stepped onto the sidewalk and began her long journey home. She'd only gone a few yards when three young men blocked her pathway. "Not again," she groaned. She'd already dealt with these three once tonight. She was seriously not up for another confrontation.

"I see you changed your mind after all," the most obnoxious of the bunch slurred. "Knew it, nobody turns down a roll with this," he grabbed his crotch and began to laugh as he took another step forward.

Bailey rolled her eyes. *Really, that's the best he could come up with?* She sidestepped his advance and tried to move past the group. She almost made it but then his buddy moved forward and blocked her again. She was evaluating her situation carefully, wondering how forceful she was going to need to be when she heard a familiar voice behind her.

"There you are," Theresa called out the open passenger window. "I thought you were going to wait by the light post." She reached across the seat and swung open the side door. "Come on, Bay, I'm tired. Say goodbye to the boys and let's call it a night."

Bailey grinned then slid into the passenger seat, closing the door quickly behind her. The three guys stood speechless as Theresa floored it, throwing gravel and dirt in their general direction. "Thanks for the save," she said turning to face her co-worker. They had never really gotten along, so she was a little surprised Theresa had come to her aid.

"You shouldn't walk out here alone at this time of night." Theresa glanced at Bailey then back to the road. "Those creeps keep it controlled inside the bar because they know what will happen if they get out of line. Rowdy or Jase would have their jewels in a ringer. Out here is another story…we're fair game."

Bailey hadn't really thought about it like that before, but Theresa was right. Rowdy scared people. He just had that quiet, lethal way about him. Max had it, too. She'd always had a false sense of security here but that was stupid. Things could have gotten out of hand back there and she owed Theresa for coming to her rescue.

"Sorry," Theresa apologized. "I shouldn't lecture. I guess I'm the last person that should be giving advice about who to trust and how to live."

Bailey studied Theresa, was there something wrong tonight? The woman was usually so bubbly and aloof. Had something happened? They weren't really close enough for Bailey to ask, but she had to say something. The woman had saved her from disaster tonight. "Just because you choose to have a good time now and then doesn't mean you're not right."

Theresa shrugged. Things weren't always what they seemed and she wasn't about to explain her circumstances to anyone. Especially not Bailey Zander. She'd always felt a little intimidated by the woman and resented that from the start. "Where's your car anyway?"

"Flat tire," Bailey fibbed as she continued to stare out the window. "I need one more paycheck before I can afford the repair."

Theresa wasn't buying it, something was off. "Well, I have to drive by your place on my way in. I'll swing by and give you a lift if you want… until the car's fixed, you know."

Bailey once again turned to look at Theresa. She'd always believed the woman was a flake, just a flighty waitress that was a little too wild for Bailey's taste. Now, she wondered. "Thanks, I appreciate it," she finally said. "Maybe we could split the gas or something. That would give me a little more time to make arrangements for the repair."

Theresa pulled into the dirt lot of the apartment complex and casually looked around. It didn't take more than a second to spot Bailey's car. Her eyes widened in surprise when she saw the damage. Bailey didn't only have a flat, someone had slashed her tires. It was pitch black out here, but the damage was obvious even with the bad lighting. "You should report that, Bailey."

Bailey reached for the handle. "I don't know who did it. What's the point?"

"How long ago did it happen?" Theresa inquired.

"The night of the game. I pissed off a couple of players… and yes the double entendre was intentional… basketball and women. Anyway, when I got up the next morning, I stepped from my apartment to find that…" she motioned to her car, "as a nice surprise. It might have been retaliation, might have just been a couple high school kids looking for an easy target. I have no idea and I don't want to make things worse." She shrugged. "I'll just save my money and take care of it after payday. I really appreciate the ride and the save, Theresa. I was getting a little worried back there."

Mount Haven

Now Theresa shrugged. "We girls have to stick together, right? Anyway, I'll be here at four, we'll talk gas later. Like I said, you're on the way."

Bailey nodded, shut the door and darted up the stairs. She couldn't get inside fast enough. She'd played things cool with Theresa, but that confrontation had shaken her. First the incident with the drunks that slashed her palm open and then this. Maybe working in a bar wasn't so wise. The men seemed to be constantly reminding her of two other men that believed women were objects and they could take whatever they pleased. She shuddered as she secured the door and began her rounds.

The instant she stepped into her room, she knew… something was wrong. Bailey rushed to the window and studied the damage. Someone had tried to break in. The only thing preventing it was the large strip of board she'd secured in the track. Another coincidence? Had the college guys been back? Was something more sinister going on here? Had Cole and Reese found her? No, she wouldn't believe that. If her stepbrother or his evil friend had located her, she'd already be kidnapped and heading back to San Diego by now. Something else had to be going on here, but what? Bailey sat on the edge of the bed, too scared to sleep. Too scared to think. Too scared to move.

* * * *

Rowdy finished off his beer and pulled out his phone. It was time to call Coop. He hadn't been hiding things from his brother, he just hadn't disclosed them. Would Coop be mad again? Probably. But that couldn't be helped. The doctor had said he needed backup.

Someone he could call if he couldn't handle the MRI again and they had to sedate him. Coop was his backup… in all things.

Rowdy pushed himself out of the comfortable lounge chair and walked to the railing, gazing out across the lake. He still couldn't believe he had such an amazing view. Once again he wondered how his life might have been different if he'd known about this place sooner. But playing the 'what if' game wasn't going to get him anywhere. He took a deep breath, pulled out his phone and dialed his brother. The phone rang twice before Coop picked up. "Hey, I was wondering what your afternoon was like today." There was no need to identify himself, Coop always checked the display.

"That's a strange question and as evasive as they come," Coop answered. "You want to tell me what's up?"

Rowdy sighed. "I have a follow-up today. I need to head into Missoula, to the clinic, and have another MRI. Last time… well, apparently I've become a bit claustrophobic in addition to everything else and they couldn't get a good reading. The nurse just called. If I can't get through this one, the doc says he'll need to sedate me. He's not willing to write another prescription for the migraines until he can study the results."

"Today should be light. I can probably shuffle things around and leave early." Coop was trying not to be angry that Rowdy had put off telling him about the test. No doubt his brother planned to go it alone.

"I'm not asking you to shuffle. I can try to do this on my own again. I just… well, I need a backup plan. If I wuss out again, the doc won't wait this time. I'll just need a ride home, that's all." Rowdy hated being a burden, but he really didn't have a choice on this one. His only other option was to call a cab and he just couldn't justify that kind of expense. Plus, he would need to get his truck home from Missoula. He still wasn't sure what to do about that, but hopefully the clinic would let him park it in the lot for a couple days. Rowdy spotted Maggie and Bryan and silently moved into the house. He did not want his nosy sister-in-law to overhear this conversation.

"Rowdy," Coop sighed again. "What time are we leaving?"

"Really, Coop. I'll just call if I can't handle it myself. I don't want you to juggle your life around and take a road trip." Rowdy ran his fingers through his hair in frustration as he plopped onto the large couch. Coop didn't have time for this and he knew it.

"Time?" Coop repeated. He was not going to argue about this. He was going to Missoula whether Rowdy liked it or not.

Rowdy realized he was once again fighting a losing battle. He rested his head against the back of the couch in defeat. "I'll need to leave here by four, but I have to stop in and talk to Jase before we go. I don't like leaving Bailey alone like this especially after dark, but it can't be helped. With us both out of town, she's vulnerable. I can't even use Knight because I don't trust him around the patrons without me there to control him. There's been more than one time lately I thought he was going to bite one of the drunks."

"And every time they would have deserved it," Coop laughed. "But I agree, Knight can't be let loose in the bar without you there. He's still got the drive and the instincts of a working dog. I'll have Mags stop by and give him a potty break around dinner time. Give me an hour to clear my schedule then I'll pick you up and we can head into town. I think we should talk to Jase before he arrives at the café. I'd like him to look out for my girl too until we get home. We both know how rambunctious that crowd can get."

Rowdy decided to try one more time, but was pretty sure he was about to fail. "Coop, are you sure you want to make the trip? I mean, I can just call if things get dicey. That way you won't have to leave town unless it's absolutely necessary."

"I'll pick you up in an hour, be ready." He hung up before Rowdy could make another argument. Eventually his brother would learn to accept help from his family graciously. Until then, Coop would just have to force it and Rowdy could deal.

* * * *

Bailey tossed the empty beer bottle into the garbage then cringed when it bounced against the wall and fell to the floor making an awful clattering noise. She couldn't leave it there, someone would trip on it and get hurt. She moved around the counter, retrieved the bottle and shoved it into the already overflowing trash can. She pivoted, took a step forward then paused. She couldn't do it. Rowdy would have a fit if he walked in and saw how cluttered and filthy the area was in his absence.

Bailey sighed, turned and yanked the plastic ties upward. The bag caught on the side of the can for a second before swinging free and colliding with the wall. She tied the red handles together and headed for the back door. They weren't really that busy tonight and those that had dropped by were regulars. Nobody would complain if they had to wait a couple extra minutes for their order. She pushed open the door and headed for the dumpster. The instant she lifted the lid on the large container, she sensed trouble.

Mount Haven

Bailey dropped the sack like a hot potato and whipped around. It was too late. A strong arm wrapped around her waist, lifting her body completely off the ground. A second hand wrapped around her mouth making it impossible to scream. She was on her own and she'd been stupid. Nobody even knew where she was. Fear turned to paralyzing panic when she heard the voice that whispered in her ear.

"Relax Tory," Reese said as he pulled his future wife's tiny frame against his chest. He was a little surprised at the instant, intense reaction his body had to the little firecracker. This was definitely going to be fun. His life was now complete.

Bailey tried to pull away but failed. Reese was turned on and there was nothing she could do about it. If she didn't get away, her worst nightmare was going to become a reality. She twisted her head to the side then screamed out in pain when someone grabbed her hair and yanked it backwards. She opened her eyes to see her stepbrother's sadistic smile just before he shoved a rag over her face.

Bailey smelled the sickly sweet order and knew instantly what it was. She'd never smelled chloroform before, but she'd seen it used in the movies. How did Cole and Reese gain access to the restricted drug anyway? It didn't matter, all that mattered right now was escape. She tried to shift and inhale around the rag, but the effort was futile. Cole had a strong grip on her hair and he was using so much force to press the rag to her face, she was sure it was going to leave a bruise. She held her breath as she kicked violently. When that didn't work, she relaxed her body completely and hoped it was enough to make both Reese and Cole loosen their grips. Within seconds she realized there was no hope. She was doomed. Apparently she couldn't outrun the monsters forever. Her head fell forward and darkness engulfed her.

* * * *

Jase glanced around and realized Bailey was missing. Where in the world could the woman be? He rushed across the room and surveyed the bar area, no Bailey. He darted behind the counter and collided with Casey. "Where's Bailey?"

"Uh… not sure," Casey said with a shrug. She glanced back at the trash can as she maneuvered around the large man and headed back out onto the floor. Once she was free of the counter she glanced over her shoulder and realized Jase was actually worried. "Try out back," she offered. "That garbage was overflowing a second ago. Maybe she took out the trash."

Jase had a sinking feeling in his gut. Something was wrong, he was sure of it. He rushed to the back of the building and grabbed the tire iron he kept hidden in the back cabinet. If he was going out there, if there was trouble, he was going to be prepared.

Jase gripped the metal weapon a little higher and tested out the swing. Perfect. He slowly slid the door open and crept silently into the night. It took a few seconds for him to register the trouble. Bailey was kicking violently as two men held her captive. Jase's hand began to sweat and the tire iron slipped an inch. He grabbed the weapon with his left hand, wiped his right on his pant leg then gripped the metal tighter. He was only going to get one shot at this. Déjà vu hit him like a punch to the gut. He'd been here before and he'd failed, which is why he was now on the run. *Suck it up, Montgomery. You made a promise and you are going to keep it. Consequences be damned.*

Mount Haven

The attack came out of nowhere. One minute Reese was setting Tory on the ground to get a better grip and the next a giant, muscular tornado was hitting him across the chest with a firm metal object. Reese went down instantly. He was on his knees, gasping for air when he spotted Cole. His friend was on the warpath. Reese tried to take a deep breath, but the pain was unbearable. He pressed the palms of his hands to the ground in an attempt to steady his body so he didn't fall over and was shocked to see Cole fly past his line of vision and collide with the outer wall of the building. His head hit the brick with so much force Reese cringed at the sound. Reese forced his eyes upwards - he had to see who had the nerve to attack them this way. The effort was painful, but he finally spotted their assailant. Unfortunately, he was silhouetted. The night light positioned just outside the back door was directly behind the man. It was impossible for Reese to make out his features no matter how hard he tried.

Jase inhaled a deep breath before taking another step forward, towards Reese. At least Cole was out cold but he was bleeding from the side of his head. Jase just hoped he hadn't killed the guy. But that was the least of his worries. Right now, he had to finish the job before he bled out. He'd expected the attack from Cole Hughes. What he hadn't expected was the large knife. Cole always was sneaky. That side blow just proved it, but Jase had a plan and it would have worked. He let Cole think he was taking him by surprise then at the last second, he pivoted and ducked. But Cole had a backup… he had a weapon, too. In the same instant that Jase struck Cole, his adversary plunged a large switchblade into Jase's forearm. He'd been aiming for his torso but Jase ducked just in time to avoid the catastrophe. Unfortunately, Cole was strong and the knife was lodged so deep in his flesh, it probably struck bone. Jase glanced one last time at Cole then focused on Reese. Hughes wasn't going anywhere, but Reese might.

Jase knew his initial attack had taken Reese by surprise and clearly knocked the wind out of him. Any second now the guy would recover and the fight would be on. He needed a plan. Jase moved toward his target, never taking his eyes off the figure kneeling before him. When he was within reach, he pivoted to the side and came at him from behind. As he grabbed Reese's hair, he kicked out and landed a solid blow to his ribcage. Reese fell forward instantly, quicker than Jase had expected. A handful of hair stuck to Jase's sweaty palm. He reached down and impatiently brushed it against his pant leg. The situation was highly suspicious, was Reese trying to lure him in for another surprise? Jase wasn't falling for it. He circled around and moved to the side watching Reese the entire time.

Big mistake! Cole hit him from behind. How had the guy recovered so quickly? Before Jase knew what hit him, Cole had his arm around Jase's neck. He was trying to cut off his air supply. Reese stood and moved in slowly. The look in his eye was calculating. Jase was in trouble and needed to act fast. If he went down, Bailey was doomed. He reached over and pulled the knife from his arm then he ducked and catapulted Cole over his shoulder. Cole landed hard and didn't get up. Jase knew he couldn't trust what he was seeing, but he needed to deal with Reese. Jase side stepped and ducked just as Reese lunged. Reese missed his target but Jase hit his. He swung his arm out and sliced Reese across his side. The momentum pushed Jase off balance and he fell to his knees. The instant his hands hit the pavement his arm gave out and he dropped the knife. It skidded across the pavement and settled next to the door, which flung open and slammed against the back wall with a resounding thud.

Jase crawled forward, protecting Bailey with his own body. He gently reached down and rolled the unconscious woman onto her back. She was out cold, a damp rag was lying at her side. She had a bruise forming on her left cheek and blood had run from her nose and dried in a stream across her mouth and down her chin. He was still contemplating what do when the area was flooded by headlights.

Coop pulled into the lot and cursed. Rowdy was clearly still suffering the side effects of the valium. "Rowdy, this is ridiculous. I'll just take you home and then I'll come back and take care of things until it's time to shut down."

"No," Rowdy growled as he pushed himself into a sitting position. "My bar, my responsibility."

"Well, I guess at least you haven't puked for the last fifty miles," Coop shook his head. He was pretty sure he had never been this unreasonable in his life.

"I'm fine," Rowdy barked as he unhooked his seatbelt and stretched. "The nausea is gone and I'm not dizzy anymore. I think it's worn off. I need to check on my people and close the place down, then I'll crash. Stop worrying, Nancy boy. You were worse off than I am that last time you got drunk."

Coop cringed at that. He had gone a bit overboard at Mitch's party but that was before they left Chicago and his family was a mess; Coop had plenty of reasons to overindulge that night. He started to turn right then immediately swerved to the left. Something wasn't right on the side of the bar. He reached under his seat and pulled out his weapon.

Rowdy was on alert. Something was going down and he was sure he wasn't going to like it. The instant Coop slammed on the brakes he was out of the car. He didn't have a gun, but that small detail wasn't going to stop him

* * * *

Things had just gone from bad to worse. Reese knew one thing, they needed to get out of there. He pushed to his feet, trying to stop the bleeding at his side and stumbled over to Cole. His friend looked up, dazed then glanced towards the approaching light. Reese reached out and helped Cole to his feet then the two of them rushed to the waiting vehicle. He was now grateful Cole had insisted they park in the trees. If they could just reach the car, they could disappear into the back woods and circle around until they connected with the dirt road they found earlier that morning. A few extra turns and they would be safely ensconced in Tory's new cabin.

Reese and Cole scurried into the darkness, each wrapping an arm around his friend in an attempt to keep the other from falling. Both men were thinking the same thing... blood didn't matter. They were truly brothers and would go to any length to save each other. Reese reached out and placed a hand on the back of the SUV for support then he fished out the keys and darted to the driver's side, releasing the lock so Cole could enter from the other side. He pulled his door shut as he turned the key, letting out a relieved breath when the engine roared to life. He didn't even wait for the passenger door to close completely before he shoved the car into drive and floored it. The tires caught and the vehicle lunged forward. Cole's hand pressed against the windshield and his body collided with the dash when Reese slammed on the brakes to make a hard right turn, but he didn't care. They had to disappear and they needed to do it fast, before someone realized what direction they had gone and tried to follow. He pushed his body backwards and twisted around to check their tail.

"I think the coast is clear," he finally said softly. "We need to be careful; don't slow down but I think we made it out without a tail."

Reese glanced around, frantically shifting his attention from the rearview mirror, to the side mirrors, to the road ahead and then back to the rearview. He agreed with Cole but they were not going to take any chances. He let off the gas and took a turn faster than was safe but he didn't want to use the brakes again. The lights would be a clear beacon, advertising to the world exactly where they were. He slid around a curve then held the steering wheel as they made a left onto another dirt road. "Help me watch for the next turn," he commanded.

"There," Cole yelled. "Slow down, man. We've lost them and I'd like to make it back to the property alive. We both have wounds that we are going to need to doctor. Let's just take a breath and decompress. Then we can fix each other up and develop a plan. I think we should call Flint."

Reese agreed. He lifted his foot off the gas and slowed the car to a more reasonable pace. Moments later they were back at the cabin. He pulled the BMW into the garage, hit the button to close the door and waited. He wanted to make sure they were safely secured inside before he exited the vehicle. Once the door hit the concrete, both men climbed from the car and stumbled inside.

* * * *

Rowdy flew from the car and rounded the corner. The scene before him made his heart stop. Bailey was on the ground, Jase was hovering over her but he was clearly wounded and barely holding his own; blood covered his entire arm and left side. The back door was wide open and Casey stood there in shock, tears running down her face. He surveyed the area and saw two men running towards the forest. When he looked closer, he could barely make out a silver or grey SUV. He had a decision to make. Chase the suspects or care for his people? His people won. He rushed forward and took Jase by the arm. His cook reacted, but Rowdy had anticipated the movement. He pivoted to avoid the blow. "It's Rowdy, I've got your back."

Jase glanced up and the light from the open door illuminated Bailey's body. Rowdy froze, was she dead? She was just lying there, completely still. Had he failed her? He promised she would be safe, had he lied? Rowdy was having a hard time breathing and he felt dizzy. Not from the valium this time. Nope. This time he was losing it because Bailey, a woman he didn't really know but somehow also knew so well, was lying before him and he had no idea what to do.

Coop was initially right behind Rowdy. He was about to move out around him when he spotted the fleeing suspects. He watched knowingly as the two men reached the tree line and climbed into a Silver BMW. "Damn it," he mumbled. How had he missed that? He took a step forward, determined to shoot out their tires when he realized a crowd was starting to form. He couldn't tell if the men had guns and with the crowd, Coop couldn't risk it. The suspects would have to wait. He knew who they were anyway. Well, he would soon enough. Tomorrow he'd stop by the motel and talk to Betty. Right now he had a crime scene to secure. He rushed to his car and retrieved his yellow tape then began running it along the edge of the building. He ignored the questions from nosy onlookers. He didn't have answers anyway.

Once the scene was sectioned off he pulled out his cellphone and dialed the office. "Matthew, I need you out at the bar and call

Chuck. We're going to need medical." He rattled off instructions then moved to Rowdy's side. Bailey wasn't moving and Rowdy looked like he was in shock. Coop recognized the signs, he'd been there himself not that long ago. He was pretty sure that was the same look he had on his face the night his brother got shot. Crouching down he rested a hand on Rowdy's shoulder and whispered softly. "Breathe, we can handle this. Whatever it is, we'll handle it. I need you to make sure your employees don't mess with anything until I can get a crew out here and gather the evidence."

Rowdy looked up, shook his head then glanced back at Bailey. Coop was right. They had a job to do. He turned to Jase and asked the question he wasn't sure he wanted an answer to. "Do you know if..." he swallowed hard and prepared to start again.

"She's not dead. She's just knocked out I think. When I came outside they were holding that rag over her face and then she just dropped. I think she's been put under chemically somehow, chloroform maybe."

Rowdy nodded and stood. Unconscious he could deal with. "Okay then, I need you to stay with her while I make sure everything else is secure." He took a closer look at Jase and realized the man had been in one hell of a fight. His arm was bleeding and he had a black eye. It was impossible to tell if the guy had hidden injures as well. Rowdy quickly undid his belt and wrapped it around Jase's arm, pulling it as tight as he dared to try and stop the bleeding.

"Thanks," Jase said glancing at his arm momentarily then returning his attention to Bailey. He might appear calm on the outside but inside his mind was racing. What was he going to do? Cole and Reese had just come to town, which meant in all likelihood Jase was a dead man. Or... he was going to wish he was. The two of them had ruined his life already and they had the power to do it again. Life in this sleepy little town had just come to an abrupt end. Once he cleared out tonight, he'd need to split. His entire family was going to suffer… again. Jase wanted to punch something. He wanted to go back in time and pummel Cole Hughes and Reese Weathersby for everything they had done to him and his family. He glanced back at Bailey and realized something. Bailey was running from Cole and Reese, too. He should have realized that, but he hadn't wanted to consider it. Was she just another one of their victims? He reached out and took her small hand in his. He may have to disappear later tonight, but for now he'd be there for Bailey, and Rowdy and Coop and Maggie. Tonight he'd be the man Cole and Reese couldn't break. Tonight he was going to be Jason Montgomery. And tomorrow? Well, he had no idea who he was going to be tomorrow.

* * * *

Special Agent in Charge, Kyle Donahue stepped through the door and glanced around. His best agent was nowhere to be seen. He once again wondered how such a promising agent could alter his life so completely for his wife. Agent Skeeter Perkin was on the fast track to something big when his newlywed internet consultant wife had been abducted by the serial killer Skeet had been tracking. Skeeter Perkins rushed home and assisted the local PD in saving the woman he loved. Then he surprised everyone who knew him by announcing he would no longer accept any assignment that took him away from home for more than a week.

Skeet's career came to a grinding halt, instantly. But Donahue had to hand it to him, Skeeter never backed down. To this day, he chose his cases carefully and had the full backing of FBI Director Stanley Burns, a close family friend who grew up with Skeet's father. As long as Burns was in charge, Agent Skeeter Perkins could be picky. Donahue had to admit that rankled a little. He wanted Skeeter out in the field. The man could find anyone given enough time, no matter how lacking the evidence. But that was not gonna happen anytime soon. He glanced up when Skeet stepped through the door and prepared to lay out their most recent case, a serial killer victimizing women from El Paso, Texas all the way to Silver City, New Mexico. He needed his best on the job even if his best insisted on working from the comforts of his tiny office.

"Before we get into whatever brought you to my humble little home away from home, I have something I need to run by you." Skeeter set his steaming cup of coffee on his desk before casually lowering himself into his comfortable leather chair.

"Oh?" Donahue asked, perplexed. He was under the impression Skeeter wasn't working on anything active at the moment.

"Yeah." Skeeter nodded and shifted slightly, making himself more comfortable. "Agent Brownlee called me about an hour ago. He's headed out to the Nevada desert, somewhere near Hiko, wherever the hell that is. At the moment he's not exactly sure what they have. What he does know is that the locals reluctantly called him in on two bodies dumped near a cattle ranch. They transported the women to the morgue and the ME found a gas receipt hidden under one of the victim's toes. The gas was purchased in California, which makes it federal. Brownlee said he'd call back when he had more, but I agreed to fly out for a day or two if he needs me."

"Fine," Donahue agreed. "Sure, that's fine. Just know, I'm going to keep you fairly busy for the next few weeks. I'm handing the Maverick Killer case off to you. You have a new priority, Agent Perkins. This Nevada thing takes a back seat to Texas. Six bodies have been located so far and the count seems to be growing. We need to close the book on this one and fast."

Skeeter nodded. He'd been expecting this. He just hoped he could close out this thing from Chicago because he was not willing to play frequent flyer back and forth to Texas. "Do I have access to the case files already or do I need to contact the locals?" He pulled out his desk drawer and slid the files on Cole Hughes and Reese Weathersby inside. Those two would have to wait for another day. He was determined to stop those monsters, but they were careful. Eventually he would catch a break, he was sure of it. Until then, life and serial killers would have to take precedence.

"You have access," Donahue assured him. "I'll be back in a few days to check on your progress. I'm heading out this afternoon. Something has come up and I need to head to Quantico and handle it personally." Then, he turned and left the room.

* * * *

Rowdy paced the public foyer, waiting for Bailey to be discharged. The hospital had decided to keep her overnight and since he wasn't a relative, he wasn't allowed in the room. If he was still a cop, that wouldn't have stopped him. But an ex-cop from Chicago didn't have influence here in Missoula. Each time the door swung open, he froze. The wait was going to kill him. He'd never been a patient man and the hospital staff had gotten on his last nerve. If they didn't bring Bailey out in the next five minutes, he was going in. He didn't care if it was against the rules. The automatic door slowly slid open and a nurse walked through, pushing Bailey in a wheelchair. Rowdy was across the room and kneeling in front of her before they cleared the doorway.

Mount Haven

Bailey tried to smile, but the effort was too much. She was exhausted, dirty, grumpy and she was pretty sure every muscle in her body ached. She closed her eyes and savored the moment when Rowdy pressed his palm over her cheekbone and gently stroked the bruise that had formed overnight. Somehow the connection made the fear subside. Fear that she had endured for the past ten hours. She still couldn't believe the staff wouldn't let her talk to Rowdy last night. She had practically begged them to let him in the room but they refused. Some stupid policy about family only. Had she known they were going to be that difficult, she would have lied. They wouldn't know if Rowdy was her brother or not. Note to self, if you are ever in the hospital again... lie and lie some more. Keep lying until they give you what you want.

Bailey opened her eyes and looked around in shock when the contact was broken. Where had Rowdy gone? The wheelchair began to move forward and she realized he had relocated to the back of the chair.

"Do we need to do anything to check out?" he asked softly.

"No, I signed everything in the room before we left. Please, just get me out of here. I don't think I can take another second in this place," Bailey said softly as she rested her head against the back of the chair.

"Amen to that," Rowdy said, laughing. The instant they were outside, Rowdy sobered. "You scared me, Bay."

"I'm sorry," Bailey said automatically. She didn't know what else to say. Things could be so much worse. Last night could have ended a lot differently than it had. If her enemies had succeeded, she never would have seen Rowdy again. That thought made her physically sick. Both the idea of losing Rowdy permanently and the knowledge of what would have happened to her if Cole and Reese abducted her.

Rowdy helped Bailey into his truck then pushed the wheelchair to the side of the parking lot. The staff could retrieve the chair if they wanted it back. After climbing in and starting the engine, he glanced back at Bailey. She looked so fragile and defeated. He hated that her fears had followed her to Mount Haven, he hated that she was terrified and he hated knowing that the monsters that did this to her were still out there. He reached over and covered her tiny hand with his palm. Bailey silently twisted her hand and linked their fingers as she held on tight. "It's going to be okay, I promise. I'm not going to let anything happen to you."

Bailey wanted to believe him, but she knew better. Cole and Reese knew where she lived. They'd been to her apartment, slashed her tires, broken her light and tried to break in through the window. She was sure of it now. Why had she dismissed everything so casually? Why had she been so stupid? "I need to tell you something," she blurted before she could chicken out.

Rowdy looked at Bailey and knew he wasn't going to like what she had to say. "Okay," he said slowly. "Go ahead."

"I've been having some trouble," she hesitated, not knowing how to continue.

"What kind of trouble?" he asked.

"I thought it was from the college guys a few nights ago. Remember, I had a little trouble with a couple guys at the bar?" she asked.

"I remember," Rowdy's mind was racing. She'd had trouble several nights ago and hadn't bothered to tell him? She promised him she'd let him know if anything strange happened. Why had she gone back on that promise?

"Well, I know I upset them so I was anxious to get home," she gulped then continued. "When I got up the next morning all four of my tires were slashed."

"What?" Rowdy practically screamed. "I mean…" he took a deep breath, trying to calm his temper. "You didn't think that was important information for me to have? I mean, one of my employees gets harassed, your vehicle gets vandalized and you didn't even bother to tell me?"

That hurt. Sure, she was Rowdy's employee but that wasn't the reason she'd promised to report anything strange. She thought they were more than that. She thought they were at least friends.

Rowdy knew he made a mistake the instant the words came out of his mouth. He pulled Bailey's hand to his mouth and kissed her knuckles. "I'm sorry, I didn't mean that the way it sounded." He was unsure how to continue. After several seconds he decided to go with the truth. "Bailey, I'm attracted to you, I want you more than I've ever wanted a woman in my life but I'm trying to keep a professional distance. You work for me, but I also consider you a friend. I'm having a hard time knowing where the line is, that's all," he glanced her way and realized she was staring at him but not making a sound. Not sure what that meant, he decided he'd said enough.

Bailey was surprised. Well, shocked really that Rowdy had admitted he was attracted to her. She'd felt it, of course. She knew the feeling was mutual but like Rowdy, she just didn't know what to do about it. And having this conversation was a little more than she could take at the moment. She was trying to keep it together, but she was so afraid. Cole and Reese were in town. She'd almost been abducted and they knew where she lived. She was alone and vulnerable. A feeling of hopelessness came over her. She hadn't felt this defeated since her father died. Bailey sighed as she remembered his favorite piece of advice. He'd told her at least a dozen times to always chase her dreams instead of running from her fears. She glanced at Rowdy and wondered, couldn't she do both? Deep down she knew it was impossible. She could never hide her feelings for Rowdy from Cole and Reese. She was putting him in danger. "It's okay, I understand. Thanks for staying, and for the ride." She had been lost in thought for so long, she almost didn't remember what they were talking about.

Rowdy let out a relieved breath and the two of them rode in silence the rest of the way back to town.

Bailey turned to Rowdy in question when he pulled onto the long drive that led to his ranch house. She loved it here, but she was confused. Why was he taking a detour? Right now she just wanted to crawl into bed and forget everything. "What are we doing?"

Rowdy glanced at Bailey, then returned his attention to the road. He wasn't taking Bailey back to that apartment. Those two thugs knew where she lived. But he didn't want to argue with her until they reached his place. Maybe she'd be so taken in by the view, she wouldn't argue. And maybe he was going to sprout wings and fly to the moon. He parked the truck and climbed outside, still unsure how to approach this problem. Or how to approach the woman inside his truck.

Bailey was taking in her surroundings. Rowdy's home was amazing and it screamed Rowdy Cooper in so many ways. The house was cozy and had a great view of the lake and the wrap around porch looked so relaxing. She wished she could just crawl into the

Mount Haven

chaise lounge and take a long nap. She closed her eyes and fantasized for several seconds before forcing her mind back to reality. She couldn't stay with Rowdy. The idea was preposterous. Living under the same roof as the sexy, appealing, and so off limits, Rowdy Cooper would make it impossible to control her emotions. She turned an exasperated look on the man when he opened her door and held out his hand.

"Come on," he persisted. "We both know you're not staying alone in that apartment until we catch those two. And I'd rather not sleep on your couch. So, here we are."

Bailey ignored Rowdy's outstretched hand and climbed from the truck. He was right of course. She couldn't stay alone and it wasn't fair to make Rowdy uncomfortable just so she didn't have to face the fact that she wanted to jump his bones. "I'll need you to take me over there eventually. I don't have anything to wear here and..." she glanced at Rowdy's jeans then back to his broad chest before forcing her eyes to his face. She inhaled sharply at the desire she saw reflected there. Rowdy immediately masked it with a cocky grin. Oh, man. This was so not a good idea.

The two of them stepped into Rowdy's cozy home. The one time she'd been inside, a tour was the last thing on her mind. Now that she had time to look, the décor was masculine but comfortable. She smiled when she spotted Knight; the large dog skidded around the corner and slid to a stop at Rowdy's feet. Rowdy patted his torso and the friendly mutt planted two paws on that gorgeous chest. Rowdy smiled as he rubbed behind the dog's ears. What Bailey wouldn't give to be a dog right now! She pushed past Rowdy and slowly moved to the couch. Dog and man followed close behind her. The instant she was settled, Knight jumped up beside her and dropped his head in her lap. Bailey rested her palm on the dog's head but was too tired to do more. She let her head drop back and closed her eyes.

Rowdy studied dog and woman for several seconds before leaving the room. He was crazy. Completely insane. How in the world was he supposed to keep his hands off that sexy body while she was living under his roof? Well, he just had to. That was all there was to it. He knew he should carry her to the bedroom but right now, he needed something to take his mind off the beautiful distraction resting on is couch. He pushed open the door and entered his weight room. Maybe if he worked out, he could enjoy a few hours of peace. Then again, maybe not. Rowdy groaned when his doorbell chimed.

Coop stood on Rowdy's front porch, hating that he had to interrupt mere minutes after his brother arrived home but he needed to touch base with Bailey. He needed to know if those two men were connected to her past, if they were the reason she was on the run. If she could identify both of them he wouldn't need to bother Betty. He grinned when Rowdy opened the door with a scowl. "Can I come in?"

Rowdy glanced over his shoulder, about to take this conversation out on the porch but realized Bailey was awake. Rowdy shrugged, aware that Andy Cooper wasn't here to talk to him anyway. He was here on official police business and his target was Bailey. He stepped backwards and opened the door wider in invitation.

"Hey, Coop." Bailey knew this was coming, but she'd hoped she would have more time. What was she going to tell these two? How much was she willing to disclose?

Coop moved to the living room and settled into one of Rowdy's comfortable recliners. "I need a statement from you and I need to know if you can identify your attackers." Better to get to the point. Bailey looked wiped out and he didn't want to drag this out any longer than necessary.

Bailey walked them through what happened that night. There wasn't a lot to tell before she passed out. She identified Reese Weathersby and Cole Hughes but didn't explain who they were or what the connection was. If he asked, she'd confess but as she glanced at Rowdy, she knew she didn't want to explain. Not yet. She wasn't ready for his reaction and she was exhausted.

"That should be enough for now," Coop decided. "I'm sure I don't have to tell you how important it is to report anything suspicious the moment it occurs." His phone began to ring. He glanced down and read the display. "Excuse me a minute, I need to take this. It's the station." Coop moved to the door and stepped out onto the front porch.

Rowdy was only half listening to his brother's conversation as he studied Bailey. "We're done here. Why don't you head to the guest room and get settled. Maggie stocked the room with a few essentials and I'll take you shopping tomorrow. I don't want you going back to the apartment yet. Not even with me there. We want to keep your whereabouts a secret for now. In a few days we can re-evaluate." He glanced up when Coop stepped back into the room. He had a perplexed look on his face. Something told Rowdy this was not going to be good news. "What now?"

Coop looked at Bailey then back to Rowdy. "I'm not sure. That was Matthew Maciver. Seems Reese Weathersby called him directly. Probably to bypass the system's recording. He said he needed to talk to me about something important and requested my presence at the station at 13:00. That's only twenty minutes from now. The man has to know the moment he steps foot in the place, he's going to be arrested. What's his game? Bailey? Can you shed any light on this?"

"Don't go!" she exclaimed bolting from the couch. "It's a trap." She began to pace the room then finally pulled up short, a shocked look on her face. "Where's Maggie? And Bryan?"

"Mags is at the house and Bryan is at a friend's. Why?" Cooper asked, even more alert now than he was after the strange call.

Rowdy moved in front of Bailey and took her hand. "Come back over here and explain. We need to know what you are thinking. What has you so spooked?"

Bailey let Rowdy lead her back to the couch. The instant she was close, she dropped onto the soft cushion and ran her hands over her face. "Cole and Reese are smart. They wouldn't make themselves vulnerable like that unless they had a plan. I escaped. They might try to talk their way out of that one and all they would have to do is call my mom and she'd back them in whatever bazar story they came up with. But there are other witnesses. You said Casey was in the doorway. Jase fought them off and both of them left evidence. That has to have them running scared. I have no doubt they are going to the station to see if they can buy you off."

"Then they just made a huge mistake," Coop grinned. "And we'll arrest them. Like I said, the instant they step foot in my precinct they are going to see what a steel cage feels like."

"They won't know that but they won't take any chances. They are smart enough to know some people do have morals. And this is a small town. They're going to have a contingency plan. Coop, Maggie and Bryan are in danger. Cole and Reese have access to money. They are rich businessmen. They have private security.

Mount Haven

Private jets for fast response times. Their security guys won't ask questions. Trust me on this, they are going to be desperate."

"You don't honestly believe those two would abduct the Sheriff's son or his wife to get what they want, do you?" Rowdy was studying Bailey. He knew she was terrified of the men, but that plan was just insane. If the two of them attempted it, they'd be signing their own death warrants. Coop was not a forgiving man, especially when it came to his family.

"I don't know," Bailey admitted. "I have no idea what they would do. I just know they will not walk into that police station without leverage. The best leverage out there when it comes to Coop, is his family."

Coop turned and took a step toward the door. Rowdy blocked his path. He stood his ground when Coop tried to shove him out of the way. "We're going to do this, but we do it right." Rowdy waited until he knew Coop was listening. Then, he walked to the small table next to the couch and pulled out a .38. He checked the chamber, showed it to Bailey then closed it back up and held it out.

Bailey stared at the gun, shocked. Rowdy could not be serious. She couldn't use that thing on a person, no matter what the circumstance.

Rowdy watched and waited for several seconds. When Bailey continued to refuse the weapon, he dropped it to his side and moved in close. He took her chin in his hand and forced her to raise her head and look at him. "Bailey, honey, I need you to trust me. Take this," he pressed the gun into her tiny hand. "Do you know how to use it?"

Bailey swallowed hard, then shook her head. She had never even held a gun before let alone shot one.

"That's okay," Rowdy gently wrapped her hand around the handle. "This is a revolver. Just point and shoot. I showed you it was loaded. Now, all you have to do is point this at your target and pull the trigger. It might be a little heavy for you, but if someone is coming at you... I doubt you'll notice. Adrenaline will kick in and you'll be fine." He let go and backed away. "I'm leaving Knight here with you. Whatever you do, don't get in his way. Once we leave, lock the door and do... not... let anyone inside. I'll announce myself when I get back and I can let myself in. Do you understand?"

Bailey just stood there staring at the gun in her hand. Had Rowdy lost his mind?

"Bailey?" Rowdy said more forcefully, he didn't have time for this. He needed to know she was going to be okay. Then, he needed to get up to the house and take care of Maggie.

Bailey jumped then looked up. Rowdy was staring at her like she was the crazy one. She nodded, then lowered herself back onto the couch. Knight moved to her side and Bailey reached down and gripped the dog with all her might. Forget the stupid gun, she had a vicious police dog for protection.

"Okay then." Rowdy moved to his gun safe and quickly spun the knob. Moments later he pulled out his pride and joy: a Remington 700 with a Nightforce scope. It was perfect for Coop because his brother owned the exact same weapon. They each had a floating bull barrel and Harris bi-pods. Coop had dialed it in himself. The two pound hair trigger was perfect for their current mission. Now he just needed to convince his brother to set up in the woods while Rowdy cleared the house. He walked forward and set the weapon on the kitchen table next to Coop.

Mount Haven

"No," Coop said and tried to turn away. He couldn't do it. He couldn't leave his wife's fate in someone else's hands, not even his brother's.

"You know this is how it has to be, Andy," Rowdy rarely used his brother's given name but he needed to get his attention. "If we are going to get through this, I need your sniper skills and you need my stealth."

Coop studied his brother. He knew Rowdy was right, but knowing and doing were two entirely different things. Waiting outside while Maggie was trapped inside their house was going to kill him. Pain radiated through his body and he wanted to reject Rowdy's plan completely. But he couldn't, because he knew deep in his gut this was the only way. He nodded once, retrieved the weapon and silently exited the house. He'd wait on the porch. Right now, he couldn't breathe, the air inside this house was stifling.

Rowdy moved to his safe and pulled out two handguns and a holster. He silently undid his belt and slid the loop through, then secured the buckle again. Next, he placed one gun in the holster and slid the second weapon behind his back and tucked it into his pants. After grabbing two additional magazines he closed the door and secured the lock. He glanced one last time at Bailey then followed his brother out the door.

* * * *

Flint Duvall stood behind the trees and watched the house carefully. Given enough time, he could determine exactly where the woman was. But he didn't have time. No, his boss... the know-it-all Cole Hughes, had insisted the hit had to occur at precisely one o'clock. That gave his team little time to scout the area before going in. He hated this kind of mission. He hated it when Cole or Reese thought they knew best. If the two spoiled rich kids would just let him do his damn job there would be fewer messes to clean up.

Flint had received the call the previous evening. He'd been frustrated to learn the two of them had tried to grab Victoria on their own. Now the locals knew them. They knew who they were and it was cleanup time. Life would have been so much easier if the dynamic duo had just called him the moment they spotted the chick. He could have brought out his team, snagged the brat and they would all be home now, enjoying the perfect San Diego sun.

Flint lowered his binoculars, turned to Lars and motioned for his right-hand man to move out. He watched calmly as Sanders followed silently behind. Noah and Terk waited patiently for their signal. The five of them had done this a million times. It was like a well-oiled machine. Flint almost felt bad about the exorbitant bill he was going to send Cole. He probably could have done this with three men, but he thought it would be good training for the crew. Seriously, what could happen with a bunch of bumbling, small-town rednecks? He moved further into the shadows and nodded to Noah. *Time to move out, boys*. The party was about to begin.

* * * *

Maggie glanced out the window again and chewed on her bottom lip. She was sure she had seen movement out by the stables. But that was ridiculous. Coop stopped in at Rowdy's then headed off to work. Rowdy wouldn't be outside, he was diligently taking care of Bailey and Bryan was at Randy Babcock's spending the night. So why was her gut telling her someone was out there? She

Mount Haven

silently crept up the stairs and slid into her bedroom. Coop kept a 9mm in the nightstand. She was careful to stay clear of the window as she crouched beside the bed and released the safety. Her heart was beating a mile a minute and she was having a hard time breathing. She had never been this scared in her life. She hoped she was being paranoid, that the attack on Bailey was making her nervous. But Maggie had never been one to jump at shadows and she was going to trust her instincts.

Her heart practically leapt from her chest when her cellphone began to chime. It was Coop, her body instantly relaxed. She'd just tell Coop what was up and he'd come straight home. Everything was going to be fine now. "Hello?" she whispered then chastised herself. Coop was going to panic if she didn't get a grip.

"Maggie!" Coop let out a relieved breath. At least she was okay. "Where are you?"

"I'm at home, what's wrong?" Maggie was instantly on alert, her troubles forgotten.

"I know that, baby, but where are you in the house?" Cooper persisted.

"Oh, well…" how was she going to break this to him? "Um…Andy, I think I saw someone outside. It scared me. I'm up in the bedroom. Don't laugh at me, but I felt safer up here. I have the gun. Can you please come home?"

"I'm here sweetheart," Coop said feeling a little better about the situation. If Maggie was in the bedroom, she'd be fine. Rowdy could go in, get her out and they could bring her back to his place. The women would be safe and secure. And until those maniacs were caught, he was not letting his family out of his sight again.

"What do you mean?" Maggie nearly moved to the window to look out but realized if Coop were here she'd never see him. Her man was a former sniper. Had her fears been valid? Was someone after her? "What's going on, Andy?"

"We think the men that tried to kidnap Bailey are here, in our yard somewhere. Rowdy and I are on it. Don't panic baby, I'm going to make sure you're safe. Everything is going to be okay." Coop just hoped he could make good on that promise.

"What about Bryan?" Maggie said, suddenly terrified for her son.

"Matthew is on his way over to pick him up. I told him to take him to the station and keep him busy until I take care of this." Coop was still second guessing himself on that one. Cole and Reese claimed they were heading to the station. In light of their current situation Coop doubted they would really show but if they did, he didn't want them anywhere near Bryan.

"Okay," Maggie let out a calming breath. If Bryan was headed to the station, he'd be safe. Her eyes grew wide when she heard the distinct sound of footsteps on the stairs. "Coop, someone is in the house," she whispered. "The stairs are creaking."

"Don't panic, Mags. Rowdy is on it. If there's someone in the house, Rowdy is there too. Somewhere. Just stay where you are and if anyone steps foot in that room, shoot. Rowdy won't come in without giving your some kind of warning. Shoot first and don't hesitate. Do you hear me honey, do not hesitate."

Maggie gulped audibly. "Okay," she finally whispered then froze. She could hear someone fidgeting outside her door. She pushed a button to disconnect the call. That last thing she or her husband needed was to deal with the phone. She silenced the ringer before slipping it onto the nightstand. She knew Coop was right, Rowdy would not enter the room without warning her first. She braced the gun on the mattress and waited. Her hands were shaking and she wasn't sure if she could hit her mark, but she would go down fighting. Her hand tightened against the grip when the doorknob began to turn.

* * * *

Rowdy followed the intruder into Coop's house. He was careful to stay several steps behind, wanting to maintain the element of surprise. So far, the guy didn't know he was being stalked. Rowdy was determined to keep it that way. Stupid criminals. He was free game now that he'd stepped inside. Whatever happened, Rowdy was justified. And the rules for a citizen were far more lenient than they were for a cop.

Once Rowdy made his way down the hallway he peeked around the wall into the foyer. The guy was nearly at the top of the stairs. Where was Maggie? Rowdy's mind was racing. Where would Maggie go if she felt threatened? Her bedroom! Coop always kept a gun close by and Maggie knew that. He took one more look up the stairs then silently moved to the landing. He knew each and every creak from sneaking up on Bryan. He wouldn't have any trouble avoiding each one. He was three quarters of the way to the top when he heard the gunshot.

Rowdy bolted forward, no longer caring if the guy heard him coming. He was focused down the hall as he came to the top of the stairway and realized the guy was still standing. Who fired the shot? Didn't matter. He ran for the bedroom then stopped when the guy slowly turned around and raised his weapon. Rowdy shot first and hit the intruder square in the chest. The guy went down but raised the gun again the minute he hit the floor. Rowdy fired a second shot into his heart and the man collapsed. Rowdy had no doubts. The man was dead. He stopped outside the door and called inside, "Magpie, it's Rowdy. I'm coming in. Please, don't shoot me, okay?" No answer, the only thing Rowdy could hear was Maggie's sobbing. "Mags, honey? I need you to answer me. I need to know you're not in shock. Please, I really need to come inside."

Maggie realized it was Rowdy calling and jumped to her feet. She vaulted over the bed and darted to the open doorway, leaping over the dead body. The instant she landed, her body collided with Rowdy's hard chest. She couldn't help it, she crumpled into him sobbing uncontrollably. Had she killed that man? She didn't think so, but she'd been too scared to look up after she fired the gun. Had there been more gunfire? She jumped back, afraid of what she might find. Had Rowdy been shot again? Was it her fault this time?

Rowdy placed his hands on Maggie's shoulders and gently turned her around. He needed to get her away from that body. He needed to get her out of this house. But he wasn't sure it was safe, yet. There was at least one other suspect skulking around outside. Hopefully, Coop would stay put. But Rowdy knew he couldn't count on that. The minute his brother heard gunfire, he'd be heading inside. Rowdy supported Maggie as they descended the stairs. Then he maneuvered her inside the large study and pushed her onto the couch. She went willingly, which told Rowdy she was not herself. He crouched down in front of her and gently took her hands in his. "You're okay, Maggie."

"Did I kill him?" she blurted.

"No," Rowdy said soberly. "I did."

Mount Haven

Maggie finally snapped out of it. She needed to make sure Rowdy was okay. She was positive now, she'd heard more than one shot. She frantically began running her hands over Rowdy's arms and chest.

Rowdy laughed. "Maggie Cooper, I am flattered, really I am, but I'd prefer your brother not walk in on you fondling me that way. One of these days he's going to get suspicious."

Maggie grinned then jumped at the sound of gunfire.

Rowdy leapt to his feet and turned to leave, then turned back and gently placed the pistol back in Maggie's hand. "Use it if you need to." Then, he ran for the door.

* * * *

Cooper waited as long as he possibly could but he was going out of his mind. Gunfire in the house most likely meant Rowdy had neutralized the threat. But what if he was wrong? What if the guy had made it to Maggie? He couldn't stand not knowing. Cooper hooked the rifle over his shoulder and moved to the right planning to slide silently from the tree. That's when he saw the second man. The guy was good and he was making his way quickly to the side door of Coop's house. At that very moment, he heard the sound of a gun to his rear. Two threats, then. Could this day get any worse?

Coop took a steadying breath and raised his rifle. He was about to pull the trigger when the man crumpled to the ground. He glanced around and spotted Rowdy. His brother must have seen the intruder and silently gotten into position without either of them knowing it. Cooper jumped from his perch and carefully made his way to the front of the house.

"Was that you?" Rowdy wanted to know. "The gunshot? It sounded like a handgun not a rifle. Was that you?"

"No," Coop admitted as he glanced nervously around them. They needed to get inside, out of the open. He was about to point that out to Rowdy when they both heard the distinctive sound of Knight's angry bark. Then a low growl echoed through the trees and Rowdy took off at a dead run.

* * * *

Matthew hung up the phone and moved to stand next to Mariah. He didn't want to leave her here, but he didn't have a choice. He stood in front of her desk for several seconds before he decided. "I have to pick up Bryan from the Babcocks'."

"Okay," Mariah said absently then looked up and frowned. "What's wrong?"

"I want you to lock the door and don't let anyone in until I get back. I'm going to call Derek and tell him to come into the office but do not open that door for anyone. Promise me you'll listen," Matthew demanded.

"What's going on?" Mariah asked again. "Does this have something to do with those men that tried to abduct the waitress?"

"Yes, Mariah. Promise me," Matthew persisted.

"Okay, fine. I'll lock the door and I won't let anyone inside until Derek gets here. But those two men said they were headed over to meet up with Coop. What do I do if they start banging on the door?"

"Ignore them," Matthew said, slipping into his jacket and heading for the back entrance.

"That's rude," Mariah countered. "And I'm pretty sure it's extremely bad customer service."

Matthew stopped in his tracks and turned to face his girlfriend. He pivoted and returned to her desk, then leaned down and kissed her soundly. "Promise me," he said again as he pulled back and studied her face. "Just please do this for me. I can't go retrieve Bryan unless I know you're safe. Coop is frantic, I can't wait or I would. Please just listen to me for once without arguing."

Mariah nodded. She rarely saw Matt this riled and it was scaring her. "I promise." She watched as the man she loved disappeared into the back hallway. Then waited, listening for the thud of the door before she stood and moved to the front door. She had just reached out to secure the lock, when the door swung open and two men stepped in. Mariah barely stifled a scream. Matthew was going to be so angry with her. She glanced through the window and helplessly watched as the love of her life disappeared down the deserted roadway. Mariah steadied her nerves and turned to deal with the terrifying men. She would not give in to her fears. "Can I help you two?" she hoped she sounded better than she felt. "I was just about to close up so you'll need to make this quick."

Cole glanced at Reese in confusion. They were supposed to be meeting the Sheriff. After the message he'd left, no law man would be able to resist. "We have a meeting with Sheriff Cooper.

There must be some mistake. I was very clear that I needed to speak with Sheriff Cooper at one o'clock today." Reese gave the woman his most menacing smile. She was already nervous, increasing her discomfort wouldn't take much effort. And Reese was all about results with very little effort.

"I'm sorry, Sheriff Cooper had to run out to the old Stoddard place. It was an emergency. Why don't you just leave your number and I'll have him give you a call when he gets back in." Mariah was scrambling for something to say that would get these men out of her office.

"I'm afraid that won't work. We simply need to speak with him today. I assume he'll be back once he finishes with this... Stoddard fellow?" Cole stepped in. If he didn't do something, Reese was going to give the poor girl a heart attack.

"Uh, yeah. I believe so." Mariah stepped backwards and slowly slid behind her desk. "Why don't I just call him and see how far out he is? That should give you an idea of how long a wait you might have."

"Sure," Cole relaxed. "Why don't you do that? In the meantime, maybe we could have a cup of coffee?"

"Oh, sorry." Mariah blushed. Not a real blush, but her cheeks were on fire because she was so distraught. They didn't need to know that. She had to think fast. If she gave them coffee, maybe she could get more evidence. Coop had said they had blood, but how many times had she seen detectives collect saliva off coffee cups? She could do this. And... if she labeled the cups and gave them to the right man, she could point out which DNA came from which man. She casually reached down and flipped a switch. Now was as good as time as any to test out that fancy camera system Coop had installed. Once she was positive the thing was recording, she rushed to the kitchen and pulled a black mug and a blue mug from the small dishwasher. Steam rose quickly, hitting her square in the face but she ignored it and brushed the now damp tendrils of hair from her eyes. She had to focus on the task at hand. Now, she would just need to mark them somehow. She peeked her head out of the small room and called around the corner. "Do you both want cream and sugar?"

"Cream and one sugar for me," Cole said with a slight grin when he noticed the scowl on his friend's face. "And my friend here likes his black."

Mariah relaxed. This would be easy. She'd just give the black mug to the guy who wanted his straight and the blue one to the cocky flirty one. Once she handed them the coffee, she'd call Matt and let him know what was going on. Blue was doctored and black was black. Easy enough. Within seconds she had the coffee ready and returned to the room. Now she just needed to make notes and later she could identify which man had which mug. She handed the cups to their rightful owners and waited. The friendlier guy took a sip and smiled. The grumpy man set his on the table and stared. Oh yeah, she was supposed to be making a call.

Mariah moved to her desk and dialed Matthew's cellphone. He answered on the second ring.

"What's wrong?" he sounded almost panicked.

"Hi, Sheriff Cooper," Maggie said immediately. She needed to alert Matthew that something was wrong. "I have two men here that say you have an appointment today at one. They got pretty lucky. I was just locking the doors when they burst inside." She listened to Matt's frantic instructions.

"Okay, I'll let them know you're a ways out. Maybe they could reschedule." She glanced at the two men and frowned. The friendly one was shaking his head adamantly. The other one was studying her with such intensity she almost dropped her phone. "Uh… looks like they can't reschedule, sir."

"Mariah, I called Derek. He's on his way over and should be there any minute. If you can just stall them until he gets there, we can lock them up for good. I'm just pulling up to Babcock's now. I need to go. We have no idea what I'm walking into here. Be careful and don't do anything rash until Derek gets there." Matthew disconnected and glanced at the ranch house owned by the Babcock family. They had seven kids and a thousand acres. Only one of the older siblings still lived at home. He'd moved back shortly after his new wife got pregnant. That was at least four years ago. For some reason he stayed, probably being groomed to take over someday. Their home was situated on the back end of Mount Haven. The chance of anyone lurking around, up to no good was about a million to one, but Matt would gather up the kid and get back to the station as requested. He was worried about his girl. This sleepy town was getting crazy and he wasn't sure he liked it.

Bryan glanced out the window and saw Matthew. His stomach clenched and he couldn't breathe. Had something happened to his family? Not again, he knew something bad happened last night, but the grownups weren't talking and Randy's mom was acting weird. She freaked out when they wanted to go to the barn. Was that phone call a minute ago something about him? He slowly walked to the front door, swung it open then stepped onto the porch. Matt was just climbing from his car when Bryan saw the man. "Matt, watch out!"

Matt spun around just in time to see the old hatchet and ducked. The weapon hit the vehicle with so much force, it lodged in the panel and wouldn't budge. Matt took advantage as the man pulled and prodded unsuccessfully. He rammed the aggressor in the stomach, catching him off guard and catapulting him backwards. The two of them landed on the hard ground with a thud. The wind was momentarily knocked from Matt's lungs, but he ignored it. He was fighting for his life and he couldn't be distracted. He just hoped Bryan went back in the house where it was safe. He risked a glance just as Michelle and her husband stepped onto the porch. The woman pulled Bryan inside, and Grant stepped forward cautiously and looked around.

Matt rolled to the side and pushed himself to his knees when the man tried to wrap his large hands around the officer's neck. This guy was not playing around. He was definitely going in a cage for assault on a PO. Matt jumped to his feet then kicked out and landed a blow to the man's torso. The guy went down again and Matt moved quickly behind him. He had his cuffs out and one of the guy's hands secured when the man swung his arm in an attempt to strike Matt on the side of the face. Grant was there in an instant. He grabbed the man's arm and twisted it behind his back. The rancher had five boys plus his grandson inside. It was a move he'd perfected years ago when the kids got a little too hot headed.

Matt slid the cuffs into place then tugged hard, forcing the man to stand. He pushed the guy forward and walked him to the back of his vehicle. There was no way he was going to transport Bryan to the station now. Once he had the guy secured, he turned back to the Babcocks. "Coop sent me out to pick up Bryan, but in light of everything I'm not comfortable transporting him now. Would you mind if I left him here with you? If you say yes, I'm afraid I'll need you to stand watch until someone can get back here for the kid."

"Don't you worry, son," Grant Babcock assured him. "Nobody's gonna hurt this boy while he's in my home. I can guarantee that." He nodded to the guy in the back of the patrol car. "Take care of the trash, I've got this. Just let Andy and Maggie know we still have him. He's in good hands. Steve should be home any minute and the rest of the boys are heading home for a visit. I've got reinforcements and the whole town knows what happens when you mess with the Babcocks."

Matt hesitated then nodded. Grant was right; with the kids at home, Bryan would be safe. The locals might know not to mess with the family, but this man was a stranger and Matt was positive he had something to do with the men that tried to kidnap Bailey. These guys were oblivious when it came to their town. That was proving both good and bad. He gave Grant one more nod then slipped behind the wheel and headed back to the precinct. The instant the car was in motion, his thoughts turned back to Mariah. He really hoped Derek had arrived and they were both okay. Matt stepped on the pedal a little harder, anxious to see that his woman was okay.

* * * *

Bailey sat horrified in the corner of the room. She was so terrified she didn't dare move. She had a death grip on Knight's soft fur when she heard the distinctive sound of glass shattering. Bailey covered her mouth to prevent the scream from escaping. She glanced at her side and studied the gun. Could she pull the trigger if she needed to? If not, she should just hide the thing to make sure the intruder didn't see it. She picked up the weapon and gripped it tightly. Knight began to growl. Bailey tried to maintain her grip on the dog, but Knight was too strong. He lunged forward and leapt in the air just as a large man stepped in the room. Knight sunk his teeth in the guy's shoulder and dragged him toward the door. Bailey watched fascinated as the dog she always considered gentle, released his hold then attacked again.

Knight released his target then waited. The man, thinking he was free, climbed to his feet. Knight growled again and leaned forward, prepared to attack again if necessary. Terk grabbed a table and tossed it at the dog, then ran. Bailey continued to watch as Knight gave chase. She heard them leave the cabin but still couldn't bring herself to move.

Terk jumped through the window, desperate to escape the dog. The boss hadn't said anything about vicious attack dogs. They were not prepared for this mission. Maybe after this fiasco Flint would listen. How many times had they begged him to rein those two idiots in? Just because they had money didn't mean they knew the first thing about security. Terk reached the forested area and reached for a large branch. If he could just get up high enough, he could shoot the mangy mutt and be done with it. He reached into his boot holster and pulled out a Glock. Bad move. The dog lunged and sunk his teeth into Terk's right thigh. Terk dropped the gun and screamed. The pain was unbearable. He had to get away from Cujo. He kicked out and the dog released his leg but then dove right back in. Terk was bleeding profusely. He had to get to his gun. He tried to fight back, but it was no use. Finally, his fingers touched the tip of the weapon and hope flooded him for a mere instant. He pushed backwards and gripped the pistol in his right hand. He was about to swing it around and shoot the beast between the eyes when the dog chomped down on Terk's wrist. The gun went off and fell to the ground. Terk's last thought was of his son. He wasn't much of a father, but if he died, the kid would be alone with his psycho mother. He had to hang on for the kid. He needed to teach him the ropes. He needed to teach him how to fight and shoot. He had so much he needed to teach him. That was Terk's last thought before his world went black.

Rowdy shot through the trees and came to an abrupt stop. Knight was in attack mode. One wrong move and Rowdy could get bitten. He slowed his pace and began giving commands. Knight relaxed and sat, never taking his eyes of the suspect. Rowdy approached and patted Knight's head. The dog was well trained even if he was retired. He glanced at the man lying motionless on the ground. The first thing he noticed was the gun. He had to move it just in case. He was about to kick the weapon to the side when Knight twisted to the side and let out a low, menacing growl. Rowdy knew that sound. He had a visitor.

Flint couldn't believe what was happening. He watched, horrified as the dog attacked his man time and time again. He pulled his gun, thinking he could get a good shot but immediately froze when a large man stepped into the forest. It was obviously the dog's owner. The dog relaxed and allowed the guy to pet his head. Flint shifted and took a step forward. The dog turned and began to growl. He was staring right at Flint. Now what? He had no idea where the rest of his crew was. This time, he was on his own.

Rowdy surveyed the area and spotted the perp. He was behind a large tree, probably thought he was hidden from view. Not from Rowdy, and certainly not from his dog. Knight took another step forward and let out a deep, threatening growl. The man ignored it. "I suggest you drop your weapon and step out in the open where I can see you. The dog is trained well and you don't stand a chance."

Flint debated. He could try to escape but the dog was certain to catch him. The car was on the other side of the property. If he pretended to surrender it might give him the advantage he needed to shoot the dog and then take out the man. He had no idea who

Mount Haven

Victoria had hooked up with, but they were not your typical backwoods hillbillies. "I'm coming out," Flint called. He took an exaggerated step to the side and dropped his handgun. He didn't need it, he had another one. Then he held his hands to the side as he slowly walked forward.

Rowdy watched as the man cautiously narrowed the gap between them. He was doing and saying all the right things, but Rowdy didn't trust him. He glanced at Knight and realized his dog didn't trust him either. Knight was on alert, his hair was standing on end and his body was leaning forward, posed to move at the slightest provocation. Rowdy turned back to the man and realized he had moved more quickly than Rowdy had expected. Just another indication the man was up to no good. Rowdy waited, anticipating something, but not knowing for sure what the guy was planning. The instant the man was within striking distance, he reached to his back and pulled a gun. He had Knight in his sites within seconds. Rowdy reacted. He tackled the man, knocking the gun free. Knight moved forward and sunk his teeth into the man's ankle. The fight was on.

Noah slid further into the thick trees and waited. He couldn't believe what he'd witnessed back there. Terk was supposed to get in, grab the girl and get out. Nobody mentioned a trained dog. He paused to listen and heard a noise. Flint had to be back here somewhere. He had no idea where the rest of the team got off to, but Terk's lifeless body was a mangled mess a few yards back. Noah swallowed and stopped, glancing around again. Men he could handle, that dog was a completely different story. It was like it was trained to attack. That thought made Noah freeze in place. That's exactly what had struck him as odd about that dog. It had to be a retired police dog. Why hadn't they thought of that? It would make sense for the local Sheriff to take in a dog once it was retired and could no longer work. But that dog had no problem working. Maybe it was an age thing. It could be that the department retired their dogs when they reached a certain age. Noah didn't really care why they had the dog on this ranch. He only cared that they did. But more importantly, he cared about avoiding the thing at all cost.

As Noah pushed forward he had a thought. He should get up high in a tree and survey the area. He could spot Flint, even if the guy was trying to hide. His boss was the best at some things, but hiding was not one of them. As soon as Noah spotted the old spruce, he prepared to scale the large trunk. Moments later he was settled securely on a sturdy branch. He pulled out his scope and began to methodically search his surroundings. Before long, he spotted his boss. The guy was wrestling around on the ground with another man. Noah set up for the shot. It was a little long, but not that difficult. He'd just need to make sure he didn't take out Flint instead of their adversary. There was no lie on the planet that could explain a dead Flint to Cole or Reese. Noah saw movement to the side of the two men and shifted his scope to investigate. The dog. And he had a clear shot. He balanced his weapon on an upper branch and dialed it in. He'd only get one chance at this and he couldn't mess it up.

* * * *

Coop glanced at Maggie then back to the window. Where was Rowdy? He was positive he'd heard a shot and his brother's absence was making him nervous. He had to do something. He slung the rifle over his shoulder and approached his wife. "Maggie, honey?" He waited, but she didn't respond. "Baby? I have to go upstairs. I know it's hard, but I need you to come with me."

Mount Haven

"But…" Maggie looked at Coop, panicked at the thought of going anywhere near that dead body.

"I know," Coop moved to stand next to her, then crouched down so he could look her in the eye. "But Rowdy is out there and I'm worried. I need to set up and make sure he's okay. I can't leave you alone. Please, trust me? Just hold my hand and don't look at it. We'll go into the guest room and shut the door."

Maggie swallowed hard then pushed to her feet. Andy was right. Rowdy had been gone a long time. They needed to check on him. She slid her hand into her husband's for support and followed him up the stairs. The instant they reached the top, she moved behind him and pressed her forehead into his back. She really did not want to see that man… that scary, evil man again.

Coop used his body to shield his wife from the carnage on the floor then pushed open the door to the spare room and gently guided her inside. He pulled the door shut and rushed to the window. After sliding it open, he gently removed the screen and set it to the side. Then he glanced around looking for something to set up on. He decided the dresser was a little taller than he preferred, but it would do. Moments later he had the dresser in place and his rifle set up to his satisfaction. He kneeled in front of the window and slowly scanned the horizon.

"How can I help?" Maggie asked, moving to stand next to her husband. "I know you told me when you were on SWAT, you had a spotter. Can I help with that?"

Coop glanced over his shoulder and studied his wife for several seconds. Once he decided she wasn't in shock, he pointed to a black bag he'd retrieved from his trunk. "Grab the binoculars out of there and help me search."

Maggie rushed to the bag and pulled out an expensive set of binoculars. She moved back to the window and positioned herself behind and slightly to the side of her husband. As she placed the lenses against her eyes, she was amazed at the clarity and magnification. Cops had the best toys! She started at the cabin and realized a window had been broken out on the side of the building. Where in the house did that window lead? The main section, most likely the kitchen. "Coop, someone broke into Rowdy's house. The window is broken out completely."

"Can you see any movement? Look in the trees, around every corner, in the bushes, anywhere a person could hide."

"I can't see anyone," she admitted, then slowly continued her survey down the trail and into the forest. As she fanned out, towards the lake, she saw movement. "Coop?"

"What?" clearly Maggie had spotted something.

Maggie silently scrutinized the area and realized what she was seeing was Knight. "Knight is out there. He's about a hundred yards from the east side of the lake. In the forest. Can you see him?"

Coop made sure he had his bearings and then slowly shifted his lens to the area Maggie was describing. The first thing he saw was Rowdy on the ground with a man. They were wrestling and fighting, but Coop couldn't see a weapon. He didn't like it, but it wasn't life threatening so he moved on. A second later he spotted Knight. The dog was alert, clearly agitated but he wasn't moving in to attack the stranger. Rowdy must have given him a command to stay. Knight wouldn't move unless he deemed the situation dire enough to disobey. He stood, moving away from the scope when movement in the far trees caught his attention. He knelt back down and trained his scope on the foliage where the activity occurred. It took him several seconds but Cooper found the sniper. The man was hiding in the trees and he had a high powered rifle trained on Rowdy and the suspect. Coop shifted and dialed in the rifle to account for the distance then slowly moved his finger towards the trigger. Just when he was about to fire, the man shifted and aimed the gun at Knight.

Coop didn't hesitate. Rowdy needed Knight for backup and anyway the dog was family. He was Rowdy's partner and he was completely oblivious to the danger. If Coop didn't remove the threat, once the dog was dead, the sniper would shift his attention to Rowdy. There was no other option, the man had to be neutralized. Coop adjusted, took a deep breath and slowly squeezed the trigger. The rifle bucked as the bullet exploded from the muzzle and traveled a true and accurate trajectory, striking the target dead center. The man instantly fell from the tree and landed with what Coop assumed was a loud thud. He couldn't hear the impact, but both Rowdy and his attacker jumped and focused their attention in the direction the man had been hiding. Coop was about to run outside, to assist Rowdy, when he remembered Maggie was standing beside him. He glanced up, expecting fear or shock, maybe even rejection. She knew what he did, but he didn't like the fact that she had just witnessed him killing a man. All he saw was determination and acceptance. His heart swelled and he remembered why he loved that woman so much. She got him. She understood him in a way nobody else ever could. He reached out and pulled her against his chest for several seconds before he gently pushed her backwards.

"We need to get to the cabin," Maggie said in such a calm tone, Coop did a double take.

"Uh... I was planning on heading out to help Rowdy," Cooper said shaking his head. Why did she want to go to the cabin?

"Bailey is alone out there. She's vulnerable. And she was probably the intended target. I think we need to get to her before you head out. I can stay with her and you can go make sure Rowdy is okay. He has Knight with him. The dog won't let anything happen to him, right?"

Cooper debated but finally decided Maggie was right. They did need to get to Bailey. "Okay," he said taking her hand as he once again slung the rifle over his shoulder. Maggie leaned over to grab the discarded backpack. Good thinking, they might need some of the supplies he kept inside. The two of them walked silently down the stairs and out the front door. Coop was on alert the entire time, but he was sure if there was another man in the area, he would have seen him. They rushed to his police cruiser and climbed inside. Coop floored it, peeling out and throwing gravel in all directions as he hustled to Rowdy's home next door.

* * * *

Matt pulled the car to the back of the station and immediately yanked his prisoner from the back seat. He entered the sally port and shoved the guy into a cell. He really didn't care who he was or why he was involved. Booking the scumbag would have to wait. He slid the door shut, careful to listen for the clink of the lock dropping into place, then headed for the front office.

Mariah was trying to hold it together. Derek was here now and the two evil men were long gone. She'd failed. They'd left before Derek arrived. Was Matt going to be angry with her? She wasn't sure she could take one of his lectures right now, her nerves were a frazzled mess at the moment. She was a secretary and dispatcher. She should not have to entertain kidnappers.

Mount Haven

Matt took one look at Mariah's face and knew she was not okay. He glanced around the office and spotted Derek. His friend had his feet on the desk as he casually scrolled through a biker magazine. Matt shook his head; the guy could relax anywhere. He glanced back at Mariah then frowned when she burst into tears. "I thought you were going to take care of my girl," he challenged Derek. A confrontation with his partner he could handle, tears... well, they just scared him.

Derek glanced over the top of his magazine, then shifted his attention to Mariah. When he looked back at Matt he was grinning. "She was fine before you arrived. I can't say I blame her. Looking at your ugly mug is enough to frighten any woman. You probably give small children nightmares."

Matt scowled, then waived his middle finger at Derek as he proceeded to cross the room. When he reached Mariah, he gently pulled her into his arms. "Shhh, babe, it's okay. Tell me what happened."

Mariah sniffled then pressed her head against Matt's shoulder. She finally felt safe again. "I tried to keep them occupied but I must have said something that spooked them. They had almost finished their coffee when suddenly the friendly one looked at his colleague with scary intensity. Then he announced they couldn't wait any longer and told me to tell the Sheriff they'd touch base with him later." She glanced at Matt, took a deep soothing breath then continued. "I don't know what happened. They just rushed out the door and sped away. A couple minutes later Derek arrived, but they were long gone."

"I checked, no sign of where they headed. There are skid marks out front but after they hit the stop sign I have no idea which direction they turned. I was coming from the south so their route took them either East or West."

Matt looked at his friend, then returned his attention to Mariah. He took her hand and pulled her to her feet as he pivoted toward the back door. "We're leaving," he said absently to his fellow cop. "The office is yours until five or until Coop gets back and tells you otherwise."

Derek glanced over his magazine then turned the page. He'd been expecting as much. The woman was a stressed out mess. Derek didn't mind. He'd just add it to Matt's tab. One day he'd need a favor and there was no doubt Derek would cash in. For now, he'd read about Harleys.

* * * *

Rowdy wasn't sure who was winning the fight. He knew if he called Knight over, the dog would get control of the situation fairly quickly. But the man had a large hunting knife and he obviously knew how to use it. Rowdy hesitated, Knight was rusty and if the man got in a good swipe, his dog would be severely injured if not killed. Rowdy wasn't willing to chance it. The situation hadn't risen to that level yet. But if he didn't get control soon, Knight would attack to save his master. Rowdy focused on the suspect. The man was severely wounded, bleeding from his nose, his mouth and a cut on the side of his face. His foot was most likely broken but yet, he still wouldn't give up. What in the world was driving him to such lengths? Rowdy loosened his grip and pivoted in an attempt to knock the man off balance. It worked, but at the last minute, the guy reached out and pulled Rowdy onto the ground with him.

Mount Haven

Moments later, Rowdy regretted his confidence. He was lying on his back, looking into the cold dead eyes of a killer. Rowdy bucked upwards in an attempt to throw the man to the side. It worked, partially. The two of them were on their sides now. Rowdy punched the man in the face. Once again, blood spurted from his nose, but the guy kept fighting. He punched Rowdy in the gut then tried to knee him in Rowdy's bad leg. Rowdy saw it coming and was able to dodge just enough to prevent a solid blow. The man shifted and adjusted his knife grip so it would have the deadliest impact. If Rowdy didn't get control of the situation soon, he was going to be dead. He glanced at Knight and smiled inwardly as his dog took a calculated step forward. With each passing second, Knight was getting closer. Rowdy didn't have a lot of time left before his partner moved in and joined the fight. Rowdy jerked and focused on the dark forest when the distinct sound of a rifle shot echoed from the distance. It was followed by a loud thud. Rowdy braced for the attack. Knight would never idly stand by once gun fire erupted.

Knight flew through the air and sunk his teeth into the man's upper thigh. As the guy tried to swing around to plunge his knife into Knight, Rowdy slid the gun from his pocket and fired. The man instantly dropped the knife and fell to the ground. Knight released his hold and took a step back, assuming the guard position. Rowdy pushed to his knees and closed his eyes. He gave Knight the command to stand down. The dog stood and ran to his master. Rowdy rubbed Knight's head and considered. His dad always told him that a good cop has instincts. Some kind of sixth sense that he never ignored. After today, Rowdy was a believer. He'd slid that gun down the back of his pants, intending to leave it there until he needed it. His shirt and his jacket would cover the evidence and he always carried a backup. He had only stepped a few paces into the trees when an intense feeling overcame him. He hadn't even thought about it. He just pulled the pistol from the waist of his pants and secured it in his jacket pocket, zipping the thing closed so the gun couldn't fall out. If he hadn't moved the weapon, it would have surely been lost in the fight. Or worse, the other guy would have found it and shot Rowdy with his own gun. A calming feeling settled over him and he wondered for just a minute, if his dad had been with him today. He shook his head and stood, determined to check on Bailey.

Rowdy heard a twig snapping in the distance and he stepped in front of Knight. If another perp was in the forest he was doomed. His only hope was to hide Knight's existence until the last minute, then send in the dog. He was about to give the command when he recognized his brother. "You know, I almost sent Knight in after you."

Coop shrugged. "That dog wouldn't bite me, not even on your command. I feed him the good stuff, remember? You... from you he gets dry dog food. Knight knows where his loyalty lies and I'm confident he would never, ever, take a chunk out of my hide."

"Is it over?" Rowdy asked soberly. He just couldn't bring himself to joke at the moment. He'd killed three men today. He hadn't had a choice, but he had still killed three men. It had been over a year since his last kill and he still wasn't completely over that one. He took a deep breath and waited for Coop's answer.

Coop nodded then placed an arm around his brother. "We didn't have a choice, kid."

"I know," Rowdy sighed. "But that doesn't make it any more pleasant to swallow."

"I have to call Sheriff Dalton in," Coop also sighed.

"I get that. It would look bad if my brother investigated a shooting at his own house where I killed three men." Rowdy didn't want Coop to feel bad about following procedure.

"That, and Knight killed a fourth guy, severed his artery and the guy bled out. Then the kicker, I killed the sniper set up in the tree. I know you heard him hit the ground." Coop ran his hand through his hair in frustration. "What the hell, Rowdy?"

Rowdy studied his brother. He had heard the thud and at the time he knew it had to be a man but it hadn't registered that Coop had to kill today, too. "Five men dead, and for what? They didn't get Maggie or Bryan." Rowdy looked at Cooper in shocked silence, asking the question without actually voicing his concern.

"Naw," Coop assured him. "I sent Matthew out to pick him up. Instead, he arrested a sixth guy. I don't know how much he'll be able to tell us but when we're done here I plan to have a little chat with Bryan's would-be abductor. I'm hoping he can shed some light on the master plan. And if we're lucky he can tell us where those two monsters are staying."

They had reached the cottage and as the two brothers ascended the stairs Maggie and Bailey rushed outside. Maggie was still holding the small .38 that Rowdy had given to Bailey for protection before setting out to hunt the men that were hunting them. He grinned as he remembered Hemingway's analogy. There was no hunting like the hunting of man. And, he had hunted armed men long enough to understand why men like him never cared for anything else.

* * * *

Hours later the bodies had been removed from the Cooper Ranch, the women had showered and the small group was headed into town for dinner. After the day they had, a little TLC was exactly what the doctor ordered. Coop kept glancing at Maggie and Bryan, but so far the two of them were holding up just fine. The last thing he wanted was for Maggie to start having nightmares again or Bryan to solve his problems with violence. His family needed this night out to feel normal again.

"Derek and Matthew said they would board up the window at my place and a friend of theirs will clean up the mess upstairs at your place while we're gone. He assured me we wouldn't even know anything happened today. Not from the evidence or destruction, anyhow," Rowdy told the car but didn't expect a response.

"We'll have a nice steak dinner maybe a little dancing with my beautiful lady and then life can get back to normal," Coop added as he subtly checked the review for anything suspicious then locked eyes with Rowdy, knowing his brother had just done the same. They may be trying to act normal, but the Cooper brothers were always cautious

Bryan groaned. He knew if there was dancing, his mom was going to make him go out on the floor with her at least once. Why couldn't they go to a place with video games instead?

The group parked the car and headed into the restaurant, determined to pretend nothing had changed. Tomorrow was soon enough to deal with reality. Tonight, they were going to dance.

Chapter Ten

Rowdy tucked Bailey in and silently crept down the hall and into the kitchen. He was restless. The events of this morning were still running through his head. He wasn't going to get even a wink of sleep tonight. His thoughts and emotions were all over the place. He couldn't deny how much he enjoyed the thrill of the chase but he preferred putting bad guys in a cage, not a grave. Feelings of regret flooded his mind, similar to those he'd experienced in Chicago. Both times he hadn't had a choice. But how many men could you kill without it having a permanent impact on your soul? Rowdy didn't know the answer to that question. And he seriously did not want to find out.

He tried to push away the thought of those men having families but failed. They did have families somewhere. He didn't know if they were fathers, husbands, sons, brothers. The possibilities were endless. But no man was an island. He walked to the fridge, grabbed a beer then slowly made his way to his favorite recliner. It was definitely going to be a long night.

Hours later, Bailey jerked awake. The familiar nightmare washed over her, leaving her with the same sense of doom she'd felt the previous night. The same feeling of helplessness she'd felt all those years ago. The dreams were nothing new. She'd had them for months after escaping California and disappearing into a harsh and unforgiving world. Now, they were back. But this time, she'd not only put herself in danger, she'd risked the lives of so many others. It had to stop. She climbed from the bed and slowly made her way to the kitchen. After grabbing a bottle of water, she maneuvered her way through the dark until she reached the large couch and settled into the corner. She slowly pulled her legs to her chest and absently gazed out the window. It struck her almost immediately that the dark nothingness staring back at her was as black and dreary as her soul. She was lost and lonely and had no idea what she should do now. Her heart ached at the thought of leaving this place. But she had to, right? She couldn't continue to put this family in danger.

"Guess you couldn't sleep either," Rowdy said softly.

Bailey jumped a mile high and let out a stifled scream.

Rowdy chuckled to himself and stood. He moved to the couch and settled in next to Bailey. The instant he landed, she moved toward him, wrapping her tiny body around his strong muscular frame. He felt her shudder then break. The sobs wracked her body as tears ran down her face in a steady stream. Rowdy didn't know how to help her, so he just pulled her onto his lap and let her cry it out as he gently rubbed her back. When she was finally finished, he stood, took her hand, and led her to his bedroom.

Mount Haven

Bailey hesitated. She was at a point of no return. It would be too hard to go back to just being friends if she slept with this man. But she had to leave anyway. Maybe it wasn't so wrong to have one memorable night before she disappeared and re-invented herself yet again. She was more than a little surprised when Rowdy pulled back the blankets and slid into bed. He pushed his body backwards until he was situated on the other side of the king sized monstrosity and patted the mattress. Bailey slowly lowered herself onto the bed, her back pressed firmly against the mattress as she stared at the ceiling. Now what?

Rowdy knew Bailey misunderstood his intentions but there was no way he was going to take advantage of her tonight. He didn't care how much he wanted the woman. He grinned when she finally laid on her back and stared at the ceiling. That was not going to do. He reached over, wrapped his arm around her waist and tugged. Bailey let out a startled yelp then turned on him. Rowdy couldn't help himself; he laughed, then with the flick of his wrist he tossed her on her side and pulled her back to his chest. Once she was settled, he kissed the back of her head and whispered in her ear. "Just relax and let it all go. I'll take care of you. Trust me, you're safe tonight. Let your mind go, hold onto the knowledge that I'm here for you. Things will look better in the morning."

Bailey doubted that, but she was willing to try anything at this point. She pressed her body closer to Rowdy's and closed her eyes. Within minutes, her breathing had slowed and her eyes drifted shut. A short time later, they were both sound asleep.

* * * *

Rowdy woke to find a beautiful Bailey wrapped around his naked chest. He didn't remember shedding the shirt, but he did recall being too hot and dreaming he was locked in a furnace. He must have removed his t-shirt right about then. He shifted, slid from the bed and moved down the hall. Knight jumped from the couch and ran to the front door. It was definitely time for a potty break. Rowdy slid the door open then stepped into the kitchen to make coffee. Once the pot was brewing, he returned to the porch and watched the sun rise over the crisp blue lake. He loved mornings like this. It was even better after waking up next to Bailey. He considered his next move. Would things be awkward after last night? He didn't see why they would. It's not like they did anything either of them would regret. Well, he might have regrets but they were noble ones and he could live with that. He turned when he heard the door open and watched as Bailey stepped bare foot onto the porch.

Bailey was wrapped in one of Rowdy's blankets as she stepped outside and smiled. The sunrise was beautiful this morning. She hated to admit it, but Rowdy was right. A good night's sleep and a new perspective greeted her this morning. She still didn't know what she was going to do, but she wasn't going to run. Cole and Reese had taken enough from her. It was time to stand and fight. She slid in next to Rowdy and turned to face him, resting one hand on the wooden railing that spanned the entire patio and waited. It wouldn't be long before Rowdy gave her his undivided attention.

Rowdy turned to face Bailey, still unsure how to proceed. He was completely shocked when she moved a step closer then wrapped her arms around his neck and pressed her lips to his. This was nothing near what he expected this morning. He knew he should push her away, he should double check and make sure this was truly what she wanted, but he couldn't. All he could do was follow along when Bailey deepened the kiss.

Mount Haven

Bailey's heart was racing and her entire body was on fire. She'd wanted this for so long but had been afraid to act on her desires, afraid to take what she knew she needed. Not anymore. The attacks from Reese and Cole and their mindless security guards proved that. Life was short, she was going to embrace it for now and deal with the consequences later. She smiled and held on tighter when Rowdy lifted her into his arms and strolled purposefully into the house, kicking the door shut as he walked. Seconds later she was set gently on the king sized bed. Rowdy pulled the blankets away effortlessly, then looked her in the eyes. He must have found what he was looking for because he took a minute to admire her body then joined her, pressing his lips to hers in a mind blowing, emotion filled kiss. Bailey stopped thinking and started reacting.

* * * *

Nearly a week had passed since the attempted abduction of Bailey and Rowdy still wasn't any closer to finding the brutes responsible. It was like they had disappeared. Vanished into thin air. Bailey had even called her mother the night before but the two friends hadn't returned to San Diego, either. That call hadn't gone well. He was still shocked and furious. The woman blamed Bailey for the mess they were in and wouldn't even consider the possibility that Cole and Reese were sexual deviants. How Bailey had grown up with that woman and turned out so… normal, he had no idea.

On the bright side, his relationship with Bailey was amazing. He had never felt this way about a woman and honestly didn't think he ever would. He hadn't been exaggerating that night when he admitted to Coop he had given up. Now, somehow happiness seemed possible. Which was beyond stupid. Rowdy knew that all the reasons he had avoided her before were still waiting in the wings. Once this was over, she could go back to her real life. There was nothing to keep her in Mount Haven when the threat was gone. But at the moment he didn't care. He pulled the salad makings from the fridge and began to prepare dinner. Whatever the future held was in the future. Tonight, he was going to enjoy the present.

* * * *

Coop hung up with the County lab and sighed. If he waited for them, he'd be dead before he got his results. He only hesitated a second then dialed a number he knew well.

"Agent Perkins," came the all too familiar voice.

"It's Coop, do you have a minute?" Cooper asked.

"Hey Coop, I always have time for you, but I have to warn you the SAC's on his way down to go over a case so I may have to cut this short and call you back," Skeet said, grinning. "So, you adjusting out there in Montana? Is being a big fish in a little pond all you imagined?" Skeet couldn't imagine leaving the city for some place as boring as backwoods Montana.

"Solitude has its benefits," Coop said, laughing.

"How's Maggie? I know you moved out there for the family. Are they all adjusting as well as you hoped?" Skeet asked, hoping Coop's family was happier than the last time he'd seen them.

"Mags is great and surprisingly, so is Bryan. We bought a couple horses and he seems to be a natural. I think it was the right thing for all of us," Coop admitted.

Mount Haven

"And Rowdy?" Skeet asked, hesitantly.

"Rowdy's adjusting," Coop said soberly, remembering why he called in the first place. "He used the money from the sale of his house to buy into a local bar and grill. He runs the bar side, Maggie runs the grill. You know she's always wanted her own place and the two of them are perfect partners. It's a great setup."

"Really," Skeet said, trying to picture Rowdy running a bar. Now that Cooper mentioned it, he thought it might be the perfect solution.

"We both know Rowdy will always be a cop at heart, but the bar's a good alternative for him. Still enough action to keep him happy, without the aggravation of the badge and he doesn't have to answer to me."

Skeet laughed. "As if that would happen. So, I get the feeling this isn't just a social call."

"As much as I'd like to say yes, I need a favor," Coop admitted.

"Name it," Skeet said immediately. Andrew Cooper saved the love of his life. He'd do anything in his power to help out his friend.

"Skeet, I keep telling you to stop trying to pay me back for Angela. I was just doing my job," Coop was frustrated. He hated using his friend for this but there wasn't any other option.

"I'll decide what I owe you. Angela is my world, you saved her. If I feel indebted, that's on me. Now, what's this favor?"

"Before we go there, you haven't said how Angie is doing." Coop was sure Angela Perkins was handling things just fine. That was just the kind of woman she was. She had been kidnapped by a serial killer and held for almost two weeks, but once she'd been rescued, she bounced back pretty quickly.

"Ange is amazing, but you know that already. She still has nightmares on occasion, but they are finally few and far between. She's started painting again. In fact, her agent is trying to schedule a big show in San Francisco. I'll let you guys know if it happens. We'd love to meet you out there and visit for a day or two."

"Send us the date. We'll see what we can do," Coop agreed. Hopefully by the time everything was finalized, this nightmare in Mount Haven would be resolved.

"Great. Now, what's the favor?" Perkins pressed.

"I have a couple DNA samples I need analyzed and run through CODIS for a match," Cooper said hesitantly. "I'm pretty sure the items I'm sending will have fingerprints as well. If it's not too much to ask, could you pull those and run them through AFIS? Mariah just completed a forensics course, but this case is too important to let her practice on the evidence. I'm pretty sure my suspects are going to pop up in one of the systems, maybe both."

"That's easy," Skeet glanced up when his secretary stepped inside the door. There was a muffled conversation then Skeet returned to the line. "Hey man, the SAC just showed up. I have to brief him on this case, could take an hour or so. Can I call you back?"

"Sure, no problem," Coop said immediately. He hated pulling his friend away from a case but this was important. "I'll overnight the samples immediately. I owe you one for this. Our lab is so backed up the ice caps might melt before I get my results."

Mount Haven

Skeet laughed. "Our lab's busy as well, but I'll put a rush on it. I could probably have the results in 72 or so."

Coop let out a sigh of relief. "Thanks Skeet, this one is personal."

"Oh?" Skeet said, intrigued. "How so?"

"It's a long story and I know you have to run so I'll try to give you the Cliff's notes version," Coop began.

"Vicky, tell Donahue I need five," Skeet said, then refocused on Coop. "Sorry. Go ahead," Skeet prompted.

"I'm not going to get you in hot water am I? This can wait," Coop hesitated.

"Naw, it's good for him. When he says jump most of these guys ask how high," Skeet said with a smile. "His ego needs a hit sometimes."

Coop laughed then continued. "A couple hotshot businessmen came to town a few days back. I ran into one at the local motel, but thought he left the following day. Turns out he just relocated. Unfortunately, I have no idea where, but his buddy Cole Hughes apparently joined him a few days later. They knocked out a waitress at Rowdy's place and tried to kidnap her. The cook stepped in and saved the day. In the process, Cole and his buddy Reese left a fair amount of blood and in Reese's case I think there's a good sample of hair as well. We also have saliva off a couple coffee mugs."

"Reese Weathersby?" Skeet asked, not wanting to get his hopes up.

"Yeah," Coop said, wondering how his friend had known that so quickly.

Skeet dropped his feet from his desk and straightened. "Coop buddy, are you telling me you have both Cole Hughes' and Reese Weathersby's DNA?"

"Uh… yeah," Coop said, confused. "You know them?"

"Do I ever," Skeet said, excited now. Vicky stepped back into the room and cleared her throat. "Hold on a sec," he said into the phone. "Vicky, tell Special Agent Donahue he might want to join me in my office. I'm going to need his approval on something." Vicky glared at him, clearly annoyed then left the room.

"Sorry about that, Coop. You have no idea how big this is. We've been watching those two for years. I can't believe they showed up in hicktown Montana, no offense," Skeet added a little ashamed of himself.

"None taken," Coop laughed. "Why are you looking at them?"

"Our best bet is to hit them with insider trading. We've got a file two inches thick on the dynamic duo," Skeet said, motioning for his boss to take a seat.

"You're not this excited over insider trading, Skeet. I know you and there is no way you have gone that soft," Coop pressed. He knew Skeeter Perkins. Something else was going on.

"Coop, I'm going to put you on speaker. SAC Donahue has joined me and he's going to need to hear what you've got to say, then approve reading you in before I can answer any of your questions."

Mount Haven

"Okay sure," Coop said, even more confused. These guys must be a big deal for the FBI to be so interested. He knew the duo was evil, he was beginning to worry just how evil.

"This is SAC Kyle Donahue, who am I speaking with?" Donahue demanded, impatience evident in his tone. He was a busy man and didn't have time for this. He'd stopped by to speak with Perkins about their current serial killer before heading home. His trip to Quantico had been productive but exhausting.

"This is Sheriff Andrew Cooper from Mount Haven, Montana," Coop said respectfully.

"Mount Haven?" Donahue asked, shooting Skeeter a warning look. "Never heard of it."

"I'm not surprised, we're barely on the map," Coop said casually. He would not be intimidated, which clearly was Donahue's intent.

"I'm sorry Sheriff Cooper, but I'm on a tight schedule and Agent Perkins and I have a private meeting scheduled." Perkins was growing more and more arrogant by the day. Donahue might have to deal with it sooner rather than later, in spite of his connection to the Director.

"Sure. No problem," Coop said, feeling sorry for his friend. It was always difficult to work for men like Donahue. "Skeet, I'll get those samples sent off today. Once they're processed just send the documentation out to me along with any hits you get from CODIS or AFIS. I'll go over it personally. I know Cole and Reese must have a history. There's going to be a hit. Sorry to delay your meeting Special Agent Donahue, I won't take up any more of your time. And do have a nice day."

"Wait," Donahue ordered. "Cole Hughes and Reese Weathersby? Are you saying you have DNA samples and fingerprints for both men?"

"I do, but I really don't want to delay that important meeting you had with Skeet any longer. I'll just check back with him tomorrow and make sure the package arrived safely." Coop was unable to stop himself. "I really do hope our small town postal service doesn't lose these. But I guess that's always a possibility when using any service. Anyway, talk to you later, buddy."

"Sheriff Cooper," Donahue said, seething. He knew he was being played and he also knew he deserved it. Once again his habit of impatience had made a simple situation difficult. "I apologize. I really did not mean any disrespect. We are in the middle of a big serial killer case and I wrongfully assumed this call was unimportant. We've been chasing those two for years but they're clever. How in the world did you get a DNA sample?"

Cooper proceeded to tell the two agents the story of Bailey's attempted abduction as well as the incident at his home, the Babcocks' and the police station.

"That means you have two samples we can use?" Donahue considered. "The blood and hair are going to be easier to test, but the coffee mugs are even better. The chain of evidence hasn't been mucked up. I'm sending an agent down to pick those up personally," Donahue considered. "Bentley from our Salt Lake office will be there before you close tonight. Do you leave at five?"

"I'll wait for him. But if it's going to be after hours I'd appreciate a call. I'll need to let Maggie know I'm going to be late," Cooper told the men. "My top priority these days is keeping the Mrs. Happy."

Both agents laughed. "I think that's all of our top priority Sheriff Cooper, or at least it should be." He glanced at Skeeter then continued. "I wish I could send Perkins out to assist you on this, but we've only scratched the surface on this murder case and I need him here."

"We're fine," Coop said, not as confident of that as he'd like to be. "Any chance you could send me some of that two inch file you've got? I'd like to know what I'm dealing with here and I think we need to warn Bailey."

"If they were strangers, how did you identify them so quickly?" Skeet asked.

"Bailey identified them," Coop admitted. "I would have been able to get Reese's info from the motel, but there's no record of Cole anywhere near this town. I'm confident they are hiding out close by, but we're still looking."

"This Bailey woman," Donahue considered. "You said she works for your brother at a bar? How did she know the two men who tried to abduct her?"

"Cole is her step-brother," Coop said cautiously.

"Are you telling me Victoria is working as a waitress in a small, out-of-the way town in Montana?" Donahue said, even more intrigued. "That's brilliant."

"Victoria?" Coop asked.

"Clearly you have a lot to learn about that family," Skeet answered. "I assume I have approval to share this file with Sheriff Cooper?" Perkins asked his boss.

"Yes," Donahue said without hesitation. "You will get everything we have. Give us a couple hours. Vicky can prepare the file while we deal with this other mess. Sheriff Cooper, please keep in touch with Perkins. I want to know the minute anything changes out there. Skeeter, I'll be in the conference room. I need to make a call before we shift gears." With that, Special Agent Donahue exited Skeet's office.

"A really big fish in a small pond, man," Skeet said, amazed. "How do you do it? Somehow you always fall into this shit with absolutely no effort whatsoever." Skeet was shaking his head.

"I really don't call two madmen wanted by the FBI attacking my family, no effort at all Skeet," Coop pointed out, annoyed.

"Sorry, I'm just flabbergasted. Vicky will get started on the file and I'm sure you're right. With DNA samples we're going to nail 'em, I'm sure of it," Perkins said, standing.

"Skeet, how bad?" Coop had to ask. "I have a couple good men out here but they're green. What am I up against?"

"Read Rowdy in," Skeet said, making a snap decision. "I know he's not on the job anymore, but it's his waitress and chances are good she's their main target."

"Why?" Coop wanted to know.

"Because she's loaded and they're stupid," Skeet said happily. "Unfortunately, their stupidity in the business arena didn't carry over to the criminal one. They don't make mistakes. I can only assume they are desperate because they just made a couple whoppers out there. As long as we've been tracking them, we have never once even been close to acquiring DNA and yet you guys have managed it twice. It's unbelievable and the lucky break we've been needing."

"What are you not telling me?" Cooper asked.

"I really do have to run, but we are pretty sure those two are serial rapists. The problem is evidence. We have one woman's statement that it was both Cole and Reese that kidnapped and raped her repeatedly but two days after reporting the incident, her car lost control and slid over the side of a mountain. Dropped close to five hundred feet and burst into flames. ME's report says she was dead before the fire started. I can't prove it, but I believe she was dead before the car left the highway. These men are bad news and will stop at nothing to get what they want. If they want Bailey, AKA Victoria, you two better stay on your toes."

"Thanks," Coop said, sinking lower into his chair. What exactly had Rowdy gotten himself into?

"Is there more to this?" Skeeter asked. "You said it was personal."

"Not really, just…" Cooper hesitated.

"Just what?" Skeeter pushed.

"I think Rowdy's falling for her. Actually I know he is. If her family's rich, chances are pretty good when this is all over she's heading home to the comfortable life of the wealthy," Cooper said, feeling defeated. He just didn't know how Rowdy would take that.

"Shit," Skeeter said falling back into his chair. "Man, she's not just rich, she's loaded. I mean multi-millions. And she owns the majority share of the business. How big of a set back? Rowdy's already been through more than any man should. How far gone is he?"

"From where I'm sitting, he dropped over the cliff weeks ago." Cooper ran his hand through his hair and sighed. "Oh, well. There's nothing we can do about it. I just hope this doesn't kill him. He's never really cared for a woman before this. Oh, he's dated and even considered a few of the women girlfriends but he's never been hooked. Not like you and I are. Bailey has that hold on him." The two of them were silent for several long drawn out seconds. "Well, this just sucks."

"I agree," Skeeter said quietly.

"Anyway, go to your meeting. Send me those files and I'll be ready when your man arrives. Regardless of the fallout, we are going to nail these two," Coop resolved with finality.

"I'll talk to you soon, read Rowdy in. The sooner the better. Maybe knowing who and what she is will prepare him for the loss," Skeeter suggested.

"Maybe," Cooper said, not believing it for a minute. Rowdy was going to be crushed. "I'll call you once I've had a chance to digest the situation and make a plan. Tell Angie hello and take care, man. Hope you get your serial killer."

"We will," Skeeter said confidently before disconnecting the line.

* * * *

Mount Haven

The following afternoon, Coop sat in his office waiting for Rowdy. He had started to go through the file but decided to wait. He and Rowdy would decipher it together. The door swung open and Rowdy walked in happy and cocky as ever. Cooper hated knowing this meeting was going to shatter his brother.

"So, what's up?" Rowdy asked, then hesitated. Coop had a thick file on his desk and he was frowning.

"Shut the door," Coop said soberly.

Rowdy silently clicked the door shut then turned to study his brother. "Just spit it out," he said, bracing himself for a blow. He'd known life was going too well. Sure, he was constantly on edge waiting for Bailey to come under attack again, but life with her by his side had become more than he'd ever imagined it could be. Fate wasn't that kind to him. Something had to happen to change his life, he'd been waiting for it, thought he was prepared for it, but now that the time had come, he wasn't ready.

"I called Skeet. The FBI sent me over this big ass file on those two men that attacked Bailey. It also has a fair amount of information on your victim. Bailey's real name is actually Victoria."

Rowdy sat down and accepted the stack of papers his brother held out for him. The first page was some kind of summary. He continued to study it, not really grasping the implication. When he reached the bottom, it hit him. "Are you telling me those two are responsible for all of this?" He shook the paper as he studied his brother's sober face.

"Those are only the ones they can connect," Coop admitted. He handed Rowdy a second sheet of paper. "These are the ones they think may have been Cole and Reese." He dropped another stack of papers on the edge of the desk. "And those are possibles. There isn't enough information one way or the other to rule them in or rule them out."

"You have got to be shitting me," Rowdy said, scrolling through page after page. "This is going to take days just to read through it all."

"I started but when I got to this, I stopped. I decided I wanted to wait for you," Cooper said, handing Rowdy a large eight by ten of an elegant woman. She was clearly rich, beautiful and haughty but Rowdy would know those eyes anywhere. He closed his eyes as he dropped the photo on top of the file. The woman in that photo would never settle for small town Montana. And she certainly wouldn't think twice about a damaged ex-cop, who now owned a backwoods bar, just off the beaten path of nowhere, USA. Before he could say a word there was a soft knock on the door. Rowdy looked at Coop who was frowning.

"I gave specific orders that I was not to be interrupted," he said, then began to push himself out of his chair.

"I got it," Rowdy said, reaching sideways and turning the knob. The instant he swung open the door, he regretted it. Bailey, no... Victoria stood in the open doorway. "They told me you two were busy but there is something I wanted to talk to you both about." She was watching Rowdy and didn't like what she saw. His expression was cold, but underneath the surface she recognized hurt. What was going on in here?

"Sorry. I need to get to the bar," Rowdy stood. He dropped the stack of papers he was holding on Cooper's desk and Bailey inhaled with a gasp.

"Rowdy," she called to his back as he made his way out the front door. She took a step to go after him but Cooper stopped her.

Mount Haven

"He needs some time," Cooper said without emotion. "Right now, he needs time alone. That's how Rowdy deals with things, how he processes. And I need you to be honest with me."

"What is all this?" Bailey asked, picking up the photo Rowdy had been holding. It wasn't as flattering as she had once believed. The woman in the photo was someone Bailey had left behind. Someone she didn't know anymore, someone she hardly recognized. She was cocky, arrogant and flamboyant. Three traits Bailey hoped she'd never possess again. She dropped the photo onto Cooper's desk and leveled her gaze at him. She wanted answers. "Where did all this come from? And why were you and Rowdy locked up here in secret, going through it?" She reached for what looked like a list and was surprised when Cooper snatched it up and placed it securely in a file, slamming the top shut before she could read a thing.

Cooper wasn't sure what he should tell Bailey, now Victoria. Was it possible she'd been involved in the financial schemes and run before she got into hot water? Maybe, but that wasn't the reason she had run. She had already explained that, and Coop believed her. Still, how much to reveal? "So, I guess it was all a game to you?" he finally asked. "Seduce the Sheriff's brother, enlist his help, and he'll be too busy to look into your background."

Bailey was hurt. Did Cooper really think so little of her? How could he even suggest such a thing?

"Was any of it real, Bailey, or should I say, Victoria?" Cooper asked, not knowing how to handle this. He wanted to pound on something, or more to the point… someone. But he couldn't pound on Bailey so he did his best to hold his anger at bay.

"Not that I have to explain myself to you, Andrew Cooper, but it was all real." She fumed when the infuriating lawman just raised an eyebrow at her. "Not the name, but everything else. Everything I've told you and Rowdy is one hundred percent true. So I'm Victoria frickin' Alexander. I haven't been that woman for years. And I didn't seduce your brother, if anything he seduced me." She motioned to the large file on Cooper's desk. "Is that what you did? Investigated me? No wonder Cole and Reese found me." She impatiently wiped a tear from her cheek and turned to leave.

"This came from the FBI. It arrived this morning," he said softly, making a decision he hoped he wouldn't regret.

That stopped her in her tracks. The FBI had a file, that thick of a file, on who? It couldn't all be her. She pivoted and slid into the chair Rowdy had vacated. "Is there anything you can tell me?" she finally whispered.

"The FBI has been investigating Cole and Reese for years," Coop said. "There was a woman…" he opened the file to look at the dates. "A Mandy Strausberg that filed a police report back… it looks like eight years ago."

Bailey couldn't breathe, Mandy had filed a report against Cole and Reese. "For what?" she finally choked out.

"You knew her?" Coop asked compassionately.

"She was a neighbor. A girl I went to school with," Bailey answered, her mind was still reeling from the news.

"A friend," Coop stated with a nod. "That makes sense."

"But she died eight years ago," Bailey said, then went visibly white when Coop didn't respond. "You think…" she pointed to the file. "The FBI thinks they had something to do with her death?"

"Not officially," Coop answered vaguely.

"Unofficially then," she pressed. "Do they think Cole or Reese caused her death?"

"I have a friend in the FBI who is familiar with this case. In fact, he's the one that sent me the file. He believes they were responsible. Mandy made an official report to the local police. She claimed she was forcibly and somewhat roughly raped by both of them. Two days later, her car mysteriously drove over a cliff. They had DNA from one of them, but once Mandy died, the case was closed. Her death was officially ruled an accident. Nobody would go near it. And the DNA was lost. It was actually never processed because the case was closed and the local police accidentally destroyed it."

"I can't breathe," Bailey said, knowing she was starting to hyperventilate.

Coop moved to Bailey's side. He sat down and gently put a hand on the back of her neck. "Lean over and take slow, steady breaths," he advised as he gently put pressure on the back of her neck.

"It's my fault she died," Bailey confessed as she sat up straight in the chair. She was crying now, big crocodile tears ran down her face and she struggled to control the shudders that racked her small body.

Cooper was at a loss; how was he supposed to deal with this woman's grief? "It wasn't your fault," he said softly, then glanced up when his door silently opened. He let out an audible sigh of relief when Rowdy stepped back into the room.

* * * *

Rowdy was angry, more angry than he could ever remember being in his entire life. But more to the point, he was hurt. Why hadn't Bailey told him who she was? He thought they'd been making progress. He thought she finally trusted him. But clearly he'd been wrong. And marching out of the room at the first sign of trouble wasn't the way to make her understand he'd be there for her. He'd only gone about a mile up the road when he flipped his truck around and returned to the station. He'd hear her out, see what the rest of the file said, then figure out what he was going to do with the rest of his life... without the woman he loved. He did love Bailey. He wasn't sure exactly when that had happened, but he loved her. Enough to be there for her, then let her walk away.

The instant he stepped back into the office he knew something was wrong. Coop's door was shut again, that couldn't be a good sign. Had he continued to study the file without him? And where was Bailey? Her car was still out front. He moved to the door and silently pushed it aside. He didn't think, he just reacted. Rowdy moved forward and dropped to his knees in front of Bailey. "Bay, what happened?" he asked as he tried to wipe the river of tears away from her face. He shot an angry look at his brother. "What happened?" he asked more forcefully.

Coop stood and closed the door. "I thought Bailey deserved an explanation," he began as he returned to sit behind his desk. "She thought we decided to investigate her. She thought that was what brought those two men into our small town. I started to explain that this file came from the FBI. That they have been investigating those two for years."

"How much did you tell her?" Rowdy asked, worried now. Bailey was not taking the news well.

"There's more?" Bailey asked, not really wanting to know.

"A lot more," Coop nodded. "I'm sorry Bailey, but there is a whole lot more."

Bailey allowed Rowdy to lift her into his arms and resettle her on his lap. He didn't say a word, just watched his brother as he ran his hand up and down this fragile woman's back. But Bailey wasn't fragile, so what had set her off?

"The first report was from a woman that Bailey knew," Cooper explained. "A childhood friend. She mistakenly believes what happened to Mandy Strausberg was her fault." He looked at Rowdy. "Mandy's vehicle suspiciously went over a cliff a couple days after she reported the incident. Skeet thinks Cole and Reese were responsible."

Rowdy cringed inwardly then gently used the palm of his hand to turn Bailey toward him. Once she made eye contact he spoke. "None of this is your fault, sweetheart. Those men are evil, they're monsters. That has nothing to do with you. You are simply another one of their victims. Don't ever forget that. Mandy may have been the first, but maybe not. I actually doubt she was. Men don't typically go from rape to murder that quickly. In fact, they don't usually start with rape. I would bet if we looked hard enough we could find other women, girls the two of them went to school with, that were sexually assaulted by one or both of them. Mandy was probably the first or one of the first actual rapes. Or, she was just the first to report it. They panicked and the only way they knew to deal with the situation was to eliminate her."

"You make it sound so cold. Mandy's not just a statistic, another insignificant case, she was my friend and she's dead." Bailey couldn't stop hot tears from returning.

"No, she's not insignificant," Rowdy said, once again hurt by her accusation. "I may not be a cop anymore, but I have dealt with a lot of victims, Bailey. A good cop never considers a victim insignificant. They might try to look at things from a distance, to analyze rather than internalize, but they are never insignificant." He tried to move her from his lap to the guest chair but she wouldn't allow it.

"I'm sorry," she said, not even blinking. "I was in shock, Mandy and I were friends. For years, she was my best friend. Then she slowly stopped calling, stopped coming around, stopped wanting to hang out with me. I was crushed and angry. She died before I could work it all out in my mind. Then I just felt guilty for hating her and losing her."

"That's understandable," Cooper said. "How old were you when she died?" He could have done the math himself, but he wanted to get Bailey talking again.

"Seventeen," Bailey almost whispered. Events were running through her head, small things that Victoria hadn't picked up on but Bailey now understood. "My father died when I was fourteen. We were close. Much closer than I was to my mother. I was always Daddy's little girl and in a way, I think my mother was jealous of the connection we had. Don't get me wrong, my mother and father had an amazing relationship." She stopped to glance at Cooper. "A lot like you and Maggie."

Mount Haven

"I'm sorry," Coop empathized sincerely. "For both of you. Losing your father must have been terrible, life changing."

"In more ways than you can imagine," Bailey admitted. She swallowed the lump in her throat and glanced at Rowdy. "Even at fourteen I wasn't convinced my father's death was an accident. Now," she shrugged. "I'm even more convinced it wasn't. I know I could never prove it. Peter hired a private investigator and the NTSB ruled it an accident, but I don't buy it."

"Why?" Rowdy asked curiously.

"They said it was a mechanical failure, something Dad's pilot forgot to check. Apparently the problem was a common one and something that would have been revealed in the pilot's pre-flight inspection. Dave was thorough. I'd been shadowing my dad since I was five. Dave never skipped an inspection, in fact we sometimes got delayed over some minor issue Dad thought was overkill but Dave insisted on safety first." Bailey wiped another tear from her face. "That's why Peter hired a private investigator. He didn't believe Dave was sloppy either."

"Could he have been in on it?" Cooper asked quickly.

"I don't know, but I don't think so," Bailey considered. "Peter is difficult and he either ignores Cole's flaws or refuses to see them, like denial. I don't know, but I think he really was my father's friend. He seemed devastated after Dad's death. He also really liked Dave and had a hard time replacing him."

Cooper was flipping through the file, looking for the data on Victoria's family. Once he found it, he studied her for several minutes. "It didn't take long after your father's death for Peter Hughes to marry your mother," he pointed out hesitantly. Should he go that one step further or would Bailey shut down or blow up at the suggestion.

"I know what you're thinking but no, they weren't having an affair before Daddy died." Bailey sighed. "Sure, it looks bad from the outside but if you knew my parents you wouldn't even have to ask that."

"Okay, maybe you could explain," Rowdy prompted.

"Like I said, they were a lot like your brother and Maggie," Bailey began. "Mom and Dad were more in love than anyone in their circles. They met and got married while they were both in college, against their parents' wishes. Mom dropped out almost immediately, college was never for her anyway. Dad finished and went on to get his MBA. He was considered golden. Anything he touched made money. He was just a natural in business and it paid off. His company was growing so fast he needed a partner. He was never home and he missed Mom and me. Peter had been pushing him for years to let him buy in but Dad always resisted. I don't really know why. They weren't what you would call close friends at that point, but they were friends. They had attended grad school together and Dad really liked Peter. Eventually Dad gave in and Peter became Dad's business partner."

"That doesn't explain the quick marriage," Cooper pressed.

Bailey sighed. "Mom was a mess after Dad died. She became so depressed, her doctor prescribed medication. She barely left the house, rarely ate and completely ignored everyone around her. Peter was there for us. We both needed him. Mom was barely living and I was only fourteen. When the bills started coming in, I didn't know what to do so I took them to Peter. He stepped in and started handling the running of the household. He was also the only one that could get Mom to eat. When Peter showed up, she actually came out of her room. It took a few months, but Peter was finally able to pull Mom out of her self-imposed prison. I think they had Dad in common. They were both mourning his death and a bond grew out of their despair. A few months later, they told me they were getting married. Mom said Peter would always be there to make sure we were okay."

"And you were okay with that?" Rowdy asked. If his father had married so quickly after his mother's death, he knew he and Coop would have thrown a fit.

"I was," Bailey said softly. "I wasn't threatened by Peter. Not in the way you would expect. Peter wasn't taking my father's place. Mom didn't love him the way she loved Dad. She was just weak and needed someone to take care of her. I knew I couldn't do it and Peter seemed to be able to. He was a friend, Dad's friend, and he seemed willing to take on the responsibility of caring for us. It just seemed like a natural step in the right direction at the time. Mom could never deal with anything unpleasant. My dad always did that, and then Peter. Years later, I realized it may not have been such a great idea."

"Why?" Coop asked, still not convinced.

"Because I think Peter expected more from Mom," Bailey glanced up looking at Cooper then turning her gaze to Rowdy. "I think Mom loves Peter in her way, but she will never love anyone the way she loved my father. I actually feel sorry for him. He obviously loved us, mostly Mom, with all his heart but he only gets pieces. Mom will never be the woman she was when Dad was alive and Peter has had to settle for what she has left. He's adjusted for the most part, but before I left I could see he craved more."

"Which only makes him look more guilty," Cooper deduced. "He wanted your mother and your father stood in the way. Once Scott Alexander was out of the picture, Piper would have been available. Maybe he coveted what your father had and believed if he were gone, your mom would turn that love and affection his way."

"I guess that's possible, but it just doesn't seem probable. I know where you're coming from and believe me, I considered it," Bailey admitted. "But the more I thought about it, the more it didn't make sense. I just don't think Peter has it in him and he and Dad really had become close friends. I'm more inclined to believe Cole messed with the plane. Probably with Reese's help. They were inseparable. Cole is twelve years older than me. He would have been twenty-six when Daddy died. I remember Dad complaining that Peter was trying to shove his son down Dad's throat and Dad was resisting."

"Really?" Rowdy said, considering. If Peter, as partner, was trying to bring his son into the business and Bailey's father was resisting, Cole may have seen that as a threat. The more Rowdy learned, the more he understood just how evil and self-righteous Cole Hughes really was. It wasn't a stretch to believe he would kill the man standing in his way.

"I'll call Skeet. He might be able to track down the investigation of your father's death," Cooper offered. "I think it is entirely possible that Cole and Reese had a hand in those murders as well. We may not be able to do anything about them, right now the deaths are classified as accidental. But at least we'll know."

Bailey couldn't stop the tears from flowing. Would her mother be able to cope with the possibility that the son of the man she was married to had killed the love of her life? And what about

Mount Haven

Peter? How would he deal with knowing what a monster Cole had become? She knew how, he'd remain in denial. So would her mother for that matter. Most likely, Bailey would end up being the bad guy in all of this.

"What's wrong?" Rowdy asked feeling Bailey tense.

"They won't believe it," she whispered. "My mom and Peter are in denial. They can't imagine Cole doing anything wrong… and Reese? No way. You have no idea how hard Mom was pushing me to marry him. She claimed I had unrealistic expectations when it came to love because of my father. She settled, I should too."

Rowdy's stomach was churning. Had Bailey been settling all this time? He had finally allowed himself to believe he'd found what Coop had with Maggie, what his father had with his mother. Now, he knew he'd been wrong. While he was falling head over heels in love, Bailey had been hiding out; settling. He always knew she might move on, run again if she got too scared. Somehow he'd convinced himself that life with him would be enough, that he could keep her safe and they would run the bar together. But Bailey was a millionaire. She would soon return to her million dollar lifestyle with her million dollar company. How could he have been so stupid?

Cooper was watching his brother. He knew he was now doubting the relationship he had with Bailey, AKA Victoria. But Cooper wasn't so sure Rowdy was reading things correctly. Only time would tell and Coop really couldn't see the woman in that photo throwing away millions to remain in such a small town, but stranger things had happened. Hadn't his mother given up the massive ranch they now occupied to move to the city for love? Coop wasn't giving up on Bailey just yet. And if he was wrong, he'd be there to help Rowdy pick up the shattered pieces of his life and somehow move forward. "Let's pick this up tomorrow," he finally suggested. "Let me call Skeet and see what he can track down for me. We have a lot of information to go over and if you're willing Bailey, I think your insight might be invaluable."

Bailey glanced at Rowdy and knew instantly something was wrong. Had she said something to upset him? Her mind was racing, going over every sentence but nothing came to her. "Okay," she agreed. A break might be a good thing. It would give her and Rowdy a chance to talk. Bailey stood and held her hand out to Rowdy. "Will you take me home?"

Rowdy studied Bailey's hand, hesitating only an instant then he gave a slight nod, slid his fingers through hers and stood. "We'll be back at eight." When he turned and opened the door, he was surprised to see Jase pacing impatiently just outside.

Jase stopped abruptly when he heard the door open. He looked up expecting to see Sheriff Cooper but instead came face to face with his boss, Rowdy. He swallowed hard then nodded. "I guess it's good you're here too," he finally said. "I'll only have to explain this once."

"Sorry man," Rowdy said, pulling Bailey from the room. "I need to get Bay home. She's had a rough day."

Jase hadn't noticed Bailey standing behind Rowdy but now that he did, he also saw evidence of the tears. It only took a second to make his decision. "Bailey? Would you mind staying, too?" He waited but only got a confused look from her. "I have something to confess, something that has to do with your family. I'd like you to hear this. I think it might explain some things."

Bailey couldn't take her eyes off Jase. He had saved her life and she had a sinking feeling that single act on his part might have dire repercussions for this man. He'd always made her

335

uncomfortable not because she knew, without a doubt, that Jase was hiding too. But because she sensed, deep down in her soul, that he had recognized her the instant she'd walked through the door. She had always been amazed that he hadn't blown her cover and had never stopped wondering why. Maybe this was her chance to find out. "I'm okay," she told Rowdy. "Let's stay, it looks like Jase has something important he needs to talk to Cooper about. He saved my life, if my being here helps somehow, I want to stay." She gave Rowdy's hand a gentle pull.

Rowdy wasn't sure what was on Jase's mind, but he could see it wasn't anything good. How many secrets did one small town hold? When Bailey pulled on his hand a second time, he turned and stepped back into the room. This time he moved to the end chair, leaving plenty of room for Jase. Bailey didn't return to his lap. Instead, she slowly lowered herself onto the chair next to Rowdy but kept a death grip on his hand. If she held on any tighter, she was going to break a finger. Rowdy leaned to the side and whispered softly, "Calm down." He gently placed her hand on his knee and smoothed out her fingers. "Whatever this is, it will be okay."

Bailey glanced up and saw Rowdy forcing a weak smile then nodded once. She would get through this. She had Rowdy by her side and whatever Jase had to say about her family couldn't be worse than what she had already learned from that file.

Jase silently closed the Sheriff's door and then lowered himself into one of the guest chairs.

"What's up, Jase?" Coop asked immediately.

Jase closed his eyes and hoped for about the millionth time he was doing the right thing. He leaned forward resting his forearms on his knees and began to tell his story, gently tracing the outline of the bandage on the back of his forearm. "I'm hiding. I'm on the run from the law," he finally told the room. "When you get the results back from that knife, the one with some of my blood on it, you are going to find out I'm a wanted man." He glanced up at Sheriff Cooper and was surprised to see his expression hadn't changed.

"Go on," Coop encouraged gently. Jase worked for Maggie and over the past month Cooper had gotten to know the gentle man enough to know that whatever run-in he'd had with the law, there was probably a good explanation. "Tell me exactly what I'm going to find and then tell me the rest. Explain what has you so nervous, Jase. I won't judge you until I hear it all."

Jase swallowed loudly. "Four and a half years ago Cole Hughes and Reese Weathersby drugged my sister at a bar."

"No," Bailey gasped as she lowered her head into her hands and rocked.

Jase glanced at Bailey then back to Cooper, confused by this reaction.

Rowdy was immediately off the chair kneeling in front of Bailey. He pulled her into his arms and rocked her silently. "Baby, look at me," he finally coaxed, waiting for Bailey to raise her head. "Please?" he asked gently.

Bailey looked up, again wiping tears from her face with the palms of her hands.

"We don't have to stay," Rowdy said softly. "If you want, I'll take you home right now. You don't have to hear this."

Bailey shook her head. "I'm so sorry Jase. I am so, so sorry."

Mount Haven

Jase sat in silence, not really understanding Bailey but realizing she knew what he was going to say about his sister. Had she known her brother was violating women and done nothing to stop him?

"Go ahead, Jase," Cooper encouraged. "Finish your story."

"Did you know?" Jase had to ask, not taking his eyes off Bailey for an instant.

She just shook her head, too upset to speak.

"I'm not going to tell you a lot, Jase," Cooper sighed. "But I will tell you that Bailey just learned some horrible things about her brother and his best friend today. I suspect what you are about to tell me will only add another victim to their reign of terror."

Jase considered, then continued. "I was supposed to meet Marnie at the bar but I was running late. I owned my own restaurant back then and a shipment was late, which made me late. We planned to have a quick drink then head into the back where the bar owner's mother had prepared a special meal in Marnie's honor. They were family friends and Marnie had just been accepted into Stanford with a partial scholarship." Jase got a faraway look and paused momentarily. "Marnie loved to draw and had been accepted into their architectural engineering program. She would have been a natural."

"Would have been?" Bailey repeated, fearing the worst. Had Cole and Reese also killed Jase's sister?

"Yeah," Jase sighed. "After what happened, Marnie shut down. She didn't leave her room for over a year. It made things worse when I bolted."

Bailey was relieved to hear the girl hadn't died but clearly she had been traumatized. And just how much had Jase lost due to her step-brother's heinous acts?

"Anyway," Jase continued, "I finally got to the bar and Marnie was nowhere in sight. The owner, Kevin immediately rushed over and told me Marnie had left with two men. He said she wasn't acting like herself and he feared they had done something to her. He recognized Reese and that was all I needed to know. Zuma Danko was hot back then and Cole and Reese frequently stopped in for dinner. They had become two of my regulars."

"Wait!" Bailey exclaimed, amazed. "You owned Zuma?"

Jase smiled and nodded.

"Oh my gosh!" she exclaimed. "Your Beef Brisket is to die for."

"Thanks," Jase said humbly. He glanced at Rowdy and grinned. "Not really a meal fit for a bar and grill, though."

Rowdy shrugged. "I don't know why not. Good food is always welcome."

Jase laughed, but then sobered realizing he needed to continue. "Anyway, I had an idea of where they might have taken Marnie. One night the two of them had come to the restaurant and bragged about having a small private party. They'd given me the address and invited me to join them. I didn't go, but the business card was still laying on my bedroom dresser. I cursed myself for the delay but rushed home, got the addy and headed off to the swanky apartment complex. When I arrived, I showed the doorman the card and he didn't question me further. As I approached the room, I spotted a bodyguard at the door." He glanced at Cooper. "This is where things got wonky. I demanded entrance into the room. The guard declined. I was arguing with him, trying to convince him my sister was inside but he wouldn't budge. He just gave me a knowing look that said he pitied me and my family, but there was no way I was getting inside. Then, Marnie screamed. I lost it. I shoved the guard, he shoved back. We fought violently and all the while Marnie was screaming and crying on the other side of that damn door. I was so focused on my sister I didn't realize we had fought our way down the hallway. When Marnie let out a gut wrenching, agonizing scream I didn't think - I just shoved the guy as hard as I could. He fell backwards and struck his head on a large marble statue.

I didn't give him a second thought. I'm not sure what that makes me, but my only thought was getting to Marnie. When I burst through the door, the scene made me wretch. I saw red and went crazy. Cole and Reese were both shocked to see me. Reese was holding her down while Cole raped her. I pulled Cole off." He glanced at the Sheriff. "I might have gone a little overboard on him. His face was a bloody mess by the time I left."

Cooper nodded, not caring that a rapist had been beaten to a bloody pulp.

"It took Reese longer to spring to action. He had to untangle himself from my sister. By the time he took his first swing, I was ready for him. Being a former marine, it was easy to neutralize him in seconds. I grabbed Marnie and headed straight for the hospital." Jase rubbed his eyes, regret showing on his face.

"It was later that night that I learned the guard had died." He glanced at Bailey, saw she was holding up then continued. "The police showed up at my house at around three in the morning. They hauled me off to the station and took my statement. I told them everything, sure they would see it was self-defense. Unfortunately,

I underestimated Reese and Cole's influence in that town. It's my fault Marnie's case never got off the ground. I led the cops to the detective handling her rape."

"I'm not following," Rowdy interrupted. "Are you saying we have to deal with dirty cops on top of everything else?"

Jase shrugged. "I don't know. Someone's dirty. Marnie's case got tossed, lack of evidence even though the doctor told me personally there was plenty of DNA. Then three days later I was arrested and charged with murder and aggravated assault on Cole. After talking to my lawyer I knew I didn't have a chance. Apparently those two had moved the body into the apartment and staged the scene like I was a jealous lover. What they were accusing me of was just sick. They said Marnie and I had been incestuous and when she hooked up with Cole, I freaked. My lawyer said I should take a plea and accept my punishment. He clearly believed I was the monster Cole and Reese claimed I was. The thought of spending the rest of my life in prison while those monsters walked free was not something I could accept. Instead, I bolted. I changed my last name and went into hiding, biding my time until I could find a way to make things right."

Cooper's mind was racing. If there was DNA evidence on Jase's sister's case, why hadn't she shown on the FBI list? "Are you absolutely sure the doctor turned the DNA over to the police?"

"Positive," Jase said nodding. "My lawyer told me the prosecutor had the results. In fact, he turned the paperwork over to my attorney in discovery. He said it didn't matter. Cole wasn't disputing he'd had sex with the girl, only that it hadn't been consensual. He claimed any injuries she had sustained must have been a result of me, not him. The attorney said the rape case was going to be dropped and the DNA would probably be destroyed as irrelevant."

Rowdy was also thinking. The DNA may be lost but the results might still be filed somewhere. It was another link in the chain that would bring those two to justice. "Coop?"

"I'll take care of it," Cooper promised, knowing exactly what his brother was going to ask.

"I understand that you need to arrest me," Jase said defeated. "There's a warrant out on me for murder. I'm a wanted felon. You can't just let that go. But I wanted you to at least hear my side of things. I also have enough respect for the two of you that I didn't want you to learn of my crimes through the system. I wanted you to hear it straight from me."

"Which is why you're not going to be arrested," Cooper resolved, standing. "Not by me. Not now and if I can help it, not ever."

"What?" Jase said surprised. "No, I can't let you do that. You're the Sheriff. You have to follow the law. The law says I killed that man and I have to be punished. I won't let you get into trouble protecting me from this. I never should have run. I should have taken it like a man."

Bailey jumped to her feet. "Are you crazy?" she demanded. "Jase, you never would have won. You never would have received a fair trial. They have money and power and it's impossible to fight them. Why do you think I ran? Because I'm family and even I couldn't fight back. I knew I'd never win. Sheriff Cooper, you will not arrest Jase for this. He's just as much a victim as his sister and all those other women. We have to stop them. We have to." She sagged against Rowdy, defeated. "What if I could have stopped it?

How many other women, other families have lost everything because I wasn't strong enough to put an end to this?"

"Stop it," Rowdy ordered impatiently. "You just said yourself that you couldn't have stopped them. If you had stayed we all know what would have happened. You may not have been so lucky the second time around. Did you even hear what Jase said about his sister? That could have been you, Bailey."

Jase frowned, Cole had attacked his own sister? No wonder it was so easy to accuse him of such unspeakable acts. Had he been assaulting his own sister all that time?

Bailey frowned at Rowdy then turned to Jase. "Cole and Reese tried to rape me three years ago, but I escaped. I knew my mother and my step-father would take Cole's side. They always did. Somehow Cole has convinced them that he is pure as the driven snow and anyone that says otherwise is either after their money or simply misunderstood his intentions. Even me. I had been preparing for that night for a long time. I think the only thing Cole has ever been denied in his life was me. Knowing he couldn't have me only made him want me more. When I came home for winter break, Cole gave me the creeps. I packed a small bag, stashed a little cash and a change of clothes and believed I'd only be going into hiding for a few days. The initial plan was to head back to college and once I graduated, I'd get as far away from that family as possible."

"What changed?" Jase asked. He probably didn't have a right to the answer, but he was curious.

"Cole bragged about their plans for me. Reese had been planting the seed for years. I knew that my mother would go right along with Reese's plan to marry me. She'd been dropping hints for months and I finally understood why. Cole also gloated about his conquest. He was going to rape me first then Reese was going to come in and 'sample the goods'. Apparently, it wasn't at all feasible for him to wait until the wedding night. They both had needs and I was just the one to take care of them. I realized if I told my parents, they would think I was crazy and irrational. They loved Reese and trusted Cole. I didn't think I had any other option. If I returned to college the two of them could find me and just pick up where they left off. I wasn't safe, I had to run."

Coop stood. "I know today has been difficult for both of you. I'm confident Rowdy will see to Bailey's needs when they leave here, but Jase are you going to be okay? Your situation is a little more precarious. If Cole or Reese recognized you when you thwarted their kidnapping attempt, they could have people after you. They would also know that one anonymous call to the state police or even the feds would land you in a cell for good."

"Which is why you need to arrest me right now," Jase pointed out, knowing it was the only solution.

"Not going to happen," Cooper said shaking his head. "What you just described to me was self-defense. I'm going to ask you to trust me on this. Give me a couple days to work on it from a legal end, but watch your back. Those two are unpredictable and they have proven time and time again they will do anything to protect their secrets. I don't want to scare you, but I truly believe your life could be in danger. Do you have somewhere to stay besides your apartment?"

"Stay at the bar," Rowdy suggested. "Max set up that small apartment in the back. I haven't done anything with it yet. It's livable, just tiny."

"Great idea," Coop agreed. "The new security system's top of the line so you'll know if someone tries to sneak in at night. During the day, they'd have to get through my brother so you'd be golden out there."

Jase scowled, "Former marine?"

Cooper laughed. "I caught that. And I'd say a former marine and a former cop would make a pretty formidable team."

Jase couldn't argue with that. He just hoped these two knew what they were doing. The last thing he wanted was to make more trouble for the family. "I'll stay in the apartment since you offered, but it's only temporary. And only because I agree those two probably recognized me and they will do anything to make me pay. But, I have a condition."

"What do you want?" Bailey asked. "If I have any say, you'll get it."

Rowdy laughed now.

"Like I said, they will do anything to make me pay. The easiest way to do that is to target my family." He glanced at Cooper. "You have any friends in California that might be willing to guard my sister and my mother? They're vulnerable and going after them would be right in line with the duo's MO."

"I agree," Cooper said, frowning. He didn't know anyone in California.

"Coop?" Bailey said instantly.

"Yeah," he answered, not really listening. He couldn't bring Skeet in on this, they were basically harboring a fugitive.

Mount Haven

"Call this number." Bailey handed Coop a note pad she must have pulled from the stack on his desk. "Ask for Bobby Carlson. I'll do the rest. Just put him on speaker."

"Who is he?" Rowdy asked, worried.

"He works for our company. Private security. My dad trusted him completely. Even if Cole has corrupted and terrorized the rest of the crew, Bobby's solid." She chewed on her bottom lip, clearly worried.

"You don't sound so sure," Cooper said, watching her.

"I'm sure about Bobby, he's a good guy and he's also a former marine. I'm just not sure he still works there. If it got too bad, he would have bailed," Bailey admitted. "In that case I can tell you all I know and maybe you can still track him down. He's solid, I'm sure of that much."

Coop picked up the phone and dialed the number. After two rings a female voice answered. "Bobby Carlson, please." Coop waited while the receptionist tried to track down Bobby.

"Don't tell him who you are," Bailey added. "Not because I don't trust Bobby, but because the phones are recorded."

Coop gave her an exasperated look then straightened and set his cellphone on the desk pressing speaker. "Hello, is this Bobby Carlson?"

"It is, can I help you?" The male voice on the other end answered.

"I need to talk to you Bobby," Bailey said. "Don't say my name. Go to Pacifica and we'll call you back in twenty minutes."

She reached across the desk and pressed end. "Okay, wait twenty minutes then I'll make the call."

"You seem pretty sure of this guy," Rowdy pushed, settling back into the uncomfortable chair. Could he be an old boyfriend?

"I am," Bailey said confidently sitting next to Rowdy. "He'll be there."

Exactly twenty minutes later Bailey was punching in another number. The instant it began to ring she set the phone on the desk and returned it to speaker.

"Pacifica," a male voice said on the other end.

"Bobby Carlson please," Bailey said immediately.

"Victoria, is this really you?" the voice inquired.

"It is, Rico. I assume that means Bobby made it over. I really need to talk to him, it's important."

"He's right here. I can't tell you how wonderful it is to hear your voice. You come back here soon, you hear? Here's your boy."

Rowdy cringed. Was Bailey in love with this Bobby guy?

"Vic?" Bobby's voice asked urgently.

"I need a favor, Bobby," Bailey said not wasting time. "There's a family in California, Marnie and Dottie Montgomery. They're in danger. I need twenty-four-hour protection on the family until I tell you otherwise."

"How soon?" Bobby asked seriously.

"Immediately," Bailey told him. "Cole and Reese have found me. They tried to kidnap me and Marnie's brother saved me. I'm afraid they are going to retaliate by harming his family."

"You're with Jason Montgomery? Are you out of your ever lovin' mind, Victoria?" Bobby practically yelled.

"Not on purpose," Jase cut in. "We just happened to land in the same town."

"Jase, man," Bobby said, a smile sounding in his voice. "Glad to hear you're still breathing."

"You sure about that, Bobby?" Jase teased, also grinning. "Didn't sound that way a few seconds ago."

"You know what I meant. It's not a good idea for Victoria to be hanging out with a fugitive. Don't worry about the kid. I'll cover her myself. If I'm lucky, the old lady will bake me one of her amazing pies."

"Thanks, man," Jase said sincerely. "Tell Ma I'm okay and somehow I'm gonna work this thing out, soon I hope."

"Will do," Bobby agreed. "Man, small world right? I can't believe you of all people saved Vic from being snatched by those two."

"Sheriff Cooper here," Coop said with authority. "Jase and Victoria seem to trust you, but I'm a little more skeptical. Mind telling me why you still work for Cole Hughes and why I should trust you to keep someone safe that he's trying to harm?"

"Sheriff?" Bobby repeated, clearly shocked. "Jase are you okay?"

"I'm not in jail if that's what you're asking. I told the sheriff everything. It's a long story, but I didn't feel like I had a choice. Anyway, he's a good man and only looking out for our safety. My endorsement isn't going to be enough. Honestly, I'd like to hear you answer that question too. How could you still work for Cole Hughes?"

"I thought I could help you," Bobby admitted. "After what happened with Marnie and then you, I almost quit. But then I realized I could do more from the inside. I was wrong. After that night, Cole never - and I mean never - takes one of us with him on personal shit. I'm still digging but so far the only thing I've found is inside trading crap. Nothing concrete that would bring them down for the monsters they truly are."

"Bobby, do you know Skeeter Perkins?" Cooper asked, already knowing the answer. He wondered how his friend had come by some of the information in that file. He was pretty sure he'd found the mole. And if Skeeter trusted him, Coop could trust him too.

There were several seconds of silence except for what sounded like choking on the other end of the line. "Who?" Bobby finally asked.

"Never mind," Cooper asked. "I'll just call him myself."

"Uh..." Bobby stalled. "Whatever, I have no idea who you're talking about."

"You might want to work on that for the future, Carlson," Rowdy chimed in. "Someone might ask you that again before this is over and you'll need to have a quicker, more believable response."

Mount Haven

"Who are you?" Bobby asked.

"Not important," Rowdy said immediately. "What is important, is guarding the Montgomerys. They need to be watched twenty-four hours a day, which means you are going to need help. Do you have anyone you trust out there that can join you?"

"Maybe." Bobby hesitated. "Vic, you know I'm willing to handle this for free, but the only person I trust to help is Dom and he can't afford to take leave without the income. Stacy just had a baby and they need the money."

"I don't want either of you doing this for free, Bobby. You're both on the clock. Salary and expenses." Bailey glanced at Rowdy then Cooper and continued. "If anyone - and I mean anyone - so much as bats an eye at the assignment, call Agent Skeeter Perkins. He'll know how to get a message to me," Bailey smiled. "I'm sure you don't know him but he's probably in the book."

Bobby laughed. "Thanks hon. Dom and Stacy are going to be stoked when I tell them you called. We've all been out of our minds with worry. Hurry home, kiddo. And Jase, the same goes for you."

"Doing my best man. Thanks for the favor, there's nobody I trust more with my family," Jase replied. "No matter what happens, tell Cole where to shove his job. You need to find something that makes you happy, life's too short. I think we've all learned that lesson in spades."

"Later," Bobby said. It didn't escape anyone that he hadn't answered.

"You know Bobby Carlson?" Bailey said, turning to glare at Jase. "How in the world did we never meet?"

"I served with Bobby. I'd trust him with my life," Jase admitted, then shrugged. "We never met because well, we didn't exactly run in the same crowds. You saw Bobby while he was on the job, we hung out when he was off. I worked long, hard hours at the restaurant and even though I was starting to see a lot more of the high class socialites at my place, I wasn't considered an equal. No charity functions for me. Anyway, I wouldn't have gone if I'd been invited. Just not my style."

Bailey shook her head then looked at Coop. "Thanks for your concern, but we really can trust Bobby. If you don't believe me and Jase, call your FBI guy. He'll confirm it, I'm sure."

"I plan to," Coop admitted. "I have a lot of work to finish up here before I can head home tonight. Rowdy, will you stop in and check on Mags? Tell her I'll be there as soon as I can get away."

Rowdy studied his brother for a long time. Coop looked beat. Rowdy knew the incident with Bryan and Maggie had really taken a toll. He was worried about his family's safety, and rightfully so. "Jase, would you mind walking Bailey to her car? I need a minute alone with my brother."

"Sure," Jase agreed, holding the door open until Bailey stepped through then silently closing it behind him.

"You're wearing yourself out," Rowdy told him the instant the door clicked shut. "I realize I'm not an officer of the law, but let me take some of this for you. I can call Skeet, maybe sift through the file and pull out the important parts. Being away from Maggie right now is going to drive you insane."

"True," Coop said with a sigh. He decided to act on his idea. "I could deputize you. I have a couple reserve positions that I can fill anytime I want. It'd be volunteer, but you don't need the money anyway."

"I'm not sure that's a good idea," Rowdy said immediately. "We both know I can't pass the physical."

"What physical?" Coop asked with a shrug. "I've been here how long and nobody has ever once mentioned the necessity for a physical."

"Coop," Rowdy argued, "I won't let you get in trouble over this. I can help without risking your new career."

"I'm not risking anything and I need you on this Rowdy. I need it to be official." Coop ran his hand through his hair and stood. "You can sleep on it if you want to, but I need you." Coop watched his brother and waited. They were a good team and Rowdy had to know in this situation, the city needed a man with experience... Rowdy's kind of experience.

Rowdy nodded once, "Okay. I hope you know what you're doing. If you get fired, I'm not leaving that cottage."

Cooper laughed and pulled a badge from his desk drawer, tossing it to his brother. "I'd issue you a gun but I know you wouldn't use it."

"I'm not wearing a uniform," Rowdy declared, turning toward the door.

"Why am I not surprised?" Coop asked, grabbing the file and following Rowdy out of his office. "We'll talk about that later. Right now all I want to do is head home and spend a little time with Maggie before I hit this file again. We'll meet back here in the morning, let's say nine. I'll call Jase's DA first thing. I can't tell you how happy that makes me. It's not every day you get to begin the morning chatting it up with an attorney. Especially one that might be corrupt, lucky me."

Rowdy held out his hand. "Let me go through that tonight. You call Skeet and get the file on the plane crash. In the morning I'll tell you what I've found and you can fill us in on your chat with the DA."

"You sure about that?" Coop said hesitantly. "Bailey is pretty upset, I'm not sure she can handle much more tonight."

"You let me worry about Bailey," Rowdy said reaching out and snatching the file. "Go spend some time with Maggie. Put this away for a few hours. We'll have plenty to deal with tomorrow."

They had reached the front door. As the two men stepped outside, Cooper warned, "Rowdy, be careful. I'll follow you home but watch your back. They know where we live."

Rowdy countered, "I know you're a big shot sheriff and all, but take your own advice man." He swallowed. "We'll get through this."

Cooper pulled Rowdy into a brotherly hug. "No matter what, I'm here for you."

Rowdy stepped back, began to turn then stopped. "I love you, too," he said softly then slowly headed for his truck.

Cooper blinked, completely shocked. He couldn't remember the last time Rowdy had expressed his love that way. He was pretty sure he hadn't done it since their mother had died. Mom was good at forcing them to express themselves. The three male members of the family had pretty much shut down once she was gone. He was

Mount Haven

learning to open up again, thanks to Maggie. His father never had and Rowdy, until this very moment, had kept his emotions locked deep inside.

"Hey Sheriff," Rowdy called from inside his truck, "you're a sitting duck out there. Get your ass in the car, I wanna go home." He laughed when Bailey shoved him. "This century would be nice," he added and rolled up the window.

"What was that about?" Bailey asked, knowing something Rowdy had said was responsible for Cooper's shocked silence.

Rowdy shrugged. "Nothing," he glanced in his rearview mirror to make sure Cooper was behind him then pulled onto the highway. Moments later he glanced at Bailey, realizing she was too quiet. When he first saw that she'd decided to ride home with him, he thought it was a good sign. Now, he was pretty sure she had only made that decision because she wasn't up to driving. "You okay?"

"Is that a punishment?" she asked, not looking at Rowdy. Her gaze was focused out the side window.

Rowdy frowned. "What are you talking about?"

"That answer." She finally turned to look him in the eyes. "I hid things from you so you're shutting me out?"

Rowdy sighed. "No, Bay." He studied his mirrors again then continued. "It was just personal." He cringed when he saw the hurt expression on her face. He wasn't doing this right. But could he keep opening up to her when he knew she was leaving? After another glance in her direction, he knew he couldn't shut her out. In for a penny, in for a pound. He'd deal with the consequences later.

Bailey wondered if her fear had ruined everything. She had told Rowdy most of her secret, but she just couldn't bring herself to tell him everything. She thought he would judge her. She worried the money would change things between them. Not trusting him had been a mistake, one she couldn't take back. Now, he didn't trust her. She didn't blame him, she deserved his silence. But she wasn't sure she could take his rejection.

Rowdy stopped in front of the cottage and climbed from the truck. He slowly walked to the passenger's side and opened the door. Bailey didn't move. "Hey?" he said softly, trying to get her attention.

Bailey had wondered if Rowdy would bring her to his cottage or drop her at the apartment. She should have known better. Rowdy would never risk her safety for anything, not even his own wellbeing. "I'll move back to my place in the morning," she said softly, finally looking at him.

"Not going to happen," Rowdy said, lifting her from the truck and cradling her in his arms. He kicked the door shut and headed for the front door.

"Rowdy! I can walk," she protested. He ignored her.

Rowdy approached the front door cautiously, listening for anything out of the ordinary. He relaxed when he heard Knight rush to the door and bark a gleeful hello. He set Bailey on her feet and carefully opened the door. Knight leapt forward, placing his front paws on Rowdy's chest. Rowdy ruffled the dog's ears then reached back and grabbed Bailey's hand. They had some talking to do before he got started on that file. He pulled Bailey with him as he walked to the couch. He placed the file on the coffee table and turned to the woman he loved. She looked so sad and he had to fix that. He reached out, placing his hand behind her neck and pulled her to him as he lowered his mouth to hers. Moments later he pulled back. "I'm not punishing you and I'm not shutting you out." He lowered himself to the couch. When Bailey didn't follow he took her hand and pulled. She still hadn't said a word. "Learning who you really are from an FBI file was tough. I'll admit that. When you walked in that door, I was pissed. I think you know that."

"I'm sorry I hurt you, Rowdy," Bailey finally spoke. "That wasn't my intention. I wanted to tell you. I almost did a hundred times."

"What stopped you?" he asked quietly.

"I was worried it would change things. I'm not that girl anymore. She was shallow and spoiled and..." she shrugged. "I don't know, full of herself. I had a lot of growing up to do. My entire life, I was sheltered and pampered. I never wanted for anything. Dad spoiled me rotten. When he died, I was alone. My mom couldn't cope but I still had everything I could ever wish for. Peter stepped in and once again my life was pretty much worry-free. Cole and Reese changed that. Going into hiding, running for my life, working for barely enough to put a roof over my head and a few scraps of food, changed me. I'm not that woman in the picture anymore. I'll never be that woman again. I know I'm asking you to trust me and maybe that's not possible, but I need you to know I trust you." She wiped a tear from her face. "And I'm sorry I hurt you. I hope one day you will be able to forgive me."

Rowdy reached out and brushed his thumb across Bailey's cheek wiping away the tears. She said she trusted him, but how could he believe that? She hadn't trusted him. He realized none of that mattered. He knew he couldn't trust her to stay, but he would trust her with a piece of his heart. "I told Andy that I love him," he shifted his gaze to stare out the window, not knowing how to continue. "Back at the station. I told my brother I love him. It took him by surprise," he shrugged.

"There is no way that Coop doesn't know you love him. I've been around you two for months. You show it in a million different ways." Bailey was confused. Why would that put such a shocked look on Coop's face?

"He knows. Just like I know he loves me, but we don't say it any more. Well, we hadn't for years. Since we've moved out here, Coop has told me a couple times, but I've never reciprocated."

"Why?" Bailey asked softly.

Rowdy shrugged. "I don't really know. We were much better at expressing our love when Mom was alive I guess. Mom was always telling us how much she loved us and how proud she was. When Coop and I got angry, she'd make us apologize. That was never enough. She'd nod then say, 'Now, tell your brother you love him.' We'd do it because it made her happy. Men don't express their emotions as easily as women do. Having Mom force it gave us an out. I guess when she died, we just all shut that part of us away."

"So, why now?" Bailey wondered.

That was a hard question to answer. "I took a good hard look at my brother and realized he needed it. The attack on his family has him stressed. He's worried about me, his family, you, this town, everyone but himself. He's worn out and it doesn't look like that is going to change any time soon. His men try, but they're no match for Reese and Cole. I needed Andy to know he's not alone. There was a night, not long after we arrived… it was the night I talked to Max about the bar. I was sitting on my front porch, deep in thought when Coop stopped by. I could tell he was stressed. Bryan was

Mount Haven

acting out and something happened on the job, I could see it on his face. Mags was at her wits' end with the kid, the whole world was weighing him down. I wasn't there for him. I should have told him that night. I should have listened to him for a change, but I didn't. Instead, he was there for me. He's always there for me. We talked about the bar and my future. That was the first time in years he told me he loved me. That was the first time in my life he'd said it without prompting from my parents. Just me and him alone in the dark. It knocked me speechless. The next morning Maggie got me out of bed, insisting she was going to be my partner. I asked her what was up with Coop and she told me he cares. She also said that Coop needed to hear I loved him, too. I brushed it aside. Convinced myself she was just being girly. Then today, I looked at my brother and realized Maggie was right. He did need to hear it, so I told him." He shrugged, embarrassed but needing Bailey to know his hesitancy to talk about that moment had nothing to do with what he'd learned about her today.

Bailey considered. She'd jumped to conclusions, the wrong conclusions. Rowdy had engaged in a very private moment with his brother and she'd intruded. "I'm sorry," she finally said, wiping the remaining moisture from her face. "I had no right to…"

Rowdy stopped her, "Bay, don't apologize." He leaned back against the couch and sighed. "You said you didn't tell me because you didn't want things to change between us. So, don't let anything change. Things are awkward, I don't want it to be that way." He straightened, turning her slightly so he could look her in the eye. "I love you." He pulled her against him when another tear ran down her cheek. "Loving you is what made it possible to open up to my brother today. Things are crazy and dangerous and I have a feeling they are only going to get worse. I need to know that we are okay. I don't want whatever this is between us to get in the way."

Bailey inhaled a long, deep breath. "I thought…" she stopped. "I mean, I was sure… when I walked through that door and saw the look on your face, I was sure you would never forgive me. Then you left and I wanted to go after you but Coop mentioned the FBI and said you needed time. I was so sure what we had was over. I knew it was all my fault. I knew you had a right to hate me, but I need you Rowdy. Not just because I feel safe with you, but because I love you, too."

Rowdy pulled her onto his lap and held her for several seconds before he spoke. Then he reached in his pocket and pulled out the badge. "Coop asked me to help him on this, officially." He placed the badge in her hand. "He's risking his career. I can't pass the physical, but he wouldn't take no for an answer. He's trying to protect me. If anything happens he wants me to be official, especially after the incident the other day. I want to do this, partly for me but mostly for Coop. I need to be there to protect my brother." He kissed Bailey's forehead. "But you have to be okay with this, too. I'll tell him no if you want me to."

Bailey was shocked. Rowdy was letting her make this decision? This was probably the most important decision of his life and he wanted her blessing before he agreed? That simple request, more than anything he'd ever said or done, made her realize the depth of his love. She knew what it would mean for Rowdy to wear a badge again. She also knew how much he needed to be there for Coop. The only way to really be there, was to accept this badge. Why would he think she'd stop him? Bailey reached out and pinned the badge on Rowdy's jacket. "Of course I want you to do this. But will you answer one question for me?"

Rowdy let out a sigh of relief. "I'll answer as many questions as you want me to."

Mount Haven

"Why would you question my support?" Bailey asked, truly perplexed.

"It's dangerous," he finally confessed.

"You are going to go after Cole and Reese whether you have a badge or not, I know that. They're going to come after you. Our relationship makes you a target, having me in your life is dangerous. That has nothing to do with accepting that badge."

"True," Rowdy admitted then sighed. "I don't know the answer to your question, exactly. Wearing that badge is an honor, but with it comes responsibility. I guess I just need you to know I don't accept that responsibility lightly. I had to kill the men that went after Maggie. You know that wasn't the first time for me. I killed a young man in Chicago before we moved here. I need you to know I may have to kill again before this is over. This thing with Cole and Reese could be deadly. With Mags it was cut and dry, a clear case of self-defense. As a cop, things aren't always that clear. I will have to make snap decisions and no matter how I explain them, no matter what the circumstances, some people will never think what I've done is okay. Especially when you add in the others. That's fine if you're a manager at a small town bar and grill. It may be a different story if you're the CEO of a multi-million dollar corporation. As much as I don't want the life you are running from to change things, it does. In ways neither one of us can control. You said yourself that Cole is a master at fooling people. What if I have to shoot him? How is that going to impact your life? Will that impact be different if I'm just a bar owner versus a cop?"

Bailey had avoided thinking about her other life. She hadn't wanted to consider what might happen and how that was going to impact all of them. But Rowdy had some valid points. His arguments were irrelevant, but she was once again touched that he would consider them. "None of that matters," she finally said confidently. "There's only one question that needs to be asked."

"What's that?" Rowdy asked, studying Bailey.

Bailey tapped the badge on Rowdy's jacket. "Is that the right thing to do?"

"Right for who?"

"Right for everyone," she said more sure of herself now. "Is it the right thing for Coop?"

"I believe so, yes," Rowdy nodded.

"Is it the right thing for you?" she asked, holding her breath. She knew it was but would Rowdy admit that?

Rowdy didn't answer right away. Finally he nodded. "For now, I believe it is."

Bailey would accept that temporarily, she'd push him on it later. "How about Maggie and Bryan? Is this the right thing for them?"

"Yes," Rowdy said without hesitation.

"Then it's the right thing to do," she told him.

"You left out the most important person," Rowdy said, lifting her hand to his mouth and kissing her knuckles. "Is it the right thing for you?"

Bailey's stomach did a little flip. Rowdy always made her feel special somehow. And no matter how serious the moment, just a simple touch could send her heart racing a mile a minute. But how to answer that question. "Rowdy, to me you are a cop whether you wear that badge or not. It shows every time a stranger walks into your bar. It showed that day you rushed to the house to rescue Maggie. It showed again today at the station with me and then again with Jase. It's the reason I feel safe with you, no matter what is happening around us. Whether or not you have a badge is irrelevant when it comes to us. I need you to know that." She waited for a response.

"I believe that," Rowdy finally said.

"So, yes. You having that badge is right for me. Do you want to know why?"

Rowdy nodded.

"The same reason Coop wants you to have it: because of the protection it provides. We both know you are going to do anything in your power to protect your brother, your family and me. You need to have the authority the badge provides as well as the protection. You can't help any of us if your hands are tied. So, accept the stupid thing already and stop worrying," she smiled.

Rowdy laughed and shook his head. "I think you have been spending entirely too much time with Maggie."

Bailey smiled back. "I don't think that's possible. She's teaching me everything I need to know about the Cooper brothers. She's proving to be a wealth of knowledge in that area."

"That's what I'm afraid of." He pressed a soft kiss to her lips then stood. "Thank you," he said sincerely. "Now, I think you should go take a hot shower and climb into bed." He glanced at the file he'd placed in front of them. He had a long night ahead of him and he didn't want Bailey to be here for it.

"Nice try wise guy," Bailey said settling back. "I already showered today and I know you're just trying to get rid of me so you can read through that file."

Rowdy shrugged.

"I want to go through it with you," she proposed, studying him.

"Some of it might be confidential," Rowdy argued shaking his head. "For law enforcement only."

Bailey shrugged. "We both know that when you read that file, a lot is going to be missing. The personal stuff, the inside take. I can help with that. I need to help with this, Rowdy. I can't change what they've done but I can help stop them. I need to help you stop them. Please don't shut me out. I admit I wasn't as strong as I should have been earlier. I knew they were evil, but I had no idea… Well, I just had no idea. They always scared me, but now I know I should have been terrified."

"Which is why you shouldn't have to hear anymore," Rowdy persisted as he settled back on the couch next to her. He was starting to cave and knew he shouldn't but if Bailey truly needed to help, he'd let her. He would never tell this woman no. How could he give her what she needed and still protect her? He sighed, knowing it was impossible. That's when it hit him. Life was going to get even more complicated from here on out. This was one more woman he couldn't say no to. Maggie was bad enough, he rarely told her no. He groaned when he realized he'd turned into his brother and his father.

Bailey was watching Rowdy, amused. Clearly he had some internal conflict raging inside his head. "Whatever it is, it truly cannot be that bad," she finally said.

Mount Haven

"You have no idea," he grumbled and shook his head. Then he sobered. "Let me shield you from this. I can go through it, find any clues that will help us and then I can give you the condensed version. If I have questions, I promise I'll ask. You don't need to know the details. It's only going to hurt you."

Bailey disagreed. "I really do need this, Rowdy. I need the details. I need to know that I went over everything with you. I need to know we didn't miss anything because I was too weak to face the truth. I love my mother dearly, but she has never been able to handle anything unpleasant. I sat in Cooper's office today and felt weak. For the first time in my life I wondered if I was more like my mother than my father. Mom would turn away from this, deny it, pretend it's not true. Dad would face it head on. I'm at a crossroads and I need to see what I'm made of. I need to know I truly am my father's daughter. Please don't take this chance away from me. I need to do this for me but I also need to do this for Dad. I need to know he would be proud of me."

"I already know your father would be proud of you and deep down you do too," Rowdy said sincerely.

"Okay then, I need to know I deserve his pride," she countered.

Rowdy took a deep breath then leaned forward and opened the file. He pulled out the first list and handed it to her. "That is the FBI's list of known victims." He watched, waiting for a reaction. "They are pretty sure those cases belong to Cole and Reese. They just don't have enough for an arrest."

Bailey shook her head. "There are more," she said, sure she was right.

Rowdy pulled out the second list. "Those are likely victims."

Bailey took the list and read the names. There were so many people she knew on here. She swallowed hard and locked eyes with Rowdy. "There are more."

Rowdy wondered how she knew that. "Why?"

"Candace Barkley isn't on here," Bailey said, ashamed she had doubted her friend.

"Who is Candace Barkley?" Rowdy asked, wrapping his arms around Bailey and pulling her against his chest. He might not be able to prevent this, but she was going to know he was here for her.

"Candace was a friend of mine while I was in college," Bailey began. "She was from a small town in Kentucky, I believe. Anyway, she was young and a little wild and away from her parents for the first time. She liked to party. She was also jealous of my money and envied the attention I received because of it." Bailey cringed, she knew she was making Candace sound worse than she probably was. "She was nice, in her way and she lived in the apartment next door. We really did get along, I don't want you to get the wrong impression."

"I understand," Rowdy interrupted. "You were friends, but not besties," he grinned.

"Please, never say that again. It just sounds so wrong coming from a man like you." Bailey smiled, she should have known Rowdy would understand. "Anyway, it was our freshman year and Candace was headed to yet another party. I had homework and refused to go with her. She was pissed but refused to skip it, so she went alone. I don't know if she thought that would change my mind or if she was just that determined to party. I stayed in my room all night. I had a term paper due on Monday. It was important to me and partying wasn't. I thought she'd come by on Sunday and tell me about her wild night like usual, but she didn't. In fact, I didn't see her for almost a week. When I did run into her, she'd changed. I asked her what was wrong and at first, she refused to say anything. When I pressed, she told me my brother was at the party. Things got out of control and she claimed he raped her. She said he had a friend with him, but she was too drunk to really remember anything about the other guy. I told her she was mistaken, that my brother was nowhere near our campus. She got angry. She said he told her nobody would believe her. The next thing I knew she dropped out. I heard she went back to Kentucky." They sat in silence for several minutes. "My brother ruined her life and I blew it off as a way to get attention. I was such a horrible, selfish person back then. You would have hated me."

"I sincerely doubt that," Rowdy disagreed. "And even if that's true, I doubt you would have liked me at my worst. I was pretty full of myself at that age, too. We all were. What matters is who you are today." He pressed a kiss to the top of her head. "I know it's hard, but that's two of your friends that those guys raped. Over the next few days, try to think of any others. Anyone that started acting strange all of a sudden. We'll get them to Skeet and see if he wants to contact them later."

"Okay," Bailey agreed, sitting up. "So, show me what's next."

Rowdy handed her the stack of possibles. He explained that there was no way to know whether those women were attacked by Cole and Reese or somebody else. Many of them were victims of one single man acting alone. That didn't seem to be their MO so most of them were unlikely. Those cases also didn't have leads that could be followed. Even if they were victims of Cole or Reese, it would be impossible to prove.

"Maybe," she said considering. "However, they are both extremely competitive, especially with each other. If one of them ventured out on their own, the other one would too. Neither one can stand being bested by the other. They would be extremely careful not to leave a trace behind, not only to avoid prosecution but to avoid the other one finding out. Or to prove their superiority."

"It's something to keep in mind," Rowdy tried to figure out how to continue.

"What?" she pressed.

"Don't take this the wrong way," he warned. "I am not saying that any of those victims are insignificant or that their case doesn't matter."

"Go on," she pressed.

"For what we are doing, what we need to know, those cases are lower on the priority list. I know that sounds bad but at some point you just have to accept that what those women experienced was tragic but it's not paramount to our case. Does that make sense?" He cringed, hoping he didn't offend her.

"I guess," she said considering what Rowdy was saying. She knew him, so she knew he wasn't being callous and insensitive. "So what you mean is that at some point we just have to accept that the two of them raped a lot of women and we may never know just how many. We have to put the one's aside that don't have enough evidence to substantiate and focus on what we do have?"

"Exactly," Rowdy said relieved. "And, we are not trying to prove a case here. It's important for us to know what kind of men we are dealing with, but I think both of us have a pretty good picture of that already. We need to find clues, not investigate the crimes.

Mount Haven

The FBI is already doing that. We're looking for anything that will help us determine where they might be, what they might be up to and whether we have to worry about other victims while they are here. Other than you of course." Rowdy's insides clenched every time he thought about what those two would do to Bailey if they ever got close enough. He would do everything in his power to make sure that didn't happen.

"Okay," Bailey took a deep breath. "Then I think we should put the rape stuff aside for tonight and focus on the business stuff. Bobby said there was inside trading. How are they using that money? Have they purchased any property close by? Did they rent that BMW or buy it? Things like that."

"Good idea," Rowdy said, flipping through pages until he reached the documents pertaining to the business.

* * * *

It was almost one in the morning and Rowdy was beat. He glanced at Bailey and noticed she was jotting something else down on her legal pad. It had only taken her about ten minutes of digging before she realized she needed a way to take notes. Luckily Rowdy had a box of his old police stuff and it contained supplies. She'd filled up at least ten pages and was still going strong. He'd snagged a smaller pad from the box and had jotted down a few things of interest.

The one case that bothered him most was a Karen Bardell. The case was seven years old. It was the next known attack after Mandy Strausberg. Rowdy didn't believe for a minute that the men had stopped their reign of terror for almost a year. The other victims just hadn't come forward, he'd bet the farm on that one. Karen was a young intern working for Drakker Consulting when the incident occurred. Peter Hughes was running the company, but he hadn't deviated from Scott's original model. *Why change what's working*, Rowdy supposed. By this time, Cole had risen to upper management. Karen didn't work directly for Cole, but she worked in the same general area.

Rowdy studied the structure of the company more closely. He was no expert but Scott Alexander's business model was definitely unique. The more he got into it, the more he respected the man. No wonder Bailey loved her father so much. He cared about people. He was a brilliant and extremely successful businessman, but wanted to help the little guy. Early on, he created a program to bring college kids in and teach them the ropes. It wasn't your basic internship either; Karen was well on her way to being one of the most desired MBAs in her field when her world fell apart.

Rowdy wondered if that was the point. Had Cole been jealous of her success? Had Karen threatened his sexist ideals and his own success? The initial detective included two notes that made Rowdy curious. He mentioned Peter Hughes and said the man had taken a fatherly interest in the young girl. There was also a note about blood found at the scene. Rowdy scoured the file for DNA results but none were found. He read through the final report and scowled. Had someone been paid off? A favor called in? The case just didn't make sense and it certainly didn't stand up to scrutiny. Days after the case had been assigned to Detective Rex Davonshire, it had been pulled and reassigned to a Detective Tim Highmore. Highmore exerted very little effort and within a week closed the case, citing lack of evidence.

Karen couldn't identify her attackers. She said she'd been drugged and everything was hazy. The blood was the only lead

Mount Haven

Davonshire had. Why hadn't Highmore followed through? It screamed cover up and that infuriated Rowdy. It was one thing for a slimy lawyer to bend the rules. It was an entirely different matter if the detective was dirty. Rowdy had no tolerance for corrupt cops. He made some notes and decided to have Skeet look into it. Rowdy skimmed through two more cases, then decided to call it a night. They had to be at the precinct by nine and if he was beat, Bailey had to be completely drained.

"You ready to head to bed?" Bailey asked, setting down her pad and stretching. "There's a lot of bad business deals and shady dealings in those files. Some of it is probably illegal, the rest needs to be dealt with immediately. If we don't stop Cole Hughes soon, my father's business is going to be ruined."

"I'm sorry, Bay," Rowdy sympathized standing and reaching for Bailey's hand. "We're going to stop him." He watched her closely as they headed back to his bedroom. "Do you think Peter would listen? I mean, if you approached it the right way, would he be open to checking? The files you have come from his company. Can you make something up, tell him a story that will explain why you have the files, and then ask him to investigate? He's a businessman too. If he spots the problems, he'll take steps to correct it, right?"

Bailey shrugged. She really didn't know how Peter would react. She'd always had a more open relationship with him than her mother. Piper Hughes only cared about image. She only wanted to hear about social climbing and ladylike accomplishments. Bailey hadn't been into tea parties and gossip sessions before she ran. She was even less interested now that she'd experienced the real world. When things settled down, her life was going to be drastically different than it had been before. And that included the company.

"I guess I could try. But, what will I tell him? How will I explain having those files?"

Rowdy considered. "Well, your location is no longer a secret, right? You told your mother where you are when you called the other night."

"Right," Bailey agreed.

"Then call someone at the company… Drakker Consulting isn't it?" Rowdy asked as he pulled off his shirt. "Call someone on the board, someone you at least like if you don't know if you can trust them. How about a secretary or your father's assistant? Anyway, call someone and ask them to send you something. Make it vague enough that they won't know you are asking for something specific but make sure at least one of those files is included. Then you can call Peter and tell him you were going over things in preparation for your return and you found something disturbing." Rowdy shrugged, "make it up from there. Tell him enough to get his curiosity piqued and then drop it. There's no better way to get a man to investigate than to drop hints and then change the subject. He won't be able to stop himself."

Bailey laughed and climbed into bed. "I guess you would know since you're a guy and all but that just sounds… silly. Are men really that ridiculous? I have to warn you, I have a great memory. I think you just gave me a secret weapon. Next time I want something, I'll have to try out your technique."

Rowdy climbed in next to Bailey and pulled her close. He was going to miss this. The closeness they shared just before falling asleep. It was his favorite time of day. "Maggie uses that one all the time with Coop. How do you think I figured it out? We men aren't that observant. It takes getting hit over the head with something before we notice. I didn't reveal anything you wouldn't have learned from my evil sister-in-law."

Bailey turned so she was facing Rowdy. She leaned in and gave him a gentle kiss. "Thank you."

Rowdy was confused. "For what?"

"For just being you. I needed to look through the files and you let me. I'll forever be grateful for that. I'm not sure I found anything that will help but there were a couple things I want to have Coop dig into… he may need to send them to that Perkins guy but it might be something." She rested her head on Rowdy's chest and closed her eyes. "Did you find anything useful?"

"I'm not sure. I found a couple things that need digging. Skeet is going to have to take those on as well. There's missing information and some of it could be huge. We'll just have to see. No more talk of rapists and business deviants. Go to sleep. We both need a break before we pick it back up in the morning."

Bailey wanted to ask what information was missing, but she was sure it wouldn't make any more sense to her than the business stuff would make to Rowdy. They would just each focus on what they did best and hopefully it would be enough. She just hoped Jase and his family stayed safe and there were no more victims in Mount Haven because of her. No matter what anyone said, it was one hundred percent her fault that those two predators were in this town. She'd never forgive herself if anyone else suffered over this.

Chapter Eleven

"I need your complete file on the Marnie Montgomery case," Coop said into the phone.

"I'm afraid that file is sealed," Assistant DA Skinner said, as he pulled out a hanky and wiped the sweat from his brow. What did some small town Sheriff want with the Montgomery file?

"Look," Coop said, growing more and more impatient by the second. "This is a courtesy call. I'm playing nice in the spirit of professional cooperation. But I'm only going to ask once, send me the damn file."

"Mr. Cooper," Skinner said, trying to sound annoyed and hoping like hell his voice didn't convey his fear. He was bluffing, but if he gave even the slightest bit of information to a cop, Cole and Reece would have his head.

"That's Sheriff Cooper," Coop growled.

Mount Haven

"Pardon me," Skinner corrected with a frown. Normally small town Sheriffs weren't this persistent. Well, if he couldn't intimidate him, maybe offending him would put him in his place. "Sheriff Cooper, as I explained, that file is sealed. Now, I'm a busy man. I don't have time to mollycoddle some small town Sheriff trying to make a big name for himself."

"Well shucks," Coop said sarcastically. "You'll have to forgive me for not being properly intimidated by such a big time city DA. I mean, any self-respecting Podunk cop would know he didn't stand a chance against a smug lawyer such as yourself. Let me try harder, maybe I can hustle up some honest to goodness fear." Coop was barely able to control his anger. "Nope, 'fraid not."

"Sheriff Cooper," Skinner said, growing more uncomfortable by the second. This was not a typical back country hick he was dealing with.

Coop cut him off. "With all that Ivy League schooling you acquired, chances are pretty good you can write. Get it unsealed," Coop growled. "If I don't have that file by five o'clock this evening, you're going to wish you never heard the name Sheriff Andrew Cooper." Coop rattled off his email then waited. "Oh, and since the instant this call disconnects I know an unscrupulous lawyer such as yourself will try to find dirt rather than do you job, I'll provide a reference. Give Michael VanLeeuwen a call. He's the DA up in Cook County, Illinois. I'm not a gambling man Mr. Skinner, but I'd lay odds you're on the take. I'm sure Mike would be more than happy to explain what happened to the last dirty lawyer that crossed me. Five o'clock and not a minute later, then I move on to Plan B."

Skinner stared at the phone, shocked. He couldn't remember the last time someone had actually hung up on him. He sighed and turned to his computer. He had work to do and he'd better do it fast.

Five o'clock didn't give him much time to come up with his own plan. And he was already wishing he'd never heard of Sheriff Andrew Cooper. Twenty minutes later, Skinner bolted from his chair and rushed to his private bath. He barely got the lid out of the way before he vomited his lunch. He was in trouble, big trouble. Andrew Cooper was not a man to be crossed. But Coop, as his friends called him, was wrong about one thing. Skinner was not on the take. Cole and Reese didn't have to pay for silence, they demanded loyalty in other ways. Mostly they just scared the shit out of anyone they came across. He pushed himself to a sitting position and leaned his head against the cold tile wall. Now what? He was screwed either way. Andrew Cooper would use the legal system to nail him good. Cole and Reese were more like Charles Manson and Ted Bundy on steroids. Cole was reckless and soulless. Reese was controlled but even more monstrous. The two of them together were enough to make the strongest of men cower. Skinner wasn't the strongest of men.

One thing was certain: the instant the two of them realized he'd provided information to Sheriff Cooper, he'd be dead. But if he didn't, he'd most likely lose his job, which would make him a liability to the dynamic duo and he'd be dead. Skinner wasn't ready to die, but if he had to go, it was going to be on his own terms. He'd long believed that Cole and Reese were responsible for the rapes and disappearances happening more and more frequently these past few years. If only he could prove it. But the two of them were way too clever. The only case that had any DNA attached to it was the Montgomery case, which is why he'd met Cole and Reese in the first place. They needed the DNA to disappear. He'd known they were lying the instant they walked in the door. But what was he supposed to do? He didn't have probable cause to force a sample from the two and the DNA collected at the scene wasn't in the system. The two of them wanted it to stay that way and after an hour in an enclosed room and more veiled threats than he cared to remember, Skinner had obliged.

Well, he wasn't going to be their lackey any longer. He would email the entire file to Cooper. The man just might have enough balls, enough character and enough street smarts to finally take those two down. And if not, Skinner had Plan B. He was a lawyer, his attack would come through the legal system. If that didn't work, at least he could deprive the monstrous duo the pleasure of killing him. He'd just have to take care of that himself, as far as they knew anyway. With that decided, he pushed himself off the floor and began making preparations. First thing, make sure Sheriff Cooper had every last shred of evidence there was against Cole Hughes and Reese Weathersby.

* * * *

Cole was furious. Reese's plan had gotten five of his best men killed and one of them was MIA. If the cops had Clyde Seskel, Cole was screwed. How hard was it to head out to a hillbilly farm and snatch a kid? Apparently just as hard as sneaking onto the property of a backwoods sheriff and snatching his wife. And where was Victoria? If she'd fled the area, they'd be less likely to find her again. He'd just lost his best PI.

"Stop scowling at me," Reese said casually as he dropped the bandage into the trash and pulled out some clean gauze. His side looked okay, but the pain was killing him. If he were home, his doctor would prescribe narcotics to get him by, but he wasn't home. He was stuck out in the boondocks with a friend that never shut up. "Must you complain every hour of every day?"

"Seriously, Reese?" Cole barked. "You're the one whining about a little pain. Poor thing never had an owie in his life. Does that little bitty cut hurt, poor baby. Maybe I could get you some aspirin."

Reese almost exploded. Cole had no idea the pain Reese had suffered in the privacy of his own home. There was a reason he never expressed emotion. The fact that he was complaining should have alerted his friend to the dire situation. Reese cringed as he doused the open wound with alcohol. He was afraid the thing was getting infected. The last thing they needed was for Reese to be down in bed with a fever. If Cole tried to run this operation, it would fail for sure. His friend had absolutely no sense when it came to precaution. He never gave the slightest thought to contingency plans or being prepared. No, Reese wasn't getting ill over this. He would endure and the minute he saw that worthless Jason Montgomery again, the man was going to pay. Not a quick, painless death. No, Reese was going to torture the guy, kidnap his mother and sister and force the man to watch as he abused them to death. Then, he might put the man out of his misery. Or... maybe not. Death was too good for the man that had sliced his ribs open and bruised his chest so severely Reese still couldn't take a deep unencumbered breath.

"So," Cole said sitting on the couch across from his friend. And at the moment, he used the term lightly. The guy was getting on Cole's last nerve. "Man with the plan, what's it going to be? We need to locate Victoria and get out of Dodge."

"I'm working on it," Reese barked out then sighed. It wouldn't do any good to take his frustrations out on Cole. This wasn't his friend's fault. Although Flint Duvall was Cole's man. But, Reese had used him a few times in the past as well. He ran his hand through his hair and stretched his legs, crossing one ankle over the other. "The first thing we need to determine is if Victoria is still in the area. Chances are pretty good that she fled. We need someone to head out to that bar and ask around, subtle like. Do we have anyone available that can assist us with this?"

"I don't," Cole admitted. "Dad has the rest of the security guys on assignments of some sort or another. The six we already brought in were the only ones I could trust completely. The rest are squeamish if it gets too intense. How about Dalton Finley? Can we get him out here and back without anyone knowing? His parole officer has him on a pretty tight leash."

"Good idea," Reese considered. He had someone he could send to convince the man it was worth it. "I'll take care of it tomorrow." He studied his friend; Cole was still having headaches. Both of them needed medical attention. Reese was worried his friend might have a concussion. He'd hit his head pretty hard on that brick wall. "How's the head tonight?" he threw Cole a bone.

Cole sighed. So, they were back to normal again. He hoped they could end this thing quickly. It had been a long time since he'd spent this much time with anyone. Cole needed his freedom. He needed privacy, and most of all he needed stimulation. None of which he was going to get sequestered out in the woods with an emotionless cyborg for company. "The head's fine. The headaches are the same, but as long as they don't get any worse I'm not worried." He was choosing to ignore the nausea and constant pressure behind his eyes he'd been experiencing the past two days. He was sure it was just a side effect of the headaches. He occasionally felt dizzy but that was probably caused by his dietary changes, not the head wound and nothing to worry about.

"Good," Reese stood. "Let's get some sleep. We can go over everything in the morning. Once Dalton arrives he won't have much time. We'll need to fly him in and out. One night tops. He can stay in the bunkhouse in the barn."

Cole stood and headed for the back room. At least the bedrooms were comfortable and they had modern conveniences. No television and they had to drive about a million miles for a gallon of milk but it could be worse. He didn't know how, but he was sure it could be worse. "Goodnight," he said over his shoulder as he slipped through the door. Solitude at last.

* * * *

Coop slowly read through the documents that DA Skinner had sent over. How had those two escaped prosecution on this? Because Skinner had let it fly, that's how. He picked up the phone and dialed California.

"I'm sorry, the District Attorney is not in today. Can I redirect your call?" The female on the other end of the line asked briskly.

"No," Coop decided. "I'll check back." He hung up the phone and sat back in his chair. Skinner was missing, Cole and Reese were missing and the evidence was piling up, fast. It was time to call Skeet back and bring him up to speed. He was about to make the call when Mariah knocked on his open door.

"What's up?" he asked as he glanced her way.

"Package for you," she held up a large brown bundle. "Must be important, I had to sign for it."

Coop stood and walked to the door, taking the parcel from Mariah and setting it on the edge of his desk. If this was the results of the testing Coop requested, Skeet had found something. He'd expected a short email not a ten pound special delivery. He removed the brown paper wrapping and pulled out a large file. Great, more reading. So far that hadn't gotten them anywhere. He moved to his desk and called Rowdy. "You still planning on opening tonight?"

"You know it's time," Rowdy sighed. "It's fine. Maggie will be in the back, away from the customers and Jase will be there as backup. If either of those two arrive, we can handle it."

"How's the leg?" Coop had to ask. Rowdy was favoring his bum leg more the past few days and Coop knew it had been injured in that scuffle with the guy in the woods.

"My leg is just fine," Rowdy said calmly. Of course Coop noticed the limp, but it was nothing Rowdy hadn't dealt with before. "You haven't seen me bring out the cane have you?"

"No," Coop admitted.

"Then there's nothing to worry about. I've got it covered. My leg's fine, my head's fine and my heart is fine. Anything else you need to know?"

Coop grinned. "Nope, that about covers it. I got a package today. I'm going to start going through it but it looks like Skeet may have tracked down that blood evidence you asked about. I'll need to read the report more carefully but that makes at least four rapes we can tie directly to the pair and at least one murder."

"And Bailey's attempted rape and attempted abduction. Now we just need to find them," Rowdy said frustrated.

"We will," Coop pulled out another file and swore.

"What?" Rowdy asked, instantly on alert.

"Well, I'll be," Coop mumbled. "It appears those two are getting cocky. Says here that two bodies were found in the Nevada desert. One of the girls had a gas receipt hidden in her sock, shoved up under her toes. The receipt was for a gas station in Texas. Skeet traced the credit card and it came back to one Reese Weathersby of San Diego, California."

"Seriously?" Rowdy perked up. The Strausberg murder was going to be tough to prove, but now they had another case to work with. They were going to nail 'em on this one. Well, at least Reese. No doubt Cole was in on the deed as well, but tying him in was going to be a little more difficult.

"I need to go through this file, there might be something here. Do me a favor - have Mags come stay at the house until you head out and then drive her over with you. I really don't want her alone right now. Bryan is over at the Babcocks' again but Maggie is home alone. It makes me nervous."

"I'll talk to Bailey, see if she wants to head up to the house and visit for a spell. I'm still going over the case files and I think I may have another lead. I'll bring it by tomorrow and see what you think."

"Great," Coop said as he lowered himself into his comfortable chair. They weren't any closer to finding the men, but once they did... those two were going away for good. "The more we have on them, the better our chances of locking them away for the rest of their miserable lives."

"Agreed," Rowdy was all for that outcome. "Tomorrow then," he said before terminating the call.

Mount Haven

Coop studied the file and smiled when he picked up the next sheet. So, Jase was now a free man. The warrant and all charges had been dropped. He looked closer at the motion to dismiss and realized DA Skinner had taken care of this the same day Coop had called. What exactly prompted that crisis of conscience? Was he afraid of getting caught or had he finally decided to do the right thing? Well, until the guy was located it was impossible to know.

Coop picked up the phone and dialed Skeet. "Got your package," Coop began.

"Interesting reading, right?" Skeet said settling in for a chat with his friend. "The Nevada case was a lucky break. With that receipt I've been able to subpoena things I never had access to before. The docs are gradually filtering in but I knew you'd want to get a jump start on those. I tracked down Candace Barkley. She never went back to college. She got a job transcribing medical records, something she can do at home. I get the feeling she's become somewhat of a recluse. I asked if I could send out an agent to take a statement and she refused. She reminded me that the statute of limitations is up on that crime and she is not willing to relive the nightmare just so we have a paper trail. I can't say that I blame her. I'm not sure I'd support a family member going through that kind of trauma for nothing. We have Bailey's account, pushing Candace really isn't going to get us much more anyway."

"I agree. Especially if she's still struggling. If she's become a recluse, she's traumatized. I just hope she has access to help. Maybe you could look into that. I'm sure the Feds have some nifty program victims can access to help them deal with trauma or some such thing," Coop considered; if Bailey were as rich as she appeared, maybe she'd front the money to help the woman. Or, the court could ask for restitution. "I know those programs typically require a report but can't Bailey file one on Candace's behalf? I mean with us locals, the complainant doesn't have to be the victim. I'd do it but that is completely out of my jurisdiction. I'm sure Bailey would give you a call if you need her to."

"I should be able to take care of it. The best way to get Candace help is to prosecute Cole and Reese and then ask the court to order restitution. I'll file the paperwork to include counseling. Just because they can't be charged criminally for that one, doesn't mean they won't have to pay," Perkins considered and began to jot down notes. He had enough from Bailey's account that he could add it to a report and file it.

"I'm surprised you haven't asked about Jason Montgomery," Coop said cautiously.

"Yes. I'm a little annoyed," Perkins admitted. "You should have trusted me. I could have made sure the warrant was recalled. Lucky for you, Skinner decided to do the right thing."

"I was basically harboring a fugitive. Do you really think I'd involve you in that? I have connections of my own, you know? I don't need my hotshot FBI friend to handle everything," Cooper teased.

"It worked out," Skeet relented. "Don't hide things from me, Coop. I need to know what's going on. I trust you explicitly, I thought the feeling was mutual."

"You know it is," Cooper said defensively. "It was about protecting you mostly. Plus, I didn't have any evidence to prove his innocence. I just knew it was self-defense. I wasn't prepared to argue my case."

"I trust your instincts, you know that too. My wife would be dead if we hadn't gone with your instincts. You could tell me OJ was innocent and I'd accept it. Just don't keep me out of the loop again. We need to be a team on this," Perkins sighed. He was annoyed, but mostly he was hurt. Coop should have included him in the plan to help Jason Montgomery escape prosecution for a case that was clearly self-defense. And it was self-defense. It was all spelled out in the motion to dismiss. Skinner cited new evidence, but they all knew the evidence wasn't new. It had just been buried for years. "There's a lot I can do from here. Strings I can pull, but I can't help if I don't know. So, is there anything you haven't told me?"

"Nope," Coop assured him. "We're still going through things. Rowdy found another hole that needs to be plugged. I'll send the details over once we nail down our questions. Other than that, it's just a waiting game."

"I hate that as much as you do, but we're getting close. I can feel it. I've been hunting these guys for so long, I won't know what to do in my spare time when they're behind bars. I've been checking the porn site. Still no activity from our man. That's unusual. I'm even more convinced he's our guy. I may never be able to prove Cole Hughes is Slick GlozzomCreeper but sometimes knowing is enough if they're put away for good."

"I agree," Coop sighed. "Now we just need to put them away for good. I'll keep in touch. On a positive note, I get to go tell Jase he's a free man." Coop hung up, grabbed his keys and headed for the bar. It wasn't open yet, but Jase was still staying in the back apartment. It would give them the privacy he needed to share the good news. And since he was there already, he might as well stay for dinner. He trusted Rowdy, but he also wanted to stay close to Maggie tonight. They would all just have to cope with his presence.

* * * *

It had been two full weeks since the attack on the Coopers. Everyone was settling back into a casual routine, but the pressure of having two men as evil and sadistic as Cole and Reese on the loose made them all uneasy. Coop, Maggie, Rowdy and Bailey were trying to relax on the front porch of the big house. Maggie was fidgeting and kept glancing at her watch. Suddenly, *Forever Young* by Rod Stewart began playing on Maggie's cellphone.

"Hello?" Maggie said anxiously.

"I guess he arrived," Rowdy said with a grin.

Maggie stood and moved inside.

Coop watched his wife step through the door then nodded. "That's Bryan. She's not dealing with this very well, but I know it was perfect timing. Bryan's been missing Troy and Sharon and Scott said Troy is depressed and moody all the time. They needed the chance to reconnect after all that happened in Chicago before we left. Plus, it makes me feel better knowing my son is about a thousand miles away right now. He's safer there than he is here. And, I really cannot believe I just said that. I never in a million years could have imagined any scenario where Chicago was safer than Mount Haven."

"We'll catch them," Rowdy promised confidently. "We're closing in. We know the car is a rental and Skeet is tracing their movement from Mexico. It's only a matter of time before something breaks."

Mount Haven

Coop watched as Maggie stepped back out onto the porch and lowered herself into the soft lounge chair. He reached out and took her hand, giving it a gentle squeeze. "I just hope it's not us," Coop mumbled softly.

"Naw," Rowdy shook his head. "We're tougher than that. Mags doesn't have the Cooper Steele by birth but she's developed it over time. I know you doubt that Magpie but it's true. Bryan is fine and we're going to end this... soon."

Maggie smiled. She loved how Rowdy could still be so positive. She also knew the men were just as terrified as she was. Their entire family was in danger. Sending Bryan to Chicago to visit Troy was the right thing to do and he was elated. It showed in the short phone call she'd just had with him. But what if something went wrong? "Are you sure there is no way possible that those two could know Bryan is a thousand miles away with non-law enforcement friends?"

Coop looked at Rowdy then back to his wife. "Well, he's not exactly away from law enforcement."

Rowdy laughed. "Yeah, when I started calling the guys to make sure they kept an eye on the kid, every one of them had already talked to the old man here," he swung his bottle toward his brother. "I've got the dog guys on it as well and I have no doubt Andy called in the Dicks."

"Of course," Coop shrugged. "My son is going to be as safe as possible. If I can't do it myself, my brothers will."

Maggie laughed. She should have known these two would call in some favors. "Thanks," she finally said. "That tells me the entire police force is watching over Bryan. He's better protected than the president."

Bailey caught a glimpse of Rowdy out of the corner of her eye. He was in pain. Was his leg still bothering him from the attack or was he getting another migraine? She studied his beer bottle more closely and realized it was practically full. Probably a migraine, then. He'd been pushing himself too hard again. If he wasn't at the bar, he was back at the house going over documents. He rarely slept and he was always on alert. Both of the brothers looked a little worse for wear these days. Bailey forced a fake yawn then gave Coop and Maggie an apologetic look. "Sorry, I'm just beat. These long days are getting the best of me. Would you mind terribly if I headed back to the house? I'd like to turn in a little early tonight."

Maggie jumped at the opportunity. "Me too," she said standing. "I've been so stressed with Bryan leaving, I haven't slept well the last few nights. I'd like to turn in early as well."

Coop and Rowdy looked at the women. Rowdy shrugged, stood and took Bailey's hand. "We'll meet you at the station at around nine, if that works."

"Nine is perfect. That will give me time to touch base with Skeet again." Coop also stood and wrapped his arm around his wife. "Goodnight. See you two in the morning."

Rowdy turned and silently led Bailey across the pathway that led home. The instant he stepped into their room, he moved to the bathroom and opened the medical cabinet. He removed the bottle of pills and shook one into the palm of his hand. He turned to exit the room and almost collided with Bailey.

"Why didn't you say something?" she asked, trying to keep the annoyance out of her voice.

"It's no big deal I'm just heading it off. I'll be as good as new in the morning." He stepped past her and strolled to the kitchen for a bottle of water.

"Yeah, right." Bailey didn't want to argue and she knew that confronting him was only going to cause more stress. They could deal with this when Rowdy was back to normal. She changed and slid into bed, planning to wait for Rowdy to join her, but she was so tired the instant she closed her eyes, she was out cold.

Rowdy stepped into the room and realized Bailey was already sleeping. So, he'd been wrong. He initially believed the yawn was all for show but clearly she was beat after all. He silently shed his clothes and climbed into bed. The new medication the doctor prescribed usually started working by now. Far better than the last stuff but tonight, the migraine wasn't cooperating. As much as he needed the sleep, he was pretty sure misery was the only thing he'd be experiencing tonight.

Bailey woke the following morning to an empty bed. Rowdy was nowhere to be seen. She rushed to the bathroom then began a methodical search for her man. She smiled at that, still amazed it was true. Rowdy was her man and if she had anything to say about it he was going to stay that way forever. She found him lying on the couch, his head covered by a large pillow. As she approached, he groaned. Not asleep then. "Do you need another pill?" she asked dropping to her knees next to his head.

"Yeah, thanks," Rowdy mumbled but didn't move.

This migraine must be pretty bad. Bailey was worried; she hoped it wasn't another episode like the first one she'd witnessed. She stood, retrieved another pill then walked to the kitchen and put on the coffee, then she grabbed a fresh bottle of water from the fridge and settled on the couch next to Rowdy. She gently pulled the pillow from his face and handed him the pill.

Rowdy forced himself into a sitting position, squinting his eyes to keep out the sun. He didn't have time for this, not now. And he couldn't be out of commission when Bailey was in danger. Once he swallowed the pill he started to lie back down but was stopped by Bailey.

"Nope, it's back to bed for you. Come on, I'll help you. I can black out the window and you'll be a lot more comfortable on the bed." She held out her hand, stood and waited for Rowdy to cooperate. For a second, she thought he was just stubborn enough to refuse. Then he pushed to his feet and slowly followed her to their room.

"I need to call Coop and let him know I'm unavailable today," Rowdy said softly as he climbed into bed. "Would you mind getting my phone and calling the number?"

Bailey pulled the covers over Rowdy and set the water and the bottle of pills next to the bed. "I'll take care of it. Just rest for now. I left the pills next to the bed in case you need them again in a few hours."

Rowdy cracked one eye and scowled. "Where are you going?"

"To the station. We have work to do and just because you can't make it, doesn't mean I have to bail as well. Trust me, Coop and I will go over the business stuff today and you two can resume the criminal stuff when you're able."

"I don't like you leaving alone. Will you at least call up to the house and see about riding in with Coop?" Rowdy sighed. The leg he could handle, but he absolutely hated the fact that these headaches put him completely out of commission.

"Okay," Bailey agreed. "But that means if he gets a call, Maggie is going to have to drive in and get me. You're not going to complain about that are you?"

"No, I just don't want you alone… ever. Please, just humor me on this. Those guys tried to grab you because you were outside alone and vulnerable. It's going to be more difficult to attack if you are always with someone." Rowdy closed his eyes and tried to breathe through the pain.

"Deal, now try to get some rest and I will set your phone on the night stand just in case you need it. Give us a few hours and then I'll come back and check on you. If you're up to it, I'll make some soup or something easy on the stomach." She leaned over and pressed a soft kiss to his forehead. "Sweet dreams, babe."

Bailey called Coop's house but got Maggie. Coop agreed to pick her up on the way into the station. Maggie was thrilled. They made arrangements to meet up for lunch before heading into the bar and grill that afternoon. Bailey felt a little weird about imposing on Rowdy's family but if it gave him peace of mind, she'd humor him for the day. Ten minutes later, Sheriff Cooper pulled up the drive and stopped in front of the door.

* * * *

Bailey and Maggie slid into the old style chairs of the diner. They had decided to skip lunch and head over for some of Skip's amazing deserts. They were so engrossed in their conversation, neither realized they were being watched.

Cole shifted in his seat and rested his head against the passenger window. He couldn't believe Victoria hadn't skipped town. She was obviously feeling just a little too confident. Well, that was going to change shortly. He wasn't sure, but he thought the woman she was with was Sheriff Cooper's wife. He'd never seen Maggie Cooper, but Victoria's companion matched the description Duvall had given. "I still think we should just snag them both," he finally said. "We planned to take the woman before, what changed?"

"We don't need her," Reese said impatiently. He was so tired of explaining himself to Cole Hughes. Couldn't the man just let him plan the missions like always? He used to be willing to go along quietly. Now all of a sudden, he had an opinion on everything.

"We still haven't dealt with that Sheriff. Why would you think we don't need her? We snatch them both, contact Sheriff Cooper and explain the situation to him. Then we split and he can find his precious wife on his own. It would be a good lesson, one he needs to learn."

"No," Reese said then turned back to watch the women through the large window.

Cole waited for more, but it never came. If Reese Weathersby didn't stop acting like such a pompous ass, Cole was going it alone from now on. He knew he could do it. Florida was proof of that. He'd been watching the news, scouring the internet. Nobody had even noticed the girl had gone missing. Yeah, their partnership might just come to a screeching halt if his friend didn't adjust his attitude. Then where would the imperious Reese Weathersby be? Trying to figure out how to lure in the women on his own, that's where. Cole straightened when Victoria and her friend exited the café and walked to a Jeep Cherokee then climbed in, still laughing and talking like they didn't have a care in the world.

Well, their life was about to change.

* * * *

The instant Bailey slid the door closed, Maggie took off. "How long do you think…"

"Here's my phone, call Andy," Maggie ordered anxiously as she glanced in the rearview and spotted the sleek BMW closing in on them. "It's programmed."

Bailey fumbled with the keys and lifted the phone to her ear.

"Hey, babe," Coop said happily. "Did you miss me already?"

"Coop?" Bailey said frantically. "It's Bailey, we need help."

* * * *

Detective Lloyd studied his file in frustration. It had been weeks since Kathy's body had been located and he still didn't have a solid lead. Forensics found plenty of DNA on the table but he'd run it through CODIS five times now without a match. There was simply no way the killer was an amateur. Well killers, his forensics team had also proven him right on that score. They had two distinct shoe prints of different sizes. Two men had gone into that cabin with Kathy, now he just had to find them. He'd been confident he'd get a response from his regional broadcast. There had to be like crimes in the area, but so far… a big fat nothing. He would not give up, he would never stop trying. Tina Langley deserved answers. He couldn't give the woman her daughter back but he could catch the men who sexually assaulted and murdered her. If it was the last thing he did, he would catch those killers.

* * * *

Reese knew the women had spotted them. He needed to act fast or they would call for help. He took a corner too fast and the wheels actually came off the pavement. He needed to slow down. How was the tiny blond out running him? Well, not for long. He floored it and grinned as he began to close the distance.

* * * *

"Tell him we're headed to the station," Maggie practically screamed.

"No," Cooper replied. "Mariah had a doctor's appointment. The place is locked down tight."

"Station is locked," Bailey announced.

Maggie glanced to the side then pushed harder on the pedal as she hit a straight stretch of roadway. It had been nearly two years since she'd gone through that EVO class in Chicago. The guys thought it would be funny to send her through first. Kind of a challenge to the rest of the men. If they didn't do better than her, they'd be razzed for life. Emergency Vehicle Operations was something every cop needed to know and her husband wasn't above shaming his men to do better. Once she'd finished her initial run, Andy had taken her through the course again, giving her pointers and improving her skills. She'd had a blast but believed she'd never use what she learned. Today, she was being tested and she was afraid she was failing. Her Cherokee was not nearly as souped-up as a fancy BMW.

"Where are you now?" Coop asked frantic to reach his wife before the two psychopaths could.

"I think she's headed to the bar," Bailey dropped the phone when Maggie skidded around a corner. Bailey swore, reached down and retrieved her cell then quickly buckled her seatbelt. "Are you going to the bar, Maggie?"

"Yeah," Maggie was gripping the steering wheel so hard, her knuckles were turning white. She had the gas pedal to the floor and just hoped the two men behind her didn't do something crazy.

"We're headed out to the bar," Bailey said as she frantically glanced backwards and realized they were not going to make it. "Coop, they're closing in on us. What do we do?"

"Tell Maggie to trust her instincts. She knows what to do," Coop fumbled to grab his police mic. "Derek, I need you to head out to Rowdy's on a 10-99 person, 10-39."

"Uh…" Derek stuttered. He had no idea what his boss was talking about.

"Oh, for the love of…." Coop stopped, knowing the traffic was recorded. "I told you guys to learn the code!" Coop barked. "Maggie is headed that way and she's being chased by that same silver BMW with our two wanted suspects. I'm further out but I'm on my way. Tell Jase to be ready in case you need backup."

"But…" Derek began.

"I know it's not ideal, but you'll have to make do until I get there." Coop returned his attention to Bailey. "Tell me where you are and what's happening now."

"We are just approaching the bridge - the one near the upper road," Bailey let out a loud, earsplitting scream.

"Bailey!" Coop called. Nothing. "Bailey!" he screamed again. Still nothing. He waited and heard the distinct sound of water running. Had the car gone over the edge? Was Maggie in the river? The drop from the bridge wasn't that far, but if they'd crashed, that meant Cole and Reese were responsible. And it meant the women were in danger. He tried to accelerate but his police car was going as fast as was physically possible.

* * * *

Bailey realized Maggie was unconscious. She frantically pulled at her seatbelt until it sprung lose. Her body fell with a thud but she didn't care. They were upside down and in the river. She didn't have much time. She crawled across the console and pressed Maggie's release. Her friend's body slid to the side and Bailey tried to catch the weight with her body as best she could. Maggie was lying at a strange angle but she was stuck. *Think Bailey!* She rolled down her window and climbed from the car, then rushed around to the driver's side and pulled open Maggie's door. Thank goodness Maggie was tiny. Bailey hooked her forearms under Maggie's arms and dragged with all her might. It took time, but Bailey finally pulled her friend to shore and collapsed on the ground next to her. She knew she needed to find shelter, some place to hide, but deep inside she also knew it was too late. She barely reacted when she heard Cole's voice.

"Sorry sis, but the game's up. I've about had it with your antics. Now it's time to pay the piper," Cole laughed.

Bailey cringed.

"So, here's what you're going to do. You are going to stand up and cooperate," Cole moved to stand in front of Bailey. "If you don't," Cole jerked his head to the side.

Bailey followed Cole's movement and spotted Reese. Fear instantly immobilized her. Reese had a gun and it was pointed directly at Maggie's head.

"If you don't, my good friend, Reese is going to blow the brains out of your friend there. I'm pretty sure she won't survive that." Cole laughed then raised his eyebrows and waited. When Bailey didn't react, he was instantly angry. She was supposed to freak out. She was supposed to cry, beg, something!

Bailey swallowed hard. There was no way out of this. Her only hope was to stall. She forced her body to remain perfectly still. Maybe Cole would think she was in shock.

Reese inhaled sharply. They didn't have time for this. Chances were pretty good that the women had called for help. Was Tory stalling or was she just afraid? Didn't matter. He had to shake her out of it. He took a step forward and cleared his throat. "Tory," he said forcefully. "I will shoot your friend in the head. I will pull this trigger and never look back if you do not stand up and head to the car. You have five seconds to respond, then I shoot. Do you understand me?"

Bailey closed her eyes and stood. She had no doubt Reese would do it. She'd spent the past several weeks going over the heinous crimes these two had committed. Killing Maggie would be easy for them. But if anyone died in Mount Haven because of her, she would never forgive herself. And if Maggie were killed, Rowdy would never forgive her. She had to do what they said.

"Good girl," Reese praised, with such a condescending tone Bailey wanted to shoot him. She'd always believed there was no circumstance that could lead her to kill another human being, but she'd been proven wrong. If she had a gun in her hand right now, she'd gladly shoot both of these men.

"I guess I lose," Cole chuckled. "I still think Reese should just shoot the bitch. Her husband has caused us enough trouble and he killed five of my best men."

Bailey studied Cole. He was serious and Reese could change his mind at any minute. "Actually, Rowdy killed them. Well, Rowdy and his dog."

"The Sheriff wasn't responsible?" Reese asked, perplexed. Who was this Rowdy? And how had he bested five men?

"You're lying," Cole shook his head. "Move faster. You're going to have to climb that embankment and no funny business. I'm watching and if you make one wrong move, your friend dies."

"Tell me about this Rowdy character. And you mentioned a dog?" Reese pressed.

Mount Haven

Could she slow down if she started to talk about Rowdy and Knight? No, they'd just shoot Maggie and both of these men were perceptive. If she started to talk about Rowdy, they would instantly know how much he meant to her. She glanced at Reese and forced her breathing to sound labored. "I can't talk and climb at the same time. Do you want me to stop or talk about this later?"

Reese studied Tory. She had changed, a lot. The old Tory would have done anything to please him. She never talked back... well, not until that night she fled. He cocked his head and studied her closer. He just couldn't decide if he liked Tory this way, or if he preferred the haughty and a little flighty girl he'd known before. Well, he didn't need to decide today. He had a lifetime to figure it out. And once he decided, that is what she would be. He'd make sure of it. He smiled at her and nodded upwards. "Climb, we'll talk about this later."

* * * *

Rowdy crawled from his bed and stumbled to the bathroom. His headache had finally receded, now he just had that awful hazy, hangover feeling. He downed another pill just to be safe and climbed in the shower. He was a little concerned that Bailey hadn't called yet, but if she was hanging out with Maggie it might be hours before they got to the bar. Those two could gossip for days. He was just wrapping a towel around his waist when he heard his bedroom door swing open. He immediately moved to the cabinet, planning to draw his gun when he heard the familiar voice.

"Rowdy, where are you?" Coop asked impatiently. He needed to pick up his brother and head to Missoula. The paramedics had insisted on transporting Maggie. He wanted to go with them but he knew first, he had to break the news to his brother.

"You know, you about got shot. You seriously should not break into my house when I feel vulnerable." Rowdy froze when he saw Coop's face. "They have her?"

Coop nodded once then moved to his brother. "Maggie was transported to the hospital. They forced her car off the road just before they crossed the bridge. I had Derek waiting at the bar but they never arrived. When I got to the scene, Maggie had been pulled from the vehicle and left on the bank. Bailey was missing."

Rowdy lowered himself onto his bed and put his face in his hands. Bailey was gone. Those monsters had her and Coop knew as well as he did what they planned to do with her. He had this violent urge to punch someone and he couldn't breathe.

Coop moved forward and sat next to Rowdy on the edge of the bed. "I know," he said softly. "Believe me, I know and I hate to push you right now but I don't have a choice. Are you going to be okay here alone? I need to get to Missoula, to the hospital and find out what's going on with my wife."

Rowdy looked up, Coop hadn't been to the hospital yet? Of course not, he'd come to deliver the news himself. His brother knew he'd been down with a migraine today and he wanted to handle the notification alone. He stood and moved to the closet, grabbing his jeans off the back of the chair as he went. "Give me five minutes. I promise, I just need to grab a t-shirt and throw on some shoes and we can go."

"I know you love her, too. I know that," Coop emphasized. "But if you're not up to this, I can tell her you wanted to come, but

Mount Haven

I made you stay home. I need you at your best if we are going to crack this case and find Bailey."

"I'm fine." Rowdy pulled on his jeans, threw on a shirt and grabbed his sneakers on his way out of the closet. "Let's go. You do recall you found me up and in the shower, right? The headache is on the mend. I just have that awful migraine hangover crap that I hate. I need to talk to Maggie. I need to see if she can help at all. Then I need to find Bailey. Every second they have her..." his voice broke and he couldn't finish the sentence.

"I know," Coop said stepping into the hall. "They're good, but we're better. You have to believe that Rowdy. We are better. We are going to find Bailey and we are going to finish this. And when you have her back, you can help her deal with whatever they put her through."

"When I have her back, those two will either be dead or in jail. There will be nothing to keep her here. I won't be helping her cope but I will save her." Rowdy moved to the door then stopped. He crouched down and patted Knight's head. "Good boy," he said softly. "Watch the house, this could be a trap. Be alert boy, go play." Most people believed that was just a good-natured way for Rowdy to say goodbye, but it was more. Rowdy was giving Knight an order. The dog was going to be on alert until Rowdy returned. If anyone tried to break in, they would seriously regret it.

Chapter Twelve

Coop stood just outside Maggie's room. The doctor had decided to keep her overnight for observation and Coop was grateful for the decision. Maggie was safe, at least for tonight. This visit had certainly been a surprise, that's for sure. Moments after being led back to the small cubicle and stepping through the privacy curtain that provided very little privacy, the doctor had returned with news. Nothing was broken but Maggie had suffered a minor concussion. Then he shocked them both when he assured them the baby was fine. Maggie was pregnant. The information seemed surreal, delivered in the tiny sterile room, nurses hustling by just outside, the sound of steel instruments clanking against rolling metal tables and the smell of antiseptic and… something else surrounding him. Coop was ecstatic, but nervous. That made this incident so much harder to accept. He should have been there for his wife. He never should have let those two psychotic freaks get anywhere near her and his unborn child. He glanced down the long, busy hallway and focused on the grey security door. Rowdy had waited for him, not so patiently he imagined, just outside that door. He could clearly imagine his brother pacing the waiting room floor a few yards away, while he worried about Bailey. No doubt Rowdy was experiencing all the same feelings, but ten times worse. His woman was missing. Abducted by sociopaths that had eluded them for weeks. Coop pulled out his phone and dialed Chicago.

"Hello?" Skeeter said groggily. "Coop, is that you?"

"I need your help," Coop choked out, suddenly very tired and extremely emotional. He had tried so hard to keep his family together, to keep everyone safe and he'd failed. He couldn't protect his family, his friends or the town.

Skeet jumped out of bed and rushed from the room. "What happened?" He stepped into his study and settled into his well-worn executive chair.

The damn broke, Cooper told him about Bailey, about Maggie being injured and about the baby. Then he told his friend just how tired and defeated he really felt. He slowly slid down the wall and settled onto the floor. "I don't know what to do anymore. I have Rowdy and that helps, but when he's down with a migraine or busy at the bar, I have a couple deputies that try hard but they're not up for this. They may never be up for this."

"And you can't let Rowdy share the burden because you are still trying to protect him," Skeet observed. "You have got to stop this Coop. Rowdy is a grown man. The two of you need each other, now more than ever."

"I know. Don't you think I know that? But Rowdy is… I don't know what? Homicidal? Self-flagellating? Stressed beyond belief. Seeing the guilt he's carrying is going to kill me. And Maggie? She thinks this is all her fault. Same deal as Rowdy. She should have been able to out-drive them. She should have noticed them sooner. She should have been paying attention."

"And you?" Skeet asked, knowing Coop was feeling just as much guilt over this as his family, maybe more because Coop was the Sheriff. In his mind, that would make it all his responsibility.

"I'm fine," he said automatically.

"No, you're not. But you will be," Skeet made a decision. He just hoped Angie would agree. "Go back and sit with your wife. Comfort your brother and talk this out. Openly and honestly. The three of you are going through hell. Band together and figure out the next move."

Coop took a deep breath and let it out slowly, then another one. Skeet was right of course. He needed to pull himself together. He'd just have to man up and figure this out. His family was depending on him. He was just glad Bryan was still in Chicago. "I know it's late, but would you mind checking on Bryan for me? I'm sure he's okay or the guys would have called but…"

"Sure, hold on. I'll call Chief Griggs right now." Skeet put his friend on hold and dialed the department's top cop.

"Uh… don't…" Cooper shook his head when he heard dead silence. Skeeter had already put him on hold. He hated knowing the police chief was going to get such a late night call, but he needed this. He had to know his son was okay.

It felt like an eternity, but several minutes later Skeet came back on the line. "Griggs said he has a man on the house 24/7. Bryan is sleeping soundly after a relatively long night of movies, popcorn and fun. You can relax, Coop. The kid is fine. I also filled Griggs in on the situation and he's going to alert the boys. Nobody will go near that house without getting the third degree and a personal escort to the precinct."

"I'd like to say that isn't necessary, I'd like to say they don't need to go that far, but I'm going to accept it. I'm going to sit back and let my friends guard my son for me. Because right now the last place I want him, is with us. It's bad enough seeing Maggie injured over this. I don't think I could take it if anything happened to Bryan," Coop said softly.

"It won't. That is one thing you can definitely take to the bank. Now, go sit with your family. I'll get with you tomorrow and see where we need to take this." Skeet hoped that was vague enough. He had no intention of explaining tonight.

"Thanks man," Coop said sincerely. "I think I'll do just that." He slowly stood and returned to the room. Rowdy was sitting next to the bed, holding Maggie's hand. He didn't even notice when Coop walked back into the room. His brother was broken, even more so than he'd been after the incident in Chicago. Life had simply dealt Rowdy Cooper one more blow than he could handle. He was staring out the window, into the darkness, a blank look on his face. His eyes were red rimmed but dry. That was so like his brother, always stoic, always in control, never allowing emotion to get in the way of determination. Coop silently picked up a chair and gently set it beside his brother. Right now, Rowdy needed his strength. His brother didn't need to know Andy Cooper didn't have any more strength to give.

Rowdy glanced up when a large hand settled on his shoulder and spotted Coop. He absently wondered how long Andy had been standing there. Minutes? Hours? He had no idea. He closed his eyes and swallowed the lump that was forming in his throat. The contact nearly made him come undone. He leaned forward and rested his elbows on his knees, as he tangled his fingers in his hair and gave a frustrated tug. He would not break down, not here, not tonight. He needed to focus on Bailey, on her rescue then her recovery. He was at a complete loss and had no idea how to deal with this. He felt like he had a hole in his soul, an emptiness that might never be filled again.

Coop watched as emotions flashed across his brother's face. Rowdy was barely keeping it together. Andy wasn't sure he could speak at the moment so he remained silent as tension radiated from his brother's body. The strain on all of them was increasing with each passing second. He had to do something, but what? Coop settled onto the chair and gently increased his hold on his brother's shoulder in a show of support and solidarity. They were in this together and Rowdy needed to be reminded of that.

Rowdy barely blinked when a single tear slowly slid down his face. How were they going to survive this? His family had been through so much. Maggie could have lost the baby today. If Bryan had been with them, what would have happened to him? And Bailey? What was his sweet, sexy and fiercely independent Bailey enduring at this very moment? Thinking about it was driving Rowdy insane.

* * * *

Skeeter hung up and turned to stand when he spotted Angela in the doorway. The instant he disconnected the call, she moved forward and sat on his lap. "Was that Andy?"

"Yes," Skeet said softly. "I need a favor."

Mount Haven

Two hours later, Skeeter and Angela Perkins entered the large airport and walked purposefully to the check-in desk. He'd found a redeye and booked it, then the fun began. He contacted Donahue and provided a quick update. His boss wasn't too happy about the late night call but agreed to send a couple agents out first thing to retrieve his vehicle. He would also call Montana and alert them to his arrival. Once that was completed, he rushed through packing and loaded their bags in the trunk. It was now after midnight and they were finally boarding the plane. Skeet just hoped he hadn't forgotten anything vital. He settled into his seat and began the long wait until takeoff. That's when it finally hit him. Where were they going to spend the night? Hopefully, Donahue thought of that and handled it remotely. If not, Skeet would see what the chopper pilot could do. He'd been surprised when Donahue offered a federal transport so casually, like the expense was nothing. Skeet knew better, but he didn't care. The Cooper brothers needed him and his wife. Nothing would stand in their way, not even logistics.

* * * *

Angie Perkins tightened her grip on her husband's fingers. She could do this. She would not show fear. Her friends needed her. She smiled when Skeet gave her hand a squeeze and pressed a gentle kiss to her temple. Her husband understood. He always understood. She was proud of herself, no panic attack, no hyperventilating, no cold chills. She'd expected at least one of those but so far, so good. She took a relaxing breath and gave herself a mental pat on the back. She could handle this. It was something she'd been wondering ever since the moment Skeet told her his plan. She hadn't stepped foot in a hospital since the day she was released. Two full weeks of torture, then recovery and years of nightmares marked her past. But here she was, taking another baby step on the road to full recovery. It felt good. No, it felt amazing! She was grinning as they stepped through the elevator doors.

"I'm proud of you, babe," Skeet smiled. "I admit I was worried, but you handled this like a pro. You are such an amazing woman, I can't even begin to tell you how much I love and respect you."

Angie smiled even bigger. Skeeter Perkins was the amazing one. She couldn't begin to describe how much love and respect she had for him. He was the perfect partner, sexy but gentle, humble but tough, sweet but demanding. He challenged her in the best possible ways. He was also very good at his job. She couldn't help but be proud. And if these two men they were chasing were half as evil as Skeet suggested, the Coopers were going to need him. She pushed up on tip toes and brushed a light kiss across his lips just as the door slid open. The couple walked hand in hand to the room number they'd been given at the front desk, neither knowing what they were going to find once they arrived.

Angela stepped into the room first, followed by her husband. She slowly perused the room, taking in the tiny family. Maggie was resting on the bed but the instant the door opened, her attention shifted to the new arrivals. She let out a surprised gasp then shot off the mattress and rushed to her friend.

Angie had only taken one step forward when Maggie's tiny body collided with hers. The two women embraced with more emotion than was warranted, but emotions were high for so many reasons. Angie patted her friend's back, thinking the hug would end but Maggie continued to hold on. "Hey Mags," Angie whispered. "It's okay. We're going to help you guys through this."

Mount Haven

Maggie burst into tears. She'd done her best to hold it together until now but this was too much. She knew she didn't have to say a word to Skeet or Ange. No explanation was necessary, the two understood the situation better than anyone should. The sobs continued as tears streamed down Maggie's face. Angie continued to pat her back awkwardly. Maggie knew she needed to stop but she couldn't.

Coop stood, walked to his wife and gently lifted her into his arms. Then, he pivoted and strolled to the bed. He didn't even hesitate, he just set Maggie down then lowered himself next to her, pulling her against him as he wrapped her in a giant bear hug and whispered in her ear.

Angie's gaze shifted to Rowdy and she inhaled sharply. She knew that look. She'd worn that look for weeks after the rescue. The only thing that could pull a person out of that kind of despair was love and time. If the men didn't find this Bailey woman alive, Angela was afraid they would lose Rowdy forever. She made her way deliberately across the room and rested her hand on Rowdy's arm.

Rowdy was now standing in front of the large window gazing at the dark nothingness outside. He jumped a little when a hand softly brushed his arm and looked up. He couldn't bring himself to smile, but he turned and focused his attention on the vibrant woman before him. "Hey!" he greeted, happy and relieved to see a friendly face, then confusion set in. "Why are you guys here?" he now spotted Skeet on the other side of the room and addressed his question to the agent.

"There is nowhere else we would be at a time like this, Rowdy. We're here for you. In whatever way you need us." He glanced at his wife then gave Rowdy a nod. Angie slid her hand in Rowdy's and gave a little tug.

Rowdy followed Angela out of the room. He had no idea where he was headed, but it didn't matter. He trusted the Perkins nearly as much as he trusted his brother and Maggie. They were all tight. Running through the fiery depths of hell and coming out alive on the other side, tends to create lasting bonds that can never be broken. Rowdy shook his head in amazement and acceptance. He should have seen this one coming.

It was over an hour later when Rowdy and Angie stepped back into the room. Skeet was sitting on the uncomfortable couch in the corner, studying something on his phone. Maggie and Coop were still snuggled up on the bed. Every head in the room focused on Rowdy as he stepped back inside the small but private space.

Coop took one look at his brother and knew talking was out of the question. Rowdy's eyes were red rimmed and Angela's were puffy, wet and completely bloodshot. He just hoped the discussion helped… both of them. Coop swung his legs over the side of the bed and took a closer look. Rowdy seemed… well, maybe a little better somehow. He wasn't as empty and gaunt looking as he had been just hours before. He was grateful for that but instantly disappointed in himself. He'd been so wrapped up in his own stress that he hadn't even considered Angela. Of course Ange could help his brother cope with this. Nobody had endured more than that amazing woman and lived to tell about it. If she could bounce back, she could certainly help his brother do the same. He owed Skeet for this and he would never forget it. He turned to his friend and gave him a knowing smile. "You in trouble now?"

"Nope," Skeet said then immediately returned his attention to his phone screen.

Mount Haven

"Am I interrupting?" Coop continued.

"Huh? No," Skeet said with a shrug.

Coop was about to push but stopped when the doctor walked in. He had some papers in his hand and moved through the crowd, approaching Maggie.

"We've checked and double checked everything. The baby is doing fine and other than a slight concussion you are also in perfect health." He turned instantly and addressed Coop. "She needs plenty of rest and if the headaches get worse or she gets dizzy, nauseous, or has any numbing in her hands or legs bring her back. Otherwise, just pamper her for a few days and she should be back to normal."

Coop grinned, "My Mags has never been normal."

Maggie punched him but climbed from the bed and grabbed her bag. "I'll be in here, changing," she called out as she rushed to the bathroom and shut the door with a loud thud.

The moment the doctor had left the room, Skeet stood and began gathering his belongings. Once everything was tucked away, he turned to Andy and tried to explain, "We flew in expecting to head to Mount Haven immediately. Donahue arranged for a chopper to fly us that last leg but when we arrived there was a car instead of a bird waiting with instructions to head to the hospital instead. What I'm saying in my roundabout way is that we have transportation but we're not exactly sure where we're going. Can we follow you out and hopefully that small town of yours has a decent hotel with a vacancy for an undetermined length of time."

Maggie stepped from the bathroom and scowled at Skeet. "I heard that. Don't think for one minute I'm going to let you two stay in a hotel. We have an amazing home if I do say so myself and guest rooms galore that are just waiting to be occupied. You guys will be the first so you'll have to tell me if I'm missing something. You are staying with us and I'm not going to argue about this, so don't even try." She moved to the bed and reached for her purse.

Coop laughed and hooked the bag with Maggie's belongings over his arm. "Don't argue with her, my friend. You'll lose. Maggie always wins when it comes to this kind of thing."

Skeet also smiled. This wasn't a loss, it was a win. Staying with the Coopers was a far better option. He'd have access to the brothers at all hours of the day and night. And Angie would be far more comfortable in a house than cooped up in a hotel for days on end. "Then I won't try. I'll just graciously accept and offer my sincere thanks for the hospitality."

"Good plan," Maggie said as she stepped into the hall. The others followed closely behind.

* * * *

Rowdy entered his home and greeted Knight at the door. His dog was obviously happy to see him. He sighed deeply and wondered if this was the life he could expect. Years of loneliness with only a dog for company. But then again, a dog's lifespan was far shorter than a human's so eventually he'd be left a grumpy, bitter old man. He gave Knight one last rub behind the ears then stepped to the pantry and dished up some food. He hadn't planned on staying away this long and he felt bad about leaving Knight locked up without a break. He knew the dog had spent the evening following his usual routine. A routine Rowdy was finally used to. Knight would relax, hear a noise, walk the area searching for bad guys, settle back down, hear another noise, conduct a search and settle again. Such was the life of a working dog, retired or not. Once Rowdy dumped dry food in the bowl, he opened his front door and watched as Knight darted across the lawn and peed on every tree. He wasn't surprised when Skeet emerged from the pathway and headed straight for Rowdy's patio.

"Miss me already?" he asked casually.

"I have a couple questions and wondered if you felt up to talking," Skeet proposed, resting his hands on the railing as he watched the dog chase a squirrel.

"Fire away." Rowdy glanced at Skeet then focused on the lake.

"Coop said Victoria was looking at the business stuff. That she was trying to track the money in an effort to discover Cole and Reese's hideout," Skeet began.

"Bailey was tracking the money," Rowdy corrected. Sure, he knew Bailey's real name was Victoria but right now he couldn't think of her as anyone but Bailey.

"Right, Bailey," Skeet corrected. That was going to take some getting used to but he could see it was important to Rowdy so he'd concentrate on getting it right. "Well, did she explain any of it to you? Did she find anything we could use? I agree with her on that one. I think the key to locating their hideout is in the books. If we find the money, we find Bailey."

Rowdy turned and leaned against the railing so he could face Skeet. "She was jotting things down, making notes. She has a whole pad filled with heaven only knows what, in there. She showed it to me once but I'm a cop, not a CPA. I have no idea where she was going with her notes and questions." Rowdy turned, called to Knight then followed Skeet into the house. Knight darted past Rowdy's leg and made a beeline for Skeet. He immediately began sniffing the visitor's leg.

"Lie down," Rowdy ordered and Knight obeyed. "Got a chicken leg in there or something?"

"I'm sure he was smelling Kathy's dog. Angie promised her sister we'd watch after the mutt," Skeet answered then moved to the large couch and took a seat.

"We didn't interrupt babysitting duty, did we?" Rowdy asked absently as he retrieved Bailey's notepad and handed it to Perkins.

"No, Kathy's due back tomorrow. Ange left a message telling her something came up and we had to bolt. The dog's fine." Skeet flipped open the pad and began to read. Moments later, he looked up and studied Rowdy. "Bailey is a genius," he flipped another page and skimmed her notes again. "I mean truly brilliant. She definitely inherited her father's keen business sense. She found things that I didn't even catch. There are a couple questionable transactions that I noted when I went through the books but most of these I never even thought of." Skeeter stopped reading and focused on Rowdy.

"Does that help us somehow?" he finally asked. He couldn't see how it would. If Bailey couldn't answer the questions, he didn't see how Perkins could.

Skeet's mind was reeling. Cole was running the company into the ground. He had to be desperate, which is probably why he'd gotten so reckless on the insider trading stuff. No, Bailey's notes wouldn't help them alone, but Skeet had an idea. "Well, that depends," he answered hesitantly.

"On?" Rowdy asked.

"On whether or not you're willing to take a little trip," Skeet said, settling back against the couch while he waited.

"I can't leave," Rowdy objected. "I'm going to find her. I need to find her, Skeet. I can't just pack up and take a trip to look into financial crap that may or may not help us with this."

"Just a short trip, in and out, but first I have a question for you," Skeet persisted.

"What?" Rowdy sighed.

"Bailey has written Peter next to some of these notes. Did she think Peter Hughes was involved? That maybe he was responsible for the bad business deals?"

"No," Rowdy said moving to sit in a lounge chair. "She wanted to ask Peter some questions. We were thinking about flying out to meet with him but she was worried about that. We decided to put it on the back burner for now."

"Worried how?" Skeet stretched his legs and crossed them at the ankles. They had a long day ahead of them.

"Worried about her mother's reaction. She called Piper after the initial attack and told her what was going on. She asked for help but Piper blew her off. She insisted Bailey was making things up and she scolded her for implicating Cole and Reese. That woman has her head in the sand and I'm not sure dynamite could dislodge it."

"Wouldn't Peter be more likely to defend his son than Piper?" Skeet asked. He had never met either of the parents but he'd studied them from a distance. Peter seemed like a straight shooter and a competent businessman but he trusted his son far too explicitly for Skeet's liking.

"Bailey was hoping with those notes he'd listen. She had a good relationship with him, she trusts in his friendship with her father, she just couldn't trust him to intervene when it came to Cole or Reese."

"So, that brings me back to my original question. Will you join me? I want to make a short trip to San Diego. I want to meet with Peter Hughes in person. I need to see his reactions, get a feel for the man. That's something I can't do over the phone," Skeet explained.

"So go," Rowdy shrugged. "I'll stay here and look for Bailey. Knight and I will do what we do best."

"I realize you have never been a detective Rowdy, I have no idea why. But your instincts are solid. I need you with me. We won't stay and in the meantime Coop will be working this, from the ground floor. He's meeting with the local realtor as we speak. You only have one motel in town and they have to be staying somewhere. It's not realistic to think they are driving back and forth between Mount Haven and Missoula daily so that leaves some piece of property they were able to acquire, or they're squatting somewhere. We need to know if anything was recently taken off the market. What homes are vacant awaiting sale, rentals nearby, that sort of thing."

"I still don't see why you need me." Rowdy wasn't convinced this was the best use of his time.

"Because you know Bailey. Because you are involved with her. Because you love her. Take your pick. We need to convince

Mount Haven

Peter Hughes this is important. We need to get him to look at this notebook. We need to shock him into doubting his son. I can't do that alone. I know the right questions to ask, the right path to lead him down but you are the one that will get him to follow. You are probably the only one that can get him to do that," Skeet sighed. "I'm going to be honest with you Rowdy. This is a crapshoot. I have no idea if anything will break through that wall he's built up when it comes to his son. But I believe it's worth a shot. I truly believe this is the best way to find Bailey. You can take Knight out to the scene but we already know everything we are going to get from there. They ran Maggie and Bailey off the road then snatched her and left in a vehicle. There is no scent to follow, no leads to process. Instead of running around chasing ghosts, let's start at the source."

"And what if he just throws us out? Then I've wasted twenty-four hours for nothing. I'm better off here, helping Coop question businesses. I'm better off..." Rowdy stopped abruptly and jumped from his chair. They had a lead they could follow. He couldn't wait for Coop and anyway he didn't want his brother around for this particular interrogation.

"What are you doing?" Skeet asked alarmed. Rowdy was up to something.

"Nothing you want to know about," he called over his shoulder as he disappeared down the hall. He needed to change and get to the jail. There was one man that could tell him everything he needed to know. Moments later, Rowdy stepped from his room and was surprised to see Skeet waiting. He ran his hand through his hair and debated.

"You can try your hardest to lose me but I'm going to warn you, many have tried. So far, nobody has succeeded. Whatever you're thinking, I'm going with you. Then we can come back here so you can pack and we head to California. Once we talk to Peter, we can either grab a hotel or catch a flight back to Montana immediately." Skeet watched Rowdy carefully; the guy was definitely up to something and he wanted to know what.

"You're not going to give up are you?" Rowdy finally said with a sigh. "I can see that. I'm headed to the jail. We still have Clyde Seskel in custody. Which begs the question why? He was Cole and Reese's man. They sent him to abduct Bryan. Why have they left him in jail all this time? Aren't they afraid of what he might tell us?"

"Maybe that's why," Skeet considered. "Maybe he doesn't know anything worth telling. He's been pretty uncooperative so far. Maybe they trust him to keep his mouth shut or maybe they made sure he doesn't have anything to tell."

"Maybe," Rowdy agreed as he grabbed his keys and walked to the door. "But I'm not banking on maybe. I'm going to know for sure."

"And how exactly do you plan to do that? Coop already questioned the guy. He's not talking," Skeet said rushing after Rowdy. He was not letting the ex-lawman take matters into his own hands.

"Again, you don't want to know." Rowdy slid behind the wheel and waited while Skeet climbed in next to him.

"Yes, I do. I understand, Rowdy. You know I understand. Are you forgetting that Angela was missing for two full weeks? That she was abducted by a madman. A man so sadistic and perverted most of us couldn't even think of the games he played for fun?"

Mount Haven

"I haven't forgotten," Rowdy glanced at his friend and gave in. Skeet was right. The man did know, and all of the things that Rowdy had imagined happening to Bailey at this very moment, didn't compare to what did happen to Skeet's wife. "I'm sorry."

"I know at this very moment you don't care about the consequences. I know you are willing to do anything, no matter what that is to get answers, but don't lose sight of who you are, Rowdy. Don't compromise yourself just to catch these suspects," Skeet advised, deep in thought then continued. "I have no idea what will help you. All I can do is tell you what helped me. I had to think of Angela's abduction in the same way I thought of all the others. I had to take a step back and analyze the evidence. I had to think of him as a suspect, a sadistic serial killer. One I had been working for months before he took my wife. We'll go talk to this Clyde Seskel character, but I wouldn't count on getting much. There's a reason he's still in jail. If he was important, he would have been bailed out the day he was arrested."

"I know," Rowdy said softly. "Don't you think I know that? But it's a place to start. So, I'm starting. If we don't get anything we can act on I'll pack and we'll go talk to Peter. Bailey was sure that with the information in that book, her step-dad would help her. If not for her, to save the lifestyle Piper had become accustomed to. So, we'll try this her way… and yours. With Coop here, I know we'll be working it from multiple angles and although I'm not a detective, I'm also smart enough to know that's a good strategy."

Rowdy pulled to the back of the station and entered the building from the rear door. He spotted Derek and approached the young cop. "This is Agent Skeeter Perkins, we need to speak to Seskel."

Derek jumped from his chair and held out a hand. "You're the one that's been sending us all those files. We're going to get them, I know it. We are going to get them… and Bailey. The two of them are going to spend the rest of their miserable lives in a cage."

"I certainly hope so," Skeet grinned. "Now, the prisoner?"

"Oh, sure." Derek went to a cabinet and pulled out a ring of keys. "I'll leave it unlocked but when you're finished, do me a favor and lock them back up. Coop just called and he wants me to head over and check out an abandoned old shack on the east end of town. I'll lock the doors so the public can't wander in and interrupt."

"Is that a good idea?" Skeet was not comfortable sending this rookie cop out to investigate on his own. "Maybe you should take backup."

"Oh, yeah. No problem. Mathews is meeting me at the end of the street. If we see anything suspicious we won't go it alone. Coop already explained what would happen if we didn't call it in before taking action."

Skeet relaxed and followed Rowdy into the back room. There was only one prisoner in sight and the guy clearly had an attitude. This was not going to be easy. Rowdy slid the key in the lock and stepped inside the cell. The tiny space was sparsely furnished. It had a single bed with a mattress and decent blankets. A table with two chairs and a urinal. Rowdy grabbed a chair and straddled it backwards as he studied the man sitting on the bed. Clyde's back was against the wall and he looked smug.

"Awe, you came to visit. How special. Any chance you brought me some treats?" He laughed as his eyes twinkled with mischief.

Rowdy was across the room in two seconds flat. He grabbed the man by the front of his shirt and pulled his face forward. "We are going to have a chat and you will tell me what I need to know. If you don't," he shrugged and released his hold. The man fell with a thud but quickly recovered.

"That's police brutality. I want this man charged. You saw what he did. Get this guy away from me," Clyde yelled as he pushed his body to the corner of the bed, as far away from Rowdy as he could possibly get.

Skeet moved forward. "I'm FBI Agent Perkins and I have a few questions for you."

The man's eyes widened then he masked his alarm with a cocky grin. "Good for you. Now, are you going to arrest this man for assault?"

"Nope," Skeet said taking the second chair and straddling it the same way Rowdy did. "I'm going to ask you a series of questions and I expect you to answer them truthfully. It's my understanding you were less than cooperative with Sheriff Cooper. I highly advise you to rethink that strategy. I need to know where Cole and Reese are staying. Are they somewhere here in town or are they commuting from Missoula?"

Clyde studied the two men. If he talked, what would he get out of it? If there was no reward, why bother? He studied the first guy and debated. He was terrified of Reese Weathersby, but he was also worried about this guy. He had that look that said he wasn't a man you should mess with.

"I don't know where Reese is staying. We weren't allowed to know. The only person that had access to their whereabouts was Flint Duvall. If you want to know where to find Cole and Reese, you will have to ask him," Clyde supplied. Anything more, any other details and they would have to offer him something in return.

"Well, since the only way that conversation is going to happen is with a séance, let's try again." Rowdy was growing impatient. This guy had to know something. He'd worked for the monsters for years.

"Flint is dead?" Clyde asked amazed. No wonder he hadn't heard a word from anyone. But why hadn't one of the other guys stopped in to give him his orders? "How?"

Skeet glanced at Rowdy then back to the prisoner. He was growing doubtful that the guy knew anything. There was a reason Cole left him here and Skeet was pretty sure it was because he was too low level to be a threat. He nodded in Rowdy's direction. "He shot him. Now, Mr. Seskel, what can you tell me? What do you know that I might need to know? Because I'm growing tired of this conversation already."

Clyde looked from Skeet to Rowdy then back to Skeet. These two weren't your typical cops. There was an underlying danger to them. One Clyde didn't want to unleash. He still couldn't believe Flint was dead, and at the hands of this stranger. No, he didn't want to cross these two. What could he tell them that would make them leave? Some kind of bone that they could gnaw on for a while. "Look," he began. "Something happened a few years back, before I was involved with the inner circle. Something that scared Cole so much he changed his op plan. Now, nobody knows where they are except Flint. Nobody has information unless it's required for them to do the job. Nobody talks, not to each other not to anyone on the outside. So I can't tell you what you want to know. I can tell you that Cole has a man, someone on the inside of the company. A money man. A guy that handles things, buys property, rents cars, charters planes whatever. This guy, and don't bother asking because I don't know his name, is Cole's go-to guy when it comes to finances. He's also a money guy in the company. That should at least narrow it down."

Rowdy slid the door open and left the cell, Skeet followed. They headed back to the main office area. Mariah was now situated in front of her computer working diligently. She was concentrating on the screen so intensely she didn't even look up when Rowdy dropped the keys on her desk. He turned and took a step forward when he realized Skeet had disappeared. Coop must be back in the office, too.

Rowdy opened the door without knocking and entered the room. Both men looked up and Coop motioned to the door. Rowdy pushed it closed then moved to the visitor's chair. Something was up. He wasn't sure he could take any more bad news.

"Skeet said he told you I went to visit Violet Coulter this morning," Coop began.

"Yeah, but from the look on your face you didn't find anything," Rowdy surmised.

"Yes and no," Coop shook his head. "Reese did stop in to see Violet. He was looking for a place to rent month by month here in town. When she told him she didn't have a listing, he freaked out... her words. She's lucky he didn't get violent, just left mumbling something about small towns."

"How does that help us?" Rowdy asked, so exhausted he couldn't think straight.

Coop studied his brother. He needed to get back in the game. His emotions were driving the bus here. He wasn't surprised, Skeet had gone through the same thing when Angie was missing. Well, he'd pulled his friend back from oblivion years ago, he could do the same for his brother now. "Rowdy, think like a cop, not a wounded man pining for his woman."

Rowdy stood and began pacing the small space. Coop was right, he wasn't thinking like a cop. Okay, Bailey needed him and the only way he was going to find her was to be a cop. He was a cop, so think. He turned to face his brother again. "So, were there listings? Did Violet lie?"

"Yes," Coop said, relieved. "Two of them. Violet didn't like Reese so she lied. She didn't want the likes of him moving to her cozy little town. But old man Wright's place out on Maple Drive was available and Zilva Tischner's place. You know the one, Skip moved over there last week. He couldn't stand living with his grandparents any longer."

"Right," Rowdy frowned and settled back into the chair. "How does that help us?"

"Because we know two things now," Skeet answered. "Reese was looking for a temporary place to stay and he didn't find one. The Tischner place is unavailable and Coop sent Derek and Matthew out to check the Wright spread once they ruled out the old shack. They're on their way back, but called in to report the place is still vacant."

"Again, how does that help us?" Rowdy said impatiently.

"Because we have a place to start," Coop threw the stack of papers he was studying across his table. "I get it Rowdy, you're worried. But seriously, stop taking it out on us. We are doing the best we can here. We're all working on it. Following leads as we find them. Do you think you're the only one upset over this? I've been up since six working on it. Maggie's an emotional wreck. Jase called, he decided to open the café for a few hours for lunch but the three of them are barely keeping it together. Theresa and Casey take turns in the bathroom and never stop crying. Skeet and Angie dropped everything to fly out from Chicago. So focus your anger where it belongs, at Cole and Reese. Stop trying to push away everyone that cares about you because honestly, I really can't take much more of your attitude." With that he stood and left the room.

Rowdy watched his brother go. Once again, Coop was right. He was so frustrated and angry at the world, he needed a target. And since he couldn't find Cole Hughes or Reese Weathersby, he was taking it out on Coop. He glanced at Skeet then stood and followed his brother. He found him outside in the small picnic area set up for employees. He was sitting on the bench, arms resting on the table, head flat on his forearms.

Rowdy stood and watched Coop for several minutes before he moved forward and joined his brother. The moment he stepped outside he knew, Coop was struggling. His brother needed him and what had he done? Made things worse. He slowly lowered himself to the bench straddling the seat so he could watch his brother. "Tell me," he said so softly it was almost a whisper.

Coop glanced at Rowdy then placed his forehead on his arms again. "There's nothing to tell."

"That's BS and you know it." Rowdy shifted, bringing his leg back around so his back was to the table as he placed his elbows on the flat surface. "I'm sorry, man. I'm sorry. As usual I got so caught up in my own grief I failed to see what was going on with you." He leaned to the side bumping Coop with his shoulder. "So talk to me. You're right, we're in this together. All the way. You can't insist I come to you with my problems when you're never willing to share your burdens with me. I know you have Maggie and that's usually enough, but clearly there's something more here. Let me help."

Coop sighed and twisted around then he too placed his elbows on the table and stared straight ahead, lost in thought. "I just keep thinking I could have lost her. We both know what kind of men those two are. They left her there, unconscious on the bank. But they could just as easily have taken her with them, or worse killed her to get back at me. I killed their man. And if Bryan had been there…" Coop swallowed and didn't know how to finish that sentence.

"I know," Rowdy leaned forward and placed his elbows on his knees. "I know. I've been thinking the same thing. Could that be another clue? You're better at this Dick stuff than me, but there has to be a reason they just left her there. They knew she could identify them, right? Or did they think she hadn't seen them?"

"I don't know," Coop said, considering that angle. He hadn't really put much thought into it before. "They had to be pissed about their men. Those two always get revenge so why not make me suffer by taking my wife?"

"Unless Bailey said something to stop them," Rowdy suggested. Bailey loved Maggie, she would do anything in her power to make sure the woman wasn't injured or killed.

"Possible," Coop nodded. "But does it really matter? Maggie still spent the night in the hospital and Bailey is… I don't know where Bailey is. And no matter how hard I try, I can't seem to catch a break."

Rowdy realized what this was about. Andy Cooper felt vulnerable and guilty. His family's lives were at stake and Coop felt responsible for Bailey's abduction. "You know…" he trailed off, not sure how to continue. "I don't blame you. Bailey doesn't blame you. Maggie doesn't blame you either. Nobody in this town blames you, Coop. You have always had unrealistic expectations for yourself. They got worse once Mom died and they ballooned into this, I don't know, invisible monster that is always chasing you, after Dad passed away."

"I saw it when we were searching for Angela," Skeet said, joining his friends. "This unstoppable force, conquering the world one case at a time. Rowdy's description is apt. It was like you were fighting some huge, invisible monster that only you could see. I didn't try to rein it in and I probably should have. Instead, I used you. I used your need to protect the world to my advantage because I knew it would help you find my amazing wife. It worked and I convinced myself that was just who you are. That I didn't need to step in. But I was wrong." Skeet sat on the other side of Coop and put a hand on his shoulder. "I was so wrong. I tried to push you in the right direction last night on the phone but I failed. Stop trying to carry Rowdy's burdens, Maggie's burdens, the town's burdens. You are only one man, and seriously… your burdens are enough."

Coop didn't know what to say. He couldn't let go. He couldn't stop helping his family. He was the Sheriff, he couldn't ignore the needs of the community. And right now there were two not-so-invisible monsters on the loose that needed to be captured.

Rowdy watched his brother and knew Skeet wasn't making any progress. He stood and moved sideways so he was directly in front of Coop. "Skeet and I are heading to California this afternoon. I need you to work on tracking down the property. They found a place, somewhere, somehow they found a place to stay. And it's not in Missoula, but the realtor might be. Contact every realtor company you can find. Get records of every transaction that has occurred in the past two months. We'll get the exact date Reese checked into the motel from Betty and go from there."

"Are you giving the orders now?" Coop straightened and looked at his brother.

"Yes," Rowdy nodded. "Skeet and I are taking the lead on this one. You need to stop trying to control everything and take a step back. You need to focus on Maggie and that unborn baby. You need to call Bryan every night and make sure the kid is okay. And you need to tell Bryan the truth, a watered down version anyway. He needs to know bad things are happening here but that it's okay because you, me, Skeet, Derek and Matthew are on it. Bryan trusts you, he believes in you. In his world, Andy Cooper always wins. If he finds out about this some other way, you are going to ruin all the progress he's made since we moved here.

Stop trying to shelter us all from the bad things in the world and start living your life," Rowdy grinned. "Bailey informed me one day that as awful as it was, I had to accept that I am merely a mortal man and not Superman. My delivery is nowhere near as good as hers was, but I think you get the message. You've always been there for me, in one way or another, even as kids. But when Mom and Dad died, you took that to a whole new level. One I'm not sure is healthy. When I got shot, I honestly believed it was harder on you than me. I found a way to go on. You? You are still living with the guilt. I don't know how many times I have to tell you to stop feeling guilty. You're a cop, I'm not. So what? So yeah, I'm taking the lead on this. But I can't do it alone. I need you and Skeet to help me. To guide me. I need you at your best because we have to think of everything. We have to stop them. We have to rescue Bailey before it's too late. Trust me Coop, have a little faith in me. I'm still a cop in here," he put his hand over his chest. "And I will not fail at this one, the stakes are too high."

"I have faith in you, Rowdy and I do trust you. So, I'll go back inside and when Derek and Matthew get back, with Mariah's help, we'll get started. By the time you return, we will know every property transaction that has occurred within 50 miles of this place." Coop studied his brother. "But I have to warn you, it might not be enough. I highly doubt they just marched in and used their own names. We'll do a search for Cole, Reese, Weathersby International and Drakker but they could have used a fake name, fake ID, fake everything. I don't mean to put pressure on you, but we need something from Peter Hughes. A string we can tug to unravel this whole mess."

"We'll get one," Rowdy said confidently and turned to Skeet. "You need to say goodbye to your wife? If so, make it quick. I'm heading to my place to grab a change of clothes and deliver the dog to the main house. Get us that transportation. We're going to San Diego." The two men walked to the truck in silence.

The minute Rowdy pulled onto the highway, Skeet let out a loud sigh and went for broke. "He's a mess. I've never seen him like this. I think there's something more."

"There is," Rowdy agreed. "He had to kill a man."

"So did you," Skeet argued. "And the two of you couldn't be more alike."

"Which is why I know how much it's eating at him," Rowdy explained. "I've been there. Not here, not recently. Somehow, once you go through that... once you accept there was nothing you could have done differently, the next time is a little easier to live with. I was a mess in Chicago. There's a reason Coop is so protective. I think he's constantly watching me, just waiting for me to break again. This thing with Bailey it brought me close. But I'm not broken yet and neither is Coop. He knows he didn't have a choice. He knows it was that man's life or mine. He knows it sucks to take a life, but it's a reality of the job. And given a little time, he'll make peace with it. Unfortunately, with those two on the loose it's going to be awhile before he can decompress. I'm worried," Rowdy admitted as he looked at the agent beside him. "I'm not sure he'll come out the other side the same man if he has to take another life so soon. Not until he can deal with the guilt, the questions, the internal debate he's wrestling with over the first one. And we both know it's entirely possible we are going to have to shoot Cole or Reese or both before this is over."

"He'll come out just fine. Maybe not the same man, maybe a better man, but he'll survive. Do you know why?" Skeet asked.

"Why?" Rowdy wasn't so sure.

"Because he has us. You, Maggie and even me and Ange. We have each gone through our own private hell and come out the other side stronger people. More compassionate but more skeptical. More humble but more determined. More sensitive but stronger. You, me, Angie we've all seen death up close and personal. Each of us views life and death a little different than we did before. This is Coop's time to search deep within himself and discover who he really is. And I for one am not in the least bit worried. If that's all that's going on here, a struggle to accept actions he took while protecting his family and himself, then Coop will figure it all out and be a better man for it. Even with everything he's seen, your brother has always been a true optimist. I hope he doesn't lose that, but maybe a little pessimism is just what the man needs to create balance."

Rowdy grinned. "Okay, Confucius. I'll drop you at the house. You have twenty minutes to get everything lined up then I start calling in favors. I want to get in, confront Peter and get out. We're not spending the night. We have too much to do here in Mount Haven to relax in sunny Cal longer than is absolutely necessary."

Mount Haven

"I think I liked you better as the low man in the group," Skeet laughed and opened the door. "Authority seems to be going to your head."

Rowdy laughed, too. It wasn't. He just needed to get back for Bailey. If she needed him, he had to be there.

* * * *

Rowdy exited the plane, still a little surprised at what Skeet had accomplished in such a short amount of time. Clearly being a federal agent had more perks than working for the locals. Or maybe they just wanted Cole and Reese so badly they were willing to use whatever means necessary to ensure their capture. Regardless of the reason, twenty minutes after Rowdy dropped Agent Perkins at the house, a helicopter arrived to transport them to the airport. Rowdy slung his carry on over his shoulder and looked to Skeet for instructions. "Do we rent a car or did you get that covered as well?"

"Donahue said there's a car waiting in the lot. We just need to find the airport security office and grab the keys." Skeet pulled out his phone and punched a few buttons on his display, a map of the airport appeared. "Okay, it's just around the corner over there I think," Skeet pointed to the right, turned and walked away.

Once the two retrieved the keys, they were directed to a parking lot. Their vehicle was located in a small enclosure where security parked. As they stepped outside into the warm summer sun, Rowdy paused to enjoy the temperatures. He figured it was high seventies, eighty tops. After the cold winter in Montana followed by a cool spring, the sun felt nice. He was gradually getting used to the cooler temperatures in Mount Haven. They were technically moving into summer there, but it was still cool at night and first thing in the morning. He smiled thinking of Bailey, no wonder she always wore a jacket. She'd come from sunny California. Montana was rainy and cold. Rowdy was used to cold Chicago winters, so it wasn't that much of a change for him, but he could see why Bailey was having such a difficult time adjusting. He instantly sobered; thoughts of Bailey reminded him of their objective. He had no idea what to say to Peter Hughes.

Skeet pressed a button and the lights flashed on a black Chevy Impala. He slid behind the wheel and waited for Rowdy to get situated. "I want to stop in at the office first," Skeet explained as he pulled onto the roadway that led to the exit. "I asked Donahue to check on a couple things and I want the answers before we meet with Peter."

"That's fine," Rowdy nodded. It would give him a few more minutes to come up with a plan. They couldn't just waltz into the man's office and tell him the sordid details about his kid. Peter Hughes was in denial - he would simply throw them out.

Moments later Skeet pulled up to a large building almost completely covered in glass except for a light brick border. Rowdy absently wondered if it was bullet proof. Most likely. Not a bad idea, protect the agents but appeal to the public. The building itself was non-descript and could have been confused with any other business in the area if it wasn't for the large "Federal Bureau of Investigations, San Diego Field Office," sign prominently positioned next to the highway. It was sandwiched between what looked like a law firm and some kind of modern looking office building. The field office was actually two buildings with a small lot out front. Rowdy followed Skeet inside hoping his friend knew where they were going. It didn't take long before they were escorted to an executive conference room and three agents walked in. Rowdy hoped they wanted to look like agents, because those matching black suits, white shirts and boring ties screamed FBI.

Skeet moved to the large table and took a seat. This shouldn't take long and the men could brief them on the highlights before he and Rowdy headed over to Drakker Consulting. "What did you find?"

One of the agents, a tall skinnier guy with a crooked nose, stepped forward and placed a large file next to Skeet. Rowdy moved to the table and settled into the soft executive chair next to his friend. Skeet opened the file and maneuvered the documents so both of them could see the contents clearly.

Rowdy skimmed the first page, but wasn't sure what it was referring to. "Financial?" he asked Skeet.

"Yeah," Skeet agreed. "I had these guys pull any and all transactions on Reese Weathersby's account for the past two months." He pointed to an entry. "There's the gas in Texas, looks like he used a rental... see, Diamond Cars in San Antonio."

"Apparently they paid a visit to a rich oil tycoon while they were in town." Agent Maitland, a short stocky guy supplied. "The police report is included. They ignored about twenty 'No Trespassing' signs, strolled to the door and demanded to see Alexia Torrin, recently married to Trenton Shapiro, the only son and sole heir to the Shapiro Corporation."

"Did they get arrested?" Skeet turned the page and skimmed the report.

"Naw," Agent Hightower, a good looking, muscular man in his thirties shook his head. "Those two talked their way out of it. The locals found the missing person report on Victoria and believed their story. Hell, it probably wasn't something they fabricated. They probably were in town looking for Cole's missing sister."

"Probably," Skeet agreed absently as he turned back to the financials and began skimming again. He pointed to an entry and looked at Rowdy. "They are shopping in Missoula. And not at some fast-food joint or a fancy restaurant. They are grocery shopping. I'd say Coop's on the right track." He grinned, triumphantly. "Now we just need to find the house."

"If it's too far out of town, some local may have rented them an old bunk house or something. We may never find them through realtor records," Rowdy argued.

"But then again, we might." Skeet closed the file and started to stand. "Thanks you guys, for all the hard work. Is there anything in here I should know immediately?"

"It's all in there," Agent Maitland said, pointing to the file. Skeet settled back in his chair and waited. "We took a closer look at the Karen Bardell case like you requested, and something popped. We didn't have time to confirm, but it looks like the Detective Sergeant in charge of the unit at the time was probably bought off. Two days after the case was pulled from Davonshire, his immediate supervisor got a personal gift in the amount of $10,000 cash. Sergeant Fred MacElroy has recently passed away but his widow claims some guy visited Fred at the office and told him a rich and distant relative died and divided his wealth among the surviving relatives. She came across as credible so I suspect that's the cover he gave so his wife wouldn't know what he did."

Rowdy shook his head in disgust; that girl's case was bought for ten thousand measly dollars. It made him sick. He knew things like that happened on occasion, but he would never understand why.

Mount Haven

Cops were supposed to be better than that. Most were, but there were also a few bad apples that somehow slipped through. And those were the ones that caused them all problems.

"Okay," Skeet nodded. "Anything else? That one seems like a dead end."

"Not quite, there was a second notation by Davonshire. I think he may have taken the blood in to be tested anyway, even though he was no longer on the case. I've sent a request to the locals to try to track it. We'll know more in a few days," Maitland added.

"Anything else?" Skeet pressed.

"Maybe," Agent Hightower answered. "We got another hit on the DNA. A couple of our guys headed out this morning to follow up. A Kathy Langley was reported missing a while back. Her mom, Tina Langley seemed to keep a pretty tight rein on the girl. When she didn't come home, Tina insisted there was foul play. Turns out she was right. Her body was found in an abandoned cabin just outside of town. A Detective Kyle Lloyd was on the case. From the reports I've received, it looks like Lloyd knows his stuff. He's been relentless in tracking any and all leads. He's run the DNA through CODIS a dozen times, but we didn't have your evidence yet." He looked at Rowdy. "Once it was in the system, he contacted us immediately."

"Let me know what you find," Agent Perkins requested. "Now, we need to head over and chat with Mr. Peter Hughes. I have no doubt he'll have all kinds of explanations and excuses for his son's recent disappearance."

* * * *

"Sounds like you guys have quite the case on those two, shouldn't be hard to prosecute once we find them," Rowdy observed as he climbed back into the car.

"I also have agents in Miami interviewing the staff at Venible Investments. So far, they look clean. I think they may just be another one of their victims. Cole went out to consult with the company on a project and I'm guessing someone let some private information slip accidentally. I know you and Coop don't care about the inside trading stuff, but it's a slam dunk. There are holes in all the other cases. The evidence is piling up and I want them on the rapes and murders. But, if somehow all of those cases tank, we still have the financial stuff."

"I agree with your strategy," Rowdy shrugged. "No, I don't want them serving time for insider trading in some plush federal prison where they get out in a couple years to live their rich and happy lives with a steel ankle bracelet. I want them in prison, I want them behind bars for the rest of their miserable lives."

"Good, then let's see what good old Pete has to say." Skeet pulled up to an expensive looking building and parked in a clean, secure underground parking terrace.

Rowdy couldn't stop looking around in amazement. The place was immaculate and the parking stalls were at least a foot wider than usual. Yeah, this place screamed money. And it belonged to Bailey. If he had any doubt about their future, any hope that somehow she'd stay with him, this just put a rest to it. Bailey Zander, or Victoria Alexander, was not going to give Mount Haven a backwards glance as she rode out of town. But that didn't matter, all that mattered right now was confronting Peter Hughes and finding out who purchased the property for Cole.

Mount Haven

---

* * * *

After introducing themselves to the perky receptionist, Skeet and Rowdy sat and waited for a meeting with Peter. They'd arrived at least forty minutes ago and still no sign of the boss. Skeet stood and moved to the counter. Before he could give his demand, the woman began to speak. "There's nothing I can do for you, Agent Perkins. I've informed Peter you are here. Now, you will just have to wait until he has an opening in his schedule. It would have been much better had you actually called ahead and made an appointment like normal people do. You seriously cannot expect a man like Peter Hughes to drop everything for a couple..." she twisted her mouth into a distorted, crooked angle as she considered. "Well, a couple of cops. You know, normal people? Mr. Hughes is a busy man."

Skeet inhaled through his nose and let out what should have been a long relaxing sigh. But he wasn't relaxed. It was all he could do not to yank the annoying woman's earpiece from her ear and scream into the microphone. Wait like normal people? Well, he wasn't a normal people. He was the Federal Bureau of Investigations and he wanted answers now. "Wrong answer, missy," Skeet barked

"What?" the receptionist asked, clearly perplexed. Probably not difficult to do with this one.

"I need to speak to Peter Hughes, now. If I am not welcomed back to his office within the next three minutes, I'm going back without an invitation. Do you understand?"

436

"No," the woman stuttered. "No, I don't understand. Mr. Hughes has a schedule to keep. I can only allow you back there when he says you can go back there."

"Two minutes," Skeet said softly. "You have two minutes and then my colleague and I will find our own way back to Mr. Hughes office."

"But you can't do that. It's against the rules," she countered.

"It's not against our rules, honey. So I highly suggest you advise Mr. Hughes of the new deadline. He may need to excuse a guest or something," Rowdy said raising one eyebrow in challenge.

The receptionist had a whispered and brief conversation through her headset then looked up at her guests. "Mr. Hughes will see you now," she glowered at them as they stood and headed for the closed door.

Skeet turned the knob and casually opened the door. Perception was everything and Peter Hughes was not going to get the satisfaction of knowing he had annoyed them. The point of making them wait was to try and get the upper hand. Well, the man was going to be disappointed. Skeet walked to one of the two leather guest chairs and settled in for a casual chat. Rowdy lowered himself into the chair next to Skeet and stretched out his legs, crossing his ankles in a show of confidence. Skeet smiled inwardly, he was definitely Coop's brother. Rowdy may never have been a detective, but he understood the art of intimidation better than most.

Peter sat behind his large desk and frowned. Making these two wait was supposed to throw them off their game. It hadn't worked. They walked in like they owned the place, all casual and confident. He had no idea what they wanted, but they made him uncomfortable. Somehow, they screamed trouble and he was pretty sure he had his reckless son to thank for this visit.

"Mr. Hughes," Skeet began. "I'm Agent Skeeter Perkins with the FBI and this is my colleague Officer Rowdy Cooper with Mount Haven Sheriff's Office."

Peter nodded in greeting but remained silent.

"We are here today to ask you a few questions about your children." Skeet watched closely, waiting to see if he got a reaction to that. It was subtle, but it was there.

"I have not seen or heard from my step-daughter, Victoria for several years now. If she is in some kind of trouble, I'm afraid I can't help you," Peter finally provided.

"And your son?" Rowdy asked, wondering how the man would answer that question.

"My son is on vacation. His friend is distraught over the loss of my daughter and after several attempts to locate her, several hopeful trips to bring her back, he is finally accepting that she is gone for good."

Rowdy wondered if the man actually believed that or if he had just put his head in the sand for so long when it came to Cole that he accepted anything the boy said out of habit. "So, you don't know where your son is at the moment?"

"As I said, he's on vacation. He's comforting a friend in need," Peter clarified clearly agitated by the question.

"I'm a little curious, Mr. Hughes," Skeet said evenly. "Most people would want to know why we were here asking about their children. They would immediately have questions, you know maybe an instant concern for their daughter's safety, especially if you haven't seen her for years. Or worry that something might be wrong with their son. You however, instantly went on the defensive. Why is that?"

"Look, I'm a busy man. As I've told you, my son is on vacation. My daughter, for whatever reason, abandoned us and has chosen not to stay in touch. She's made a conscious decision to break her mother's heart. So unless there is something else I can do for you, I must ask you to leave." He glanced at his watch then back at the men. "I have an important meeting in five minutes that I need to prepare for."

"I'm afraid you'll have to cancel that meeting, Mr. Hughes," Skeet said forcefully. "We are not even close to being finished and I don't plan to leave until you decide to cooperate."

"Unless you have a warrant for my arrest, I'm afraid you are mistaken. I have no intention of cancelling my meeting and I don't see how I can help you further," Peter pushed. He may be intimidated but he would not just roll over on command.

"That's your choice," Rowdy shrugged. "We thought you would be more comfortable talking here but I have no problem moving this conversation to the field office. More questions for you to deal with on your return, but I actually prefer conducting this type of inquiry in an interrogation room."

The room was silent for several seconds. It was Peter who finally broke the silence. He took a deep breath and released it. "Okay, clearly I handled this meeting the wrong way. I'm a businessman. My job is to negotiate. I normally insist on starting the meeting with the upper hand. Please, tell me why you are here. Does this have something to do with Victoria? Like I said, we have not had contact with her in years."

"Actually, she contacted her mother a few weeks ago," Rowdy corrected, waiting to see how Peter reacted to that revelation. Why was he pretending he didn't know where Bailey was?

"That's impossible, Piper would have told me if Vicki made contact," Peter said confidently.

Skeet shifted and considered. This was an interesting new twist. So, Piper hadn't talked to her husband about the call from Victoria. "Victoria did call her mother, Mr. Hughes. There was no longer a reason for secrecy. The two men she was hiding from, had not only located her but they made an unsuccessful attempt to abduct her. She called her mother for help but was turned away."

"That's ridiculous, Piper loves her daughter. She would never turn her away, not after missing her all these years. You must be mistaken." Peter's mind was reeling. These two were awfully confident that Victoria had called her mother.

"I overheard the conversation. Victoria called her mother from my home. There is no mistake. Piper Hughes not only turned her daughter away, she scolded her for implicating your son and his friend, Reese Weathersby, in her attack."

"What are you talking about? That's absurd. Reese loves that girl and Cole has been so concerned about her disappearance that he's paid a private investigator over fifty grand to track her down. There is no way the two of them attacked her. She simply misunderstood their intentions. If they tried to abduct her, it was only because they wanted to bring her home safely." Peter's heart was racing. Why had he been left in the dark on this? Cole hadn't called to say he found Vicki and Piper hadn't told him about her daughter's call. His wife had been acting a little strange lately. When had that started? The night of the gala… approximately two weeks ago.

Skeet pulled Bailey's notepad from his briefcase and set it on the large desk in front of Peter Hughes. "I don't know your daughter, sir, I don't know you either. But my research leads me to believe the two of you were fairly close before she disappeared. If I am correct, I think you will recognize that handwriting as Victoria's."

Peter reluctantly took the pad and flipped open the cover. He inhaled sharply, it was Vicki's writing. He'd recognize it anywhere. So, his best friend's daughter had been located. Then why were these two men here? He was about to close the binder when a notation jumped out at him. He studied the figures and notations Victoria had made, then he turned the page. No, this wasn't possible. One particular entry disturbed him the most and next to the notation, off to the side Victoria had written 'Peter'. He looked up at the two cops and swallowed the lump forming in his throat. "Why was Victoria going through company records? And how did she get them for that matter?"

"She got them from me," Skeet answered evenly.

"You? But wouldn't you need a warrant to access my personal business records? I would have been advised if such a demand had been issued." Peter was frantically considering the possibilities.

"If I obtained those records on my own, yes. I would have needed a warrant. However, someone inside your company provided them freely. Someone who was concerned over your son's activities. Someone who decided to do the right thing and access information from the inside then turn it over to the authorities," Skeet provided.

"I have a mole in my company?" Peter asked absently.

"I find it interesting that the only thing you seem to be surprised about is my informant, not the illegal activities of your company," Skeet pressed.

"What? Oh, well I..." he looked back at Victoria's notes and frowned. "I'm going to need to look into this myself to see if she's correct. Vicki has been gone a long time." Peter trailed off. Clearly not comfortable voicing the last of his thoughts.

"And Cole is the only one with high enough access to pull that off," Rowdy supplied. "You are still trying to protect your son."

"Not the only one," Peter also had access, but he hadn't done any of this. If it was true, Cole was running his business into the ground and doing it illegally. His company could be in a lot of trouble. Trouble that consulting firms like this one, didn't recover from. If their clients didn't trust them, their business would be ruined. And who would trust a company in trouble for insider trading and dishonest business practices?

"Well, from my research the only other person with that kind of access is you." Skeet waited. "I'm not going to ask you if you did it, because I can prove you did not. Which brings us back to the situation at hand. Do you have any idea where your son is, Mr. Hughes?"

"No," Peter said, looking up. He was instantly alarmed at the worried look on both of the men's faces. "This is not about poor business practices, is it?"

"No," Rowdy grunted. "Your son and his friend, Reese, abducted your daughter. She's in danger and we need to find her immediately. So if there is anything you can tell me, anything that will help locate the two of them, you need to tell us now."

Peter furrowed his brows. Why would the boys abduct Victoria? "When?"

"Victoria was traveling in a vehicle with the local Sheriff's wife, Maggie, yesterday afternoon. Cole and Reese ran her off the road, forced her vehicle into a river and then left Maggie unconscious on the riverbank. They disappeared with Victoria. We know they haven't left town because the roads are being carefully monitored by the sheriff and his men," Skeet provided. "So, I am going to ask you one more time, do you know how we can find your son?"

Peter was shaking his head, Cole wouldn't do what they were suggesting. If he'd found Victoria, he would have brought her home immediately. His stomach roiled and he was sure he was going to be sick. A little nagging voice at the back of his mind rejected his conclusion. Cole had always had an unnatural obsession with Victoria. That is why Peter had such strict rules when it came to Cole's interaction with the girl. He needed time, he needed to corner Piper and find out exactly what Victoria had told her. He needed these men out of his office. He took a deep breath, hoping it would calm his nerves and looked Agent Perkins in the eye. "I have no idea where my son is. He was extremely vague when he left. He wouldn't even guess at when he would be home. I can only tell you what he told me: he was going to help Reese. They had recently traveled to Texas on a lead about Victoria. They were sure they had found her. When it turned out the woman was not my daughter, Reese left upset. He is in love with that girl and planned to marry her. Out of all of us, I believe he took her disappearance the hardest."

"Right," Rowdy said sarcastically.

Peter looked at the man more closely, then it hit him. The cop was in love with his daughter. Was the feeling mutual? "I don't know what you mean by that. I can only tell you what her mother and the boys told me. I admit I was not as observant or attentive as I could have been at the time. Victoria was in college and the business was struggling with the downturn in the economy. We didn't have a lot of interaction. I had hoped that would change once Vicki graduated and came to work with me. She was brilliant, just like her father when it came to business. Then, she was just gone."

"Did you ever wonder why? Ever stop to consider why a girl with so much going for her would just vanish like that?" Rowdy asked, angry now. The man was not going to listen to a word they said. Bailey was right, when it came to Cole, Peter Hughes had a serious case of denial.

"Mr. Hughes," Skeet interrupted. Rowdy was letting emotions dictate his actions at the moment and that was only going to get them in trouble. "I was told there is a man here, in your company, that would have helped Cole with some financial transactions. A money guy, someone he trusted that might have helped him while he is on this… vacation. Can you please tell me who that is? I need to talk to him immediately. I need to find out if in fact someone is helping Cole obtain property or cash while he's away."

Peter knew exactly who would have helped Cole, but he wasn't willing to provide a name until he talked to Frank Mandel himself. He'd always thought the guy was trouble, but he had no reason to get rid of him. Plus, Cole insisted he was good at his job and they needed to keep him around. Was that because Cole knew something Peter didn't and was using that knowledge to manipulate the man? He hated to think poorly of his son, but how many years, how many problems did Cole have to cause before Peter accepted who and what Cole really was? "I have no idea, but I'd be happy to look into it. Maybe you could leave me a card or something and I'll call you if I learn anything that will help."

The man was lying. Rowdy had no doubt. The guy knew exactly who had helped Cole, but he also recognized the signs. Peter Hughes was not going to give up the name. No, he wanted to protect his son and would probably talk to the guy in person before sharing anything with the police. It was a risk, Hughes could destroy any evidence available in an attempt to protect the kid, but Rowdy didn't think so. Something told him that Peter also loved Victoria. Maybe after he digested everything, he'd be in a better frame of mind to help them rather than hinder. Rowdy looked to Skeet and nodded.

Skeet reached into his wallet and pulled out a business card. Obviously Rowdy had come to the same conclusion he had. They were not going to get any more information from Peter Hughes today. He only hoped after talking to his wife and the mystery man in the company – oh, there was no doubt Peter Hughes knew exactly who had helped Cole from the inside -that the guy would do the right thing. If not, they were back to square one. Skeet stood and dropped his card on the desk. "We'll be in touch." Then he reached out and retrieved the notepad.

"Can I keep that?" Peter asked.

"No," Skeet answered. "We still need it, our investigation is ongoing. But I will have my secretary make copies and email them to you. They should arrive this afternoon," then he turned and followed Rowdy out of the room.

Mount Haven

They silently exited the large building and walked slowly to the car. Rowdy climbed in and slammed the door in frustration. "He might eventually give us what we need, but it's going to take time. Time Bailey may not have."

"I know," Skeet said turning the key a little too hard. The engine started and he pulled from the lot. The car slid sideways leaving skid marks in its wake. They had both hoped Peter Hughes would listen to reason. Instead, he'd buried his head in the sand and dismissed them. "I guess we head back to Mount Haven and see what we can do to help Coop."

Rowdy pulled out his phone and dialed his brother.

"Any luck?" Coop asked in greeting.

"Nope," Rowdy replied. "Anything on your end? Peter Hughes is still in denial. He may come around, he may not. For now, we're on our own."

"Shit," Coop sighed. "Well, on this end we are going through records. I've contacted every realtor from here to Missoula and on down to Conner. The last of the transactions just arrived. Mariah is sifting through them for anything that could connect to Cole, Reese or either of their companies. We are starting with any property purchased or rented within a fifty mile radius. Derek and Matthew have also contacted every hotel and motel in the area. I'm confident they are not renting a room. So, that leaves real-estate. Jase called, he wants to come in and help. Maggie decided that until Bailey is found they are only offering dinner and only for two hours a night. Theresa and Casey are also coming in to help. I've got Maggie in my office looking through the financials Skeet sent. There may be something that didn't register with Bailey, because it was common knowledge... a company, an affiliate office, something that we can look for. It's a long shot, but we're going to find her, Rowdy. I promise, we will find Bailey."

"I know," Rowdy agreed. He had no doubt they would find Bailey. That wasn't the question he always asked himself. He just wasn't sure they would find her in time. They could already be too late. Not knowing what she was going through, what those monsters were doing to her - that was the question that haunted his every minute.

Chapter Thirteen

Maggie was tired and bored. Sure, she had a business degree, but she hated doing the books. Plus, she was terrible at it. She didn't understand half of what was in this file. She was more of a seat of her pants kind of businesswoman. She could out negotiate with the best of them and had no problem creating an atmosphere that would attract customers. Finances and numbers were all Greek to her. She jumped when the door to Coop's office swung open and her husband stepped into the room.

"Any luck?" he asked as he settled into the comfortable guest chair.

"No," Maggie said, defeated. "I don't understand most of it. The numbers don't make sense to me so I'm going through corporations. I was thinking maybe these guys created a dummy corp, some affiliate office they could funnel funds through that wouldn't be easily tied to Reese's organization. But I really think this is a long shot. We have all the records from Weathersby

International because of Skeet's subpoena but only a few from Drakker Consulting. Only the files that the informant was able to retrieve. What if the money came from Cole, not Reese? Then all of this is for nothing. Then we are wasting valuable time because in all likelihood the answer is not in here."

Coop stood and moved behind Maggie. His wife was tired and that always made her grumpy. He reached out and gently began messaging her shoulders. "That's investigative work, babe. You follow the leads, go through what you have and when you've exhausted all possibilities you move on to something else. It's a slow and agonizing process, but it works. Trust me, I've been doing this for years. Sure, it takes time. That's why you are working this angle, I'm working a different angle and I have Derek and Matthew physically checking every vacant property within a hundred miles of here. We have also circulated their photos to all our residents and have the community watching for the men and the car. They are still close by, I know it. And, if they try to leave, we'll have them. Until then, we keep doing what we're doing and hope we catch a break."

"I'm not really that patient, Andy. You know that." She growled out loud and lowered her head to the desk. "I want to find her now. I want you to go out and put a bullet through those men's heads and rescue my friend. And I keep wondering what kind of person that makes me. But each time I tell myself I need to have more compassion and I need to love those who hurt me, I remember what they tried to do. Those monsters tried to abduct me. They ran me off the road and left me for dead. They tried to take my child. They tried to kill you, kill Rowdy, and kill Knight. They messed with my family and I just can't find it in myself to care. Somehow putting them in jail for the rest of their miserable life doesn't seem like enough."

Mount Haven

Coop leaned down and kissed the top of her head. "Let's go home. It's late and Skeet and Rowdy should be arriving any minute. This can wait until morning."

Maggie sighed then stood. She let her husband take her hand, guide her out the door and settle her in their car. Tomorrow was going to be another long day. But tonight was going to be equally long. She was so terrified of what her friend was going through right now. There was no way she could relax until Bailey was rescued.

* * * *

Reese was in pain. Excruciating pain. He glanced at his side and knew his wound was becoming infected. He'd done his best to keep it cleaned out and slathered it with that stupid goo each day, but the antibiotic ointment wasn't working any longer. The cut was now warm to the touch. It was also red and had become swollen and tender a few days ago. Reese had tried to put ice pads over the bandages, but it didn't seem to help. He'd also developed a serious fever that over-the-counter pain killers couldn't touch. He needed a doctor and he needed one now. But he couldn't just waltz into a hospital and ask for assistance. Knife wounds had to be reported to the local police. And the local police were looking for him. Otherwise, they would already be back in San Diego. Once they secured Victoria, they had intended to get out of town but the instant he saw the police car, he panicked. Cole suggested they head back to the cabin then one of them could investigate. Reese had stayed with Tory, securing her to the bed while Cole drove the dirt road that intersected with the highway that led out of town. A patrol car was waiting. A quick check at the other side of town told them the only two routes out of this stupid, backwards hellhole were blocked. They had to wait it out. Reese was sure if they gave it a few more days, the coast would be clear. It was a small town, they couldn't afford to station their entire police force at the exits forever. But in the meantime, he had a serious problem. So, now what? He'd already scoured the shed where they'd found the chloroform but there was nothing out there that would help.

Could he drive to a nearby town and threaten a doctor, nurse, vet maybe? It would be risky, but he was sure they were looking for the silver BMW. All he had to do was get to that abandoned farmhouse where he'd spotted the beat up old truck, and use that to sneak out and find a vet. It would have to be a vet. The instant he left, a doctor or nurse would call the authorities. But a vet, they worked with animals. They understood natural selection, survival of the fittest. A vet might keep his mouth shut long enough for the trail to grow cold. Reese had no intention of providing any kind of information that would lead the cops to him in any way. He'd provide a fake address, fake name and fake explanation. A vet would be more likely to accept his lies.

Now, what to do about Tory? He couldn't take her with him, but did he trust Cole enough to leave her here? Cole wanted her and he'd waited too long for this moment. Reese hated knowing he had to move forward with the deal he'd struck years ago. He hated the thought of his friend going anywhere near his woman. But if he got it out of his system now, while Reese was away, that was it. Cole only got one shot and then Tory was off limits forever. He just wouldn't think about it. He wouldn't give Cole permission but he wouldn't forbid it either. Once it was done, it was done. Ignorance was bliss. Reese would just force himself to believe Cole would wait. Then if he returned to discover he hadn't, well... then the whole thing would be behind them for good. "We need food," Reese said casually. "You stay here and guard her, I'm going to find something to eat. Then we need to start planning our escape." Guarding Tory should be easy enough. They had moved the single bed into the living room and handcuffed her to the decorative metal frame. Then they'd secured the bed post to the fireplace. She had nowhere to hide and no chance of escape.

Cole studied his friend. Reese didn't look well. Was he injured, too? Cole's headaches were getting worse and the dizzy spells were becoming more frequent. He actually fell down in the bathroom when he leaned over to wash his face this morning. The pressure behind his eyes was now a constant annoyance. Because of that he couldn't read his friend's expression. What he could read was his body language. Reese was in pain and Cole wasn't entirely sure the man was simply going out for dinner. But did he really care? Reese was getting on Cole's nerves more and more with each passing day. He desperately needed a break from his friend. The man was an insufferable ass, just like his father. Ironic really, Reese hated Carlton Weathersby with a passion, but he acted more and more like him with each passing year. Cole wondered if their friendship would survive this trip. Maybe, if they could just get back to their normal lives. Lives where they only encountered each other a few times a week and during one of their special ventures. Yes, things would be fine once they returned to San Diego. They would both be happily married and their extracurricular activities would resume as they always had. Life would be perfect. That brought his thoughts back to Victoria. If Reese left, maybe he'd have his chance at the woman. He could finally have what he'd been denied all those years. But did he want to rush it that way? He had no idea when his friend would return. And if Reese saw him getting too rough with the woman, he'd intervene. Cole knew his friend was having second thoughts, just like he was having when it came to Reese and Sissy. Just another good reason to act on his needs while his friend was away. "Sure, will you grab some beer while you're out? Better yet, see if they have a decent bottle of scotch. The grocery store probably won't stock anything remotely palatable, but do me a favor and look will you?"

"Sure," Reese said, pulling on his jacket before he exited the cabin. He knew he'd have to stop in at a grocery store, otherwise Cole would know he wasn't shopping for food. But that cheap crap they carried wouldn't satisfy either one of them. Maybe the vet would have something better. He could always look. Now, he just had to find his target. It couldn't be anyone here; the locals seemed to like their sheriff a little too much. He'd have to travel out of town, somewhere on the way to Missoula would be best. An out of the way town that was far enough off the beaten path that they had never heard of Sheriff Cooper. He slid into the vehicle and started on his way. Finally, he was going to get some relief for his pain.

Reese pulled onto the adjoining dirt road and cursed. He was sure he was being followed. Would officers be waiting if he connected with the paved highway? How had this happened? It was a small town. They were all supposed to be stupid and easily fooled. But maybe that's where he made his mistake. It was a small town. Everyone knew everyone and life was so boring they had nothing better to do than stick their noses where they didn't belong. He made another turn onto yet another dirt roadway and then made a second sharp right. He had a map and GPS, so he could drive like this for hours. Then, once he was sure he'd lost the pesky do-gooder, he could head back to the cabin. They'd just have to have canned soup for dinner and he'd wait for another day to seek out his vet.

Reese had been driving for over an hour when he finally felt confident he'd lost the tail. He slowly maneuvered onto the familiar trail that led back to the cabin. He thought of Cole and Tory and his anger spiked. Had Cole been enjoying his wife while Reese had been frantically working to lose his pursuer? If Cole had touched his woman, had spent the past hour in ecstasy while Reese spent it in pain and frustration, Cole was going to pay. He stepped on the gas, anxious to return and check on his woman.

* * * *

Bailey watched Cole very closely. There was something wrong with him, but that wasn't going to stop his attack. She could see it in his eyes. She twisted her wrist again and winced, accepting the fact that she was never going to get free of the cuffs. She could feel the liquid slowly run across the back of her hand and knew she'd cut her flesh with the metal binds again. Her arms were starting to tingle from being secured above her head. No matter what Cole did, she would fight him. She didn't care about the consequences. Somehow, she was going to win. Fear engulfed her. If she couldn't win, she was still determined to survive. Women had been raped before. They had found a way to get through it, move past it and evolve. She could too. Her mind shifted to Rowdy. She loved that man. He was everything she'd ever wanted in her life and never believed she could have. He had to be a wreck right now. She knew he would blame himself for this. Rowdy Cooper was a savior and the fact that he couldn't save her was going to haunt him forever. For that reason alone she was determined to recover. If she didn't, Rowdy wouldn't either.

Cole approached the bed and grinned. Cocky little Victoria was terrified. His body should have reacted to that fact alone, but his head was throbbing and the pain was excruciating. This was his chance to have her, to get even for teasing him year after year. The woman knew what she was doing, even as a teen. Every time he came home for a visit, every time he stopped by on a weekend away from the rigors of college, she was there. Her friends were there, teasing, taunting and flaunting those little bodies in those skimpy bikinis. Well, Mandy Strausberg had paid for her behavior hadn't she? And Victoria was going to pay, too. He just needed to do something about this stupid headache. Cole moved to the bathroom and opened the cabinet. He flipped open the bottle of over-the-counter meds and downed four of them. That should do it. He paused, when was his last dose? He'd taken four of them earlier, but that must have been hours ago because his head felt like it was in a vice. Or was it this morning? He knew he'd taken his first dose this morning when he got up. Oh, well. He shrugged, hopefully they would only take a few minutes to work. In the meantime, he could still have a little fun.

Bailey didn't take her eyes off Cole. He disappeared into the bathroom but moments later reappeared. The look on his face terrified her but she would not let him see that. She would be strong and she would find a way to get through this. Maybe if she envisioned Rowdy, that would give her the strength to do what she had to do. She swallowed hard as Cole stalked toward her. It was as if she was the prey and he was a violent, determined predator. Well, he was a monster. Bailey jerked and kicked as hard as she could when Cole reached the bed and undid her jeans. He was laughing as he yanked the garment from her body. They caught on her tennis shoes, which seemed to annoy Cole. Good. Bailey considered how could she use that to her advantage?

Cole moved to the foot of the bed and tried to release the jeans. He couldn't think and the fact that the stupid things were caught on her shoes annoyed him. He grabbed one leg and yanked, Bailey's shin slammed against the wooden frame and she screamed out in pain. Again, that should have excited him but it only made him more frustrated. "Stop it!" he yelled as he forced her leg against the bed. He pulled off one shoe, then moved to the other. As he released Bailey's leg, she pivoted and swung one leg over his head.

Mount Haven

He was stuck between her shins, held in place by the stupid jeans. Bailey now had the upper hand.

Bailey was surprised that move had worked. She knew it was worth a shot, but she seriously believed all she was going to do was make Cole furious. Once she had his head between her ankles, she used all her weight to pin him to the bed. Then she tightened her grip, hoping the pressure would knock him out. She was trying to cut off his air supply but was pretty sure she was failing.

Cole was furious. Bailey's tactics should have been easy to counter. But with the pounding in his head, the pressure behind his eyes and the nausea that had hit, he couldn't get a good grip on her body. His only hope was if she tired before he did. Bailey shifted and forced his head into the long wooden beam that ran across the foot of the bed. Pain radiated through his entire body and he thought he was going to black out. Something was seriously wrong with him. He needed a doctor. He felt so weak all of a sudden. He would think about that later, right now he needed to get free from his violent, terrified sister. Before he could come up with a plan, he heard the distinct sound of the door colliding against the far wall. Reese was home. Cole relaxed, grateful his friend had returned.

Bailey was getting tired, but she knew she could never give up. She had to keep fighting, she had to keep Cole away from her. She was actually starting to believe she would win when the door flew open and an angry Reese loomed in the opening. Bailey watched in shock as he marched across the room and grabbed Cole by the back of the neck. In one fluid motion he yanked his friend free of Bailey's legs and tossed him toward the fireplace. Cole stumbled, lost his footing and his head collided with the rock hearth. Cole's body instantly went limp as it fell to the floor. Bailey screamed, turned her head to the side and covered her face with her arm.

Victoria's reaction enraged Reese even more. She was upset he'd rescued her? Was she enjoying Cole's game? Enjoying their time together? Did she secretly want Cole as much as he wanted her? In Reese's mind, she was already his wife. He had thought the connection would be a onetime thing, but how could he ever trust them together? He reached down and grabbed Cole's limp body and threw it onto the bed. Cole could spend his one night with Tory, unconscious for all he cared. Reese pivoted and stalked out of the cabin, slamming the door as he left.

Bailey began to cry. She glanced at Cole, then quickly moved away from his body. She didn't know if he was dead or just injured, but either way she didn't want him anywhere near her. She used her feet to push her body into the corner of the bed and dropped her head to her knees. She was doomed. Eventually Reese would return and from the crazed look in his eyes when he left, she would certainly be punished severely.

* * * *

Maggie, Coop, Rowdy, Angela and Skeet sat around the large dining room table sorting through paperwork. They had already gone through all the listings once before, looking for the obvious. Now, they were looking for anything else. If Cole and Reese had purchased or rented a house using a realtor, they hadn't used their real names or either family business. So the group was now looking for corporations, small companies, or anything that looked like a fake name.

"I can't take this anymore," Maggie said, standing. "I need snacks. Does anyone want anything to drink while I'm up?"

Mount Haven

"I'll take a Coke," Angie said shaking her empty can.

Rowdy glanced around and saw they could all use a refill. "I'll take care of the drinks, you conjure up some food. I'm starved." He had just reached the end of the hall that led to the kitchen when the doorbell rang. He glanced at Maggie, then Coop and slid his .40 from its holster. Everyone they knew was already here. The only exception was Coop's deputies and they would have called before stopping by.

Coop and Skeet were on their feet and behind Rowdy before he reached the door. Rowdy reached out to turn the knob then shifted and moved against the wall. He took a deep breath then glanced back around to see where Maggie and Angie were. The women had retreated into the study. Good, they were safe. Rowdy slowly reached out and slid back the curtain on the small side window that framed Coop's door. He immediately let out a relieved breath and returned the gun to its holster. Coop and Skeet did the same, but wondered who could be waiting just outside.

Coop decided the best way to find out was to let them in. He flung open the door, expecting to see someone he knew but hesitated when he spotted a man and woman he'd never met on his porch. He looked back to Rowdy in confusion.

Skeet was shocked. He never in a million years could have seen this one coming. After his initial confusion, he took a step forward and held out his hand. "Peter, Piper, this is a surprise."

Peter took Skeet's hand then waited as his wife stepped inside. They were both tired and he was still angry at Piper, but that renewed confrontation was going to have to wait. Right now, they had a crisis on their hands. If anything Victoria had told her mother was true, she was in danger. He still couldn't believe Cole was

458

responsible for the financial mess at the company. They were in serious trouble and Peter had doubts they would ever recover. But Cole was responsible, for everything. Frank Mandel had confirmed it. He provided Peter with stacks of documents. Hidden inside was information that Peter was sure would lead these officers to Cole's location. He and Piper had argued about his decision for the past several hours but Peter was not going to back down. He owed it to Scott to save his little girl. He had promised his friend he would protect her, and he had failed. If Piper wasn't willing to do what it took to save her own daughter, Peter would have to take care it. He'd always known Piper was weak, for lack of a better word, but he had no idea just how weak. He'd watched Scott handle everything for years but his best friend hadn't let on just how high maintenance his wife really was. Was that because things had been different with Scott? Maybe it was time to admit that as well. Peter's life was not anywhere near what he had planned. He always thought he would have a loving wife, a son he could be proud of, grandbabies. Now, his son was a criminal, his company was in trouble and his wife… well, she was Piper. And for about the hundredth time today, he wondered if that was enough.

Maggie stepped from the study and greeted their guests. Had Bailey's parents really come for her? Come to help? She couldn't think of any other reason they would be here. Maybe Rowdy's visit had made a difference. "Go ahead and make yourselves comfortable. I was just about to throw together a snack. Can I get you something to drink while you wait?"

Rowdy smiled. Maggie was always the hostess. "Mr. Hughes?" Rowdy paused but when Peter didn't reply, he moved to the liquor cabinet. He surveyed the contents momentarily then pulled out a bottle of scotch and turned, holding it out in question.

"Oh yes," Peter finally acknowledge the gesture. "Thank you. Piper will have a glass of wine if you have it."

Coop disappeared down the hall. A short time later he returned with a tray of freshly cut cheese and crackers and a bottle of wine. Maggie followed, carrying some kind of tiny meat tray and two Cokes. She handed one to Angie and one to Skeet. Then she sat in their extra-large lounge chair and waited patiently, Coop moved forward and silently joined her.

Rowdy grabbed two beers from the small refrigerator under the drink cart and popped off the caps. He casually handed one to Coop then moved to a second lounge chair. Peter and Piper sat nervously on the large couch, leaving the loveseat for Angie and Skeet. Nobody spoke, they just waited for their visitors to explain why they had flown all the way to Montana without notice. The couple didn't seem to be happy about the trip.

"I'm sure you are wondering why we are here," Peter began. "Well…" he glanced at Rowdy then to Skeet. "After the two of you left, I had a heart to heart with Frank Mandel. He's one of the accountants at Drakker. He denied it at first, but he finally admitted that he has been helping Cole transfer funds to a dummy offshore account for years."

Rowdy sat up straighter. If they could find the account, they may be able to find the recent transaction and determine where Cole and Reese were… where Bailey was.

"I know you are going to need details and I'm prepared to turn over anything you need, Agent Perkins. But for starters, I brought these. I have Nancy looking for anything else you might need but I think this will get you started. Frank said he included everything, but I'm sure you can understand why I'm not willing to take his word for it. If there's more, Nancy will find it."

Skeet stood and took the papers Peter had presented. He glanced down and studied the top page for a minute then looked up at Peter in shock. The information in these documents alone could put Cole away for years.

"Yes, I know." Peter lowered his head in shame.

Piper began to sob.

"What is it?" Coop finally asked.

"Company transactions, things that are illegal. Money that has been shifted and moved to avoid detection." Skeet looked back at Peter. "Was Frank responsible for this?"

"No," Peter said softly shaking his head. "Oh, Frank did the moving and the buying but it was all ordered by Cole. My son was not only involved in all of that, but he was also embezzling from the company. I have a right fine mess to deal with, but first I think we should focus on Victoria." Peter shot an angry look at his wife then turned back to the group.

Rowdy caught the exchange and cocked his head in thought. Was it possible that Peter had been kept in the dark about the threats, the attack, everything? "Why?" Rowdy finally asked.

"Why what?" Peter asked, clearly confused.

"Why are you here now? You practically threw me and Skeet out of your office yesterday and she…" he nodded at Piper. "She rejected her own daughter when Bailey called for help. She sided with Reese Weathersby and your son. She told Bailey to just suck it

Mount Haven

up and go home and do whatever she had to do. Bailey was supposed to feel lucky to marry into a wealthy family that clearly wanted her. If rape and violence was the life you wanted for your daughter a few weeks ago, I'm wondering what changed."

Piper sucked in a shocked breath then continued to sob.

"I know you will never understand Piper's motives, I'm having a difficult time grasping them myself but deep down, she wanted what was best for her daughter. She was misguided and naïve when it came to the boys but she would never knowingly put Victoria in danger." Peter was sure the man must be over exaggerating the situation. Cole was rambunctious and spoiled, but rape? His son wouldn't… but then a memory hit him and he began to wonder, still he would never hurt Victoria. "I get the impression there's more. What can you tell me?"

"Mr. Hughes, do you really think that is a good idea?" Skeet glanced at Piper and almost felt sorry for the woman. "I mean, I think your wife has had about all she can take right now."

"Of course," Peter glanced at Piper then back to the men. "We came straight here because I was under the impression this was urgent. If you don't mind, we will just head back into town and see if we can find a motel." He stood and waited for Piper to follow. "I'll get Piper settled then return for the details."

Rowdy hesitated, then plowed forward before he could change his mind. "I have plenty of room at my place. Why don't you stay with me until we locate your daughter?" he turned to Coop and Maggie. "I'll need you to watch after Knight, if that's okay. I don't know how he will react to strangers in the house. He's been pretty high strung lately."

Coop nodded, surprised by his brother's offer.

"Are you sure?" Peter asked, studying the man closer.

"Yeah," Rowdy shrugged. "Just let me move my dog and I'll show you the way."

"Mr. Cooper," Peter cleared his throat. "Uh, well… it seemed… well, I got the impression while you were in San Diego that maybe there was something between you and Victoria. Am I right?"

"Yeah," Rowdy confirmed just before he walked out the door. There was no way he was going to discuss his relationship with Bailey with her parents before he knew what was in their future. Of, if they had a future.

Peter turned to the rest of the room. "Did I do something wrong?"

"No," Maggie assured him. "It's just that Bailey and Rowdy's relationship is fairly new and with her on the run and hiding out and… well, being rich…"

"You keep talking about this Bailey person. Can I assume you mean Victoria?" Peter asked.

"Oh, yes." Skeet glanced up from the file he was still reading. "Victoria has been going by a new name in an effort to remain undetected."

"Why would she do that?" Piper asked, looking to Peter for guidance.

"I imagine because she was on the run, Piper." Peter shook his head, what in the world was it going to take for Piper to admit her daughter fled out of fear? "Anyway, back to Rowdy. I'm guessing he doesn't know how this is all going to work out," Peter supplied in understanding. "Well, I don't know if it helps, but Vicki has always been... I don't know, a bit of a romantic I guess. Her father taught her that, I think." He glanced at Piper then continued. "Anyway, if she truly loves that man out there, the choice will be easy for her." Peter frowned. He'd been counting on Victoria to help him turn this thing around. That might not happen, now. If she'd found love, they just might lose her forever. Especially after the way Piper had treated her when she called and asked for help.

Moments later, Rowdy was back with Knight. The dog stepped into the house and immediately focused on the strangers. He tugged at his leash but Rowdy gave a command and Knight reluctantly followed his owner up the stairs to Bryan's game room. Rowdy shut the door and returned to the ground floor, motioning for Peter and Piper to follow. The three of them walked silently to the cottage.

"You have a very beautiful view," Piper commented as they ascended the stairs and stepped into Rowdy's home.

"There's a guest room at the end of the hall on the left. Bathroom has an entrance from the bedroom and the hallway. I have my own, so you won't have to worry about privacy." He turned to head back up to the house but paused when Peter spoke.

"Once I get Piper settled, I'd like to return to the house and discuss the situation in more depth. Will that be okay?" Peter asked, watching the stoic man carefully.

"Sure," Rowdy shrugged. "I have to warn you, though... you aren't going to like what you hear." He glanced at Piper, sighed then left the house. It was obvious the couple needed a few minutes of privacy to work something out.

Peter found himself alone with his wife and for the first time since they'd been together he had no idea what to say to her. He felt more alone right now than he'd ever felt in his life and wondered, again, if it was even possible to repair the damage. Or, if he wanted to. He knew Piper loved him, in her way, but it no longer felt like enough. He wanted the fairytale. A wife that was in love with him, a wife that cherished him, a wife that gave as much as she received. He no longer believed Piper was capable of that kind of partnership. He reached down and retrieved their luggage then carted it to the guest room. He couldn't worry about his marriage right now. He needed to worry about finding his late friend's daughter.

Peter stepped from the room and wondered where Piper had disappeared to. Oh, well. She knew what his intentions were. When she realized she was alone, she'd also know where he was. He stepped onto the porch and spotted his wife in what looked like a comfortable patio chair. "I have no idea how long I'll be. Don't wait up." He turned to descend the stairs but paused when she called out to him.

"Peter?" Piper asked. "Before you go will you tell me why you hate me?"

Peter ran his hand through his hair in frustration. Having this discussion was going to delay his return, but he couldn't leave her believing he hated her. "I don't." He turned and moved to stand in front of the railing, leaning his body against it for support. She was still crying, but not uncontrollably now. Wet tears just leaked from her eyes and she looked up at him in desperation. Seeing the woman he loved like this was breaking his heart, but he had to stand strong. "You already know why I'm angry."

"I thought I was doing the right thing," she argued. "I thought it was what you would have wanted. The things that man said about your son. Cole couldn't…" she swallowed hard and shook her head in denial. "There has to be some other explanation. Reese wouldn't hurt Victoria. He loves her. Cole is her brother, he's her older brother. It's his job to look out for her, to protect her. He wouldn't hurt her. You can't seriously believe he would."

Peter realized Piper was looking to him to clear her conscience. She'd ignored her daughter's plea for help and she needed someone to tell her she'd done the right thing. But she hadn't and he would not shelter her from this. He'd done far too much sheltering where she was concerned for decades. "I have no idea what Reese Weathersby is capable of and neither do you. What I do know is that Cole has become arrogant and selfish. He has risked everything, do you understand that Piper? My son has destroyed us. And still you sit there in denial. You had better start accepting reality my dear because soon, very soon, we are going to have to make some dramatic changes. Your life is going to change forever. And there is nothing that I, or anybody, can do to stop it."

"It's Cole's life too, why would he destroy his own future? Why would he risk all that he has that way? I just can't believe he would do that. There must be another explanation," she maintained.

"And that is the conundrum. You want to live blissfully in the dark and pretend that nothing unpleasant is possible. I, on the other hand, am forced to face reality," he straightened. "I suspect I will be late, don't wait up." Then Peter Hughes turned and disappeared down the trail that led to Sheriff Cooper's large home. He could hear Piper's sobs as he walked away.

Rowdy, Skeet and Coop were in the study when Peter returned. They were deep in conversation, trying to decipher the documents Peter had provided and wondering how much to reveal to Cole's father in one sitting. Just the evidence they had about the rapes was going to upset him. If they dumped the murders in his lap too, he may not recover from the blow.

"I'm not a weak man," Peter announced as he stepped through the door. "I know there must be a reason you are so worried about Victoria." He glanced at Rowdy then back to Skeet. "You decide where to begin but I need to know. I need to know what else my son has been up to other than the financial exploits."

The three men settled in for a long night of explanations.

"Before you start," Peter said lowering himself to the large couch. "You mentioned the possibility that Victoria could be raped by Reese. I know it's probably none of my business but do you have reason to believe that boy is a rapist? I would assume if you had evidence he would have been arrested already."

"Not just Reese, Mr. Hughes, Cole is also involved as well. The two of them have been a team for a number of years. You are aware of a situation eight years ago? A woman filed a report with the local cops about being raped by Cole and Reese. A man died and the girl's brother lost everything," Skeet probed, wondering how much Peter would admit to knowing.

"You must be referring to the Montgomery case," Peter guessed as he moved back to the large couch. "The DA assured me that was her brother, not my son. Not Reese. Her brother was abusing the girl and if I recall, he disappeared after charges were filed against him for murder. He also killed one of our security guards, a man that was acting as Cole's bodyguard at the time."

Skeet dropped a file on the table and waited. Rather than explaining the evidence and the situation to a man who desperately wanted to believe in his kid, Skeet would let the evidence speak for itself. Then they could talk. That particular file not only had Marnie

Mount Haven

Montgomery's information, it also had all the reports and evidence they had collected regarding Mandy Strausberg and the notes Bailey and written up about her college roommate, Candace Barkley.

Peter slowly picked up the folder and began to read. His eyes grew wide and he swallowed hard. Page by page, he looked through the documents, each one more damning than the last. By the time he was finished, he couldn't breathe. He felt dirty. Dirty, ashamed and extremely nauseated. He was going to be sick. "Bathroom?" was all he could get out as he jumped to his feet and looked around.

Coop pointed to the hallway. "The bathroom is just outside the door to the right. One door down. Take your time."

Once Skeet heard the bathroom door slam shut he turned to his friends. "He's going to be a while. Let's continue looking at the stuff he brought with him. He said this Frank guy sent information that might lead to where they are staying. We might as well dig in. It might take us some time to find it."

"If Frank knew anything, wouldn't he have revealed it to Peter?" Rowdy asked.

"Not likely," Skeet shook his head. "I've dealt with guys like Frank too many times to count throughout my career. There was a reason Cole selected him. A reason Cole felt confident using him to funnel money and hide bad business deals. The guy is dirty in one way or another and Cole knew it."

"And that means his loyalties lie with Cole," Coop provided. "Are you saying he gave us what we need, but he buried it? Or that he didn't give us anything, just wanted to waste our time?"

"He probably provided it, he'd be afraid to flat out refuse an order from his boss. Provided, but buried. Peter said he didn't have time to go through it before he left, so this Frank guy wasn't exactly forthcoming with information. We are probably going to have to dig. And that could take all night."

"Shit," Rowdy said as he plopped back in his chair. He had selected a large stack of papers and slowly begun to peruse them not knowing exactly what he was looking for. Coop and Skeet followed suit. It was going to be a very long night.

* * * *

Where could Cole be and why wasn't he returning his call? Frank was frantic to reach his boss and college buddy. They had partied together since they were young. Then, when Frank found himself jobless and hiding out from his former employer, Cole had offered him an olive branch. A way out of his current mess and a chance to get back on his feet. Of course, he'd jumped at the offer. Now, it was his turn to get Cole out of trouble and the man wouldn't return his calls. He downed another shot of Patron; the high quality tequila went down smooth and ultimately did the trick. He was finally tipsy. Frank needed a strong buzz to get him through tonight. His world was dangling precariously over another edge and he needed Cole to assure him they would be fine. But Cole had disappeared. Ten messages over two days and the man was ignoring him. Was that a sign he should run? He glanced absently at the brunette that slid in next to him, then ignored her completely and motioned for the bartender to bring him another drink. He was so uptight that the woman didn't even tempt him tonight. He had a decision to make, and if Cole didn't return his call within the next twenty minutes he would move on to plan B, a flight to Switzerland. Cole wasn't the only one skimming the books. The difference was, Frank had learned from his mistakes. This time, the money would never be traced back to him. This time Cole would take the fall alone. Frank wouldn't exactly be living the life of luxury, but he wouldn't be behind bars and he wouldn't be desperate or desolate either. Frank glanced at the clock, fifteen more minutes.

* * * *

Bailey could hear Cole's phone vibrating in his pocket. That was the second time she'd heard the distinct noise in the last half hour. Cole hadn't moved. Not even his phone got his attention. She glanced at him lying there next to her and wondered if he was still alive. Did she really want to know? Not enough to move over and check him for a pulse. Plus, could she really get a reading with her foot? Since she was still handcuffed to the headboard that would be her only option. If he was faking, he might take her actions as a sign of weakness. She anxiously glanced at the door and wondered how much longer before Reese returned. She'd seen the man angry before and knew without a doubt that when he returned, all hell was going to break loose. She just hoped somehow she would survive the storm.

* * * *

The men worked well into the night. Maggie and Angela had reluctantly retired at midnight, succumbing to the constant pressure from their husbands. Maggie hadn't fully recovered from her accident and Angela was worn out from jetlag and the overwhelming anxiety she'd experienced leading up to that hospital visit. It was nearly two in the morning when Coop finally stood and declared he was heading to bed. Skeet looked up, considered then followed his friend up the stairs. Rowdy took a minute to finish the page he was studying then glanced at Peter. The man gave no sign he was planning to leave.

"I know you just got here and you want to push through this, but we really should try to get a couple hours of sleep. The three of us have been at this more than forty-eight hours. We can't go on much longer. We can crash for two to three hours at my place, then we can head back up here and resume where we left off. In addition to the nap, I desperately need a shower." He stood and waited for a response.

Peter looked up, saw the determined look on Rowdy's face and decided not to argue. "I'm not going to get any sleep tonight, do you mind if we bring some of these back with us? I can keep searching until I get tired."

Rowdy hesitated then gave in. "Just write Skeet a note letting him know which files you took so he doesn't panic when he finds them missing."

Peter scribbled something on a blank pad then set the note on the top of the tallest file. He grabbed an empty glass and set it on top of the note. When he glanced up, he saw Rowdy was smirking. He shrugged, "I just want to make sure it's still there when they wake up."

"After you," Rowdy pointed to the door. "I need to lock up."

The two men entered the cottage and Rowdy flipped on a lamp. The room was eerily quiet. "So, help yourself to whatever you need. You've found the bathroom and…" Rowdy trailed off. This man and his marital problems were none of his business. "Look, I have no idea what is going on with you and your wife and I don't want to know. But, I sensed some underlying tension. If you're trying to avoid her, just sleep on the couch. It's extremely comfortable and there are pillows and blankets in that closet. Don't stay up all night to keep up appearances. Your marriage is your business."

Peter sighed as he lowered himself to the sofa then dropped his head on the back of the couch. "What marriage? Piper agreed to be my wife because she was lonely and afraid. I thought in time, she'd grow to love me but apparently not. She's naïve, extremely gullible when it comes to the boys and... self-absorbed. Yet, I still love her... more than life itself."

Rowdy hesitated, then moved to sit on the chair across from Peter. "I don't know either one of you. I do know Bailey, though. And she loves you both. She trusts you and she was very adamant that her mother loves you, in her way. If Bailey can see it, if she can believe it after being away for over three years, I'd say you have something worth fighting for. Especially if you love her as much as you say you do."

"Mr. Cooper," Peter began.

"Rowdy, please. It makes me cringe every time you drop that Mr. Cooper crap."

Peter smiled. "Okay, Rowdy it is. I can admit that I was intrigued by Scott's wife from the beginning. Well, not in college but later after they had both matured. Not in an inappropriate way, but in a mystified way. It was obvious how much he loved her and the feeling was mutual. They dated casually in college as far as I knew and I'd seen them around a few times, but I hadn't met her until one night at a business social. They were married by then and it amazed me that he was just as successful in his personal life as he was in his business ventures. It didn't seem fair somehow. I briefly wondered if his wife had something to do with that. At the time, my life was far more complicated. My marriage had already fallen apart. Cole was ten years old and suddenly overnight, he was living with me. I found myself in a situation I never imagined; a single father trying to raise a kid, and forge a career. His mother wouldn't tell me what happened, only that she was finished. And she was; Cole has not talked to her for years. Unless he lied about that, too.

Anyway, that night is when I approached Scott about a partnership. He resisted, but I could tell he was interested. We hadn't been close for years, after graduation we each went our own way and basically drifted apart but he didn't say no so there was hope. Eventually, we joined forces and Drakker Consulting was the best firm out there for a lot of years. Then Scott died and things got complicated again. I had to hold the company together and work through the difficult transition. And Piper and Victoria had to move on without Scott. He was such a wonderful father, and husband I suspect."

"Bailey told me about that time. She also said you were there for them. Their family was falling apart and you stepped in and held it all together," Rowdy supplied. The guy truly looked miserable.

"Yes," Peter said as he continued to look at the ceiling. "There were people… co-workers, business associates, fake friends that speculated. Nobody said it to my face, but I was surrounded by people who had doubts." He suddenly sat up straight and looked Rowdy in the eyes. "I loved Scott like a brother. We had become so close by this time. You have a tendency to do that when you work so closely with someone day after day, year after year. Anyway, I loved him like he was family. I missed him so much. It's ironic I guess. I was grieving over his shocking, unfathomable death. But I was struggling to deal with the loss of so much more than my best friend, because of my best friend." Peter knew he probably wasn't making any sense. "I'm sorry, I'm keeping you up. I didn't mean to."

Rowdy shook his head. "I think maybe right now you are going through something just as difficult. I think you need your friend now more than ever. He's not here, but I am. Sometimes it helps to verbalize things, even if you do that with a stranger. I'm willing to listen as long as you need me to. It's not like I'm going to sleep anyway. I'm not going to rest until I find Bailey and see for myself that she's okay. Mr. Hughes, I'm sorry you had to find out about your son this way. It's a lot to take in."

Peter smiled. "If I have to call you Rowdy, you are required to call me Peter."

Rowdy laughed. "Okay, I can do that."

Peter sighed. "I appreciate the offer but I think I've reminisced enough for tonight. I'll just finish looking through this stack then I'll try to get a little sleep."

Rowdy studied Peter Hughes and realized Bailey was right about him. Peter was a good, hard working man. His only crime was loving his son too much. And that love had led to trust and leniency. It was unfortunate that trust had been given to the wrong kind of man. Rowdy could see in a way, it was still there. Peter was trying to accept the evidence in front of him, but somehow he still believed in his son. Rowdy had seen it a million times on the job. Parents in denial, didn't overcome years of repudiation overnight. "Okay, well if you decide you don't want the couch and you're not ready to make nice with your wife, I do have another small room. The bed's only a single, but it's clean. I set it up for Bryan just in case he wanted to spend a few nights over here."

"Bryan?" Peter asked, immediately looking up from his task.

"Oh yeah, Bryan," Rowdy confirmed. "He's my nephew. He hasn't actually used the bed so the sheets are new, so are the pillows."

"How many siblings do you guys have?" Peter asked, thinking it would have been nice to have a brother growing up. Well, it would be nice to have a brother to lean on right now.

"Just the two of us. Mom and Dad have both passed away. Coop is the only family I have left." Rowdy swallowed.

"Then Bryan belongs to Andy and Maggie Cooper?" Peter furrowed his brows. He hadn't seen a child all night.

"He does, but he's visiting friends," Rowdy provided, seeing Peter's confusion. "A friend from our old town called and asked if the kid could visit. With everything going on here, we all thought it was a great idea. Especially after those two tried to have him kidnapped."

"What?" Peter yelled. "Sorry, I mean what?" he added at a normal tone.

Rowdy settled back in. It was time to tell Peter just what his kid was up to. He started with the attempted abduction at the bar where Jase had thwarted their efforts then he explained how the security guys had made a calculated and coordinated effort to kidnap Maggie, Bryan and probably Bailey.

Peter stopped him. "What happened to the men? The security guys. Do you have their names?"

"Uh, well… there is one housed in town. In jail. His name is Clyde Seskel. He's been cooperating, well sort of. So, Coop probably won't ask the judge to hold him over until trial but we want him out of our town. If you can make that happen, we'd be extremely thankful for your assistance."

"You said sort of cooperating. Do I need to have a personal talk with Clyde? I know he's afraid of Flint, but I also believe he has a wife or girlfriend at home. He's probably not too happy about losing his job," Peter considered. "What about the others, the ones that came after you guys up here? Are any of them in jail?"

"No," Rowdy closed his eyes and forced himself to continue. He went through the deaths, not in detail but enough to help Peter understand Rowdy and Coop didn't have a choice.

"Dead. All of them?" Peter whispered. "I never did like that Flint Duvall. He was another man Cole said he knew. My son insisted we award the contract to his company and I gave in, but I never trusted the man. In fact, I was getting suspicious. Cole paid Duvall over fifty thousand dollars to find Victoria. And as far as I knew, he didn't have the slightest inkling where that girl had been. I should feel sad, I should feel something, but I'm just thankful none of you were hurt. I'm sorry for all this. My family has caused more than a little trouble for this cozy little town. If I can do something to make it up to you, please don't hesitate to ask."

"I'd say you are doing it right now, Peter." Rowdy glanced at the paperwork. "You didn't have to provide all of those. You certainly didn't have to fly out here so quickly to deliver them in person. And you didn't have to join us tonight as we tried to track the smallest of clues. It's enough." Rowdy stood and pivoted toward the hallway. He'd only taken two steps when Peter stopped him.

"Have they killed anyone?" Peter swallowed hard as he asked the question that had been bothering him all night. He silently waited, afraid he didn't really want to know the answer but knowing there was no turning back. "I know Agent Perkins believes they were responsible for Mandy Strausberg's death, but have there been others? Women they killed while they…" he couldn't finish. Moisture gathered in his eyes and he rapidly blinked back the tears.

Rowdy studied Peter for several seconds before he responded. "I'm afraid the answer is yes. I'm sorry, but yes. We are positive there were at least two. Another one in California is looking like it could be their work as well. I know you don't want to hear it, but…"

"No," Peter stopped him. "Maybe in the morning. Maybe I will be able to hear it in the morning, not tonight. I suspected, I had to know, but I truly hoped you would say no. I was silently praying they hadn't progressed to that point yet. Rowdy, I'm sorry but is there any way you could leave me alone now? I just realized what an amazingly awful father I am. I'm a failure. My son is a monster. He's destroyed my business, my family, my life. The son whom I have loved from the moment I held him in my arms is a genuinely evil, vile creature and I have no idea how to deal with that." He still held out hope the deaths were accidents.

Rowdy took another step toward the hallway then stopped. "I know it's hard, especially tonight when you have learned so many things about your son. So many awful, ugly things that you never knew, never could have thought possible, don't want to accept, but Peter, you have to believe in yourself. You are not the failure. You loved your kid, there is no crime in that. Sure, you may have been less than strict with him but so what? You loved him, you nurtured him, you helped build an amazing company. A company you planned to pass onto him someday. I guess what I'm saying is that Cole enjoyed the benefits of your labor. He was raised by at least one loving parent and went to the best schools. You are not responsible for what he became. What you are experiencing is normal. I've seen it before. Trust me, you are not the first parent in the world to discover their child did not grow up to be the upstanding, loving man they had hoped for. He made bad choices, not you. And I need your head in the game tomorrow. I need you rested and fresh because we still have a lot to go through if we are going to find Bailey."

Peter took a deep breath and tried to calm his raging emotions. He studied Rowdy then nodded. "You're right. I can deal with the reality of my son's life later. Right now I need to find my girl, Scott's daughter, Piper's little princess." He smiled. "The Princess that wasn't, if you ask Bailey." He decided to try on the new name and wondered if Victoria would keep it or go back to her given name when they found her. "I can see now why it was so important you find her. I'm sorry I wasn't more cooperative yesterday."

"I didn't blame you for that," Rowdy replied honestly. "I expected it. I was just hoping I would be able to get through to you. I was hoping to push you enough to investigate. Bailey was positive if you would just start looking, you would do the right thing. She was right. Now, goodnight Peter. I'm going to leave you alone like you asked. Tomorrow morning is going to come quickly."

Chapter Fourteen

Rowdy woke, showered and moved into the kitchen for a much needed pot of coffee. He hadn't gotten a bit of sleep, not really. Just dozed for a few minutes before he jerked back awake. He glanced at the couch and spotted Peter. So, the guy hadn't gone to bed then. Hopefully, Peter could eventually work things out with Piper. Rowdy was still a little angry with her for upsetting Bailey and he was sure he would never understand the woman, but there was something about her that made a guy want to protect her. He couldn't really explain it, she just seemed extremely fragile and appeared to need a little extra.... TLC maybe? Rowdy shrugged and began to make the coffee as quietly as he could.

Peter sat up and realized his host was in the kitchen. They needed to talk... before Piper awoke. He'd spent a fair amount of time thinking about Piper and his marriage last night, including the advice that Rowdy had given him. Unfortunately, he hadn't come to any conclusions, but he did know that Piper was a mess. He also knew he couldn't walk away without trying to help her. He wanted to be there for her. He thought he should, but right now he couldn't. So, he'd deal with the problem he could resolve and work on the rest later. He slowly made his way to the kitchen table and pulled out a chair.

Rowdy had just finished throwing together the pot of coffee when he heard a chair slide across the kitchen tile. He turned to see Peter staring out the window at the lake. Rowdy didn't blame him, he really did have an amazing view, especially first thing in the morning. His house faced west, so they had amazing sunsets, but the mornings were also enchanting. It was so serene and peaceful compared to Chicago. Rowdy loved to sit on the front porch and watch as the sun rose over the mountains and landed on the crystal clear water of the lake. Sometimes there was a slight breeze but most mornings, the surface was like a thin sheet of glass making the sunrise dance gracefully over the surface. And the wildflowers here were amazing. Rowdy loved the Indian Paintbrush the most with its vibrant red flowers and dark green stems. The contrast was a large part of its beauty. He didn't know the names of any of the others, but they definitely added character to his home.

Peter waited until Rowdy settled into the chair across from him before pulling out the file. "I think I might have found something."

Rowdy waited silently.

"Okay, it's a long shot. I'm going to need Skeet's help to track it, but last night I was thinking of something that Piper said. She wanted to know why Cole would risk his livelihood. He's destroyed our company and I never stopped to wonder why. I'm not sure the why matters, but that brought me to a different question. How does he plan to finance his escapades once the business folds? Oh, I'm sure Cole believes he can fix this. He's been buying and selling illegally for months but he had to have a plan. I considered Reese and that's when I remembered Carlton complaining that Reese was running their company into the ground as well. Carlton secretly told me that he was no longer leaving his corporation to his son. Apparently he found some up and coming hotshot kid that has a lot of promise. Anyway, that's when I remembered Sissy. I can't believe I forgot her all this time. I mean, she's supposed to be marrying my son in a few months."

Rowdy grinned. "Okay, Peter. I realize you have not had an ounce of sleep, but I have to tell you man, you are rambling something fierce and I haven't had coffee yet. Please get to the point already."

"Sorry," Peter nodded. "Victoria's trust." He pulled a sheet of paper from the stack and shoved it towards Rowdy.

It was a spreadsheet and it had a lot of rows and columns that didn't make a lick of sense to Rowdy. He was a former cop and current bar owner from Chicago. Not a freakin' accountant. "Sorry, that doesn't help me."

"It will help Agent Perkins. How soon do you think we can head up? He's going to have to call James and get the bank account number, but I can help with that." Peter was still thinking.

"Can you maybe give me the dumb guy version?" Rowdy growled as he stood and pulled two cups from the cupboard. He poured the coffee then reached in the fridge for a carton of half and half. On his way back to the table, he snagged the container of sugar. "You think they bought or rented the place with Bailey's money?"

"I'm sure of it." Peter spread the paperwork out on the table. He pointed to an entry several weeks back. "That's Frank's code for

Bailey's trust. I know because I'm the one that set it up. We used it to pay her tuition, books, apartment expenses, whatever she needed. I came up with Scotland Fairies in honor of Scott, and the fact that she was always like his fairy princess. Anyway, look at this entry. Scotland Fairies made a money transfer here for one hundred and fifty thousand. That sounds like a down payment to me."

Rowdy looked at the man like he was crazy. It sounded like a house to Rowdy.

"I know it's a lot but when you look at the next entry... that's over a million. Cole and Reese have purchased property. They own a house nearby, which is why nobody has seen them... they used Bailey's money to hide their trail."

"Bring your coffee, you just got it to go," Rowdy said, snatching his mug and the paperwork off the table and moving toward the door. Both men stopped abruptly when they stepped onto the porch and spotted Piper. Had she overheard their conversation? Did it matter? Rowdy couldn't think of anything they said that would be a problem. "Morning. Sorry, but we need to talk to Agent Perkins. There's coffee made if you want it." Rowdy was off the porch before he thought of the question. "Piper," he asked as he turned to face her. "Did Bailey have unrestricted access to her trust fund?"

"Yes," Piper said, studying the attractive young man. "Why?"

"Did anyone else have access to it?" Rowdy asked, ignoring her question.

"I did," Piper narrowed her eyes and waited for an explanation. When Rowdy didn't answer she grew impatient. "Rowdy Cooper, why do you want to know about Victoria's trust?"

"Honey," Peter answered. "This is very important. Someone has been withdrawing funds from Victoria's account. Did you take any money, any at all, out of Victoria's trust? Maybe to pay off the school tuition, buy her a place where she could live if she returned? Anything? Did you make any preparations after she phoned you?"

"No, I already told you that." Piper's gaze shifted from her husband to Rowdy and back to Peter. At least he was talking to her. "What is this about?"

"Someone has cashed out a substantial amount of money from that account," Peter replied absently. "Victoria was on the run but someone would know if she was the one accessing her fortune. I can guarantee she hasn't touched it."

"Victoria would not touch that money. Not until she came home. She knew her father set that trust up to make sure she could get through college and have a decent start. Sure, Scott Alexander knew she was going to take over his portion of the business one day, but he wanted her to have a buffer. Money that was hers, free and clear of the business. 'Mad money', Scott used to call it. I would never touch that money and Victoria... well, she was going on about being attacked and broke. I think she even said something about not touching that account. What exactly do you mean by 'substantial'?"

"That's not important," Peter turned and descended the stairs. "We need to talk to Agent Perkins."

Piper rose and moved gracefully to the door. Rowdy could hear her mumbling but couldn't quite make out what she was saying. Something about pig headed men, stubborn and secrets. Rowdy chuckled to himself. She sounded like Maggie. For the first time since meeting Piper, he saw a glimpse of Bailey.

Mount Haven

Peter and Rowdy rang the bell. The last thing they wanted to do was waltz in and see a couple of women less than ready for mixed company. Maggie opened the door and smiled in greeting. "Where's Piper?"

"Oh," Peter choked on his coffee not expecting that question and at a loss of how to answer it.

"She's still at my place," Rowdy answered for him. "Is Skeet up? We need him to look at something and get his nerd squad working early."

"You know he hates it when you call the FBI's Cyber Division that," Maggie scolded. "I have no doubt they worked hard to achieve that level of success in the computer world."

Angie stepped into the room and gave Rowdy a hug. "Which is exactly why you should keep it up." She laughed and winked at Rowdy. "He's still a hotshot in his circles, hardly anyone gives him a hard time these days. It's good for him. In fact, we should definitely visit you guys more often." She moved forward and gave Maggie a hug. "This view is amazing!"

"Coffee?" Skeet asked as he stumbled to the chair. If he'd gotten three hours of sleep it was a miracle. It was always difficult for him to acclimate to a new bed. Another thing he didn't miss about his old life. Flying from place to place had gotten old fast, but he'd kept it up for the money and the prestige. Speaking of prestige… "Ange, did I just hear you encouraging Rowdy to call the guys the Nerd Squad? Because we both know how hurt they are going to be when I tell them you've joined the dark side."

Angie laughed and set a cup of coffee in front of her husband. "Then don't tell. Problem solved."

Coop zombie-walked into the room and settled into a chair. He glanced up, grateful when Maggie pushed a steaming cup of coffee under his nose. "Thanks, babe."

"Why are we all up?" Maggie asked, glancing around the room. "I mean look at us, we barely got any sleep but every one of us rose before the sun this morning."

"Stress," Angie suggested. "We can sleep next week. What's on the agenda for today? How are we going to find Bailey this morning?"

"I know we need to get started on that paperwork in there, but I thought I'd go over to the cottage and visit with Piper for a bit. Ange, do you want to join me?" Maggie asked.

"Actually," Peter interrupted. "I think I found something. If I'm right, we don't need to go through paperwork. We just need to get Perkin's men on it and then the waiting begins."

"What did you find?" Skeet asked. Excitement instantly replaced discouragement as Peter explained the entry and his theory.

Coop was listening to Peter and concentrating. Had he seen Scotland Fairies on any of the realtor printouts? He was pretty sure the answer to that question was no, but he wasn't willing to go by memory. He pushed back his chair and stepped into the other room. He was shuffling through files when Rowdy stepped in.

"Great minds think alike?" Rowdy asked. "I was just trying to remember if Scotland Fairies was on any of the paperwork. I can't remember seeing it… at all. Do you?"

"No," Coop admitted. "But I doubt we would. I mean those two have been careful. They're just as sloppy as any other criminal, but they are careful. They would try to hide their purchase. Cole knows about Scotland Fairies and he would want to hide the theft from his father. Skeet is going to have to send everything over to Washington. He'll want the best guys on this."

"I'm not so good at waiting, you know that." Rowdy plopped down on the couch and opened a file. "It's driving me insane. The not knowing. We have to find her, Coop."

"We will," Coop picked up a file and joined his brother. "I promise, we will."

* * * *

Maggie and Angie stepped from the shelter of trees and continued up the stone walkway towards Rowdy's. The instant the cottage came into view, they saw Piper. Bailey's mother was spread across the wooden porch swing, gazing off toward the lake.

"It's beautiful isn't it?" Maggie asked softly as she ascended the stairs. "I fell in love with this place the instant I saw it. I don't think any place on earth could entice me away."

"It is," Piper agreed as she lifted a handkerchief and gently patted her face. She hadn't stopped crying since Peter had arrived home to confront her about her daughter. Why did Victoria have to be so difficult? It wasn't bad enough she'd disappeared, now she was tearing the family apart.

Maggie and Angie settled into Rowdy's Adirondack chairs and waited. When Piper didn't engage them, Maggie decided it was up to her. "You have been crying a lot since you arrived, Piper. Do you want to talk about it?"

Piper was surprised at the girl's nerve. She was beautiful, tiny and excessively nosey. "It's private."

"I understand," Angie nodded. "But I also know that when your family is in crisis, it's better to talk about it than shut down. Nobody can deal with something this stressful alone."

Piper considered, but eventually gave in. This was no different than her monthly book club back in San Diego. Oh sure, the group liked to read. But, they liked to gossip and brag even more. Piper had no intention of bragging or gossiping but these two were obviously happy in their marriage. Getting a little advice from them couldn't hurt. "You're right, of course. I just don't understand Peter. He's so angry with me. It's cruel, really. I don't understand it."

Maggie was floored. Was this woman for real? "Let me get this straight; you are not upset over Bailey's abduction? You are upset because your husband is angry with you?"

"Well, yes," Piper said. Wasn't that obvious? "Victoria probably just ran away again. I really don't see why all the fuss. Peter isn't like this. I have no idea what's gotten into him. But if Cole does in fact have my daughter, they are probably home by now. He's a loving brother. He has always watched out for Victoria. She's safe… she's just fine. But there's something wrong with Peter. Do you think he might be ill? I mean, something must be wrong. Do you think he needs to see a doctor?"

Angie was watching Piper. She was a pretty good judge of character and it was becoming more and more evident that Piper was simply in denial. "Why is Peter angry with you?"

"Oh." Piper thought about it before sharing. "Well, he thought I should have told him that Victoria called. He said it was unforgiveable of me not to tell him Cole had attacked my daughter and was here, in Mount Haven, stalking her."

"Well, he does have a point," Maggie provided. She couldn't believe she'd taken time away from their search to comfort Bailey's mother.

"But I don't believe Cole did any of those things, so why would I upset my husband with false accusations?" Piper argued.

"I'm confused," Angie said, taking a deep breath. Either this woman was an idiot or she simply could not live with the knowledge that her husband's child was a monster. Angie was pretty sure it was the latter. "You are Bailey's mother. It's your job to protect your daughter yet you keep implying she lied about the attack, that she lied about Cole's intentions, that she lied about her fear of Reese Weathersby. Is your daughter a liar, Mrs. Hughes?"

"No," Piper said immediately then realized what she had done. If Victoria hadn't lied, then Cole and Reese were after her. They had attacked her. But she couldn't accept that. She had allowed Cole into her home, into her family. If he attacked her baby girl, that meant Piper had failed her child. She thought of Scott and the special connection he had with his daughter. Piper had been a little jealous of that connection at first, but she accepted it because she knew, without a doubt, Scott loved her too. He just treasured and adored his daughter. Eventually Piper had realized that love didn't alter or lessen the devotion he had for his wife. Scott would be so disappointed in her if she had put their only child at risk. No, Cole could not be dangerous. They all had to be wrong about that.

"Quite the conundrum, isn't it?" Angie grinned. "Mrs. Hughes, this is not your fault. This is Cole and Reese's fault. But make no mistake, Bailey is in danger. There is no telling what those two men are capable of. I suggest you accept that, somehow learn to live with it and start helping us instead of hiding out with your head in the sand." Angie knew she was probably being too hard on this woman, but credulous people like Piper just pissed her off.

Maggie wanted to like Piper Hughes, she really did. But right now, she could barely stand looking at the woman. She was more concerned about a little fight with Peter than the safety of her own child. Maggie stood and moved to leave then changed her mind. "I know this must be a difficult time for you but I'm finding it hard to know how to help you. For some reason you don't want to accept how evil those men are. You will need to know. At some point you are going to need to know. When that moment arrives, you know where to find us." Maggie stepped off the porch and disappeared down the walkway.

"Goodbye, Piper," Angie tested. When she didn't get a response, she too stepped off the porch.

"Peter is barely talking to me," Piper admitted. "He acts like he hates me. Victoria is missing, all of you think Reese a monster and according to Peter, his son has ruined us financially. If I accept what you are telling me, even one little nugget of what you are telling me, where does it stop? How do I move forward?" Piper looked earnestly at Angie then began to sob. "Where does it end? When my first husband died, I was barely able to get out of bed. If I lose Peter and Victoria… and Scott's company? How do I get out of bed in the morning?"

Maggie hadn't left, she'd waited for Angie just out of sight. When she heard Piper's agonizing questions and then the sobs, she returned. She didn't stop, she just walked up the stairs and pulled the woman close. Angie joined her and the three of them sat there for what seemed like an eternity while Piper Hughes came to grips with her new reality.

* * * *

Bailey had no idea where Reese was and she didn't care. Knowing there was a special kind of hell for men like Reese Weathersby brought her comfort. She gritted her teeth and rode out the pain as she tried to shift into a more comfortable position. She'd been right, Reese was livid. When he'd returned from his walk, the fury had grown exponentially. He stepped into the cabin, took one look at Bailey and Cole then went berserk. One of her eyes was swollen shut, her ribs were so painful it hurt to breathe, and her abdomen was killing her. She just hoped he hadn't damaged any internal organs. At least he had unhooked one of her arms. She glanced at Cole and wondered if he was still alive. He wasn't moving, but last night she'd broken down and finally checked for a pulse. She was pretty sure he still had one, but it had been weak and difficult to find. She didn't know what the hell had come over Reese, but he was a crazy person. It was impossible to decide which Reese scared her the most. She could either get beaten to death or the pervert might sexually assault her, which would be even more violent and traumatic. There were just no good possibilities to hope for. Her only hope was that somehow Coop and Rowdy would find her. She knew they were good at their job. But was anyone that good? She didn't even know where she was, how could they? She felt a deep, gut wrenching sense of despair that flooded her soul and stomped out every last shimmer of hope. Bailey's heart ached, she missed Rowdy and his family. She felt so alone.... on her own yet surrounded by monsters. She was desperate and vulnerable and held captive by a lunatic. The only thing she knew for sure, was that life as she'd known it was over for good. And with that thought, Bailey began to cry.

* * * *

Reese paced behind the cabin. He couldn't go back, not yet. His anger was out of control and he'd almost killed Tory. His beautiful, precious future wife and he'd almost lost control to the point of no return. He wanted to scream at the world. He was becoming his father. The man he hated. The man that had ruined his childhood, had chased off his mother and had become the bane of Reese's existence by controlling every aspect of his business life. He hated him, loathed him with every fiber of his being yet, hours earlier he had acted just like him. How had that happened? When had it happened? He'd ask Cole, but he was afraid of what his friend might tell him. Anyway, Cole was still out cold. Reese wasn't sure what that was all about. He hadn't hit his head that hard, had he?

Reese turned and punched the outer wall then cursed as pain radiated up his arm. He glanced at his knuckles and realized they were bleeding... all of them. Just another reminder of his brief but lethal loss of control hours earlier. He would have to go in sometime. He needed to clean the cuts and now he was going to need an ice bag. But if he stepped through the door and saw Tory caring for Cole again, could he rein in his temper? And that was the problem, Reese really didn't know the answer to that question. He hadn't planned on punishing Tory last time. But when he'd stepped back into the room and spotted the two of them lying on the bed together, he lost it. Why hadn't Cole moved? Tory's bed was the smallest and the least comfortable. So why was Cole still occupying it? Because he wanted free and ready access all night, that's why. The idea of Cole being with Tory was driving Reese insane. Even after pacing the woods for hours as he waited for the sun to rise, his blood still boiled at the thought. He really needed to get a grip. They had a deal. One time and then nothing…forever. So why did Reese feel so threatened now that the time to pay up had come? He turned and leaned against the wall and tried to evaluate the situation logically. For the first time in his life, he didn't have the answers.

* * * *

It took nearly two hours for Skeet's team to come through. But they had come through and in a big way. They traced the money from Bailey's account to the Caymans to Australia and a few other countries that didn't matter. What mattered was it stopped in a popular bank right in the center of San Diego. Agents Maitland and Hightower had done the rest. Now, they had a name. The fake company's name Cole or Frank had created for the account. Speaking of Frank, he was missing. Skeet believed the dirty money man had skipped town. He was probably out of the country by now. But Frank Mandel was not their concern. Finding the property purchased by that business was their priority at the moment.

The small group was gathered around the large dining room table. Jase had outdone himself. The talented cook must have spent all night creating every finger food imaginable for the group. Coop and Rowdy had just finished distributing drinks when the doorbell rang. Once again, the three lawmen tensed and glanced around the room.

"Stay here," Coop ordered the women then moved to the door.

Skeet checked the window this time then smiled. "It's Piper. We have to stop meeting like this."

Coop grinned and opened the door. Piper stepped hesitantly into the house.

Peter stood and wondered what had brought his wife out of the comfortable cottage. Lounging on the front porch with a good romance was more her style. He'd figured she could keep herself occupied for days. He just hoped they didn't need that long.

"I'd like to help," she announced to nobody in particular. "Victoria is my daughter. I want to do my part to help locate her."

Maggie and Angie smiled and the men looked at each other in confusion. Maggie acted first. She stood and walked to Piper. "Here, there's a chair next to me. We've figured out where the money came from and how they hid the purchase. Now we just have to go through all these realtor records to find the company."

Piper relaxed. She should have known Maggie would welcome her with open arms. The walk over had been tense and nerve wracking but this tiny woman had a way of making people feel welcome in the most trying of circumstances. She glanced at her husband and cringed. He did not look happy to see her. Well, too bad. He was the one that said their life was about to change. She just hoped he would still love her as she slowly learned to reclaim control of her life. It had been too long. Somehow after Scott's death she had completely lost sight of who she was. She'd coasted along letting her husband make all the decisions. She believed it was easier that way, but in the process she had become a stranger. A woman she didn't recognize. A woman that had been taken in by a pretty face and lies. If Reese Weathersby was the monster Victoria described, not the sweet boy he pretended to be... he was going to rue the day he'd messed with her family. She was strong... deep inside where nobody but her knew it, but all the same, she was strong. And she was a mother. Not even the men in this room had any idea how powerful and lethal that simple role made a woman. Well, they were about to find out. Especially if they tried to dismiss her.

"Okay then," Coop said recognizing the expression on Piper's face. It was that look that women seemed to be born with. The one that said shut up and accept it. That's exactly what he planned to do. "We need to divide up these files. With all of us working, we should be able to find Aqunullity Mazuma pretty quickly."

"It's in there," Maggie affirmed. "I remember highlighting it. I was marking any companies I hadn't heard of before to do a more thorough search the next time around. I remember that one because I wondered what they did or produced. I just wish I could remember which realtor did business with them." She glanced at Coop, then Rowdy and Skeet. "I think you should leave this to us. Angie, Piper, Peter and I can find the company. We have a lot of files but if we split them between the four of us it should go pretty quickly. The three of you need to develop a plan of attack. We all know that once the property is located Rowdy is going to fly out of here like a bat out of hell."

Rowdy narrowed his eyes at Maggie. Was she implying he should stay behind?

Maggie stood and moved next to Coop. "My amazing husband told me how he wanted to rush in, guns blazing when he found out I was trapped in the house alone and Flint Duvall and company were after me." She wrapped an arm around Coop's waist. Coop pulled her close and kissed the top of her head. "Rowdy, you stopped him. You forced him to come up with a plan. A logical plan. One that he hated, but he also knew it was the best way to deal with the threat. Now it's Andy's turn to step up and develop a fool proof plan that will ensure Bailey's safety and capture the bad guys."

Angie looked up and focused on her husband. "That's why we came, isn't it? We are here to ensure this situation has the desired outcome. Coop and Rowdy did the same for you when I was in danger. The three of you together are unstoppable. There is no one alive that can plan an op better than you three. Go plan. Let us find the property. Come up with a mission plan that ends this thing peacefully so we can all get on with our lives."

"The women are right," Skeet said looking directly at Rowdy. "You know they are. Let's head to the study. We need to start gathering resources and developing an action plan. Obviously specifics will have to wait until we know where they are but there's a lot we can do. For starters I want information on the area law enforcement personnel. We might need help. Let's figure out who to call for backup."

The three men silently left the room. Maggie heard Coop talking about Matthew and Derek and what role his two deputies could play in all this. She couldn't hear specifics but Maggie knew her husband would want to include them and protect them at the same time.

"Okay then," Piper sighed. She turned to Maggie and smiled. "Thank you for the warm welcome." She glanced at Peter then immediately looked away. Her husband was studying her intently. Piper had no idea how to explain things to him so she decided to avoid the topic altogether. "Where do you want me to start?"

Angie passed over a file. "We are just skimming through the records one company at a time. There are more realtors in this area than I would have imagined. This shouldn't take too long though. All we have to do is go down each list until we find Aqunullity Mazuma. The name is so unique it should jump out at us immediately."

Mount Haven

"Okay," Piper said accepting the file. "What is Aqunullity Mazuma anyway? Did Cole or Reese threaten them into funneling money or something?"

Peter continued to watch Piper, amazed. Was it possible his wife had finally accepted the situation for what it was? He truly hoped so. They had a long way to go if they were going to save their marriage and he truly didn't know if that was possible, but this was a promising first step. "Cole had Frank Mandel steal funds from Vicki's trust. They funneled it through various accounts in an attempt to hide their activities but over two million landed in an account under the name of Aqunullity Mazuma in a bank located in our home town. From there, they simply transferred the funds to a local realtor and purchased property to hide out in while they did surveillance on Victoria. Coop had the roads blocked almost instantly so we are fairly confident they are holding your daughter on the same property. We just need to find it."

Piper closed her eyes and inhaled several breaths to calm her nerves. It was so difficult to think of Reese and Cole going to such lengths to harm her daughter. She truly had been hiding in the closet for years, but that all changed today. She would face the world head on, no matter how unpleasant. Her daughter's life might depend on it and she owed it to her late husband. Scott would be so mortified if he knew what a failure Piper had been since his death.

Peter returned his attention to the paperwork before him. He knew that look. It was the expression Piper got when she was thinking about Scott. He shouldn't be surprised that at a time like this she would think of the husband she had loved... still loved. But at the moment it didn't matter. Watching her as she reminisced about some distant memory twisted the knife in his heart a little more. Peter actually rubbed his chest as the pain of his current situation intensified. It was all he could do to sit there quietly as he skimmed list after list looking for the offensive company name.

It was nearly an hour later when Angela suddenly jumped from her chair and announced she'd found it. She rushed to the study to notify the men. That's when the house turned from intense focus to loud but controlled chaos.

Skeet pulled up a detailed and classified map of the property on his phone. "This isn't going to work. I need a computer. We have to scroll so far in to see the details, we only get a small snapshot of the place."

Skeet disappeared up the stairs then returned with a laptop. He quickly connected his office MiFi to the computer and logged into the encrypted server to access the FBI's secure mapping program. The men huddled around the small screen studying every detail. Twenty minutes later Coop sat back in his chair and ran his hand through his hair in frustration. "It's not going to be ideal, there are so many things that could go wrong with this mission." He looked at Rowdy and knew his brother was itching to leave. "I'll set up here," he pointed to a large tree situated to the right of the front door of the cabin. "I won't know the distance until we arrive. From here it looks about a hundred yards away. That's doable. We're going to use our radios, our frequency. I'll let Mariah know so she can monitor and record. Let me go grab my spare walkie from the car. Rowdy, you'll need the one I gave you a couple weeks ago. I only have one extra and I need to give that to Skeet."

Rowdy nodded. He was going to need to stop at home before he could head out anyway.

Mount Haven

"Okay then." Skeet stood. "I have to make a couple phone calls and change, we head out in…" he glanced at his watch. "Let's say fifteen minutes from now."

Rowdy also stood and exited the house. Coop could advise the women and Peter of the plan. They would need to stay at Coop's, inside, until the mission was complete. Once they had Bailey back and Cole and Reese in custody, the Hughes could decide their next move.

Piper watched the men scramble around the house, loading up weapons, ammo and miscellaneous police gear. She was worried about her children. Yes, Victoria was hers by blood, but Cole was also her son. She'd accepted him as part of her family the instant she'd met him. He wasn't as openly affectionate as his father but he was refined and sophisticated. Cole Hughes was the walking definition of debonair. Women loved him and men envied him. Too bad he wasn't as chivalrous and gallant as she always believed. Still, she didn't want anything to happen to him. She wasn't sure Peter would survive if Rowdy or one of the others had to use lethal force to stop his son. Piper began to pace nervously, wondering how long this would take and how she would handle the interminable wait.

* * * *

Coop shifted, dialed in his weapon then picked up his walkie. "Car one to dispatch."

"Go ahead," Mariah answered immediately.

"Is everything set up?" Coop knew they wouldn't need much from his employee but he wanted all communication between the group recorded.

"Affirmative," came Mariah's reply. "Oh, and Lieutenant Jakab Brant from Missoula called. He's on his way with an eight-man team. He insisted you wait until he arrives but I explained the situation and suggested he expedite."

"Copy," Coop replied. Good, they had backup coming. The op would probably be over by the time they arrived but at least it was something. Skeet also had a team of agents heading in from Salt Lake. Unlike Missoula, these were highly trained SWAT members who were proficient in dealing with hostage and barricade situations. The two groups would probably arrive at about the same time. Which would be too late to stop the current op plan. Agent John Hensick had ordered Skeet to wait or face disciplinary action. Unfortunately for Hensick, Skeet had a high powered protector. FBI Director Stanley Burns was on board with Skeet's plan. The Perkins' longtime family friend understood the situation and agreed that waiting was not an option. Coop suspected Director Burns also knew Skeet well enough to understand that he'd act on this with or without approval. If Coop was right, Burns was doing what was necessary to protect Skeet from repercussions. If it were anybody else, they would have been ordered to stand down. But Skeeter Perkins was like a son to Burns, and the director had been present during the crisis with Angela. He knew full well that Rowdy and Coop had saved Skeet's wife. Now it was time to return the favor and Stanley Burns would not stand in Skeet's way. Coop was grateful for the support but he still believed he and his brother had simply done their job that day. It wasn't necessary to repay them for anything.

Mount Haven

"Dispatch, Perkins. I am in position," Skeet announced over the air.

"Copy Perkins," Mariah answered. "Car 6," she inquired.

"Go ahead," Derek replied.

"I have advised the residents along Granville Drive that you are in the area. They've been ordered to stay inside with their doors locked." Granville was the dirt roadway that led to the target. There were three houses at the far end, just off the paved roadway. Their occupants were curious but agreed to remain inside until advised it was safe to leave. Mariah was worried about Derek and Matthew. Well, to be honest she was worried about everyone. The Coopers hadn't lived there long but everyone had accepted them as part of the town. She knew they had experience, big city experience but the men they were hunting were dangerous. Cole Hughes seemed cordial enough, but that Reese Weathersby was evil. She'd sensed that about him the instant he stepped into the station. Everyone was on edge. Things like this didn't happen in Mount Haven and the residents were anxious for the crisis to come to an end.

* * * *

Rowdy led Knight into the thick trees surrounding the cabin. This was going to take a coordinated effort. Skeet and Coop were in position, now it was his turn. He glanced down at Knight; the dog was in work mode. It may have been over a year since the duo had officially worked a situation together but some things never changed. Knight was alert. He tugged at the leash as he frantically studied the area. Rowdy knew the dog wasn't just watching for a threat, he was scenting the air for any indication there was a bad guy hiding in the woods. He slid behind a tree approximately fifty feet from the back door and waited.

It only took a couple seconds for Knight to settle and focus on the target. Rowdy pushed his transmitter and whispered into his headset, "Car fifteen in position." He waited for dispatch to acknowledge his traffic then called to Coop, "Car one, Car fifteen."

"Go," Coop answered absently as he surveyed the area. He wasn't seeing any movement inside the building.

"What's your twenty?" Rowdy needed to know exactly where his brother was before this thing got started.

"Two at eighty," Coop replied. He spotted Skeet crouched about thirty feet from the side of the house. Now they just needed Matthew and Derek to check in and they could put their plan in motion.

Rowdy relaxed. Coop was only eighty yards out, easy shot for someone as proficient as his brother. Rowdy visualized the map they'd studied all afternoon. Coop was somewhere facing the front door of the cabin. Most likely to the east because it would give him a clear shot to the building. He probably had a visual inside the target as well. "Any movement?"

"Not so far," Coop answered softly. "I don't have eyes on the west side of the target but I have a clear view of the east side. No movement. It looks like a kitchen window but I can see the open living area and the fireplace pretty clearly." Coop started to respond then stopped, he needed to relay the information but he didn't want Rowdy jumping the gun.

"Car five in position," Matthew announced. His heart was beating and his palms were sweating. He'd gotten into law enforcement because he wanted to help people but he'd never imagined something like this could happen in Mount Haven.

"Copy, Car five," Mariah answered.

Perkins shifted the weapon slung over his shoulder. Once Derek called in, this was going to go quickly. Matthew would call out over the bullhorn, which everyone knew Reese and Cole would ignore. Then all hell would break loose. Skeet just hoped the good guys all walked out of here on their own. He didn't really care what happened to Cole Hughes or Reese Weathersby. He froze at Coop's whispered update. The information surprised and confused him.

"I have eyes on our victim," Coop announced.

Rowdy tensed.

"It looks like she is handcuffed to a bed. I can't see it very clearly but it looks like a small bed with an iron headboard. She's secured to the headboard."

"10-85?" Rowdy asked.

"I can't tell," Coop lied. There was no way he was going to divulge Bailey's condition. Rowdy would blow the op and put them all in danger. "I can see a man lying next to her. I think it's Hughes, but I can't see Weathersby anywhere. Hughes is either injured or sleeping. Either way, he's not moving."

Rowdy tightened his grip on Knight. It was nearly time to act. He just kept telling himself their plan would work. It had to. He just hoped Bailey didn't get injured in the process.

"Car six," Derek announced. "I've arrived."

"Copy," Mariah said softly. Things were about to start now.

"Car one," Derek continued.

"Go ahead, Derek," Coop answered.

"I was delayed because I had to wave off a media chopper. Is there any way we can designate this a no fly zone? The pilot was pissed, but he complied. We both know the station is going to send him back this way though. That kind of noise is going to hamper our efforts. Not to mention the fact we don't need it on the news if any of us has to neutralize a threat."

"Agreed," Coop responded. "Dispatch, did you copy that? I need you to send out a press release to the area stations."

Skeet waited for Coop to finish then advised. "Car one, let me handle that. I can have Salt Lake put the stations on notice. They won't argue with the feds and Mariah is busy enough."

"Copy that," Coop agreed that was a better idea. Also, it left Mount Haven out of the loop. If the media squawked, the FBI would have to field the complaints. "Dispatch cancel that request, the feds will handle this."

"Copy," Mariah said relieved. The last thing she needed to deal with right now was a bunch of reporters asking questions.

Skeet pulled out his phone and found the Salt Lake Field Office. He briefed them on the situation, provided their GPS coordinates and requested they make the distance significant. Derek was right, they didn't need the media getting their hands on a shooting if they could prevent it. Once that was complete, he waited for Matthew to start his announcements.

Mount Haven

"Car six, Car one," Coop called.

"Go ahead, sir," Derek answered.

"Let us know when you are in position. On your cue we're ready to go."

"Copy, give me two minutes and I should be set." Derek was moving as quickly and quietly as possible through the forest. These guys had picked an ideal location. He was just thankful it wasn't fall or the crunching leaves would be heard a mile away but in late spring the ground was soft and pliable. If Coop and company hadn't moved to town, he was sure they would be in over their heads. Former Sheriff Jaffrey Walters had been nothing more than a slick politician. He didn't have the first clue when it came to police work. Derek wasn't judging, the man had lived his entire life in Mount Haven where normally nothing worse than a brawl between drunk brothers happened. But the guy was a tyrant. He was the most narcissistic man Derek had ever had the displeasure of knowing. He'd been thrilled when Mayor Jon Herlin was elected. The community knew the man was going to force Sheriff Walters into early retirement and look outside the city walls for a replacement.

Derek moved in next to Matthew and nodded. The mission was a go. His friend would try to negotiate and Derek would have his back. He mentally tried to visualize where Coop, Rowdy and Skeet were. If Coop was eighty yards out from the front, he was to Derek's left. Skeet was on the east side of the building and Rowdy was somewhere in the back with his dog Knight. Derek's heart was racing as adrenaline pulsed through his body. He knew this was routine for the Coopers, but for him it was a first. He just hoped it worked and he made it out alive. He was too young to die in a gunfight with a couple of sadistic perverts. He unclipped his holster and pulled out his weapon. Better to be prepared for anything, right? He reached down and pressed the talk button. "Car six in position."

"Car five, start the announcements," Coop ordered. He wondered how long before Missoula arrived. The situation wasn't ideal. He needed an IC and it couldn't be him. It would be impossible for one man to command the situation and function as a marksman. But he was out of bodies so they'd just have to make do. He waited as he heard the distinct sound of Matthew Maciver speaking into the bullhorn.

* * * *

Reese jumped to his feet and moved to the end of the hallway. How had the police located them? He glanced at Cole, the man still hadn't moved a muscle. Reese was starting to worry. Had the blow to the head killed his partner? No, he wouldn't believe that. Cole had to be okay. Maybe receiving another blow so soon after the hard hit Cole took that night at the bar had been too much. He was probably just unconscious, but that didn't help Reese. He glanced at Tory and once again his anger spiked. The woman was now alert and clearly pleased by the arrival. Reese clenched his hands by his side and forced his mind to relax. He would deal with Tory later. Right now, he needed a plan. He was good at planning. He could do this. The two bit hellhole these people called a town, only had so many officers. One was clearly in front, making absurd demands. Where were the others? Where was the Sheriff? That was the man Reese was afraid of. He had originally believed Sheriff Cooper was just like all the other small town cops he'd encountered over the years. But clearly he'd been wrong. The man must have taken a job from a big city somewhere and settled in Podunk for some reason.

Mount Haven

Okay, think, Reese. You've gotten out of worse situations, you can get out of this one.

He glanced once again at Tory and realized she was smug. The conniving woman was enjoying this. She'd probably instigated it somehow. Reese took a deep breath, renewing his previous conviction to escape capture and punish Victoria. His confidence plunged when he heard the officer's next words.

"This is Officer Matthew Maciver with the Mount Haven Sheriff's Office. You need to leave all weapons inside and slowly exit the front door with your hands up. We have the building surrounded. If you cooperate, I can ensure your safety. If you don't comply in the next five minutes our officers will have to come in after you. If that happens, I cannot guarantee your safety. Again, Cole Hughes and Reese Weathersby come out with your hands up. You now have four minutes to comply."

Reese paced the hallway, how was he supposed to come up with a plan in a measly four minutes. It was impossible. He didn't even have a weapon. Their only gun was still in the car. He hadn't considered the possibility that the police would locate them. How had they found them anyway? One thing was clear: if he surrendered he wouldn't be harmed. If they came in after him, he might be. But if they came in after him, it might explain Cole's condition and Tory's. His lawyers could blame the amateur police for both injuries. No, he was staying put. Anyway, they might be bluffing.

"One minute," Matthew announced. It was clear the men were not coming out. That meant Rowdy and Knight were going in.

"Get ready," Skeet announced. He was taking the lead now. Coop had to concentrate on the targets and Rowdy was going to have his hands full as well. "Once the last minute is up, I'll deploy the distraction device through the side window on three. Rowdy, you and Knight enter through the back as planned and I will make my way onto the porch to open the front door. Coop, that should give you a clear view into the cabin."

"Copy," Rowdy replied as he straightened and moved forward slightly. Knight was anxious, so was Rowdy for that matter. This would be over in a matter of minutes. He just hoped they achieved their desired outcome.

"Cole Hughes and Reese Weathersby your time is up," Matthew announced. "This is your last chance to obey my command. Come out with your hands up."

No response.

"Three, two, one," Skeet counted down over the air then raised the weapon and fired a round. The small projectile shattered the window and landed in the center of the room. Light erupted as a loud boom echoed throughout the forest. The cabin shook and the walls rattled from the power of the blast. Skeet had never actually deployed a bang before. But he knew what to expect. Coop and Rowdy had walked him through it a dozen times today. Plus, he'd been on scene at ops before and knew they were loud and bright and powerful. Being the one to actually deploy the thing was amazing. A thrill that was difficult to describe.

Reese fell to the ground. Were they blowing up his house? Then it hit him, he'd heard of tactical teams using a loud device to distract the occupant so they could send the team in from another direction. That must be what these officers were doing to him now. He jumped to his feet and darted for the front door. As he reached for the handle he realized he'd peed his pants. He glanced back and saw the dog. Embarrassment left him as fear took over. Reese hated dogs.

* * * *

Bailey jumped about a mile high when the window shattered and the tiny bomb exploded in the room. She covered her face with her arm and waited. Chaos erupted around them and still, Cole didn't flinch. She was afraid that meant he hadn't made it. Peter and her mother were going to be devastated. Bailey knew somehow she would be blamed. Somehow this was going to be all her fault. At the moment she didn't care. All she cared about was getting out of this place alive. She choked back tears. Rowdy had come for her.

* * * *

Rowdy released Knight and followed his K9 partner across the backyard and to the closed door. He didn't bother trying the knob. In one fluid motion, he kicked out and the door flew open hitting the back wall with a loud thud. Knight was across the room before Rowdy registered the scene completely. Bailey was sitting on a bed in the living room nestled in the corner between the wall and the large bed frame. She had pushed her body into a sitting position, which must have been difficult with her hand hooked to the bedpost like that. She had her elbows resting on her knees and her face was buried in her one free arm. The flash-bang must have scared her. But she had to know they were here for her. Rowdy looked closer and realized Bailey was only wearing her t-shirt and panties. What did that mean? Was he too late? Rowdy's heart beat faster and anger engulfed him. If Bailey was injured, if she'd been violated, Rowdy would personally make sure the man responsible paid dearly for his crime. Where were the men anyway? Rowdy pulled his eyes from Bailey and spotted Cole. The man was lying across the bed, unmoving. Was he already dead? That was a strange twist, one Rowdy would consider later. Right now, he had to find Weathersby. His eyes traveled across the room and landed on the vile man just as Reese flung open the front door and hurled himself onto the porch. Knight followed.

* * * *

Coop kept his eyes trained on the front of the building. He could still see through the window clearly. It took a couple seconds for his eyes to adjust after the bright flash of the bang but the scene remained the same as before. Then suddenly, Reese was in his sights. Should he finish this? One slight squeeze of the trigger and Reese Weathersby would be history. The problem would be solved permanently. But Coop couldn't do it. Oh, he had cause and no jury in the land would convict him of wrongdoing. He would be justified in killing the man who held an innocent woman hostage - that was one of the rules of engagement. The hostage taker was always fair game. But Coop knew he would never be able to live with himself if he took out Reese just because he could. Rowdy and Knight were inside and Skeet was slowly making his way across the front porch. Killing the maniac wouldn't be morally right and Andy Cooper had honor and integrity. He had to let Rowdy and Skeet resolve this peacefully. They could take Reese into custody and the justice system would sort it all out. Coop inhaled, exhaled, inhaled and exhaled again. He needed to relax. He needed to monitor the situation until its conclusion. He wouldn't take the man out callously but if there was danger, if there was any possibility one of his men could get injured, he'd act without hesitation. He could live with that. Suddenly the front door flew open and Reese flew through the air, landing on the front porch, Knight emerged a second behind him. Coop grinned. He loved that dog.

* * * *

Skeet was making his way cautiously across the front porch when suddenly the door flew open and Reese Weathersby landed at his feet, Knight on his heels. Skeet froze. Would the dog recognize him or view him as a second threat? Skeet wasn't about to take the chance. He dropped his arm, lowing his weapon to his side as he spoke. He wasn't worried, Coop had his back. One wrong move and Reese would be neutralized. "Reese Weathersby, you are under arrest," Skeet studied the dog. He knew Knight was well trained. Today, it showed. The dog was standing just outside the door, waiting but clearly in attack mode. His ears were standing straight up and his body was leaning slightly forward. One wrong move and Reese would have a chunk removed from… well, somewhere. Skeet really didn't know where the dog would connect. He pressed the button on his walkie and waited for the delay. "Rowdy, the suspect is down but we need you to control your dog. Derek and Matthew are here, ready to make an arrest, but none of us want to get bitten."

Rowdy hesitated only a minute then turned and started toward Bailey when he heard the traffic. He hated leaving her, but Hughes didn't look like a threat and Knight needed to be contained. He grinned, pretty sure the dog had everything under control. Reese didn't stand a chance against Knight. But Rowdy didn't want to risk the others. One wrong move and Knight wouldn't care if you were friend or foe, stitches would be needed. Rowdy loved this job, he especially loved working with his K9 partner, and knew Knight was happy to be back on the job. Rowdy loved being a cop and missed the thrill of the arrest but he also knew when this was all over, he'd turn in the badge. He was a bar owner now. And even though this op had turned out okay, he would still never pass a physical with his leg. And it didn't matter what Coop said, that was a deal breaker. He was going to put his foot down, for his brother's sake. Coop would push things with the mayor and it might cause trouble down the road. No, Rowdy's cop days were over now and he knew it. He stepped onto the porch and called Knight to his side. The dog immediately joined Rowdy, but his attention never wavered from Reese. Knight didn't trust the man and it showed.

Rowdy watched Reese as Knight moved to stand beside him. He casually reached down and snapped the leash onto the dog's collar with one hand as he gripped his pistol in the other. The instant the dog was secure, Derek and Matthew approached Reese, planning to cuff him and transport their prisoner to jail. Things didn't go as smoothly as they hoped. Derek knelt next to Reese and reached for his left arm. Once he had a good grip on it, he swung it backwards securing it behind his back. He was completely taken by surprise when Reese reached out with his right hand and retrieved Derek's weapon from its holster.

Derek panicked and lunged. Reese raised the pistol and fired.

Coop was watching the scene before him. It appeared to be under control but he wasn't taking anything for granted. Until Reese was handcuffed and in the back of the cruiser he was going to be prepared. Rowdy stepped from the cabin and instantly called Knight to his side. He had just finished attaching the dog's leash when Derek and Matthew moved forward. Coop tensed as he studied the group in his scope. Derek forgot to snap the strap that held his weapon in place, or he wanted easy access. But that could be dangerous. Coop forced himself to breathe and watch. "Just cuff the man and pull him to his feet. Another few seconds and everything will be fine," Coop whispered to himself. But it wasn't. Coop shifted and focused on Reese. The Sheriff knew the exact moment Reese decided to act. The man's eyes changed as he studied his surroundings, then he yanked the cop's gun from its holster. Coop trained his gun on Reese and prepared to fire.

Anyone watching Rowdy would think he was ignoring his dog. But he wasn't, he was in total sync with his K9 partner and both of them were on edge. Reese was up to something, Rowdy could feel it. So could Knight. Rowdy tightened his grip on the leash, if Reese did something stupid, Rowdy would need to control the dog. He shifted his grip on his weapon, prepared to use it if necessary. It was. Reese waited for just the right moment, then he reached out and slid Derek's gun from its holster. Derek lunged forward, probably in a futile attempt to recover the lost gun but Reese raised the pistol and fired.

Derek didn't see Matthew react. His only thought was *get my gun back.* He lunged at Reese, believing he could take the man by surprise before he reacted. He'd been wrong. He was flying through the air when Matthew's body collided with his. Matthew must have lunged before Derek had. The two deputies hit the railing with so much force the weathered wood cracked and gave way. Both men fell over the side of the deck, hitting the compact dirt with a thud. They both tensed and tried to untangle themselves when they heard the distinct and unmistakable sound of gun fire.

Reese's bullet hit the side of the cabin and lodged in the thick wood panel. Derek was lucky Matthew had reacted so quickly. Otherwise, he might be dead. Rowdy wasn't going to wait for Reese to get a second chance. He raised his pistol and fired. The bullet struck Reese in the chest at about the same moment a second round collided with his skull. Rowdy looked toward the trees, knowing his brother was responsible. So, Coop wasn't going to be spared the misfortune of taking another life after all. Maybe Rowdy would claim his bullet had hit first. But would it matter? Probably not. Not with his brother. Coop would have to somehow deal with the knowledge that he had taken another life. Rowdy hated knowing what his brother would go through, Coop was still coping with the jumbled emotions of the last shooting, but it couldn't be helped.

Skeet reached Rowdy and wondered if Coop was on his way. Reese might be dead, but Cole could still be a threat. It was more likely that Coop had remained in position, waiting to see if Cole tried something, too.

Rowdy gave Knight a tug and wondered if the whole, passed out on the bed thing was a cover? Was Bailey really still in danger and Rowdy had just walked by and left her alone with a madman? He turned, ready to dart inside when Skeet grabbed his elbow. Rowdy pivoted in anger but froze when he saw Skeet shaking his head with his finger to his lips. Okay, they were on the same page but Skeet was actually thinking… Rowdy not so much. Which was something that could get them all killed. He gave Skeet a nod and waited for the agent's signal.

Skeet moved in next to Rowdy, grateful the man had recovered so quickly. None of them had expected Reese to act so rashly. His stupidity had gotten him killed, but Cole could be just as reckless. They needed to be smart. Something the youngest Cooper had clearly forgotten. Moments earlier Rowdy nearly took action, based purely on emotion. If Skeet hadn't stopped him, Rowdy would have bolted through the door without knowing what was on the other side. The former SWAT cop knew better. Skeet studied Rowdy's face until he was positive the man was back in control. Then the two men moved to the door, Skeet on one side, Rowdy on the other. Before Skeet made his move, Coop's voice echoed through his earpiece.

Mount Haven

Coop still had a clear view inside. Cole was not a threat, well he wasn't moving anyway. It could be a trick but Coop didn't think so. He glanced back at the porch and realized Skeet and Rowdy were worried about Hughes. "Cole is still lying on the bed in the same position he's been in since we arrived. Either he's injured in some way or he's playing possum."

Skeet signaled for Rowdy to go first and he followed close behind. As the two men entered the cabin, Rowdy dropped Knights leash making sure the dog could react instantly if needed. He wasn't sure if Cole was faking an injury of if the man was really unconscious... or dead. If he jumped up with a weapon, Knight would be on him in two seconds flat. He glanced at Skeet then nodded. Skeet and Rowdy cautiously approached the bed. When Cole didn't move, Skeet poked him with the barrel of his gun. Still nothing. The two men looked at each other each one contemplating their next move.

* * * *

Bailey felt more than heard Rowdy approach the bed. She peeked through her arms and realized they were worried about Cole. "He's injured," she croaked out and realized her throat was dry. When was the last time Reese had given her something to drink? Last night and it had been Cole, not Reese, that had provided it. She raised her head and winced when Rowdy saw her face. His gentle, compassionate gaze turned stone cold and she was thankful they had already arrested Reese. Or had they? There was a reason the men had been firing their weapons moments earlier. Maybe Reese was dead. She looked up and studied Rowdy hoping for a sign. For half a second she was confused. Rowdy wasn't moving near her. Then, once again she remembered Cole. "They got into a fight, well not

514

really a fight. Reese came in and got angry with Cole and shoved him across the room. I think there was already something wrong with Cole. He stumbled and his head collided with the stone fireplace. Reese tossed him onto the bed and Cole hasn't moved since."

Rowdy reacted to the news. He was at Bailey's side the instant he realized there wasn't any danger. He glanced to the side and spotted Skeet as he turned Cole onto his back. The agent could deal with the suspect, Rowdy wanted Bailey free from her binds and in his arms. He pulled out his handcuff key and frowned. The key fit, but the cuffs didn't budge. Of course, they were over-the-counter restraints, not police issue. He pivoted, the key must still be on Reese's body. Before he even took a step, Coop entered the room and held out the key. Rowdy snatched it and released Bailey's hands. Once again, his blood boiled at the damage to Bailey's wrists. If Reese wasn't already dead, Rowdy would kill him with his bare hands. He was so furious, he could barely function.

* * * *

Bailey didn't care what she looked like. She didn't care about the pain. The instant her arms were free, she wrapped them around Rowdy's neck and held on tight. When Rowdy wrapped his strong arms around her body and pulled her forward, she screamed out in pain. Rowdy jumped and tried to release her but Bailey refused. She didn't care about the pain, she needed Rowdy. She needed to feel his strong arms wrapped around her, she needed to know she was safe.

Rowdy was barely holding it together. Bailey had been beaten so severely, one eye was swollen shut. Her wrists were a bloody

Mount Haven

mess and the instant he wrapped his arms around her, he realized she must have some kind of damage to her torso. Reese Weathersby had no idea how lucky he was. The monster's death had been better than he deserved. Rowdy twisted and sat on the edge of the bed, gently settling Bailey onto his lap. He slowly ran his hands over her arms, her sides, her back feeling for anything broken. He was a little surprised when the room suddenly filled with additional people.

"Sir," a paramedic crouched in front of the couple. "I need to get her onto a stretcher and check for internal damage. Can you please help me out here?"

Rowdy glanced up and realized the Missoula guys must have brought medics with them. He slowly stood and gently set Bailey on the waiting stretcher. As he tried to straighten, Bailey refused to let him. She had her arms locked around his neck and wouldn't let go. Rowdy chuckled a little then leaned in and whispered in Bailey's ear, "Baby, I'm not going anywhere. But these guys need to make sure you are okay. I've got you. I promise," he pressed a gentle kiss to her temple, then her forehead and once again tried to stand.

Bailey heard Rowdy, she understood exactly what he was saying, but she didn't want to let go. She tightened her grip for a second then logic set in and she released her hold. Rowdy immediately took her hand in his and waited while the medics asked her questions. Moments later they were loading her into an ambulance. Terror gripped Bailey's mind and she refused to let go of Rowdy's hand. But as they lifted her into the ambulance she was too weak to hold on and the connection was broken. The medics climbed into the back of the vehicle and started to close the door. Bailey screamed.

Rowdy couldn't stand to see Bailey so scared. He wanted to hold onto her, to assure her everything was going to be okay. The medics said he could ride in the front of the vehicle, but not the back. If he wanted to accompany her to the hospital that was his only option. He wanted to. He glanced back when he felt a hand on his shoulder. Coop, he should have known his brother would be close by.

"Go on," Coop nodded to the ambulance. "I've got things here. Reese's body will be handled by the feds and Cole is alive… barely. He's also being transported, but there's not a lot of hope. I'm afraid he's probably not going to make it." The two brothers watched as the medics slowly pulled on the back doors, ready to secure their patient and rush to the nearest hospital. Then Bailey screamed.

Rowdy was flinging open the doors and climbing into the back before anyone knew what he planned. He immediately rushed to Bailey's side and took her hand in his. "Hush," he soothed. "Bailey, it's okay. I'm here. I'll always be here. It's okay."

"Don't leave me," Bailey choked and gripped Rowdy's hand harder.

"Never," Rowdy leaned down and gave Bailey a feather light kiss on her lips then he stood and glared at the two medics. "I'm not leaving. You'll have to arrest me if you want me out of here."

"Not a problem," one of the medics shifted and made room for Rowdy to sit. "But you do have to ride on this bench. The driver won't move an inch until you are settled in your seat."

Rowdy lowered himself onto the bench and for about the hundredth time wondered what Bailey had gone through. He was terrified of the answer to that question and refused to ask. He just sat there holding her hand, their eyes locked on each other as Coop closed the back doors and the driver pulled away from the cabin. It turned out to be a long, bumpy ride back to the highway. The two men worked frantically to set up an IV then sat back and comfortably waited. They were used to this, Rowdy wasn't. Moments later he realized they must have given Bailey something for the pain because she relaxed her grip and slowly drifted off to sleep. "Is she okay?" he finally asked.

"I don't think she broke anything and there doesn't appear to be any internal bleeding, although we can't tell that for sure. We're taking her to the local clinic, from there a helicopter will transport her to Missoula. You're going to have to find your own way out there. I'm sorry but nobody is allowed in the chopper besides the doctor and his nurse. There's not room for another passenger and they calculate fuel based on the patient's weight. Any deviation will put the flight at risk."

"I understand," Rowdy nodded. He didn't like it but if Bailey was out cold, she would never know. They could get her into the ER quicker and make sure she didn't have a bigger problem. He and Coop would stop by the house, grab Maggie and Bailey's parents then head into the city. He pulled his phone from his pocket and dialed his brother.

* * * *

The dispirited group silently stepped through the doors of the hospital. The seriousness of the current situation dampened the pleasure of having Bailey safe. She was injured, one man was dead and another fighting for his life. Sure Cole and Reese were bad guys, but they were human beings with family who cared. And Cole's family was part of this group. Peter hadn't said one word since learning of his children's condition. Piper cried the entire way to

Missoula. And Skeet and Angela prepared for another stark reminder of the past.

Skeet moved to the small reception desk and began to ask questions. The rest of the group waited a few steps behind. Finally, after what seemed like an eternity, Skeet returned with a room number and directions. They slowly made their way down the hallway until they reached the elevator. Skeet turned to Peter and Piper. "Cole is in room 426. I'm afraid the news isn't promising. Maybe you should go there first."

Piper looked to Peter for direction and wondered if that was the wrong decision. She was trying to take control of her life but at this moment, she had no idea what to do. She needed to see Victoria, she was desperate to know that her daughter was okay. But she also knew Peter needed some time with Cole, especially if his son was not going to make it. "Peter, I think we should go directly to Cole's room. We can drop back down to see Victoria once we have a better understanding of what is happening with Cole."

Peter was in a daze. If he'd been himself, he would have been impressed with Piper's willingness to take charge, but he wasn't himself. So, he simply nodded and let his wife take the lead. When the elevator reached the third floor, everyone but Piper and Peter got off. The remaining couple rode to the fourth floor in silence, neither one knowing what to say to the other to make this nightmare palatable.

The instant they walked into the room, Piper knew there was no hope. She slowly made her way to the bed with Peter by her side. Piper reached out and brushed the hair away from Cole's face. She blinked rapidly trying to fight the tears. Peter silently took his son's hand and gazed out the window. Memories of his son growing up flooded his mind. Happy memories, birthday parties and trips to amusement parks. He hadn't had a lot of time for his son, but he'd tried. He'd done his best with the hectic schedule he was burdened with. Running a company took time. Could that be the reason Cole had gotten involved in all this… malarkey with Reese? Peter had no idea. He'd never know. Because Cole was not going to wake up. As he studied his son's face, that fact became a little more obvious with each passing second. His son was dying and there was nothing Peter could do about it.

The couple jumped a little when the doctor walked in. As the man explained their son's condition, the hole in Peter's heart got bigger. He felt like he was drowning in a black hole of despair. Should he call Cole's mother? Would she even care? Peter tried to focus on the doctor's words but his mind was stuck on "brain damage" and "never recover". He blinked and forced himself to listen.

"It appears your son suffered a previous injury, a subdural hematoma," the doctor explained.

"What does that mean?" Piper asked.

"Basically that Cole had a less severe injury prior to the attack last night. I'd say at least a couple weeks ago. His brain had a very slow bleed. He most definitely would have felt some symptoms from the injury. Probably headaches, dizziness, confusion and forgetfulness. That sort of thing. This second injury exacerbated the problem exponentially. I doubt the outcome would have been any different; even if we were able to treat him right away."

The hospital could keep Cole alive on life support but the neurologist was sure Cole would never recover completely, if at all. Peter had a decision to make. He dropped into the closest chair and wept.

Piper sat with Peter for nearly an hour before she excused herself. Once in the outer hallway, she looked for a quiet alcove where she could make the calls in private. She decided to call Sissy first. The girl was going to be devastated but it couldn't be helped. It would have been better to break the news in person but Piper didn't have that luxury. The phone rang twice before Sissy picked up. Moments later Piper disconnected. She was drained and a little worried. Sissy and her parents were flying out this afternoon. Piper supposed that was best. The girl needed closure and seeing Cole one last time would give her that. Piper just hoped the family could take the news… all of it. Because there was no way anyone could shield them from the horrible rumors that were sure to circulate throughout the area about the serial killing rapists that had been stopped by the local police. She took another deep breath and dialed Cole's mother. This call was going to be even more unpleasant but for different reasons. Lulu was a selfish, arrogant socialite. She was not going to be happy. Cole's death was going to be the talk of the town and her popularity was actually going to take a hit over her son.

After ten minutes of listening to Lulu blame Peter for the man Cole had become, Piper hung up. She still had no idea what her husband had seen in that woman. Her personality was toxic and always had been. But was Piper that much better? She'd been weak for years, only thinking about her own reputation, never wanting to disrupt their precarious place in society. When had she become that woman? When had she lost sight of who she really was? Probably when Scott died. How had Peter tolerated her for so long? And why did he still love her when she was such a burden? Piper took a minute to compose herself before stepping back in the room. She was surprised to see her husband standing at the window. He turned to face her when she walked through the door.

"There's nothing more we can do for him now. It's time we joined the others. Bailey needs us." Peter moved toward the door.

Mount Haven

"Why are you calling her that, too? I know why the others do, but her name is Victoria." Piper tried to hide her irritation but knew she had failed. Victoria had always liked her middle name better than her first but Piper refused to allow it. She'd named her daughter Victoria for a reason. The name portrayed confidence and sophistication. Bailey was... common.

"Because I believe that is what she prefers," Peter looked at his wife, then glanced at their joined hands. He didn't remember making the connection, had Piper initiated it? "And from now on, I plan to listen to my daughter. If we had done a little more of that, this whole mess might have been avoided."

Piper inhaled sharply. Did Peter blame her for all of this? Maybe he did hate her. How could she fight that? How could they function in a marriage if Peter despised her? But the worst part was knowing he might be right.

* * * *

Angela stepped into the room and spotted Bailey. Memories flooded her mind and she froze. The girl was a mess, just like Angie had been so long ago. She could do this. She could walk into the room and provide moral support for her friends. She'd never met Bailey Zander, but that wasn't important. Rowdy was her friend. Rowdy and his brother were there for her and Skeet when they'd needed them most. Now, she was going to be there for Rowdy... and Bailey if she would let her. Angie had a unique insight, one she was more than willing to share with this strong but damaged girl. She turned and smiled at her husband when Skeet wrapped a protective arm around her waist. Her man always knew what she needed. She had no idea if it was because he was going through the same emotions she was, or if he just knew her better than she knew herself. She rested her head on Skeet's shoulder and waited. Rowdy was approaching the bed. He obviously needed a private moment with the woman he loved. Angie glanced around the room and spotted Maggie and Coop. Maggie was crying into her husband's chest, Coop had a stoic and slightly angry look on his face. Angie was sure if Coop could go back and kill Reese Weathersby all over again, he would.

Rowdy stepped to the bed and took Bailey's hand. She was still sleeping; the medication they had given her must have been strong. He glanced around and spotted a cushioned chair and reached for the seat, dragging it with one hand across the slick floor.

Coop saw what Rowdy was doing and he immediately came to his aid. He moved behind the chair and easily pushed it into place beside the bed. Rowdy sat with a mumbled "thanks" then returned his attention to Bailey. Coop glanced around the room, feeling a little lost. He returned his gaze to Maggie, took her hand and led her to the couch near the window. Once he settled into the corner of the uncomfortable seat, he pulled Maggie onto his lap, leaving plenty of room for Skeet and Angie if they wanted to join them.

Skeet gently guided his wife to the couch then he too sat and pulled her onto his lap. They might be here awhile and seeing Bailey so battered and bruised brought back unpleasant memories. Bailey hadn't been tortured the way Ange had, but this incident was going to leave scars. The same as it had with his wife. Oh, she was coming along…better than he had hoped. But she still had nightmares sometimes. Skeet was worried seeing Bailey like this would bring them back in the coming nights. It couldn't be helped. Angie had insisted on being there for her friends. So they would muddle through it, the same as Bailey and Rowdy would need to.

Mount Haven

Everyone in the room looked up when Peter and Piper entered the room. After several minutes Rowdy broke the silence. "You okay?" he was talking to Peter, but he included Piper as well.

Peter nodded as he approached the bed and studied Bailey's injuries. "How is she?"

"The doctor said she's fine. They gave her some pretty strong pain killers and that's why she's sleeping so soundly," Rowdy provided. "She has a couple cracked ribs but none are broken. Her face is probably the worst. Her cheek bone is fractured and she's taken some pretty severe blows to her abdomen. There's a lot of bruising on her stomach and ribcage. When you take her back to San Diego, she's going to need TLC for several weeks."

"I'm not going to San Diego," Bailey whispered. The entire room went quiet, everyone staring at the patient.

"Of course you are, dear," Piper soothed. "We'll take care of everything. Don't you worry about a thing, Victoria."

"I prefer Bailey. And I am not moving back to California. I belong here, in Mount Haven. I'm staying here," she insisted.

"But Victoria," Piper began.

"Bailey," Peter interrupted. "She said she prefers Bailey."

Piper shot her husband an angry look then continued. "You should have graduated with your MBA years ago. It was your father's dream for you to take over once you had your degree. That's been on hold for nearly three years. It's time to return, to rebuild the company. You have to come back to California, honey. You can't just abandon Peter like this."

Rowdy didn't know what to say or do. Was it possible Bailey would stay? But why? If she was sacrificing for him he couldn't allow it. He knew what it was like to give up everything, he couldn't let Bailey do that for him.

"Don't worry about the company, sweetheart," Peter moved to stand directly across the bed from Rowdy. He took Bailey's hand in his and gently rubbed circles over her palm. "I can handle it. You do what you need to do to be happy." He glanced at Rowdy then back to Bailey. "The two of you seem happy. Foster that, worry about that. I can take care of the business."

"That's not what I meant, Peter," Bailey started to shake her head then winced. She was so uncomfortable, she wanted to sit up.

Peter grabbed the small remote and began playing with buttons. It took him a minute but he was finally able to raise the upper part of the bed, placing Bailey in a more comfortable sitting position. "Better?" he asked handing her the remote.

"Much, thanks," Bailey smiled at her step-father. "I'm not giving up on the company. I'm not abandoning you, Peter. I can handle my responsibilities from Mount Haven. We are a consulting company, we can operate from anywhere."

Peter nodded.

"Victoria," Piper began to argue but stopped when Peter gave her another angry look. "Oh seriously? Bailey then."

"I'm not going to argue about this, Mother." Bailey would not let her mother run her life.

Piper sighed then moved away from the bed and settled into a visitor's chair. Victoria was still upset, they could talk about this later. Their life was in San Diego. Bailey would accept that once she was well.

"Peter," Bailey began again. "I hope you aren't angry but I called Tony Nazario."

"I'm not angry." Peter sat on the edge of the bed. "In fact, I've called Tony several times over the past three years. The company profits weren't what I expected and I wanted to hire him to find out why. I had no idea my own son was skimming on a regular basis. Anyway, Tony won't help us. He made it very clear the last time we spoke that he is happy where he is and I should stop calling."

"Well," Bailey said hesitantly. "That wasn't exactly true." She studied Peter apprehensively, not knowing how he'd take the information.

"Go on," Peter encouraged.

"Well, he wasn't happy. In fact, he's been actively looking for a new prospect for the past year. I think I have him convinced we're a perfect fit."

"Then why?" Peter stopped. "Cole?"

"I don't know what happened. Tony won't tell me. But the two of them got into it Tony's senior year at Stanford." Bailey fought to remember the details. "I do know he attended a party in Monterey and Cole and Reese were there. I always thought it had something to do with me. Tony was protective of me and I thought maybe they said something that pissed him off. He already knew I was afraid of them, so it wouldn't take much. Anyway, in light of what we've all learned recently, I think it was probably something more substantial. Tony turned you down because of Cole."

"I see." Peter couldn't think about his son right now. Thinking of Cole brought the knowledge that he was going to have to make a decision and he wasn't ready to do that. "Bailey, what did you offer Tony? I mean, the company is in trouble. I'm not sure we can match what he's making in New York."

"We haven't talked salary, but he knows he's going to take a cut," Bailey assured him. "The cost of living is less in Montana anyway."

"Montana?" Peter considered. The lease was up on the large office building they were currently housed in. He'd considered moving, rather than renewing anyway. Could they set up their home base in Missoula? He didn't see why not. Maybe the change would do them all good.

"Well, I know you might want to stay in San Diego and I think we could make that work but I'm not leaving. I love it here and…" she glanced at Rowdy. "And I have some unfinished business I need to take care of."

"Who is Tony?" Rowdy scowled. Was Bailey bringing an old boyfriend to town to help her sort out her financial mess?

"Tony's a friend," Bailey grinned. "We were best friends when I attended Stanford, while I worked towards my MBA. Tony graduated the year before I would have. He instantly moved to New York. He's brilliant and just what Drakker needs right now."

"I thought you were brilliant and just what Drakker needed right now," Rowdy was worried. When this brilliant businessman returned, would Bailey realize she didn't want to be stuck in Mount Haven for the rest of her life?

Mount Haven

"I'm going to take Maggie down and see if we can find some coffee," Coop said as he stood and tried to send exit vibes to Skeet. Rowdy and Bailey needed a few minutes alone.

"Yeah," Skeet stood as well and took Angie's hand. "I'd love a cup right now."

Peter looked from Coop to Skeet and back to Rowdy. Okay, he could take a hint. "Piper and I could use one, too." He stepped to the door and waited for his wife. She scowled at him, clearly not happy about being forced to leave but she eventually followed. Once again, Peter wondered if their marriage was going to survive. He wanted to work things out, but he also wanted to know he was important to his wife. Not just an easy meal ticket.

Once the group left the room, Bailey reached for Rowdy's hand. "Are you upset about Tony?"

"No," Rowdy considered. He wasn't upset, just worried.

"Then what? There's something going on and I need to know what," Bailey pushed. "Tony is a friend, that's all. I need his help. He is brilliant when it comes to business. He's spent the past five years working for a company that saves corporations that are in trouble. We're a consulting firm, but Tony is a fixer. He's already looked over some of the documents we got from Skeet and had some preliminary ideas on how to turn things around. We need that right now. Once it becomes public that Cole was involved in so many illegal activities, our clients are going to get nervous."

"Bailey, you don't need my permission. Do what you need to do. It's your company, it was your father's company. I know you need to do whatever's necessary to ensure it's a success." Rowdy settled back in his chair, not sure how to sort through all his feelings. He had accepted the fact that Bailey was going to leave him once he rescued her. Now she said she was staying but what did that mean for them? He knew what he wanted. He wanted to make Bailey his wife. But what did she want?

"No. You're right, I don't," Bailey agreed. "But I would like your support. I'm getting the feeling you feel threatened by Tony and that's just absurd. Tony is a friend, nothing more. I need him to help me with the business. I need you in every other way. Do you understand?"

"No, not really," Rowdy confessed. What exactly was she saying?

"I've been scared," Bailey began. "Scared of so many things. Scared to get involved with you because I didn't want your family hurt by my problems. Scared of Cole and Reese, scared of my parents' reaction. Scared of what would happen when this was all over. I refuse to be scared any longer, Rowdy. So I'm just going to get this out there and deal with your reaction. I love you. I've loved you for a very long time. I kept thinking it wasn't fair to you, to tell you how I felt when so much was uncertain but I sat in that cabin and berated myself. I didn't know if I was going to make it out alive and if I died, you would never know how I truly felt about you. So, there it is. I love you. Whatever it is you are thinking about Tony, forget it. I love you."

Rowdy stood and pressed a gentle kiss to Bailey's lips. He wished he could hold her, but he knew the kind of pain she was in and there was no way he was going to make things worse. He rested his forehead against hers and sighed. "I love you too. More than I ever thought possible. I was so sure I was going to lose you. I thought…" He swallowed hard. "Well, I thought once the threat was over you would want your old life back. Mount Haven isn't glamourous. I can't give you high-society parties and champagne."

Mount Haven

"True," Bailey grinned. "But you can give me tequila shots and whatever's on tap."

"I'm serious, babe." Rowdy kissed Bailey's temple before he returned to his chair. "I'm not some brilliant business guy. I'm still getting the hang of running a bar in a small town."

"I love that bar," Bailey frowned. Was this all because an old friend was coming to town or the money? "You do know Peter and I are about broke, right? You saw the books. You know the business is in trouble."

"I also saw your trust fund balance. You are not even close to being broke." Rowdy wasn't intimidated by the money. He didn't care about that. He just didn't feel like they'd had a fair shot yet. She was on the run, then they were chasing her hunters. Now, things had settled down and he wanted her to himself but he was going to have to compete with an old boyfriend.

"True," Bailey conceded. "But if the money makes you uncomfortable, we won't touch it. I've lived off my salary for three years now. I don't care about any of that." She studied Rowdy. This wasn't about money. "This is still about Tony."

"How long did you date him?" Rowdy finally asked.

"We never dated," Bailey said, grateful they had decided they would never be anything more than friends. She understood now and she didn't blame Rowdy. If some old girlfriend of his showed up, she'd be upset too.

"Never?" Rowdy pressed. "I find that hard to believe. I am a guy and I know what college is like."

"Never," Bailey said airily. "I think initially Tony was trying to hit on me, but I was such a mess, he realized pretty quickly that I needed a friend. He filled that role for the first year we knew each other. At the end of my first year in grad school, Tony asked me to an event he was attending. I was technically his date, but we instantly knew there would never be more. We continued to hang out until he graduated. Then he moved to New York. I got through most of my last year, but dropped out before I completed my final two courses. I'd like to finish those and hope I can take them online. It seems such a waste to throw away all that effort and not graduate."

"I agree," Rowdy hadn't gone to college, but he thought Bailey should have the chance to finish. She'd been running for her life. Surely Stanford would understand.

"Tony tried to keep in touch with me while I was on the run, but I never responded," Bailey continued. "When I met him I was a mess. I didn't have any close friends, for some reason whenever I got close to a girl they turned away from me after a while. I know why now, but at the time I thought it was me. I met Tony on my first day at Stanford. I felt so out of place and alone. He walked into our Business Finance class and sat next to me in the back. I could tell he was the type of student that normally sat up front. Then he turned to me and welcomed me to Stanford, claiming he had been assigned as my mentor for the semester. I didn't believe him of course, especially when he asked my name. I said Bailey; I'd always liked my middle name better than Victoria and I thought 'what the hell'. I was in a strange college, nobody knew me and I could be anyone I wanted to be. I later went back to Victoria but Tony has always called me Bailey. So, when he emailed me while I was hiding I panicked. Cole was amazing with technology and I was sure he could hack into my email and locate me. So I ignored Tony, but knowing I still had a friend was the only thing that got me through some of the rough times.

Mount Haven

Tony sent me emails fairly regularly, which is why I knew he was open to something new. I really hope you understand why I need to do this, Rowdy. Tony is going to have to take a huge cut in pay and I'll probably end up signing over some of my stock to make things fair. But Rowdy, I really do need him to get through this storm. Even with Tony on my side and Peter, I'm not sure we're going to keep the company running. It will kill me if I fail my father that way. I need your support. I'd really like you and Tony to be friends but I need you to be okay with this."

Rowdy studied Bailey for several minutes and realized he would do anything for her. Even agree to something that might end up breaking his heart. "I'm okay with it. And I'm here for you." He linked their fingers then brought her hand to his lips and softly kissed each knuckle. "I love you, Bailey. So I'll try to get along with this Tony guy. But if I get even the tiniest inkling he wants to hit on you, I'm going to hit on him… and not in a good way."

Bailey laughed. Men! "Deal," she finally agreed. Now, time for the big question. "So now that I'm not in danger, do I have to move back to that tiny apartment?"

"No way," Rowdy said immediately. "You're mine, sweetheart. All mine. If you're willing, I want you with me forever."

"Good," Bailey sobered, not sure how to respond to that.

Rowdy studied Bailey. He needed her to know how he felt about her. "I know it's been a strange, bumpy road. I know I did everything in my power to keep our relationship professional at first but Bailey, I need you to know you're it for me. I want time with you. I need time. I need to be able to hold you and love you and keep you safe. I need to date you, pamper you and get to know the real you, all of you. I think we've had a pretty good start, but you have been hiding. From your family, but also from me. Move in with me, let me love you, let me discover everything about you." And let me show you I can be enough, Rowdy thought but didn't dare say it out loud. That would come with time.

A tear escaped the corner of Bailey's eye. Was this wonderful, amazing, sexy man really declaring his love for her in such a simple yet powerful way? Yes, he was. And she was going to grab on tight and hold onto whatever this was for as long and far as it would take her. "I accept," she smiled. The first real smile she'd had in a very long time.

The couple talked well into the night. Rowdy explained what had happened while they looked for Bailey and how Peter and Piper ended up in Montana. He told her about the troubles between her parents and filled her in on the story behind Skeet and Angela. Somewhere in the middle of it all, the others came back then said goodbye to spend the night in a hotel. Bailey knew the following day was going to be difficult for Peter. Sissy and her parents were flying in and those close to Cole would have to make a decision. She just hoped her mother would rise to the occasion and be there for the man that had always been there for Piper and her daughter.

As night fell and the hospital grew quiet, Bailey looked into the eyes of the man that she loved and knew, deep down in her soul, that everything was going to be okay. They were going to make it. A memory hit her suddenly and she smiled. Maggie was right. The Cooper boys were tough, obstinate and extremely sexy on the outside but Rowdy was like Coop on the inside. The brothers were soft as marshmallows with hearts of gold. And in her mind, that was just perfect.

Epilogue

Two weeks later, Rowdy was preparing the bar for opening when a good-looking, well-dressed man stepped through the door. Somehow he knew this was Tony Nazario. He took a deep breath and prepared to lie through his teeth. Bailey claimed she was put off by Rowdy's confidence, but Tony was more cocky and self-assured than either of the Cooper brothers. It was immediately obvious Tony was used to getting his way, Rowdy was sure of it. The man headed straight for the bar and slid onto a stool.

"You must be Rowdy," Tony raised an eyebrow. He grinned, knowing Bailey was right. Rowdy wasn't at all sure he wanted Tony intruding on his turf. Too bad. He was about to poke the guy a bit when Bailey stepped from the backroom, spotted Tony and smiled. It was good to see her smile again. He expected her to give him a proper greeting but instead she moved behind the bar and wrapped an arm around her man.

"This is Rowdy," she gave Rowdy a slight hip bump in warning. "Rowdy, this is Tony Nazario."

"Yeah. I figured that one out on my own, babe." Rowdy grinned down at Bailey and gave her a gentle peck on the lips. "Maybe you should go say hello." The two of them locked eyes for several seconds before Bailey nodded and turned.

Tony watched, stunned as Bailey slowly moved around the bar and came to stand directly in front of him. It was blatantly obvious these two were in love. It shocked him speechless for a minute and he was instantly glad he'd been interrupted. If he got on Rowdy's bad side, he might just lose Bailey's friendship for good. He wasn't an idiot, the woman sent him a very clear message the moment she walked through the door. He was happy for her. Bailey deserved to find love. She deserved to be cherished and Rowdy clearly cherished her. He pulled her into a hug, careful not to hurt her ribs then brushed a kiss across her forehead. There, that should be brotherly enough for the hawk watching from behind the counter.

Bailey slid onto the stool next to Tony. "I am so glad you finally arrived. Peter and Mom have gone back to San Diego. I pitched your proposal to him the night before he left. He's thinking on it, but I'm pretty sure he's hooked. The lease is up on that monstrosity in San Diego anyway. I always hated that building but Dad and Peter loved it. Now we just have to find a suitable building in Missoula. After the funeral, Peter is going to start his tour. I just hope this works."

"It will," Tony assured her. Peter was going to visit each of their clients personally and explain the situation. He would also offer a break on any contract that Cole had handled personally. Their company was in trouble, but Tony was positive the fallout would be minimal. Lucky for them, the FBI wasn't going public with what they had found on Cole and Reese and the insider trading or the illegal money transfers. With Cole and Reese deceased, there were no charges to be filed. And Bailey and Peter were keeping the embezzlement under wraps. They were the only victims so nobody else needed to know. If Cole had survived, this would have been a lot worse. Tony would never be that insensitive, never mention that fact to Peter or even to Bailey, but it was the truth. "How's Peter doing?"

"He's maintaining," Bailey frowned. "Sissy and her parents agreed with Mom and Peter so it made the decision go a lot smoother. They held out nearly two weeks before they took him off life support. The funeral is on Tuesday. Rowdy and I will fly out tomorrow and see what we can do to help over the weekend. So, if you need anything from me before next week we better take care of it today."

The front door opened and Theresa stepped into the dimly lit room. She loved her job. These days it was the only thing she loved. Life inside this building was entertaining and predictable. Outside, was more than she could handle most days. She would never tell anyone just how serious her troubles were. Mount Haven was a happy little town where people believed hard work and dedication were rewarded with success and happiness. Little did they know just how tragic life could really be.

Theresa had only gone two steps when she spotted the sophisticated man at the bar. He was casually talking to Bailey and Rowdy and wearing an extremely expensive suit. Could he be an old friend? The man was stunning and hopefully just passing through. Her heart beat a little faster and she swallowed the lump that was forming in her throat. She had only experienced this strong of a reaction to one man before in her life, and Theresa knew just how toxic that situation had turned out in the end. She would not allow herself to fall into that trap again. She was still paying for the first mistake, she was pretty sure she would never survive a second. Regardless of the danger, Theresa could not take her eyes off the sexy, cocky specimen sitting so confidently at the bar. His dark brown hair was styled in a classic crop cut that was a little messy on top but trimmed on the sides in such a way that every hair remained perfectly in place. The man was sporting that GQ tight beard that made Theresa want to run her palms slowly across his face and then kiss him silly.

Now she was being silly. She took a deep breath and approached her boss, doing her best to ignore the eye candy that was now scrutinizing her. Theresa expected to get one of two reactions, blatant interest or disgust. But this guy wasn't openly showing either. Just another thing that drew her in... and made her want to run. This guy was danger with a capital D. "Morning," she hoped she sounded casual. "Need any help before we open?"

"Hey Theresa," Bailey said turning to face her co-worker. She wouldn't exactly call her a friend, yet. But ever since that night Theresa saved her from those drunken men, the two of them had been getting along. "Come meet Tony Nazario. Tony, this is Theresa Regan, one of our waitresses."

Theresa chuckled, figures. The guy had a catchy name to go with his custom tailored suit and cocky grin. She looked up and quickly looked away. The man was still studying her, she felt like a bug under a microscope. Yeah, she definitely needed to stay away from this guy. She reached out her hand for a polite shake, better to get the niceties out of the way, then she could bolt. When his large hand encircled hers, Theresa felt a jolt all the way to her toes. The instant attraction scared her so badly that she quickly pulled her hand away and practically ran to the back room.

Tony frowned. He was still trying to figure out the woman that he'd just met. Nothing came to mind. He'd spotted Theresa the second she'd stepped into the bar and at first he pegged her as another bar bunny. A loose woman who was probably a dim wit and a slut. But when he looked closer, he realized that was a front. She wore tight skirts and low cut shirts as a shield. From what, he had no idea but her eyes screamed tragedy. For some reason, Tony had always been a sucker for a pretty face in need. Wasn't that how he'd met Bailey all those years ago? She'd been more tragic than most but this woman…the waitress, was a mess. He wondered if anyone else noticed it.

Tony glanced around and decided he was the only one that realized Theresa was acting. Bailey and Rowdy seemed oblivious to the fact. Maybe because they were so caught up in each other they missed something that obvious in others. Tony gave himself an inward shake. He was here to do a job. He was here to get his friend's business back where it belonged. Then he'd have to decide… stay in Missoula working for Drakker, or move on. He had plenty of time to make his decision. What he didn't need right now was a beautiful woman that screamed disaster. He would definitely be staying away from one Theresa… what was her last name? Oh yeah, Regan. Theresa Regan. So why was he staring at the back door anxious for her to return?

THE END

A Dog Named Knight

We started together in seventy-eight
We were young, eager could hardly wait

Began our tour next to Max and Thor
Worked long and hard to find our place in the Corps

Drilled and trained 'til we got it down right
A rookie handler, a dog named Knight

Out on the street and after dark
We patrolled State and Redwood and a place called Lark

Our tour in the Corps was hard but fun
A burglar could hide but dared not run

A riot in Magna a shooting on Main
There was plenty of blood mayhem and pain

A burglar in a school a man with a gun
I was scared to death but you were having fun

Responding to stabbings robberies and a fight
Me with my badge and a dog named Knight

Worked well together you and I
For me it was exciting for you the praise high

Get challenged at a kegger too much ale
A stop at St. Mark's then it was off to jail.

Mount Haven

The shift was graveyards from dusk to first light
Now a veteran handler a dog named Knight

Every year in the State came Olympic dog trials
You'd be wearing medals I'd be wearing smiles

Competition was keen your performance bold
Came time to retire you wore medals of gold

Your career was a long one full of wins and success
You served with distinction were ranked among the best

But now it was over time to retire
You were getting older losing your fire

Retirement was hard didn't fit your style
Restless and willing but had run your last mile

Then you were gone... old age put you down
It was hard for me not having you around

No longer at my side gone from sight
But forever in my heart lives a dog named Knight

- by R. Lee Smith

Deputy R. Lee Smith & Knight
Dog and handler team 1978-1985
Salt Lake County Sheriff's K9 Corps, Utah